Falling From Grace

S.L. Naeole

Falling From Grace

S.L. Naeole

Visit my website at www.slnaeole.com
Visit the official website for Falling From Grace at www.GraceSeries.com

Printed in the United States of America

First Printing: July 2010

ISBN 1453626336

Printed in the United States of America.

Falling
From
Grace

S.L. Naeole

For my wonderful husband & my mites

"Thus, in discourse, the lovers whiled away
The night that waned and waned and brought no day.
They fell: for Heaven to them no hope imparts
Who hear not for the beating of their hearts."
Al Aaraaf—Edgar Alan Poe

PREFACE

His beauty was painful to take in, even as his passion pulled from me a cry of agony. Captured in his frozen eyes was the light of every star ever born, and every wish ever made. His beautiful smile stretched cruelly across his face as he took in the panoramic of my fear.

There was lust in his eyes that begged him to be quick, but there was no need to rush; he had all the time in the world, while I had only the time he spared me. His beautiful smile grew as my breathing quickened.

A comforting caress as he leaned into me, a promise of nothing but suffering and death on his lips as he said my name lovingly. I was pinned to my fate—this was to be my last embrace—I welcomed it as the bitter flood began.

GRACE EXPECTATIONS

I dread Mondays.

And the incessant buzzing of my alarm clock heralded it like some newly crowned king. What idiot had set that thing for—I peeked from beneath my pillow at the clock sitting on my dresser, mere inches from the foot of the bed—five-thirty? It couldn't have been me; not in a million years. I wasn't ready, not for today anyway, and I definitely wasn't ready for it to start at five-thirty. The darkness of early morning still blackened my window.

As a rule, Mondays don't start until the sun comes out. Oh, who was I kidding; it was September…in Ohio. There wasn't going to be any sun for another hour at least, and in less than three, I'd have to face the world again. Summer was over and my senior year was starting, just as my life was ending.

It was unavoidable, this first day of school after a lifetime of memory making; all those whispered secrets and shouted declarations between friends were as permanent as time. And yet, nothing could be as permanent as broken promises, or my shattered heart, broken by my best friend. In truth, my only friend; the only person in the world I trusted, who knew me inside and out and who looked past what the others saw as freakish.

Graham Hasselbeck wasn't just my next door neighbor. We grew up together. He had been my childhood playmate, the two of us inseparable all our lives, from diapers to puberty. It goes without saying then that we had the same tastes in just about everything two friends could share. Even fate seemed inclined to throw us together when we started school, with the both of us being assigned to the same classes from kindergarten through high school.

Our life's milestones seemed to run in time together as well, since we learned how to ride our bikes together, broke bones together, even got sick together. We were beyond close, our bond too strong and significant to break.

Even when he grew taller than me and everyone else, when he took off the braces that straightened imperfect teeth while mine still displayed that heinously embarrassing childhood gap, when he became popular with everyone while I lagged behind, when all of the girls noticed his dark blonde spikes and green eyes, and no one noticed me at all—Graham had remained my best friend.

And this summer together, like all of the previous summers before, had been spent hanging out, just being with each other, just being friends…up until two weeks ago. That was when he stopped taking my phone calls, and when he started leaving his house before I got up, only coming home long after my curfew kept me indoors.

That was after I broke the cardinal rule of friendship and told him I was in love with him.

It sounded reasonable enough, telling the person you've known since forever that you're in love with them, especially since I was. And why not tell him? After all, he knew everything about me. Every secret, every obvious and invisible flaw, and every screw up were all well documented in our memories, if not in photo albums created solely for blackmail use at a later date. I had been nothing if not unbearably and unfailingly honest with him.

And perhaps that was where I had gone wrong.

With a dismayed groan I thought back to that moment, that crucial blip in time when I'd finally found the courage to tell Graham how I felt. We had been sitting on the hood of his Buick Skylark, which used to be his dad's. The rusty green coupe with the dented passenger door had been our home away from home when Graham's parents were fighting—which seemed to happen on a daily basis now—or when my dad had his girlfriend over to visit.

The car was a birthday present his dad had told him when he'd given it to him two years ago. Graham had just made captain of the football team—the youngest ever at sixteen—and had also just passed his driver's test. It was a defining moment for him, and receiving that car was like being given the world. Of course, it didn't go unnoticed that Graham's dad had also just bought himself a brand new truck right around that time.

Richard Hasselbeck wasn't exactly trying to hide that fact from his son, but he also didn't come right out and say it either. I had called it tacky, but Graham had gone on and on about the freedom we now had to go to the mall—which we never did—or go to the Indian Mound park to throw the ball around—which I could never quite do without him complaining that I *"threw like a girl"*—or go to the cemetery to visit the graves of my mother and his grandmother—a monthly ritual for us.

But at that moment, right then and there that car was my platform, where I stood as the executioner put the invisible noose around my neck—and released the trapdoor.

"Graham," I started, my voice quivering from the chaos of my nerves. I took a few deep breaths to calm them while I braced myself against the windshield. Its smooth, sloped surface did nothing to comfort me or give me any real sense of stability; I was just fearful that without it, every word that came out of my mouth would send me flying backwards in retreat—rocket propulsion via the pouring out of my heart.

He glanced over at me and smiled cockily. Call me a simpering little girl stuck in Cinderella mode, but I loved that smug smile of his. Then again, so did every girl over the age of twelve within a five mile radius. The way his cheek dimpled ever so slightly, teasing me with the promise of its depth never failed to make me forget just what it was that I had wanted to say

"What's up, Grace?" he asked in a stunted tone, taking note of my awkward tension and adjusting his posture in kind. He leaned back, as though bracing for the emotional upheaval that he could sense was on the brink of breaking through my awkwardly feminine defenses.

I started to speak, but my tongue grew heavy and dry in my mouth as doubt began to slip in. I had replayed the speech over and over again in my mind, imagining what I'd say and what his reactions would be. But I'd never vocalized them, never stood in front of a mirror and said them out loud just to hear what they sounded like, and now it appeared that the internal fuse that existed solely for this purpose had shorted out on me, causing me to stare at him dumbly.

"Grace? What's up?" he asked again, sensing my caution and frowning in response. When had I ever held back from telling him how I felt, he'd probably wondered. His confusion was warranted; I knew that I wasn't acting like myself and that was putting him off.

If this was going to go well, I would have to put myself back together otherwise I'd never make it beyond just sitting there. After taking several more calming breaths, I swallowed my doubts and decided right then and there to wing it. Seizing my moment of renewed strength, I took the first hesitant step towards my running leap of faith. *Olympic medal of openness, here I come.*

My mouth opened, and the words tumbled out.

"Graham, I love you-"

I quickly bit down everything else that wanted to join those four words, a jumbled mess of disclosure catching in my throat and nearly causing me to choke.

I wasn't that brave…yet.

For one agonizingly long moment he said nothing, and the silence felt like it would strangle me. Or it could have been that I was just holding my breath while waiting for a response.

His face was an ever growing map of emotions, and though I professed to know him better than anyone else ever could, even I had to admit that I couldn't see just where exactly he was going to land. This was the first time that I had said those three words to him in a tone that wasn't playful or mocking—the way you're supposed to say it to your best friend—and I knew that it had caught him off guard completely because he'd never been at a loss for words before. In one fell swoop, I had managed to do the impossible and silence Graham Hasselbeck.

After what could have been a lifetime or perhaps seventy-two seconds—give or take a minute—he sighed…somewhat reservedly. "Ditto, Grace."

The ground rumbled beneath me, opening up a hungry chasm that awaited my next move.

And then Graham smiled.

So I leapt. "I'm also *in* love with you," I whispered, just loud enough for him to hear. Maybe too loud. Out of habit, I had closed my

10

eyes when I had begun to speak, but at that moment I needed them to be open, needed to gauge his reaction. I didn't want to miss anything; I needed to see his face, see his eyes when he heard my confession.

And I didn't recognize it at all.

He was looking past me, avoiding eye contact as his face held on fast to a blank expression, though I could see a slight puckering between his brows as he struggled with some inner turmoil. I wasn't used to this, to seeing him so aloof, and it was one of the most terrifying moments in my life. For reasons unknown I began see my life flash before my eyes—Graham was in almost every scene, filling them up like the sun fills up a frigid morning with its warmth—and those images were slowly being eaten up by hungry flames of doubt that clawed at my heart as it beat slowly, almost painfully in my chest.

He carelessly shoved his hands into the pockets of his jeans in some vain attempt to keep them occupied. "Grace..." he sighed.

Maybe he muttered it. I don't remember which because the next few minutes destroyed me to my very core and prevented me from being able to distinguish anything apart from how dark and desolated my world was becoming. The sudden feeling of loss as all the blood in my body started to drain away to some unseen place was causing an acute buzzing to flood my ears. It blocked out everything but the sound of my entire world being knocked off of its foundation—the very thing that kept me from falling into that chasm that waited patiently for me to stumble—and crushing my hopes as it landed on my heart.

"Grace, I...I don't know how exactly to put this without hurting your feelings...but I don't feel the same way about you."

He paused for a minute, the blank expression finally cracking, revealing a very incredulous, very angry scowl upon his face. I was taken aback by the sudden shift in his emotions as he barked, "You should have known better than to be so stupid! We're in two different leagues, Grace. We run with different crowds—or, at least I do. You've been struggling to keep up since the sixth grade and I've been weighed down with this friendship for too damn long. You've been holding me back, and now you gotta tell me you're in love with me, like that's supposed to mean something? What are you thinking?"

11

He shook his head, muttering to himself as he ran his fingers through the crisp spikes of his hair over and over again, frustration wracking him in ways I had never seen before. He slid off of the hood, landing on the sidewalk with very little grace, too upset to care, and started pacing, his hands alternating between jamming themselves into his pockets and running through his disheveled hair.

I watched him, unable to say anything, unable to find the strength in me to argue in my defense because I knew that he was right. I *had* been holding him back, and we *were* in different leagues. We always had been. I just didn't think that any of that had mattered to him before.

After several minutes of pacing, his head bobbed down once with such finality that it made my heart skid to a halt. It was as though he had just won some silent argument he'd had with himself and was agreeing with the outcome, and I knew that whatever that outcome was, it wouldn't bode well for me.

He lifted harsh eyes to mine, his mouth opening just wide enough to let the words tumble out as quickly as they could, if only to keep from prolonging the inevitable, or perhaps from saying something worse. "This has got to end now. We can't be friends anymore, Grace. We can't be anything anymore."

And so my future had been decided, I realized, and he had been the one to make the decision.

I didn't know what my face read at that point, if it showed anything at all because in that moment I embodied what the proverbial "they" meant when *they* said they felt numb. It's how you're supposed to feel after your heart takes an emotional beating and then decides to escape, abandoning you, leaving you to fend for yourself without the aid of love and hope to keep you going.

Whatever it was that Graham saw in my face then, it gave him enough reason to pound that final nail into my coffin, sealing it shut from everything that was good, everything that had been us up until that point.

"I didn't know how to tell you this when school was over— didn't want to, really—but I got accepted to NC Prep. They've got an amazing football team, and the only way I'm going to get scouted is if I'm playing for a ranked school. It's my one shot out of here, so that means I won't be going to Heath this year."

He paused to reach into his jacket pocket with a clumsy hand and pulled something out, shoving it towards me with such blatant disgust I could almost taste it. "Here, take it," he said to me as he pushed it against my hand, never once reacting to the way I flinched at the contact.

Call it being childish, call it just plain stubbornness, but I refused to accept whatever it was he was trying to force into my unwilling grip, clenching my fingers so tight I knew my knuckles were turning white from the effort.

My head turned from side to side in utter refusal; I didn't want parting gifts, as though I was the second runner-up on some game show. This was my life he was destroying, my heart he was breaking— couldn't he see how humiliated I was? How horribly and hideously inadequate he had made me feel now that not only had he reminded me that I wasn't popular or pretty—or even liked—but that he'd also reinforced that fact by informing me that he couldn't even stand to be in the same school as I was?

"Take it, Grace," he demanded as he pried open my fist and pressed the small object against my palm, closing my stiffened fingers around it. I took it numbly, my arm dropping dead at my side in defeat. I didn't even bother to look at it; I was too busy staring at the stranger standing before my eyes.

"Grace," he continued, his voice softer now, his gaze drifting downwards toward some unseen object that had no real purpose other than to keep him from having to look at me, from having to see the hurt he had caused me.

"I guess I should have told you this a while ago, but I suppose now's as good a time as any, and I don't want you to find out from anyone else because I know that that would be worse than finding out like this. See, I've been dating Erica Hamilton for the past six months. I didn't want tell you about it because…well, I guess I kinda already knew how you felt, and didn't want you to get hurt."

13

Didn't want me to get hurt? The rough exhalation that came out of me told him clearly that it was too late for that.

He sighed, as though a huge weight had been lifted from his shoulders, and ran his fingers through his hair again, calming it down some, only to cause it to stand up at weird angles when he struggled with what he had to say next.

"Erica and I…well, she and I have gotten pretty serious—really serious actually—and she thinks that it wouldn't be right for me to stay friends with you. And now that I know for sure how you feel, I know that she's right. It's not right, and it's not fair to you, or to me.

"She also said that it would be wrong of me to keep some of the stuff you've given me—like that-" he motioned towards the object that he had forced into my hands "-she said that I needed a clean break from you, to rid my life of everything that you'd ever given me. And so I thought that maybe you'd like that back, instead of me just throwing it away."

I didn't want to look down at what was in my hands and affording him my reaction. Instead I simply nodded.

Truth was, I was afraid of finding out what he had returned to me. What had I given to him that wasn't deserving of being thrown away or completely destroyed, like he had just done to my life? He couldn't be giving me back my heart; that lay in a pile of ashes in my lap.

"I have to get going, Grace. I gotta go pick up Erica at the mall; we're having dinner with her dad. It's her birthday today." He started to walk away then, but suddenly stopped and turned to face me, a wistful smile on his face.

"Um…have a great rest of summer, 'kay? Maybe I'll see you around. Or something."

With a wave, he was gone, back into his house to await my departure. At least he wasn't just standing there, waiting for me to leave. Or better yet, at least he hadn't told me to leave. No, he had done me the favor of leaving himself, one last act of kindness from my now former friend. At least, that's what I told myself.

It was in that moment of comprehension that I knew I had not only lost my best friend, but I had also lost most of my summer as well. All of those moments, those memories that I had stored in my mind, that touched my heart in so many different ways, were becoming distorted now, like an over pixilated movie. All of our conversations, our inside jokes, our confidences replayed in my mind, and all of them were now taking on new meaning for me…because all of them were now meaningless to him.

I was now the inside-joke: His and Erica's. And whoever else knew about this. Of course, it was a given that everyone else already knew. Why wouldn't they? I wasn't popular and they were. Two different leagues, he had said: the reality and the fantasy. But I never wanted to be anything other than Graham's friend. Even with loving him, I valued his friendship so much more. Now I didn't even have that.

As I got off of his car and walked towards my house, I started analyzing the past several weeks in my mind. Had we really spent the summer together like my memories had foolishly led me to believe? Every single day, they told me. And that's how it looked from my end…at least it did on the surface. He would meet me at the small library I worked at every morning, hanging out for a bit before leaving right after lunch for football camp.

When we went camping with our dads every other weekend, something that hadn't changed since the two of us were in middle school, he had never given a sign that he was distracted by a missing girlfriend. It was only afterwards, when we got home that he'd disappear for several hours, leaving our dads and me to unpack and clean out the gear.

We'd watched campy old movies and held a Rocky Horror Picture Show marathon at the beginning of summer break, holding it at the end of the month like always—it was a Grace and Graham tradition to call each other Rocky and Frank all day until one of us forgot, at which point that person got punched in the arm—because we were buds, Grace and Graham, best friends since forever. But he said he was busy with football and helping out his dad at the store last month, and so he asked for a rain check. I had never thought to question any of that until

15

then.

I calculated the time in my head as I walked towards my front door and the numbers only added to my grief. The burnt out hollowed shell of a person I was when I entered my room was completely unrecognizable. Everything suddenly hurt and I needed to lie down.

I remained that way for the last two weeks of summer, getting up only to head to work at the library, knowing that there was no chance that I'd run into anyone from school there.

My dad, the only other person in my life—in my existence really—had made several attempts to comfort me in his own little way, but quit trying altogether when he received no encouragement on my part. When he couldn't get an answer out of me as to what had happened after asking on several separate occasions, he went and spoke to Richard. I knew that his goal was to find out what had transpired outside that day to turn me so inside out, but he wouldn't get a straight answer from that avenue either. Richard couldn't tell the truth if it killed him—he was a natural born liar.

Dad eventually guessed what had happened, though. He wasn't blind. He'd noticed Graham's absence just as surely as he noticed the absence of my sarcastic comments, my ability to laugh at his corny jokes, and…well, me; perhaps even more so, because the absence of Graham meant the absence of Richard as well.

Richard and Dad had become fast friends after they had both moved here to Heath with their wives: Dad and mom came from California—Dad was coming to work as a manager for a chain grocery store—and Richard and Iris from Nevada, Richard having just purchased a small auto dealership near Newark. Both were avid football fans, but only Richard was blessed with a son who would fill Friday and Saturday nights with high school games to cheer at.

James and Abigail Shelley, on the other hand, were blessed with a daughter they named Grace, after the three Greek Goddesses; Mom had been a lover of all things Greek, which was odd considering she was Korean.

Now see, the three Graces are supposed to be these symbols of beauty and fertility, of peace and friendship, and charm and creativity.

16

This Grace, the version I grew up to be, while not ugly, is far from being even remotely similar to what one would describe as beautiful. I've got a slightly wide forehead—I've been called a five-head a few times, if that means anything. I've got dull brown hair that seemed to suffer from fits when the weather isn't cooperating. My brown eyes are rather unremarkable and owlish, a pretty lousy compromise between my mother's dark brown and my dad's bright blue. And the freckles scattered across my pale skin seem out of place for my dark coloring. Suffice it to say, I'm an odd mish-mash of my mixed parentage.

And, unlike most girls who lived in Heath, I didn't take ballet, or jazz, so I wasn't graceful. I didn't enter pageants or talent contests for sashes and trophies, so there went my charm and creativity. I didn't go to gymnastics, or take swimming lessons, or any of those things that little girls did with their mothers standing by, watching proudly. I was content with my books, my poetry, and my movies. Most importantly, I was very happy being a best friend to Graham. But what symbol of friendship could I be with no friends to speak of at all now? The only thing I had ever been successful at, I had failed the minute Graham had left me.

Lying in bed and remembering so much had me trembling with undeniable and bitter grief; the feeling of loss still felt so new. It was easy to choke on it, to suffocate on its core of bitterness. Its hold on me was so strong that I was bawling and hiccupping like a baby into my comforter, needing it for its imaginary strength almost as much as I needed it for its ability to muffle my sobs. I was in near hysterics…again.

How would I go back to school? How could I? The only person who had ever talked to me *just because* would no longer be there. I also couldn't avoid the fact that the person who I partially blamed for all of it—his girlfriend Erica—would, joking and sharing snide comments with the friends I now knew had all been having a good laugh at my expense for the better part of a year.

"Pity, party for one, your table is ready," I mumbled into my pillow.

Monday.

17

I think I'll hate Mondays for the rest of my life.

POSITIVE

With a resigned sigh, I dragged myself out of my bed. It was the first time in nearly forty-eight hours that I had done so for reasons other than to use the bathroom. The ever looming return to school had kicked my depression into high gear when the last weekend of summer started.

I needed to take a shower and wash the stiffness out of my body, as well as my face. Dried tears could iron a face flat, my mom used to say, and she had been right. Plus, I couldn't face this horrible first day looking my worst, even if my worst was only second place to my best. I looked at myself in the bathroom mirror and recoiled at what I saw. Ugh, I was ghastly. There were lines imprinted on my face from the creases in my pillowcase, and my eyebrows were all spiky and pointing in odd directions. I definitely needed to shower and shave. And brush my teeth. Ew—I've never been a stickler for personal hygiene on an OCD level, but there was something to be said for having smooth armpits and legs, and clean teeth and hair. Gross! At the moment, my teeth felt like they'd been soaking in sludge, my hair…it needed prayers. My legs and armpits? Big Foot would be frightened.

I climbed into the shower and sat on the little bench that was molded into the shower wall; I waited for the hot water to hit me. I had to stand up to readjust the angle of the showerhead, but after a few minutes, I was as close to content as I could possibly be with the world outside waiting for me to face it or return to cowering beneath my blanket.

While brushing my teeth in the shower, I did a very—and highly unusual for me—girl-type thing and thought about what it was that I would wear. I hadn't bought anything new this year. Dad didn't have the money for anything other than secondhand when it came to my

the dead needed breakfast. At least, my stomach thought so, if its grumbling was any indication.

I grabbed my brush, resigned with the fact that I'd fallen into a new routine that ran parallel to my old one—just emptier—and headed down the steps to the small kitchen below, where the smell of buttered toast and coffee made my stomach rumble once more like a starved animal contained within another starved animal.

"I'm ready. What's to eat?" I asked in as cheerful a tone as I could muster. Dad turned around, shocked at my appearance. Had I really looked that hideous before that a simple shower could cause such a reaction?

"Um…I'm making egg-in-a-hole and some bacon. You want some?" he asked me, showing me the pan with the egg that had been cracked into a hole cut out of a slice of bread, then pointed at the pile of bacon sitting on the table. "I can make you something else if you want. I think there are some toaster waffles in the freezer."

I shook my head. "What you're making sounds just fine, Dad." And it did. It smelled wonderful. Not eating for a few days would probably have made my boots seem edible—add some new potatoes on the side and you'd have a gourmet meal—but this, this was bacon fat heaven at the moment. I sat down at the small table that filled up half of the kitchen and glanced over at the clock. It was just a little past seven. I had an hour to eat and get going. We didn't live that far from the school, but I had to watch the time. Today would be the first time in over a year that I'd be walking to school.

"So, um, G-Grace," Dad's nervous speech began as he slid a plate in front of me. "I wanted to know how you're feeling…um…about…you know, school and everything."

"I'm fine, Dad," I said, only half lying. I grabbed my fork and started to lean in towards my breakfast, fully intending to concentrate on eating and *not* talking.

He watched me as I went through the motions—I was so unlike my mom that he could read me like a book. "No you're not. You don't have to lie to me, hon. I'm your dad. You can tell me if you're not feeling up to this yet. It's just the first day, nothing really important going on, right?"

I shook my head even though inside I was thinking that my entire senior year wasn't really that important. "I'm fine, Dad. Really—I can do this. It's just school. H-he's not going to be there anyway, so it'll be alright."

He regarded this with shock marking his face. "What do you mean he's not going to be there?"

Hadn't Richard told him? Why wouldn't he have bragged about his son getting into one of the most prestigious schools in the state, with an even more prestigious football program? "Um, Graham was accepted into NC Prep, Dad."

A moment of silence passed, and then Dad threw down the spatula, splattering the table with grease and bits of egg. "I cannot believe that sonnuva...I cannot believe he lied to you like that." His voice was drowning in anger, choking on it. I felt the same strangling sensation in my throat.

"What do you mean, he *lied* to me, Dad?"

Graham wouldn't have lied to me about not being at school with me, would he? My mind raced around the fact that our entire summer— perhaps our entire friendship—had been a lie; the facts were staring me in the face, and yet I just couldn't accept it.

"Grace, Graham isn't going to NC Prep. No one is. The school is no more—defunct. It's been closed down for three weeks now. Janice told me over month ago that it had lost a lot of money on some big investments and couldn't afford to operate anymore."

Janice was Dad's girlfriend of the moment. Aside from being the one to last the longest among all of Dad's girlfriends, she was also the school nurse at NC Prep; how had I forgotten that?

"So Janice is now out of a job?" I asked, trying to buy some time to process this bit of information. If the school was closed, that means that Graham would be attending Heath High School...with Erica...and...me. The forkful of eggs and toast in my mouth suddenly felt like lead; it weighed down my tongue, and the metallic taste of something I didn't recognize filled my senses as they clobbered each other to occupy space in my already confused mind.

I was so consumed by this new piece of information that I barely heard Dad as he answered me. "Technically, she's been out of a job for a while now. She's having difficulties finding other work, both in Heath and Newark, and she's getting desperate. Her unemployment is set to run out soon."

He put his hand on my shoulder, pressing down in what should have been a reassuring gesture, but instead felt more like he was holding me down for what he had left to say. He looked into my eyes once more, hesitant, as though he knew that what would come next would cause a negative reaction. "Grace, I asked Janice if she'd like to stay here with us until she can get back on her feet. I wanted to tell you a week ago, but you were still in such a state, I couldn't bring it up."

Stupid Graham. Stupid North Cumberland. Stupid me. Look at me—reduced to juvenile insults. Why did I have to open my mouth? All it ever did was disappoint me in some way.

"You invited her to live with us? Without talking to me?" I was incredulous. I was angry. I was…hurt.

He looked down at the table and stared at his plate, now full of cold, greasy eggs surrounded by stale toast. "Janice needs a place to stay, Grace. She's been out of work for too long, and she can't afford her mortgage on top of all of her other bills. You're almost an adult, getting ready to head off to college, to a whole new life without your old man. I didn't think that it would be a big deal if she stayed here."

Janice. Janice "*Du Jour*" Dupre. Janice "The-woman-who-wants-to-take-my-mom's-spot" Dupre was going to be moving in to my mom's home. Sleep in my mom's bed. Cook in my mom's kitchen. The thought disgusted me. The betrayal to my mom turned the already congealed blood within me to ice. Could things get any worse?

Dad took a deep breath, exhaling it slowly while his hands gripped the table, preparing for what came next.

Of course. Things could always get worse.

"Grace. Listen. I care about Janice a great deal. She's funny and she makes me laugh, and that's not something I have done a lot of since your mom died—you know that better than anyone. Your mom will always be your mom, nothing can or will ever change that, and I

24

will always love her, but Janice is giving me a new start…at a lot of things."

Your mom? Suddenly she's no longer just "mom". She's *your* mom. And new start? At *a lot* of things? What *things*? What could he possibly need a new start at? The warning bells starting going off in my head. The knocking at the door of my consciousness turned into banging: insistent, desperate. A question quickly formed in my mind, a frightening question that I had to voice. I had to hear the words, even though I knew the answer before they ever left my lips.

"Dad—is Janice pregnant?"

His wide-eyed stare, coupled with his silence was, ironically, pregnant with the answer that I dreaded. He slowly nodded his head.

My face burned from embarrassment and anger. "Why, Dad? Oh my God, aren't you guys old enough to know how to use a condom or birth control pills?!"

Okay. I admit that I went too far, but what was I to do? My forty-seven-year-old father had just knocked up his girlfriend!

I sensed it before I saw it; Dad's face turned several shades of red before settling on a near ketchup-like color, and it couldn't have been more of a warning than if he'd actually had it tattooed on his forehead: I was about to get an earful.

"Grace Anne Shelley, don't you ever speak that way to me again! I won't be disrespected in my own home; you will do well to remember that, young lady. Yes, Janice *is* pregnant, and how that happened is none of your damned business! Yes, she *is* moving in with us in three days, and I expect you to be respectful to her, if not friendly, because this is *my* house, and when you disrespect someone *in* my house, you're disrespecting me."

I stared at his face, his nostrils flaring so wide that I considered shoving some bacon up there just to get him to stop talking about respect and houses, especially when he was planning on disrespecting Mom's memory by bringing *that* woman into *her* home. I really didn't like to pay much attention to him when he was angry. It saved me from having to relive the words he'd said later. The words he was about to say now.

"I love you, Grace Anne. I have loved you from the first moment you entered into this world, probably before you were even born. You're the best thing I've ever done, the best part of me and your mom. You make it easy to love you; you're a lot like your mom in that regard. But while it's easy to love you, Grace, it's very difficult to like you. It's hard. You make it so difficult with your expectations, your guilt!"

He shook his head, his disappointment clear, and then said quietly—almost too quietly—but not quietly enough, "Perhaps it was best that Graham ended your friendship. You always expected more from him than he could give you, especially after Mom died."

I felt my fingers dig into my thighs under the table and winced; my once numb body had started feeling again. It was feeling the burn of anger, betrayal, and…pain. But this time I wasn't going to let it turn me into a ball of gelatinous Grace. Instead, I got up, ignoring the outraged expression that crossed over Dad's face.

Déjà vu had me walking upstairs to my room. But rather than throwing myself on my bed to cry myself senseless again for another two weeks, I grabbed my book bag, tossed in my wallet and my binder, grabbed my MP3 player, and left.

The clock read twenty past seven.

I was going to be early to the worst day of my life.

ERICA

I stood in a line, invisible while in plain sight like any other day. Over half of the senior class was either in front or in back of me, all of us clamoring for our class schedules like junkies looking for a fix. Everyone else who had already endured the wait stood off to the side, comparing classes together. The typical questions were being passed around: who was in whose class, who would sit next to whom, who was going to be closest to the doors for a ditch day success, and who had free periods.

All I wanted to know was if Dad had been right. Would Graham be here? And if he was, would we be in any classes together? It was a strong possibility and I didn't know how I'd be able to handle that. Seeing him would be difficult enough. My heart, still nothing more than a cold pile of ashes, did nothing at the thought.

And then there he was, standing next to a beautiful girl with a halo of blonde hair that hung down her back like a gold curtain. They had their heads bent towards each other, comparing schedules and laughing, completely oblivious to the icy turmoil that raged within me just a few yards away. When she looked up at him, he smiled down at her, his hand reaching up to stroke her hair. His fingers trailed to her waist, and she leaned into him, her arm wrapping around his in return. I, in turn, felt nothing but the cold September air around me, still warmer than I was on the inside. But death wasn't supposed to be warm unless you were heading straight to Hell, right?

Well, I was in Hell. A cold, dead, Graham-holding-onto-a-beautiful-blonde-Erica filled Hell.

A little cough from behind me alerted me to the fact that I was next; great, caught daydreaming again. I hurried forward and quickly whispered my name to the registrar whose name I could never remember, despite seeing her every single year for the past four. The difference between the two of us was that while people avoided me because I was odd, they avoided her because of how mean she could be if you dared to cross her. It was the main reason she was as popular as she was. No one felt brave enough to stand up to her; beauty and money were intimidating things.

And she was certainly beautiful. The ice blue eyes that glared past heavy lids were so full of malice, one often felt like they had no choice but to continue to look at her for fear of havoc she'd unleash if you did not. Her smile was full, but upon closer inspection it was plain that she did so through gritted teeth, as though expressing genuine pleasure was somehow painful or annoying.

I stared at her, trying to find a reason to like her, if only to make it easier to see why Graham had chosen her. Did she have a redeeming quality of some sort that I didn't see that Graham did? Everyone knew she was rich, and obviously she was beautiful and popular, but was that it? Graham had never been *that* superficial… On second thought, she did remind me of one of Graham's favorite actresses who was always casted as the cold, calculating high school villain. Maybe that was it. He liked the beautiful girls with the flawed personalities. I was just flawed.

"Did you see him? Oh my GAWD, he was beautiful! HAWT!" Erica gushed. "I think Graham was getting jealous that he was staring at me for so long. Oh-Em-Gee, those EYES! I swear, they were so amazing! It felt like he could see right into me!"

Another voice replied, "I know! He stared at you for, like, *ever*! Like you were something he wanted to eat! And Graham should be jealous. Hell, *I'm* jealous! He's not the cutest guy in school anymore!"

More giggling filled the room.

I wanted to gag.

"Speaking of Graham, did you see that freak friend of his? She ran right into that new guy and it was like she bounced off! He repelled her like he had some super power against freakiness or something! Hawtman!" the other voice laughed.

I could see Erica through the crack between the door and the frame of the stall. She was staring in the mirror at her reflection, a twisted smirk on her face.

No. Her eyes were focused somewhere else. She was staring...
At me.

She could see me, knew I was there. She pulled up her lips into
a very cruel smile and spoke, "Graham and Grace aren't friends
anymore, Becca. He ended their friendship a couple of weeks ago when
I told him it was her or me." She began messing with her hair. The
long, blonde strands shimmered like spun gold, even under the
fluorescent lights of the bathroom; the type of hair that Graham always
said he hated, but the exact same hair that he had been playing with just
a few moments ago.

A snickering-snorting sound followed. "He chose you over his
best friend? Girl, he must love you. Those two have been tight since
diapers!"

Erica nodded, still staring at me, the cruel, warped smile
distorting the beauty of her face. "Of course he loves me. He told me
that there's no one else who makes him feel the way that I do, that he
trusts more than me. He said there's no competition when it comes to
me and how he feels. And really, why would there be? I mean, look at
me! I at least look like I have girl parts!" she cracked, pushing her
breasts together and making a moue with her lips, winking—whether at
her own reflection or at me I didn't know.

Girl parts—apparently another reason why I wasn't quite fit to
play the part of Graham's girlfriend and Erica was. I knew that I wasn't
curvaceous. In truth, I was more like the rectangle to her oval; corners
where there should be curves. I had breasts, but they just weren't made
of quite enough of the stuff that guys liked to gawk at. I'm fairly certain
that I look passable in a bathing suit, but I'd never grace the cover of
some swimsuit magazine. I didn't really think that that had any bearing
on Graham and me, but looking at Erica's body, how her little pink top
and her brown corduroy skirt hugged her shape, I understood that I
wasn't physically attractive to Graham either. It just kept piling on,
didn't it?

Erica put her hands down and started digging through her bag.
"Did you know that she told him she was in love with him the day he

33

ended it? He told me about it afterwards and we laughed at how pathetic that was. God, she's desperate. He even told me how he always felt sorry for her because her mom had died and everything—but that just proves what a good guy he is doesn't it? So goddamn charitable.

"He said that her mother was some illegal immigrant or something, and that she probably died from some disease they have in those third world countries that had been dor-something…I don't remember what it was he said, but she probably had it when she was pregnant, and now Grace might have it, too. Isn't that…*sad*?"

She pulled out a tube of gloss and started to swipe her lips with it, puckering and pouting, apparently gauging the level of coverage. She smiled, and then frowned. Too much gloss—a large amount had landed on her teeth; a nice, hot pink chunk. Despite the rage that was boiling inside of me at the blatant lies that she was telling, I couldn't help but smile a little at that.

Becca broke in then, her high-pitched voice causing me to grit my teeth. "I thought her mom died in a car accident. Some freakish explosion or something. Hmm. Learn something new every day. Wait—she actually said she was in love with him?"

Erica nodded again, quickly wiping away the foreign pink spot on her teeth with some tissue she pulled out of her bag, and smirked. "Of course, I wouldn't be surprised if she tried to attach herself to this new guy. Did you see the way she looked at him? Like a dog in heat; how pathetic. If Graham doesn't want her, what makes her think that this guy would give her the time of day?

"She probably just wants to be his friend, just to be able to say that she was friends with the two hottest guys in school. Of course, from the way he was looking at me this morning, I don't doubt I could take him away from her, too. Not that she'd even be able to catch his attention. Not in *those* clothes anyway."

Take who away from me? Was she talking about the gray-eyed god that had somehow gotten my heart beating again without so much as a word? The one who I had absolutely embarrassed myself in front of? The one who made my knees feel like they were made out of water?

Ugh…she was right. I am pathetic.

"Did you hear his name, though?" the Becca person asked, leaning forward to inspect her makeup. I saw her then. Her hair was just as blonde as Erica's, but with dark roots peeking through, and it was cut short in a sloping bob. Her eyes were dark, like mine, and void of any real sincerity. She had berry stained lips, and when she reached up to touch them, as if checking to see if the stain would rub off, I noticed her nails were painted the exact same shade.

"Uh-uh," Erica responded, shaking her head while still watching me. "I was too busy staring at his eyes when he told Graham. Something about those eyes just makes me want to do whatever he wants. Anyway, he'll probably tell me in class. I think we have sixth period theater together. I took a peek at his schedule while he was talking to Graham. Did you know he speaks with a British accent?"

"No way! That's hawt!"

Somewhere deep, under all of the rage and sadness that was pulling me under, I made a mental note to somehow develop a pill that made the word "*hawt*" impossible to utter by vapid blondes… especially the bottled variety.

"I know! I can't wait to hear his voice again. It was like listening to melted honey," Erica moaned, licking her gooey pink lips.

The one named Becca cackled. A genuine cackle. I half expected her skin to explode into bright green warts and a pointy black hat to magically appear on her head as she flew around the bathroom on her broomstick. "You're such a slut! Please tell me, what does '*melted honey*' sound like, Mrs. Shakespeare?"

Erica shrugged. She looked at me once more. "It sounds hot and slow and sweet…a lot like Graham when he's kissing me. Mmm…I wonder what the new guy kisses like. If his voice gets me all hot, imagine what his lips are like!" She turned her body sideways in the mirror, sucking in her stomach while examining her figure. "I wonder if he'll be like Graham. Graham's obsessed with making out— wants to do it all the time. He especially likes kissing *this*." She slapped her rear end on that last word in emphasis.

With a shrill peal of laughter, the two of them left, the

resounding cackles bouncing off the walls long after they had gone and the door had closed.

Long after the bell had rung.

Long after I had stopped fighting the tears.

SO WE MEET AGAIN

I entered my homeroom class five minutes before it was time to head off to first period, my face a puffy, blotchy mess. I didn't even bother to try and set myself to rights. No one would notice me anyway.

Mr. Frey was, as I expected, asleep at his desk. A piece of paper was perched carelessly on his face, rising and falling with each snore; it had the words "I'll teach when I'm sober" written on it in red ink. The raucous nature that is every homeroom occupied by Mr. Frey didn't skip a beat when I walked in. Like some amorphous being, it accepted me without a ripple of distortion. I somehow found an empty desk and proceeded to wait until the bell rang to proceed to first period. All around me, I could hear the laughter of friendship, the stories that were told filled with fond memories, and I felt my spirits grow heavier by the second.

With nothing left to do but wait, the thoughts that I had tried to avoid came barreling through my mind. Graham was here, and he had lied to me. Well, of course he had *lied* to me. But to do it while trying to making it seem as though he was finally being honest was a double lie. And to hear that Erica was now interested in this new guy… Oh Graham. He broke my heart for a girl that was already looking to replace him. I felt the ashes in my chest begin to get soggy…as though I was now crying on the inside.

Just when I was sure that my body would explode from the seemingly endless internal flooding, the bell signaling the end of homeroom rang mercifully. I was off to French class. Madame Hidani would provide a respite from the tortuous reminiscing. She knew how to keep a class in hand and focus our attention onto more important things. Like vowels.

I walked into the familiar classroom, feeling a bit better as I saw the long list of tasks we had to complete by the end of today's lesson.

No small talk allowed here. It was straight business with Madame Hidani. There would be no time to think. No time to listen. No time to feel. It sounded like heaven.

A group of girls were gathered around a central figure at the front of the classroom, near the poster of Manet's famous print, "*Le déjeuner sur l'herbe*". I didn't spend any time paying attention to their giggling and chattering and took a seat in the back of the class; the same seat I had occupied last year; the same seat where I had helped Graham pass each and every single French test we had. I shook my head again, forcing the thoughts about him out of my mind. I wouldn't be thinking about him for the next hour, I vowed to myself.

The bell rang, and the gaggle of girls at the front started to disperse. I reached into my book bag and pulled out my binder. A writing assignment had been placed up on the board, and Madame Hidani was doing her best to calm down the chatter so that we could focus and begin. Well…so that everyone else could focus and begin. I was ready. More than ready to not have to think about Graham, my summer vacation, or blondes with perfect bodies and pink lip gloss on their teeth.

Or, at least I thought I was.

There on the blackboard, in clear chalky words was our assignment. In French, we had to give a two page description of our summer break.

Even Madame Hidani had turned on me!

I groaned and quickly looked around to see if anyone had heard me. I swallowed down a gulp of shock. Rows and rows of heads were turned, facing me. Was there not a single soul in the school who didn't know what had happened? I counted eighteen pairs of eyes all looking in my direction. Eighteen *female* eyes.

Of course they were all female. French was a romantic language, and no seventeen or eighteen-year-old boys were interested in romance. They were interested in cars, and breasts, and breasts on cars. And it was because of this bit of knowledge that I could say, quite honestly to myself, that it was no wonder that they were all staring…those eighteen pairs of eyes weren't staring at me. Of course not. They were staring at *HIM*.

A warm, pulling sensation in my solar plexus forced me to turn my head towards my right. The only seat next to me, the one that Graham had filled just one year ago—the one that had been empty when I walked in—was now occupied.

It was the gray-eyed god, and he was staring, his silver eyes locked on me. I felt just as uncomfortable then as I had in the bathroom with Erica staring at me in the mirror. Moreover, I felt embarrassed. Could it be possible that I was feeling more self-conscious than I had when I thought that all of the eyes were on me? I blushed just then, and knew that the answer was yes, I was.

"So we meet again," he said to me softly, a hint of wry humor tingeing the bass in his voice. His accent was something you'd only hear on television or the radio: clean, smooth, very English. And he smiled—an earth stopping, breath stopping, universe stopping smile.

I swallowed—it sounded loud enough to wake the dead. It was definitely loud enough to startle me. "Are you talking to me?" I croaked, another rush of heat flooding my cheeks as I heard the nervousness in my voice.

He nodded. And then, impossibly, his smile grew. "I don't recall anyone else bumping into me and leaving before I could offer assistance. Or, at the very least, introduce myself."

I didn't think that I was capable of blushing so often, in such a short period of time. My heart wasn't exactly in the best shape to be sending any unnecessary blood anywhere else but to my brain and my limbs—it already felt as though that was putting an extreme strain on my entire body—yet the blush came so easily, as if from some magical spring of embarrassment. "I apologized for that." I said quickly. Too quickly.

"You sure did, Grace," a girl I knew as Lacey Greene who was sitting directly in front of me snickered. "But it was more like the sound that comes out of a constipated cow."

As quickly as my cheeks had warmed by the rush of blood, they turned to ice by the loss. I turned to look at her but she had eyes only for our new classmate, seizing the opportunity afforded to her by my reaction to her flippant comment. I turned back to look at him. Gone was his smile, replaced by a grim line and a disgusted glint in his eyes; it appeared that he agreed. I *had* sounded like a constipated cow.

I turned my attention back to my paper. I wrote my name down in the upper right hand corner, the date, and the period with some antiquated pencil that I found in the bottom of my bag. I titled the assignment and started thinking of a way to tell Madame Hidani that my summer had been one big practical joke on me, and that the only friend I had in the world had been pitying me this whole time.

After a few minutes, I couldn't see my paper anymore. Tears—heavy and thick with grief—were blurring my view of just about everything. But they did not fall. Remarkably, they remained contained, merely teasing me with their weighted sting. Surely they would not fall before a roomful of catty girls, most of whom had always hated my close friendship with Graham, would they? Of course, it wasn't really as close a friendship as everyone thought it was, so they couldn't have wanted that, could they? No. I was sure that no one would have wanted to be made to look as foolish and gullible as I had.

But then again, this was Graham Hasselbeck. It didn't matter if he forgot your name; it was enough that he had at least acknowledged that you even existed. And he had always seemed to look beyond the fact that I lacked any outer beauty, still finding me wanting in some way, even if only in friendship. To them, that was him being charitable; an admirable trait in any guy, much less the most popular guy in school. And still I wondered…would he still be in my life had I chosen to keep my feelings to myself?

No. Erica had been quite clear on that. He would have done it sooner or later. I just gave him the opening he needed.

The bell rang—the tone shrill and piercing—wrenching me from my thoughts. Had the hour gone by already? The clock perched on the wall certainly seemed to think so. I heard Madame Hidani call for our papers to be brought forward to her desk…all two pages. All around me groans and complaints were being uttered—apparently I wasn't the only one who hadn't done the class assignment.

I looked down at my blank sheet of paper, having written just my name and title. Only…it was filled with writing—my writing. When did I write this? I skimmed it over quickly and recognized bits about working at the library, saving money for school… How?

Seeking some kind of obvious answer, I looked at the seat in front of me, knowing that it would be empty. I turned to the seat next to me. It, too, was empty.

Perplexed, I began gathering up my things. With shaky hands I grabbed my paper and handed it to Madame Hidani who smiled at me upon seeing my lazy scrawl. "Fantastique!" she cheered in her lilting French. "You're only the second person to turn this assignment in, Mademoiselle Shelley."

"Who else turned in the assignment?" I asked, hoping that the curious tone in my voice masked my nervousness. I didn't believe for a second that I wrote what she was holding in her hand, but there wasn't a single other person in the room who had put any effort into the assignment, from my understanding, so…

"Oh, the new student, Monsieur Bellegarde also turned his paper in. Five pages, if you can believe it!" she crowed. She held it up so I could see. The neat and elegant handwriting was beautiful, and completely unlike anything I had ever seen with its loops and curls that looked more like something that came out of an eighteenth century history book. He had written five pages of that? As if she read my mind, she nodded. "He spent some time in France while abroad—his mother is a native of France—and so this was child's play for him. I think I'll have to come up with much more difficult classroom assignments if I'm going to keep him interested, eh?" She seemed giddy at the prospect. I cringed.

Excusing myself, I lugged my book bag over my shoulder and headed off to Mrs. Hoppbaker's class, saying a quick "*Adieu*" to Madame Hidani while pondering what exactly had transpired while I was lost in my thoughts. I knew that I didn't write that paper. At least…I think I didn't. It *was* my handwriting; I couldn't doubt that. The Ls were tilted to the right, and the Xs were crooked, just like they always were. I remembered seeing that. But why didn't I remember writing those Ls and Xs?

Mrs. Hoppbaker's class was half full by the time I got there. Of course, it being an elective math class, it was filled with those who should be more comfortable with someone like me, but my friendship with Graham had alienated that crowd just as surely as it had alienated the popular kids—I was no man's land when it came to friendship.

Sighing, I took yet another backroom seat and started copying the year's syllabus down on a sheet of paper pulled from my binder. I took no notice of the absence of a very large presence until the bell rang.

"Good morning, class. My name is Mrs. Hoppbaker, and I am so skinny, you could blindfold me with dental floss," said a very familiar voice from a very unfamiliar body.

"Mrs. Hoppbaker?" a boy I remembered as Ian asked incredulously, his mouth hanging open with the same shock that the rest of the class was buzzing with.

The thin woman with the beautiful chestnut hair and glowing skin the color of a summer peach smiled at him. "Yes sir, Mr. Thompson. It's me, Mrs. Hoppbaker. Over one-hundred pounds lighter, healthier, and just as funny as ever if I do say so myself, although modesty isn't one of my virtues, so I hope none of you were expecting that."

My jaw was touching my desk. I could feel it. She was beautiful! Not that she hadn't been so before she lost the weight, but the amount of confidence she exuded, coupled with the loss of a whole person in body fat looked incredible on her!

She spent the first fifteen minutes of class time answering questions about her weight loss, which came thanks to the gastric bypass surgery she had done the day school was let out three months ago. How in the world does someone lose over a hundred pounds in three months someone asked. Exercise, eating right, and lots and lots of extracurricular activities came her reply—I didn't want to guess as to what those activities could mean.

It was no secret that Mrs. Hoppbaker and Mr. Hoppbaker were

in love. They were the only people to ever have been kicked out of the Indian Mound Mall movie theater for making out. Of course, Mrs. Hoppbaker and Mr. Hoppbaker had both weighed the equivalent of six people at the time, and a great to-do was made of it, but in the end they both said that they should have kept it a little more PG and a lot less NC-17.

I was so amazed at the transformation in her that I failed to notice that while everyone else's eyes were on her, one pair was on me. It wasn't until I heard my pencil drop onto the floor and bent down too retrieve it that I turned to see them: A pair of gray eyes, focused so intently on my every move, I almost stopped breathing.

"I might sound like a broken record here, but so we meet again," a soft, soothing voice spoke.

My attempt to sit up was so abrupt, my head connected with the corner of my desk with painful accuracy. The sound seemed to reverberate around the now silent classroom. When did the questions for Mrs. Hoppbaker stop? Why did they have to stop now—right when I happen make a fool of myself all over again? "Idiot," I mumbled to myself as I grabbed my head with my left hand.

The giggling and laughter that erupted surrounded me, and the suffocating feeling of embarrassment began to overwhelm. A warm hand reached over to cover my free one just then and time seemed to stop. Everything was blurred by a misty haze while electricity seemed to shoot between the microscopic space between our hands—a human Jacob's ladder—the current bouncing between the two of us as I slowly raised myself upright. My breathing eased, my head stopped hurting, and my left hand dropped down. I looked into those gray eyes again, not exactly sure what I'd see, but positive that whatever it was it would never leave my mind for as long as I lived.

"Not gray…silver…" I whispered, burning the mysterious shade to memory before he could blink—before I could blink.

The sound of the bell woke me from my dreamy fog. Class was over; how did that happen? How did I manage to daydream through two classes in a row? Everyone was standing up, grabbing their books and heading off to their third periods. I looked over to my right at the empty desk. Had I imagined it all? Had I been daydreaming and everything that I thought had taken place…hadn't? I looked towards the front of the classroom at Mrs. Hoppbaker. Nope. She was still thinner and beautiful.

I stood up and dreamily headed out the door to my next class. What was my next class? I had been so preoccupied by the sight of Mr. Branke's name on my schedule that I had completely skipped over it. I scrambled into my book bag for the small sheet of paper and scanned the class list. There was a big, blank spot where the period before lunch was supposed to be. A free period! There was a God!

I headed towards the school library on anxious feet. It was my sanctuary. It was where I knew that I wouldn't run into Graham or Erica, and I was sure that I wouldn't run into the new boy either. I walked through the double doors of the school library and took a deep breath—the smell of books was always comforting. I had made a vow with myself at the beginning of summer that should I ever become filthy, stinking rich, I'd buy myself a million books, if only to smell them. Much like people loved the smell of new cars, I was enthralled by the smell of the written word.

I found a table near the restroom and plunked myself down onto a chair, tossing my book bag onto the ground. I took out the pencil that I had used in French class and stared at the tip. It was still sharp— barely used. Did I have an unknown pen that I'd absentmindedly used instead? I rummaged through my bag, turning out its contents in vain. A dollar and some odd change, a paper clip, three rubber bands for my hair, an old gum wrapper, my MP3 player and my binder full of paper were all that were there. I didn't even have a single book.

Perplexed, I placed everything except the trash back in my bag, and continued to stare at my nearly unused pencil. I knew I had written my name and date, title and period on my French paper. I knew that I had gotten through at least three points of the syllabus for Calculus.

The syllabus—it was still in my folder! I quickly took it out again and opened it up. There, staring up at me on the first page was the exact same syllabus, written in my hand; thirteen points of classroom discussions, testing, and assignments, described in detail; I could only remember writing the first three.

There was something fishy going on and I didn't know what to make of it. Perhaps it was everything I had gone through these past few weeks. Maybe all of this stress…maybe it was making me zone out and I was simply writing out of reflex. Some people are capable of driving home long distances without realizing it after great stresses in their lives. Why not writing? It seemed rational enough—if I said it enough times, maybe I'd start to believe it. And why not? The entire school already thinks I'm pretty damn gullible now, so I should be able to convince myself of just about anything.

Like how the gray-eyed god had been in two of my classes and he had deliberately sat down next to me in both of them…and had spoken to me…twice. And he touched my hand; I didn't imagine that. Oh no. He really had touched my hand; his hand was warm, soft…not like the calloused hands of my dad, or even Graham. With that brief contact, he had somehow compressed the scattered ashes in my chest back into a solid mass, the force of it causing it to ignite. And it burned, still. With his pewter eyes and his warm hand, he had rendered me speechless, clumsy, breathless…and whole.

And I still didn't know his name!

What was it that Madame Hidani had said his last name was? Bellegarde? He was half French? What else did I remember about him? What color was his hair? I remembered fluttering, like a bird's wing—it was black. His hair was definitely black. That meant that those slate eyes were rimmed with black lashes. What about his face— what did it look like? Chiseled? Slightly. There was softness in his face…his smile. The smile that had made me forget how to breathe, or blink, it was so beautiful.

I felt my breath catch and my heart race as I remembered how it only grew when I had asked him if he were talking to me. It seemed an impossibility that he was referring to me when he uttered those few, mundane words that seemed to alter my world in less than a nanosecond. Meet again? Had we ever even met? Surely he couldn't consider my rudely bumping into him and then running away like a coward actually "*meeting*"…right?

Then again, he was part French, and even Madame Hidani made it a point to bring up the fact that the French are known to seem rude to those that have spent lifetimes dealing with courtesy and etiquette rules handed down by custom, as we in America are known to do. Perhaps he thought my bumping into him was familiar? My running off was glad tidings?

I shook my head at the insanity of the notion. No. What I did was rude in any language, any country. I was fooling myself here. It wouldn't do me any good to muddle my head with more inane notions with three more classes to go, and the one I dreaded the most coming up immediately after lunch.

I shuddered at the thought of Mr. Branke's creepy smile, his hairy arms, and his monstrous hands. I doubted that he'd focus as much attention on me this year—now that I was the laughingstock of the entire school there really wasn't any appeal left at all, if there had been any to begin with. But I could still mentally prepare myself for this while I had the chance.

Before I knew it, the bell was ringing, signaling the end of third period and the start of lunch. Nothing, absolutely nothing epitomized high school as one's own personal Hell like cafeteria food. There was just something about it that exuded torture with promises of terrifying consequences once consumed.

I looked around and saw that all of the students were being ushered out of the library towards the cafeteria. I grabbed my bag and headed glumly towards the aroma of what promised to be nothing but bland and slightly burnt food, another body among the masses headed towards our gastronomical slaughter. I stood in line, tray on the ready, trying to decipher what exactly was what, and what exactly was safe. I grabbed a baked potato because aside from not cooking it completely, there wasn't much one could do to screw it up; a bowl of chili, because cumin could save just about anything; a carton of milk, just in case the cumin failed, and headed towards the cashier. The middle aged woman behind the register was busy smiling and laughing with whomever it was that stood in front of me. I waited patiently as he gathered his change and placed it into his wallet. A nice wallet. Leather.

Expensive.

He turned around and faced me.

My gray-eyed god was standing in front of me, a tray of food in his hands, a bemused smile stretched across his face.

I felt a jerk within me. The fire in my heart started to grow. It was hot. No, not hot—it was burning.

I could feel the heat rising in my chest, that scorching sensation climbing the walls inside of me to reach the outside. I felt it burn through my clothes, scalding hot and real. And…it smelled like chili?

It had happened in an instant: One minute I was staring into the deepest pool of pewter—the next, I was wearing a very hot bowl of chili on my chest, while the hands of this beautiful stranger were on the back of my tray, now pressed against the burning spot that spread across my shirt. His fingers were touching mine, cool, soothing, contrasting quite loudly with the searing pain that was creeping across my chest and down to my abdomen. *That feels nice…*

His eyes widened in shock, and he stepped back. If not for the burning—burning from the heat of food, to the burning of eyes staring in my direction, and finally the burning of embarrassment at having been so unbelievably clumsy—I would have whimpered at the loss of that small amount of comfort I received in our contact. But I had to step back into reality and realize that I was now covered in spicy tomato sauce in front of the entire student body, and that I didn't know how it happened.

I heard a snort behind me and I turned to see Erica and Becca standing there, the two of them red-faced, trying very hard not to laugh…or look guilty. Graham stood stone faced behind the two, staring at the only thing that could keep attention focused away from me.

I turned back around to see for myself. He was kneeling, scraping the mess onto *his* tray!

"What are you doing?" I hissed as I bent down to remove the bowl and ruined chili from his tray and place it back onto mine. "This is my mess. I will clean it. Stop it—people are staring!"

He removed the bowl from my tray and placed it back onto his

47

while staring at me with a bemused gleam in his eyes. "I'm cleaning up *my* mess."

I glared at him. Silver eyes or not, he wasn't going to do this to me—he wasn't going to martyr himself in front of the entire cafeteria for Super Freak. "It's my chili, my bowl, my mess. I should have been more careful and paid attention to what I was doing." I reached for my bowl, prepared for him to argue again, but this time he didn't stop me. He didn't say or do anything as I placed the bowl back onto my tray. He simply waited until I was done, and then he stood up and left.

"Looks like even the new guy can't stand being around you, Freak," Erica's voice announced loudly, her tone full of mocking satisfaction. A few people around us tittered, while someone made an obnoxious sound in response. "Could you hurry up and clean up your mess so that the rest of us normal people can eat?"

Behind her, Graham's face was deadpan. It hurt.

I said nothing, just continued to clean up what I could, then headed towards the trash bin and emptied into it the remnants of my uneaten lunch. I mustered up what pride I could and, with my head held as high as possible, walked out of the cafeteria—and out of the school.

I didn't know where I was going, but I knew it wouldn't be to Mr. Branke's class smelling like chili and reeking of embarrassment. I couldn't go home, either—Dad was already upset with me, and I was equally upset with him, if not more so. While there was a good chance he was at work, if he weren't, coming home from school because my shirt was covered in food wouldn't exactly be conducive to repairing our relationship. I just had to be…away. I couldn't take another second of listening to Erica's voice, or seeing Graham pretend that I didn't exist. And I definitely couldn't stand to have *him* bear witness to the ridicule that had become my norm.

I hitched my backpack up higher on my shoulder and trudged down the sidewalk that would eventually disappear into a rocky shoulder and lead me towards the small public library that hid in rural Heath. I know Miss Maggie, the little old librarian who had been working there for the past thirty years wouldn't mind me showing up a few hours before school was supposed to let out. I just had to figure out how to get a change of clothes. I couldn't sit in an air conditioned room full of books smelling like I needed some sour cream and chives to go with my shirt, but going to the mall— which was in the opposite direction—wasn't an option either.

I had only been walking for about a mile, and was so lost in my thoughts that I didn't hear it approach: The low rumble of a vehicle that didn't sound like it belonged on a sidewalk, and yet was. I turned around and exclaimed, very loudly, "Oh dear bananas."

There on the sidewalk was the gray-eyed stranger. He was on a matte, midnight-black motorcycle that looked too expensive for any average adult to own, much less a high school kid, and he wore a jacket that was just as dark. His eyes peered out at me, framed in the black window of a helmet. He looked like black flame.

With a tick of his head, he motioned for me to get on.

"Are you nuts?" I shouted, shocked and incredulous.

He again motioned for me to get on, his head jerking more determinedly.

I turned around and walked in the opposite direction, which was exactly where I did not want to go: back to school. I didn't realize that he was right behind me again until I heard him rev the throttle. I turned and looked at him, furious that he hadn't gotten the clue the first time. Once again, he motioned for me to get on.

"Why?" I asked. Who was I to him?

His response was another turn of the throttle.

I made an attempt to reverse my present course and head back in the direction of the library when he made that black monster beneath him growl like something I had never heard before—a shiver ran down my back, but was it out of fear or…anticipation?

"Fine!" I shouted at him, "But don't you complain that your jacket stinks of beans and beef afterwards!" I climbed hesitantly onto the back of the bike, angry, confused. I looked down, my hands dangling clumsily at my sides. How do I hold on? The engine roared and the bike lurched forward—I realized as soon as my arms wrapped around him to keep from flying off that this was how it was done. An automatic response, I told myself. But the feeling of my arms around

49

the waist of this person was too delicious to be automatic. It was...phenomenal. I could feel the warmth from beneath the jacket radiate outward towards my skin, causing it to prickle with goose bumps.

We were flying. That's what it felt like. He was traveling so fast, I couldn't make out anything recognizable. So many questions flew through my head, like the buildings and trees that whipped by, each one blending into the other.

Where were we going? What was his name? Where did he come from, and why did he follow me? Would there be any way for me to change out of my chili-infused clothing? So many questions I wanted to ask him, but over the roar of the bike and the padding of the helmet, I knew that he wouldn't have been able to hear me, nor I his answers.

I simply rested by cheek on his back, knowing that there really wasn't anything he could do to stop me and held on tighter, enjoying this rare and unusual moment for as long as it lasted. I accepted that whenever I returned down to earth, the harsh reality that was slowly becoming my life would swallow me up whole and all I'd be left with was this memory.

I didn't want to move when we finally slowed down and came to a stop in a gravel filled parking lot that fronted what appeared to be a very large park. I hadn't been here before, and surely there wasn't much that I hadn't seen in Heath, what with having someone like Graham Hasselbeck as your best friend—*former* best friend. There wasn't a sign or any type of logo that hinted at a name. It was just a large, open field with a few picnic tables, a solitary bench, some enormous rocks for climbing and sunning yourself, and a playground with a swing set. The parking lot had four tall light poles in each corner that looked like miniature versions of the one that illuminated the baseball field behind the school.

As soon as I heard the engine turn off I hopped off the bike; it was as though the last bit of stored energy my legs contained had turned them into springs. He followed, although his movement was much more fluid—used to it. That's what it was. He was used to riding the bike, the feeling of that powerful vibration turning his insides to foam.

My legs felt permanently bowed, and they rattled like a penny in a coffee can after what could only have been a ten minute ride. I was embarrassing myself. Again.

"I always wanted to know how it felt to be a human compass," I muttered as I held onto my thighs in a vain attempt to keep them from shaking.

I could hear his muffled laughter and I looked up as he removed his helmet, my mouth suddenly still…gaping…dry.

Dear God in Heaven, how could someone be so beautiful? And what on earth was he doing here with me? Rather, what was *I* doing here with *him*? His hair, I realized now, was slightly longer than what was considered trendy here in Heath, and it was wavy. A chunk of it hung over his right eye, like a black velvet curtain hiding a star performer on the magnificent stage that was his face.

His nose, often a body part that looks so foreign on the human face, looked as though it had been sculpted from the same travertine stone of his skin. His cheekbones were high, sharp…almost dangerous. But his mouth—that *was* dangerous. Of that I was certain. His lips were full, poised at the ready to kill me with a smile. I knew it was coming any second now. How many times had I died today with just one quick twitch from his lips? This time, I was ready…a willing victim.

He looked at me. I closed my eyes, prepared. I took a deep breath, and then…

"So we meet again."

I opened my eyes and blinked.

Was this the only thing he knew how to say? A face so divine, a mouth so lethal, eyes so deep and mysterious, and when he speaks with that glorious voice that made my legs begin to tremble even harder—not from the bike ride, but from something else altogether—he has nothing new to say?

"Don't you know anything else to say other than '*so we meet again*'?" I yelled. Why was I yelling? I was furious, that's why! "You have no idea who I am. I certainly know a lot less about you, so tell me why would you follow me, tell me to ride with you on your-your-your

51

death machine, and then choose *that* to say, with everything else that I'm sure you want to know?"

He folded his arms across his chest and smiled. He was amused!

"Why are you smiling? This isn't funny. I'm in the middle of God knows where-" I eyed him up and down "-with God knows who, and I stink of beans and *beef*!"

For whatever reason, my mouth was moving on its own, the words falling out like the bottom had been torn out of a rusty old coffee can filled with secrets. "My best friend—well, he's not my best friend anymore, and he probably never really was—hates me. My father is starting a new family without me with a woman I cannot stand. I just ditched my first day of school…for the first time…*ever*; and the only thing you can say to me is '*so we meet again*', as if that is somehow the most important, most relevant phrase in the history of the spoken word?"

I was breathing hard; all of the angry feelings that I had dammed up within me were leaking, oozing out of every pore, slowly deflating the balloon I had felt growing inside of me, suffocating me. I had never really done it before—yell at someone for no reason other than because I was angry—it felt good. "I'm through being the damn punch line for everyone's jokes, so you can wipe that stupid smirk off of your face. You're new here so you're seventeen years late for the joke anyway."

He took a step forward, the slight motion causing me to take one back for some nameless reason. "I don't recall you responding in a very pleasant manner when I said it the first time, and I received no response the second time, and now after saying it again this third time, you give me a response in the form of a little tantrum. You should be glad that I'm amused, rather than turned off," he answered me, calmly, matter-of-factly. He reached for the seat of the motorcycle; lifting it, he removed a small bundle from within and handed it to me. "And, just in case I was rude by not introducing myself earlier, my name is Robert N'Uriel Bellegarde."

Robert. Now I knew something that Erica did not. I knew his name. I felt the beginnings of a reluctant smile form on my lips, but I quickly squashed it. "So you *do* know more than four words of English. Good. That'll make it easier to yell at you later—I hate yelling at people who can't understand what I'm saying," I joked nervously, grabbing the item in his hand. "What is this?"

He shrugged his shoulders. "You complained about smelling like beef and beans. That's an extra shirt I carry with me in case I ever need a clean one, and it just so happens that today, I do. Or, at least, you do."

I looked at the bundle of cloth in my hands. This was a shirt? But it felt so…nice! Soft, like an old t-shirt, but it wasn't old, faded cotton with some cheesy screen print on it. I was a stranger to anything different. This shirt, if one could call it that, was a gunmetal gray, shimmery, and smelled…it smelled incredible. I looked up at him, wondering why he would give me his shirt when he didn't even know me. What was I but a nobody to him? I looked around nervously and laughed; where was I going to change?

"I'm not a fan of chili—the smell offends me—so I would appreciate it if you would change; we're completely alone here, so you can change right where you are. I'll turn my back, if that will make you feel better." He paused and looked at me, his expression bemused, contemplative. "And I *do* know you, Grace. You're not the nobody you think you are."

I didn't even notice that he had answered the questions in my head before I had had the chance to ask it out loud until later.

SECRETS

He turned around so that I could remove my now crusty, chili-drenched clothing with some semblance of modesty. The shirt was probably impossibly stained now—there was no saving it—so I just balled it up and threw it into a nearby trashcan after using it to wipe up the chili that had leaked through onto my chest. I quickly slipped on his shirt, gasping at how silky it felt against my skin. It definitely was far more expensive than anything I owned. It hung like a sack on my body, though; trailing down to my thighs, the collar hung low over my chest. I looked down and sighed. There really was nothing there to cover anyway, so why try and be modest?

"Okay, you can turn around now," I told him, confident that I was looking as decent as humanly possible.

He put his hands into his pockets and slowly turned to face me. The look on his face didn't reveal to me anything as to how he felt about the way I looked in his shirt. Of course I would look hideous in it; the color was wrong for me, if I paid any attention to that sort of thing to begin with, and there was no shape to it—or me for that matter.

"Thank you for the shirt," I said, not quite sure exactly what to make of his vacant expression. "And I'm sorry about your jacket and the...er...tantrum."

Nothing.

"I do want to know where we are, though. I want to know why you picked me up. I want to know how you knew what I was going to ask before I asked it. And...I want to know why me. Why me of all people?" I rambled.

His smile returned. This looked promising. "So many questions from someone who couldn't even say hello. Well let's see if I can answer all of them to your liking. We're at the Bellegarde family retreat, I picked you up because you shouldn't be walking alone, I read your mind, and because you're different. *Very* different."

Did he just say he *read* my mind? "Wait a minute. You *read* my mind-" saying it out loud didn't make it any more believable "-you actually *read* my mind?" Didn't convince me that second time either. "And what do you mean, I'm '*different*'?"

"*Very* different," he corrected.

"I heard you the first time," I snapped. "What exactly do you mean by that? And answer me about the mind reading thing!" I was glaring at him, annoyed that he had me sounding like a parrot. I didn't like these up and down emotions that he was causing in me, either. One minute I was ready to melt into a puddle at his feet. The next, I wanted to rip his eyes out of their sockets. This wasn't me at all, and I didn't like it.

He started walking towards a bench, motioning for me to follow, and then sat down. "I can hear your thoughts just as clearly as if you spoke them aloud, Grace. And," he paused for effect, "you *are* very different. You're not like the other girls in school at all. Actually, you're not like any girl, period."

Well that was no surprise. "Everyone knows that I'm not like the other girls in school. It's called being ostracized, Robert." How weird that felt—saying his name so casually, like we had been friends for ages…it came out so naturally, I felt giddy and embarrassed all at once. I turned my face away as I sat down, not wanting to see the reaction to my use of his name. Of course I feared the likely rejection of my assumed familiarity, but more than that, I feared that I might see the opposite…and hated myself for even thinking such a possibility could exist.

I continued talking while staring at my shoes, "How can you hear my thoughts? Can you hear what I'm thinking right now?"

I looked at him and focused, my eyebrows drawing together with deep concentration. *Is this coming in loud and clear to you, breaker-breaker?*

He laughed. It was a very rich sound—vibrant and multi-faceted, like an audible prism—I marveled at the way it seemed to fill my head with its resonant tone. "I hear you loud and clear," he replied to my silent question.

Gape mouthed, I stared at him.

What's four plus four?

"Eight."

Who wrote the Star Spangled Banner?

"Frances Scott Key."

Why did the rooster cross the road?

"Because it was stuck in the chicken."

How are you doing *this?*

"I was born with this ability."

My mouth was gaping so widely, I felt like an open back door. *You were* born *with it?*

He nodded. And then I heard a voice inside my head. It sounded tinny…strange…faint. Slowly it grew louder. Stronger, until it was, as Robert had described, as clear as it if were spoken aloud.

And now, Grace, you can hear my *thoughts.*

I fell off the bench. A loud "umph" came out of my mouth as I landed on the hard ground in complete shock. He laughed at me again, only this time I heard it twice, like an echo both outside and inside of my mind.

"You…you're in m-my-my head!" I gasped.

So I am.

"Stop it!" I shouted. I grabbed my ears with my hands, as though that would work to keep him out, as if he were merely throwing his voice, rather than his thoughts. And then, just to make sure, I started la-la-la-ing. It wasn't my finest moment to be sure, but this wasn't exactly the time to be wowing a judging panel.

Why is it easy for you to accept that I can read your thoughts, but not that you can also hear mine?

"Who said that I accepted you reading my thoughts? For goodness sake, people aren't supposed to read other people's thoughts! And I wasn't born with this…this…*thing*! Why should I accept hearing your thoughts?" I shouted, exasperated, annoyed…frightened.

"Grace, I told you that you were different. Most girls would be trying to think dirty thoughts around me—most girls do no matter

56

what—but not you." He knelt beside me on the ground. He put his hand under my chin and lifted my face so that I could look at him. Or that he could look at me. Secretly, I hoped it was the latter.

"It is," he reassured me, grinning when he saw me grimace—a reaction to him hearing what I didn't say. "I don't want to scare you, Grace. I cannot explain to you how, but I just knew—deep inside of me—that you'd be able to learn of my secret, and keep it. The way a *friend* is supposed to."

Was it really that simple? All he wanted was a friend? If that was it, why did I feel so disappointed?

"I want *you* as my friend," he said, smiling as he offered me his hand.

"Okay, look. That's really going to annoy the crap out of me," I told him, taking it and pulling myself up to a standing position. "My thoughts are my own. I'm sure you wouldn't like someone always digging around in your private thoughts, would you?"

He shrugged, his expression stoic. "My sister is always in my thoughts, needling her way to find out bits of gossip, or secrets she can blab to one of her girlfriends. It's no big thing. If there's something I don't want her to know, it's not that difficult to keep hidden." He looked down at my hand, still enclosed in his, and smiled again.

I forgot what I was going to say because I, too, was staring down at our hands joined together. I didn't realize that I had never let go...and that he hadn't either. I also didn't know that when touching like this, skin to skin, I couldn't stop the influx of thoughts that passed between the two of us.

It flowed like water into my head—filling up crevices that had been empty for longer than I had been alive—as my mind seemed to drain of everything it had ever contained to make room. His voice filled my head, roaming around in my mind, echoing, calling, searching...searching for what? I was starting to feel full, stretched too tight. I felt my face pinch, wincing as the pain was beginning. It was throbbing, merciless...the pressure was increasing at an enormous rate and it didn't seem close to abating any time soon. I could see his face, his wide, fear filled eyes; he was hearing my inner cries of pain, and they were hurting him.

You…need…to…let…go…Grace.

And then he was gone.

Everything was gone.

ℜ

I was lying on a bench, something hard beneath my throbbing head. I felt something dripping from my face—it being wiped up by something cool and wet. I could smell the rusty tang of blood, and the syrupy sweet smell of something unfamiliar. My eyes opened to two big pools of liquid mercury staring worriedly into my face.

"Are you okay?"

I tried to sit up, but I couldn't move—something was holding me down. I looked back at those liquid pools and realized that at the way they were angled, I had to be lying down in his lap. My eyes flicked down to my chest, and saw his hand was pressing down on my abdomen. I turned my head and saw his other hand was holding down my left shoulder. I couldn't get up because he was holding me down.

I looked up into his face once more and said in a shaky voice, "I'm fine. I just need to sit up."

He looked reluctant to let me go, but eased his grip on me and slowly helped me into a sitting position. The dizziness that engulfed me was troubling. I felt like I had been drained of all my strength and energy—not unlike how one feels after not eating all day. I looked at Robert's hand, the one that I had been holding when my mind started suffocating—that's what it was, my mind had suffocated—underneath the rush of his every thought. In it was a cloth that appeared to be stained with blood…but whose?

"It's yours. Your nose started bleeding right after you fainted," Robert answered guiltily. He seemed very pale, his voice just as shaky as mine. Of course he would. He'd been in my head, shared the same fear, saw everything in my head go black…and he'd shared my pain. That would be enough to scare anyone out of their wits.

I reached for the cloth he was holding and looked into his face.

I decided to try something. I needed to focus on something. I looked at his lips—too distracting—his nose, yes, his nose would work. It was a mighty fine looking nose, but when I blocked out everything else, it was just a nose, and I could concentrate. *Is it still bleeding?*

Not anymore. It stopped just before you woke up. And thank you about my nose.

I was so amazed, I actually blushed. Where once I might have been terrified—even mortified—now I was in utter and complete awe; he could hear my thoughts, and I could hear his. This was a genuine connection. With someone I didn't know at all.

"What do you want to know?" he asked me, turning so that he could face me more comfortably, gearing up for a long discussion it appeared.

"Um…well…you said that you were born with the ability to read minds. Why? And why can I now hear yours? Can I hear anyone else's? This would have helped me out a great deal a few months ago if so. And what *was* that—when I passed out—why did that happen?" I rambled quickly as the questions rushed out one after the other. I felt unable to stop it as I looked at him and waited for him to answer before the inquisition could continue.

"You can hear my thoughts, Grace, because I allow you to. You can *only* hear the thoughts that I allow you to. As for the other…I can't tell you that now. You already know more than I was willing to reveal," he whispered, looking past me at some unseen thing with such sadness in his eyes, my fingers itched with an unfamiliar longing to hold his, to comfort him in some way. "I *will* tell you that I am your friend, Grace. You now know a secret about me that no one else outside of my family knows, and I'm trusting you not to share it with anyone."

He was trusting me… Who trusted me? Not even Graham had done that, and he knew me better than anyone.

"It's not my secret to share, Robert."

Cautiously, I held out my hand, scared that what had happened earlier would happen again if he did, but more afraid that he wouldn't accept it at all. Why should he take my hand? He had just met me— what did he know about me? And what if what had happened to me frightened him, proved just how much of a freak I was? Could he really trust someone like me?

I know everything I need to know to trust you. His voice filled my head and he took my hand, as if to confirm, to acknowledge our fast formed friendship. *You can trust me, too. I will not betray you. I am nothing if not a loyal friend and guardian.*

"Um…thank you," I said to him, my voice tinged with disbelief, and looked around us, needing a distraction from his hypnotizing stare. Hadn't he said this was the *Bellegarde* family retreat? "Does this place belong to your family?" I asked aloud, knowing he had heard my thoughts before they had reached my lips, but feeling a need to fill the silence, I uttered them anyway.

"Yes. This area has been in my family's hands for centuries," he confirmed. "My mother's family inherited it, as well as the surrounding forest and waterways, so this is pretty much all ours." His swung his arm out in an arcing motion, referring to all of the greenery that lay before us.

I glanced over at the playground and raised an eyebrow. "What's with the swing set and see-saw?"

He laughed softly, "Well, we rent this area out a lot for large corporate gatherings, family reunions, weddings, etc… My mother realized that there'd be children who would be playing here too, so she had the playground built for them. She loves children. She'd have had a small army of them if she could." He motioned to a gazebo that seemed to be nestled between a pair of tall trees, almost invisible from where we were sitting, despite its size. "That is where most of the weddings are performed, and then the receptions are held right over there." He pointed to a wide open space to the right of the gazebo that seemed to stretch on forever. "It's nice and flat; perfect for dancing."

I could picture it, the extravagant weddings that were held here in such a vast and open space. I could see the tents pitched up, twinkling Christmas lights strewn up everywhere, the tables and chairs covered in yards and yards of white silk, and everything scented with flowers of varying shades and blooms. It took me a few minutes to realize that the images were too crisp; it was all too clean to just be my

60

imagination. These were memories.

I looked at him, and he grinned. *I thought you might need a little help.*

My jaw fell at the insult. *I do* NOT *need help with imagining a wedding here*

He shrugged his shoulders. *Fine.*

And the image was gone, as if he had pressed stop on a DVD, and all I was left with was a blank screen. *That was rude!*

You said you didn't need help imagining a wedding here.

I suddenly wondered when I it was that I had become comfortable with speaking to him through my mind. We had had almost an entire conversation without speaking a single word, and instead of frightening me like it should have, it annoyed me.

Easier than it sounds, huh?

I glared at him. "I prefer talking. People will think I'm even crazier than they already do if I remain quiet for long periods of time because I'm having a silent argument with you."

I stood up and stretched my legs—oh that felt good! I started to walk away before realizing that he was still holding my hand. With one blindingly quick tug, I was back on the bench sitting next to him. I blinked in shock, not just by his reaction to my attempt to leave, but also by the fact that despite the strength necessary to have done such a thing, his arm had barely moved. I would have been more convinced of him brushing aside a spider's thread than him somehow forcing me to sit beside him. And yet, despite my shock, none of this seemed to be of much interest to him as he remarked to my observation.

"No one is going to think that of you. Not anymore," he said as he looked at my face, the mischievous twinkle in his eyes betraying the serious line of his mouth. I could have sworn I knew how to breathe—I had been doing it all my life, after all—but for some reason, I couldn't remember how at the moment.

"Grace, I am your friend. I won't let people treat you like that anymore," he vowed, the seriousness shifting now to his eyes. "You are too good a person to have people take you for granted."

"How are you going to stop people from doing what comes so

61

naturally to them?" I snorted.

He ignored that and continued. "I know the hurt you've felt, and I've seen how you've been treated. It won't be like that anymore. I promise."

How could a mind reader protect me from the hurt that I already feel? How could he protect me from the memories permanently burned into my mind? How could be prevent the snide comments, the jokes, or the memories from crushing down on me tomorrow, when it started all over again? Truth was that he couldn't. He couldn't change the fact that no matter what time I went home today, Graham would still be my next door neighbor who wanted nothing to do with me, or that my dad was still going to let that viper into my mom's house.

Want to bet?

My mouth became the perfect "O". "No, I don't want to bet. If knowing you read minds is too much information already, then I probably don't want to know the rest anyway; and if that's the case, I will just have to ask you to stay out of my business." Boy, this friendship thing was getting off to a rough start. I've yelled at him more times in the past hour than I ever had at Graham in our entire lives.

Before I could utter another word, my stomach decided it was time to interrupt us. The rumbling sound was quite loud, and embarrassing, but a testament to the fact that I hadn't finished breakfast, and didn't even get a chance to start on lunch. The sun was heading westward, sinking ever so slowly, so dinner was around the corner. Was I going to miss that, too? I thought not. "Robert, you need to take me home. I'm starving, and it's getting late."

He stood up and pulled me up with him without an ounce of effort. Our hands had never separated throughout the entire conversation, I noted, and blushed. "If I must. But first, I want to make sure you realize that it's okay to yell at me if you want to. You don't have to keep it in like you did with Graham. I am your friend now. I accept you for what you are."

My eyes bulged. *Would you* stop *digging through my memories? If you want to be my friend, you're going to have to realize that friends don't do stuff like that!*

62

His laughter was soft. *Most friends also can't literally read each other's minds.*

Ok. He had a point. *Just don't do it anymore. It's creepy. And annoying.*

He nodded his head and we walked towards his motorcycle. His helmet, which he'd hung on the handlebars, was handed to me. I looked at it questioningly. "Don't you need it?" I asked.

"No. I have a hard head." He climbed onto the motorcycle and started it up. The loud rumble vibrated through me and my legs, remembering how it felt to get off, seemed to have formed an opinion of their own that they were not climbing back on. Trying to stall, I put the helmet on, not bothering with adjusting my hair, resulting in my vision being completely distorted by wayward strands covering my face. He sighed, and pulled the helmet off of my head. He pushed my hair back and replaced the helmet. He pushed the visor down, turning everything a muted dark gray, and yanked me onto the seat behind him.

Take *that*, legs.

I figured you needed a little help.

Yes. This mind reading thing of his was definitely going to get annoying.

Wrapping my arms around his waist again, I held my breath as he revved the engine and we took off. Like lightning, we streaked across the road, everything a blur once again. I wondered what had happened to the chili that I was sure had stained the back of his jacket, deducing that he'd probably cleaned it while I was passed out.

I closed my eyes and suddenly I could hear—no—*see* his thoughts, see all of the events that had occurred today through his eyes while we rode. He was standing in line, his vision set on a beautiful blonde girl standing off to the side with her boyfriend. It was Erica. He felt warm, happy.

He turned to the person who was standing in front of him. She had brown hair, the color of mahogany, and she was wearing an old t-shirt. She had chosen it for comfort, he could tell, because it wasn't like anything anyone else was wearing. She was whispering to the woman in front. The woman looked confused and needed her to speak louder.

She did, saying her name. Grace…

"Oh honey, I know who you are. You're Miss Grace Shelley. My, you've grown over the summer, haven't you, sweetheart?" the woman in front said loudly. The name seemed to trigger a wave of fire through him, and he relished the burning, as though he had been starved for the heat. He continued to stare at the back of her head. Willing, waiting for her to turn around, fighting the urge to *make* her do so.

She reached behind her head to pat her hair. It wasn't hair she was feeling at all. It was a tangled mass of unruly knots that she had completely forgotten to brush that morning. He could feel her embarrassment, hear it. He reached forward to touch her hair ever so quickly as she stepped forward to talk to the lovely lady handing out class schedules once more. More warmth filled him as he inhaled deeply the sweet fragrance of it. When he removed his hand, the tangles were gone.

I blinked. He could do a lot more than read minds!

More visions appeared. He was walking to his homeroom class, seating himself next to a girl with short, blonde hair. She was smiling so widely, her ears were part of it. He smiled back. It was such a bright smile it was reflected in her eyes. His warmth flowed outward, and the blonde girl started perspiring—you could see she didn't care. She introduced herself, but he was listening to her thoughts; she wanted to know everything about him, his name, where he came from, but most importantly, if he had a girlfriend.

It sickened me to know that I had that in common with her; I, too, was curious about that last part. I felt him shake his head in the negative—reading the thoughts in my mind as he played back his own— and I felt some sense of relief that should have, but didn't feel out of place or awkward.

The vision behind my closed lids shifted and he was now surrounded by girls. Giggly, giddy, glorious girls. He liked girls, judging by how much he laughed and smiled with them. He glowed with warmth. A soft pale white surrounding him, fluttering in and out as they touched his shoulder, batted their eyelashes, lightly brushed against his side, the flirting not subtle at all, but not blatantly obvious either. Then his focus shifted to something else—no, not something—it shifted to *someone* else. He excused himself and walked towards the back of a classroom, taking a seat next to the person who had captured his attention.

She looked so sad, so forlorn. *Grace...* He wanted to reach out and touch her hair again. But there were no more tangles. He could see the tracks of dried tears on her cheeks, and he had started counting. What was he counting? He shook his head at the figure that he came up with. He had counted the number of tears that had flowed down her face.

The girl sitting next to him looked up and turned to face him. Through his eyes, she was surrounded by a soft white halo, and the warmth he had felt earlier around all of the other girls seemed to pale in comparison to this new heat, a blaze burning deep within him, threatening to turn him into living flames. It felt good. He welcomed it. He took in a deep breath, his nostrils flaring as he inhaled the fragrance that was her hair, her skin, her breath...her. *Grace...*

He spoke to her, amused at her shocked reaction. He spoke again, his gaze locking with hers, trying to reassure her without words or actions. She stumbled over her response, and then blushed. The flames licking at his skin grew even higher. Another girl sitting in front of her said something she thought was amusing in its cruelty. Its iciness dampened the heat enough for him to turn away and take a good look at the girls surrounding him now. All looked at him like he was the latest trend that they had to have...and he was on sale. Their thoughts were all the same. *Nothing different here.* It never was. Beautiful faces, but the thoughts were all predictable and mundane.

He turned to look at *her* again. She was bent over her paper, lost in thought, and she was chewing on the inside of her cheek. She was thinking about something painful. It hurt him, feeling the despair she was experiencing, and what he heard, what he saw in her mind tugged at him, made him want to comfort her in any way possible.

He could see glossiness surrounding her eyes and knew them to be tears. She was on the verge of crying. Her pain was so acute it caused his breathing to get ragged, as though he himself were feeling the hurt that had welled up deep inside of her. He looked at what she had been staring at—her paper. It was blank with the exception of her name and assignment title. It would be enough, he decided.

Quickly, he dug deep into her mind and pulled out moments from her memory that didn't involve the source of her pain. He willed them to the paper sitting in front of her, bending them to her curvy and slanted handwriting until they filled up the front and back neatly and effortlessly. She wouldn't need to have failing her first classroom assignment hanging over her, not feeling the way she does. The bell was ringing, and images shifted. Another classroom, and she was there again. He felt the fire surround him as he tried once again to talk to her. He didn't understand why his voice sounded so shaky.

I smiled at that thought. It had sounded steady as time itself to me.

She was focused on the teacher speaking at the front of the class. He needed to distract her somehow. He saw her pencil resting at the edge of her desk, and called it over with a gentle crook of his finger. Obediently, it rolled off the desk. The sound of it hitting the cold tile below was enough to tear her eyes away from the chatter going on between teacher and students.

She reached down to pick up the traitorous writing tool and looked up at him. The flames around him danced with glee. She stared at him as he tried, once again, to talk to her. Her response was slow in coming. She seemed frozen. And then she moved so quickly, he couldn't see it happening until it was over. She had tried to rise—too fast, too nervous—and she hit her head on the edge of her desk, a complaint tumbling from her lips.

Instantly, one of her hands was at the contact point—trying to hold in the pain, or prevent it from coming at all—unwilling to allow anymore tears. Immediately, his hand was there, covering hers, offering what level of soothing comfort he could without scaring her.

There were titters around them, but he didn't notice who was laughing; he didn't care. He just wanted to lessen her pain any way he could. Soon, the hand on her head lowered. She was close to smiling now. It was almost enough. And then she spoke once more, telling no one in particular that his eyes weren't gray at all. No. They were silver.

Suddenly, the visions were gone. My mind was empty once again, save for my own thoughts. We weren't moving anymore. How much time had passed since he started his vision sharing? I looked up and saw my house. How had he known where I lived?

Do you even have to ask?

Of course I didn't. What he couldn't get out of me the conventional way, he could surely learn from me in another, more intimate manner. I looked at my house. The garage door was shut, which probably meant that Dad had indeed gone to work and wasn't home yet. Good. I wasn't ready to face him anyway. I climbed off the back of the monstrous bike and wobbled a bit before his patient grip helped steady me; I knew my legs weren't going to cooperate with me, fully mutinous now that they had been forced against their will to endure that seemingly endless vibrating.

I pulled off the helmet and handed it to him. "So…um, thanks," I said, unsure where to proceed with this oddly formed and sudden friendship, or how to process all of the new information I had just gleaned through him sharing his memories. I grabbed the hem of the shirt he had given to me to wear. "Um, I'll get this shirt back to you tomorrow."

He took the helmet from my hands, looking not at me, but at my home. "Don't worry about it. I have at least five more of those at home. You're going to be alone…"

I shrugged my shoulders. "No big. I've spent a great deal of my life that way. I'll see you at school tomorrow then." I started up the walkway, turning as he revved the bike.

Thank you, Grace…for allowing me to trust you with my secret.

I watched as he sped off, watched as he disappeared from my sight—watched with a small smile on my face as I thought, *it's my secret now, too.*

A SMALL KINDESS

I clutched my new secret to myself as I walked into the dark house. I saw the clock on the wall said it was a quarter past six, and knew that Dad would be home in less than an hour. I considered making dinner for the two of us, but I was just too hungry and quickly made myself a tuna sandwich instead. I plopped down on the sofa and flipped on the television, looking for anything that could be the white noise I needed to process all of the events of today.

He had said that I was different. *VERY* different he had emphasized, and so I was, like a dodo amongst the peacocks. But he was the truly different one. He could read minds! He could send thoughts into others' minds as well. He could…write papers in another's handwriting just by thinking about it, and turn a tangled mess of hair into something neat and presentable. It was as if he were some kind of magician.

I snorted at that. Magic? What was I, six? There had to be some logical explanation. Maybe he was showing me what he wanted to: a mixture of fact and fiction, to test me, test my loyalty. Well, even if people would have believed me, I wasn't going to go blabbing to the world that he could read minds. I'm sure that he knew that I wouldn't. It may not have been thought directly, but my subconscious would have definitely not have allowed for it. And he had already delved deep in there several times today to have known this.

I looked down at my hand. The one he had held for so long while sitting on that bench together. I brought it to my face, as though the warmth that had spread through it was still there, and would reach out and burn my cheek, half expecting to catch a hint of his smell. I wrinkled my nose as the pungent aroma of tuna and pickles rushed up and around me. No mystical, magical scent here.

68

I looked down at the shirt he had given to me to change into, wondering when it was last that he had worn it. I pulled it to my face and rubbed it against my cheek. It felt unbelievably soft against my skin, and I could imagine him on the other side of that fabric, his warmth radiating through, into me…

I don't know how long I stayed like that—my thoughts lost in my imagination and daydreams—but when my eyes reopened, I was on my bed in my room. How did I get here? I looked at the digital clock that sat on my desk, its red numbers bright in the darkness of my room reading thirty minutes to midnight. Daydreaming about Robert had cost me five hours? I looked down at the clothes on my body. I was no longer wearing his shirt. Instead, I was in my usual bedtime uniform of boxers and a white tank top.

I suppose that I had fallen asleep on the couch and Dad had carried me upstairs and changed me. I flipped on the lamp that sat on the nightstand next to the bed. With a surprised laugh, I realized that I felt bereft without Robert's shirt. I didn't know why, but I needed to hold it, feel it. Perhaps it was because it was the only proof I had that today had even happened.

I stood up and walked over to my dresser. Had Dad placed it there? The basket that had been there this morning was still there, but Robert's shirt wasn't in it. I went to check my laundry hamper. It wasn't there either.

I started downstairs and froze when I heard the sound of talking. I recognized Dad's voice; it sounded like he was asking a question but wasn't getting an answer. Was he on the phone? I continued down to see who he was talking to at this time of night. It was not like him to be up so late.

He was sitting on the couch, a laundry basket to the side of his knees, folded clothes piled on the coffee table in front of him. He was talking. But he wasn't talking to anyone on the phone. He wasn't talking to anyone. There wasn't anyone else there.

"Dad?"

He looked up at me and smiled sheepishly. "Hey Grace. You're up."

I nodded. I picked at the hem of my boxers, trying to figure out how to ask him if he'd been talking to himself. Well. Not exactly talking to himself; rather, having a full blown conversation with himself. "Um, Dad...who were you talking to? Just now?"

"I-I was talking to Mom," he said softly, sadness plain to see in his eyes. "When it's just me and I'm doing things that we used to do together, it's like I can feel her here, and so I-I talk to her."

Well. That was a surprise. I knew he folded laundry to remind himself of her, but I didn't know he had conversations with...her, too. "What were you talking about wi-with Mom?" I asked, slowly lowering myself down by his feet, opposite of the now empty basket.

He started placing the folded clothes back into it while trying to find the words to answer me. When he had everything cleared off of the table, he turned to look at me. "Grace, I was telling your mom about Janice, about the baby, and about how much I worry about you." He grabbed something from the top of the pile of clothes in the basket and handed it to me.

It was Robert's shirt.

"I know that Graham broke your heart, Grace. I know how deeply hurt he left you. I saw it with my own eyes. But I worry about your actions as a result of that pain." He gestured to the shirt in my hands. "You were wearing that when I came home. It's not yours. It's not even a girl's shirt. Where'd you get it?"

I squeezed my hands around the soft fabric, wondering how to go about explaining the day's events in a way that didn't sound crazy. "A friend gave it to me to change into after I spilled chili all over my other shirt." There. Simple. Easy. The truth.

He looked at my face, and I knew he'd see that I was being honest. I didn't expect him to realize that it was only part of the truth. "Graham told me you went off with some guy after ditching school."

My eyes grew wide with shock. And, anger. "You spoke to *him*? After what he did?"

He blushed, embarrassed at his betrayal and my reaction to it. "I had to. I got a call from the school saying you missed the second half of the day, that you had skipped school altogether. You've refused to make any girlfriends, so I had to speak to the only person I knew went to school with you."

He reached out to pat my head, like he used to when I was younger. I jerked away. He sighed. "I know how you teenagers can react when things get difficult. You want to make yourselves feel better any way you possibly can. I don't believe you'd ever do drugs, Grace, but there are other ways to feel better…" his voice grew softer.

Now I was embarrassed. Was he suggesting that I'd had *sex* with some random guy because Graham had hurt me? I looked into his face and that's exactly what I saw. I could feel anger and rage bubbling up within me.

"Was that why you changed my clothes, Dad? To *inspect* the goods? To see if I had been *spoiled* by my need to feel better about having my best friend betray me, my father saying that it's hard to like me and that it was a good thing that he had hurt me?" I stood up, my hands shaking from the intensity of the betrayal. "I got *this* shirt from a *friend*. While you may feel that people can't like me, there's one person who has proven you wrong. He likes me, Dad. Genuinely *likes* me, and he helped me today when I was feeling like absolute *crap*."

I stared angrily at my dad, shocked and hurt that he could think I'd have sex with some stranger just to get over Graham. "I didn't have *sex* with him. Unlike someone *else* in this family, I don't need to do *that* in order to feel better."

I headed back towards the stairs when he shouted my name. "GRACE ANNE SHELLEY, YOU STOP RIGHT THERE!!"

Tempted to keep on walking, but understanding the consequences if I did, I stilled my feet, my eyes drifting to the rough edges of carpeting that butted up against the stairs.

Heavy breathing and mumbled counting were all I heard for a few minutes. Finally, he spoke—his voice much calmer…

"I didn't change you. Janice did that. She told me to let you sleep, that I could talk about this with you in the morning." The melancholy tone with which he spoke kept my eyes glued to the floor—I wasn't willing to look into his face and see the same in his eyes.

"I told her this morning that you weren't happy about her

coming to live here. With us. She said she doesn't want to move in if you don't want her to, that she doesn't want to be a part of this…life, if you don't want her to be. She doesn't want to come between us, Grace."

I looked at Dad and choked on the words that I had prepared in my rebuttal. His eyes were pleading—his face full of grim lines and a wan smile.

I remembered that look. He'd had the same expression when he first saw me in the hospital and, seeing that I was fine, had held onto some desperate hope that they had been wrong about Mom. Was it that desperate that he be with Janice? Was he that deeply in love with her that losing her was like her dying?

I turned and sat down on the bottom step. This was confusing me. I hadn't known that Dad's feelings for Janice were so strong, so serious. But didn't he say he cared for her a lot this morning? Yes. He did. Sex? Sure, I knew they were having sex. He never brought her over here for that, but he never lied to me about spending nights over at her place either. I just didn't know that it went beyond that.

So here it was. He had finally found someone to fill that void that had been in his heart since Mom died. And I couldn't stand her. I looked over to Dad, looking so small in his inner pain. He was losing a future with a new love and another child. And all because I didn't like Janice and had an unreasonable fear that she was trying to replace my mom in his life.

How selfish was I being? Graham's face was suddenly in my mind. He had never tried to work on a compromise with Erica about me. He just chose her. I wasn't even part of the equation anymore, and that had hurt me. Never mind the fact that I loved him. That didn't even factor into this problem because he hadn't known that when he'd made his decision; but if he had, he still would have chosen her over me. I knew that much.

But Dad had made the same decision this morning, hadn't he? He had underestimated Janice though; she was the kink in the gears. She had decided not to come between the two of us. She had sacrificed security and love and who knows what else so that I could be happy, even though I hadn't thought twice about her happiness, too consumed with what my mom would have thought about all of this. We both were thinking of the exact same thing, only from different ends, and we both had come to the same conclusion.

Only trouble with that is that now that I had gotten what I thought I wanted, I wasn't happy. I hadn't thought about what kind of effect it would have on Dad, and I just didn't want to see him hurt anymore. He'd spent too much time alone after Mom had died. Everyone said so. Said it was "unnatural" for a man to stay single for so long. Then said it was "sinful" when he started dating again in earnest. He couldn't win for losing. But none of the relationships ever lasted long. I was always the issue.

No one wanted to be the mother of "Grace the Freak", the gangly, weird looking girl who had somehow survived a horrible car without a single scratch on her while her mother burned to death.

But Janice was willing. She wanted to be a part of Dad's life as much as he wanted to be a part of hers. She just didn't want it so badly that she'd come between the two of us. I saw that now. I saw all of it, and I felt ashamed. I was being just as cruel as Erica…as Graham. I shook my head. I would stop it.

"Dad," I began, trying hard to find the right words to express my remorse and guilt. "I think you should tell Janice that it's okay if she wants to move in. She makes you happy, and that's more than I've been able to do this past week. I can't find a reason to hate her for that, and I'm sorry I tried."

I tried to gauge his reaction, see if what I had to say would please him. "You deserve to be happy, Dad. You deserve to have a second chance, just like everyone else. She's your second chance. I see that now."

His face was pinched, his shoulders were still hunched, and the words that I had hoped would have changed his entire demeanor weren't enough. I suddenly felt worse.

"Grace, this isn't something you can just fix by saying she can stay now. This isn't high school, this is real life. She's leaving, Grace. She heard back from a school up north that had a job opening and was

73

just waiting to see if things could be worked out here. She came home with me to talk to you, but when I saw you dressed in some guy's shirt, I couldn't think about anything other than who you'd been with and why you were wearing his clothes-"

"I told you Dad, he gave it to me because I had spilled food all over my other one." I interrupted, wishing that I hadn't thrown away that shirt just to reassure him.

He nodded his head, an automatic reaction. He took a deep breath and sighed. "It doesn't matter anymore, Grace. Janice has made up her mind. Look, I'm tired. I think I'll head up to bed. Don't stay up too late."

I scooted over on the bottom step and watched as he passed me by, looking dejected and absolutely miserable. My relenting on Janice was too late. My moment of unselfishness didn't come soon enough, and knowing that I had been a factor in my dad's unhappiness was weighing down on me with an incredible amount of pressure. Watching him slowly climb up the stairs, I knew I had to do something. I just didn't know what. Not yet, anyway.

I was galvanized into action as soon as I heard his bedroom door close upstairs, the clicking of the lock giving me an idea. Quickly, I went to the phonebook in the kitchen. I found the number I was looking for and started dialing like mad.

The ringing was torturous. I willed the person on the other end to answer while I ran over what I was going to say. Three rings. *Answer*. Four… *ANSWER*!!

"Hello?"

I let out a whoosh of breath, so relieved to hear that voice for the first time in my life, I actually started giggling.

"Um…hello? Who is this?"

"J-Janice? It's me, Grace," I blurted out, afraid I'd start giggling again and she'd confuse me for some prank happy teenager, or some psychotic clown-faced killer.

I could hear her breathing on the other end, somewhat annoyed, rough, and was convinced that she was about to hang up on me when she started talking. "What's the matter, Grace? It's very late. Is something the matter? Did something happen to James?"

I took a deep breath, sending out a silent prayer that I was doing the right thing, and started. "Janice, I wanted to tell you that I'm sorry. I'm sorry for what happened tonight. I-"

She cut me off. "Grace, did your dad tell you what happened? Look, Grace, what happened tonight wasn't your fault. Your father and I, we-"

It was my turn for interrupting. I didn't want her making up her mind before I had even had a chance to change it. "Janice, please. Let me finish. It's taking a lot for me to do this, but it's for a good reason, believe me." I waited for her to say something but when all I heard was silence, I continued. "I wanted to tell you that I'm sorry for what happened tonight. If I had been awake, I would have told you that I *do* want you to move in with my Dad, and start your new little family together."

I surprised myself with how convincing that sounded, believing in those words myself. "You make my dad happy. He told me so himself twice today, told me how much you mean to him, and that's not something that I take lightly. He wants you in his life. He *needs* you in his life, Janice.

"It was wrong of me to have gotten so upset this morning when he told me about the baby…and you moving in. I was angry and upset about my own problems, and I didn't want to see how much he wants this, *needs* this because then I'd have to think about someone other than myself and I couldn't not be that selfish. Not then. But things have changed, my eyes are open now and I see that I was wrong. You're good for him, Janice. I'd be blind if I didn't see that and admit that now, no matter how I feel.

"I'm asking you—no, begging you to not leave my Dad, Janice. He deserves to be happy. He deserves to be happy with you. I was being selfish about everything, and I'm very, *very* sorry about that. You have to stay, Janice. We both want you to stay."

I could hear her fidgeting with the phone, as if she were trying to find something else to do to keep from having to respond to me. Finally, she spoke. "Grace, I'm supposed to drive up north tomorrow morning to sign my contract papers. It's going to be very unprofessional of me to just not go."

I felt my stomach hit the floor. She was still going? She was talking about professionalism when my father's heart was at stake? She was…wait. "Janice…? Does this mean you're staying?"

A small sigh reached my end of the phone. "I love your father, Grace. He makes me happy, too. I want a future with him—with the both of you. You're a part of James…maybe the best part. The best part, he tells me. I cannot have him without you, and I wouldn't want to. If you are sure about this, if this is what you want, then yes, I'm staying."

I did a quick dance on the kitchen floor at that. There was no rhythm to it, but who needed that when you had just ensured your father's happiness? I had been prepared for a battle; I didn't expect it to be so easy. "Thank you, Janice, for doing this. It really means a lot to me."

"Thank you, Grace. Thank you for doing this."

She told me that she'd be here in the morning to tell Dad that she had changed her mind, and that we had talked—in that order—and then we hung up. I was feeling very good. That small act of kindness had changed my whole outlook. All of the events of today had changed my whole outlook.

After two weeks of doing nothing but crying, moping, and feeling sorry for myself, not to mention a day of hurt, embarrassment, and incredible secrets, I suddenly felt unbelievably tired. Going to bed now would bring tomorrow that much faster…and tomorrow I would see Dad's smile return to his face. Tomorrow I would have a friend, an ally at my side, whose secrets I was now a part of. Tomorrow, I'd begin a new chapter in my life. It sounded so good, I was in my bed and asleep in a heartbeat.

LOST AGAIN

When my alarm went off at six, I felt amazingly refreshed. I rushed through my shower, brushing my teeth at the same time. As soon as I had rinsed the last bit of soap off, I was out, pulling my clothes on and struggling against the friction of dry clothes against wet skin. I ran a towel through my hair and then fought the angry tangles with my brush. I looked at my reflection in the mirror. I had chosen my favorite t-shirt, black with the head of one of my favorite movie characters, Jack Skellington on the front, smiling his crooked jack 'o lantern smile, and my favorite pair of jeans. A black belt surrounded by grommets, and a matching bracelet were the only accessories I dared wear. I knew my limitations.

I ran downstairs, walking into the wall of aroma that was canned cinnamon rolls and brown and serve sausages. The typical Tuesday breakfast never smelled so good.

Dad was sitting at the table, newspaper in hand, sipping a cup of coffee while the cinnamon rolls baked. In a cup of warm water in front of him was the frosting packet, ready and waiting to be squeezed onto the doughy goodness. Dad looked up from his paper and gave me the usual once over. I was used to it, and waited for the normal response to my shirt and jeans combo, but today, nothing came.

"Morn, Dad," I said cheerfully, hopefully.

"Good morning, Grace," he replied, a stark difference in his tone compared to mine. He went back to reading the paper. Not wanting to burst out and announce that Janice would be over in a few minutes, I grabbed a mug from the dish rack, walked over to the coffee pot and poured myself a cup. I added the creamer and sugar slowly, counting each spoonful, doing my best to occupy my mind so that my mouth didn't start moving before my head could tell it to stop. When the oven timer went off, signaling that the rolls were done, I rushed over to take them out.

Before I realized what I was doing, I had my unprotected fingers on the sizzling hot pan, and I screamed. I felt myself being pulled towards the sink, and cold water was pouring on my ever reddening fingers. It should have felt soothing, but all I could feel was the burn beneath my skin, beyond the reach of the water. That was how Janice found us, both of us too preoccupied to hear the doorbell. She quickly went to the freezer to grab some ice out of an ice tray and placed them into a dish towel that had been near the sink.

"Let me see, Grace," she said, soothingly. I gave her my hands and she placed the now cold towel on my fingers.

It stung and I flinched away, but she held fast. I didn't want her to think that I flinched out of rejection for her, so I grit my teeth and allowed her to help. She asked me if I was feeling woozy, if my fingers were feeling numb, if I felt nauseated. All par for the course for a nurse, I suppose. When she was satisfied that my hand had been thoroughly cooled, she asked me where the first aid kit was located.

I gestured towards the top of the refrigerator where the red box was located. She told me to hold the cloth and ice in my hands while she grabbed the box. Rummaging through it, she found a roll of gauze, some sterile pads and some ointment. She removed the towel and ice then and proceeded to apply the ointment, pads, and wrapped my fingers individually. "They'll be easier to clean this way." She said when she was done.

"Thanks, Janice." I said, wiggling my fingers, glad that at the very least, I wouldn't look like a mummy with mittens.

It was then that we both realized we had an audience.

Dad was staring slack jawed at the two of us as though he'd never seen us before. Truthfully, he'd never seen us act so friendly towards each other. Ever. Frankly, I was trying to remember the last time we had even spoken to each other and I was coming up empty, my mind drawing an absolute blank.

Taking my cue at the look on his face as he gazed at Janice, I gingerly grabbed my book bag with my bandaged fingers, and headed towards the back door. "Well, um, I think I'll catch some breakfast at school. Bye Dad." I kissed his cheek. He was still too stunned to do anything other than nod. "Bye, Janice. Thanks again," I called as I left the house, hoping that they'd have a lot to talk about and all the time in the world to do it.

I walked around the side of the house, smiling to myself. It was odd how *good* it felt, seeing the two of them together. Wasn't it just twenty-four hours ago that I couldn't stomach the thought? I shook my head, ashamed at my selfishness. He needed to be happy. He deserved to be happy.

Who deserves to be happy?

I stopped short, stunned at the strange voice in my head. No. Not strange at all. It had been there yesterday. But he had also been right in front of my face, too.

"Robert?" I called out nervously. I walked towards the driveway, past Janice's little SUV, and there he was, sitting on that death machine. My legs started quivering at the memory. "What are you doing here?"

"You didn't answer my question. Who deserves to be happy?" he said, folding his arms across his chest.

"My Dad, if you must know. He and his...um...girlfriend are moving in together." I replied. *Why didn't you just go digging through my head to find out, instead of asking me?*

He shook his head. "You said not to do that anymore, remember?"

Oh.

He laughed. "Now, to answer your question, I'm here to see if my new friend wanted to ride to school with me."

I felt the warmth flow through me, blooming in my cheeks, rushing to my toes and fingertips. I winced at the pain that suddenly shot through my hands. "Ahh." I cried, dropping my backpack onto the ground.

He was off the bike and holding my hands before the sound had finished leaving my throat. I blinked as I looked at the spot where he had been and where he was now, and wondered how he had moved so quickly. His hands were cradling mine; he was looking at the bandages, and then into my eyes, asking me silently for the story. I concentrated, focusing on the events that led up to Janice putting the bandages on, hoping he could see them as clearly as I had seen the thoughts he had projected into my mind yesterday.

He pulled us down to the grass, both of us on our knees; He started removing the bandages that Janice had so neatly wrapped my fingers in. "Robert wha-"

He shook his head, warning me to be quiet. When the last ointment drenched pad had been removed, and the now angry, blistering skin was exposed, he hissed.

My eyes grew wide at the sound, and a slight tremble ran through my body. I was tempted to yank my hands out of his, but he read my thoughts as quickly as they had appeared and he clamped his fingers around my wrists like vices, locking them in place.

Slowly, he lowered his head towards my hands. I stopped breathing. I don't think I could've started again even if I wanted to. He pressed his lips against the bubbles that were slowly appearing and blew on them. I stared in complete awe. Who would do something like that, much less to someone like me?

I should have been grossed out, but I was too busy trying to keep myself still; my entire body was growing warm and I was fighting the urge to run away as his lips continued to press against the red flesh of my hands. He continued to blow on them and it slowly dawned on me that the heat that I was feeling was no longer stinging, but rather comforting. He pulled his face away from my hands, looking down at them and smiled, his grip loosening.

I snatched them out of his quickly, not wanting him to continue to view the ugly blisters that were beginning to form, and braced myself for the pain, but there was none. Curious, I looked down at them. They were…fine! The redness was gone, there were no blisters—no pain. I looked up into his face, looking into the deep pools of his eyes, asking him for an explanation.

That's for a later date. I didn't want you holding onto me with your hands in pain. You might fall off.

80

"But you will tell me," I demanded.

He nodded and then stood up, offering his hands to help pull me up. The strange mixture of awe, curiosity, fear, and something I couldn't place that I had felt yesterday on the ride home returned to me like a tidal wave, nearly causing me to stumble. He sensed this, and didn't let me go as he grabbed my back pack before the two of us walked to his bike. He placed my hands on the seat. *For support.* He pulled something off of the handlebars and placed it on my head: the helmet, of course.

You ready?

I smiled, pretty sure that he couldn't see it behind the visor and mouth guard. It felt good to smile at him, even if he couldn't see it.

I see it. Let's go.

Yes, that was definitely going to get on my nerves.

He climbed onto the bike, waited for me to follow, and then turned the key and started the engine as soon as I had done so. Out of the corner of my eye, I caught movement a few yards away. A pair of green eyes were staring at the two of us. Angry green eyes.

Before I could take a better look, we were off. The wind whipped around me, getting very cold as we traveled at who knows what speed. I just knew that I was riding on the back of a very expensive motorcycle, my arms wrapped around someone I had met only yesterday who knew more about me than I did about him, and I was fine with it. Perhaps my reputation for being a freak wasn't undeserved after all.

You're too critical of yourself.

I know myself better than you do. I let the words bounce around in my head. *I've been called a freak since I was seven-years-old—since my mom died—but I didn't do anything that was freakish in any way until yesterday, when I got on your bike and let you invade my mind like a parasitic worm.*

I felt his body shake. It took me a while to realize what he was doing, but when I did, I couldn't help but feel a bit miffed. He was laughing! *You were only too willing to allow me to* 'invade' *your mind. But it was necessary, Gee, to be sure that I could trust you with my*

81

mind.

Why are you calling me 'Gee'? No one calls me that. It's an interjection, for crying out loud.

His body was shaking again. Why did he think I was funny, when that was the furthest thing from my mind? *I'd bet that you're probably the only female at that school who would take offense to me giving her a nickname.*

Why would I want a nickname anyway? I like *Grace.* It's the name my mom chose for me. It's different. I pouted. An actual, bona fide pout. *Is it because it doesn't sound like 'Erica' or 'Becca'? It's not girly enough for you?*

His head moved back and forth in disagreement. *I happen to think your name is lovely. Grace is a name that few can carry without contradicting its definition. You've managed to epitomize everything that that name stands for, and I much prefer it over Erica and Becca.*

We were nearing the school now, and I could see that Robert on his bike was drawing a lot of stares from the students who were outside. They were staring at me, too, I realized as the looks of adoration towards him turned into something much darker when their eyes focused on me. The initial joy I had felt while riding with him was instantly stamped out by embarrassment once more. Self-conscious as always, I lowered my head, turned away from the school, and tried to pretend that I was alone while Robert maneuvered the bike into a stall in the student parking lot.

As soon as we had come to a stop, I was climbing off the seat. My legs weren't so mutinous now, having had two previous trips that were twice as long under my belt, but I still felt unsteady. I fumbled with the helmet, not wanting to remove it and expose the complete abstract sculpture made up of my human hair beneath it, yet not wanting to look even weirder by keeping it on long after stepping away from the bike. I knew it wasn't shielding my identity from anyone. These kids knew me as soon as they saw my shirt. Only Grace the Freak would wear a secondhand t-shirt with a skull on it, as if I were mocking death, while everyone else wore their best department store brand clothing.

I like your shirt. That's one of my favorite movies, too.

Robert was standing there, waiting for me to stop fidgeting with the helmet. Once I did, he placed his hands on either side of it and removed it slowly. As soon as it was off, my hands were in my hair trying to smooth out any knots that had formed there with my fingers. What they met with were silky strands that weren't out of place in the slightest. I stared at him, remembering the vision he had shared with me yesterday. He had reached out to touch my hair, and the immense tangle that had been there had disappeared. My jaw dropped. That hadn't been a phony vision at all. He had really done it.

You've guessed my secret. I'm Vidal Sassoon.

I fumed. "I don't think this is funny. You're trusting me with a lot of secrets, Robert, and I don't even know what it is that I'm keeping to myself!" I tried to keep my voice down as low as possible. I didn't want others to hear our conversation, but I also didn't want to have this conversation with him silently in front of everyone. Let them think me a freak for wearing a black shirt among a sea of pink. Just don't let them think of me as a freak because I can read minds.

You can't read minds, though. You can only hear what I want to share with you.

I glared at him, unable to say anything, by thought or voice.

Well, you aren't a freak because you can read minds, since you can't. That's what is bothering you, right? You're afraid that they'll think you've got this freakish gift or something? Well, don't worry, because you don't. Your head is just as boringly normal and utterly predictable as theirs is in their minds

His words hurt. They weren't any different in tone than what I had heard every day for the past ten years, but for whatever reason, they were able to cut me like no one else's could. Lifting my chin up, determined not to cry, I grabbed my backpack from his hand and threw it onto my shoulder before turning around and walking away.

I could hear him calling for me. He was actually shouting and not trying to throw his thoughts into my mind. But I was too angry to let him in there. I slammed that door shut, locked it, and the key was now resting comfortably in my back pocket. People were turning their heads to look at me, then towards him. He must not have noticed because he continued to call after me, running now. I kept on walking.

I half expected him to grab my arm and make me turn around to face him. Isn't that what guys did when they wanted your attention? When they were rejecting your rejection? But it never came. I kept on walking, and he stopped calling out for me. I walked through the school doors, down the long hallway leading to the cafeteria, and headed towards the counter to buy a bowl of powdered scrambled eggs. I took my eggs and sat down at an empty table at the far end of the cafeteria; as far away from the doors, and people, and disappointment as possible.

I knew I wasn't a mind reader. I was being sarcastic in my own thoughts, for crying out loud. If I can't be sarcastic with myself, who in the world could I be sarcastic with? But did he have to call me boring and predictable? Just like them? I'm sure that they would have told me to take that as a compliment, that I should only be so lucky. Lucky to be what, exactly? Someone like Becca? So self-absorbed, she's oblivious to everything around her? Or like Erica? Mean and spiteful and as close to evil as one could get in high school?

I sighed. She was also beautiful. In truth, anything that was the opposite of what I was had to be beautiful since I seemed to be incapable of drawing the attention of the opposite sex in any capacity other than friendship, and even that was up for speculation. I was too skinny, too plain, too quiet, too smart…too different. I was also too weird. The only girl in Heath to have never been friends with another girl—instead depending on the most popular guy in school for all the companionship I received, and being so blinded by that very companionship, I mistook it for affection.

So much for being too smart. I snorted. I got the joke now, the joke that I'd been the butt of all summer. I could afford to be humble, now that there wasn't anything else to be. Would it turn out that Robert was also in on it somehow? That the reason he hadn't continued after me was because he was having a nice laugh with Erica about how big of a sucker I was?

I shook my head. I might not know much about him, but something inside of me told me that he wasn't the type to mess with people's minds like that. Not when he could so easily read what was

84

inside of them.

When the bell rang, I gathered the thoughts that I had strewn across my mind, tucking them someplace safe. I wasn't going to be taking any chances that Robert wouldn't try to sift through them and pluck out things to prove just how boring and predictable I was.

I walked into Mr. Frey's class, choosing an empty seat near a rear window, and placed my head on the desk, tuning out the chatter that was going all around me while Mr. Frey snored soundly at his desk. I had nearly perfected the silence when a hand gently touched my shoulder.

I raised my head to see who it was. It was a girl I recognized, but couldn't quite remember her name. She had very familiar features: tip tilted almond-shaped eyes, hair the color of jet, straight and thick, a round face that complimented her round mouth that was pulled up in a friendly smile, and a small nose, all set on a backdrop of perfect porcelain skin the shade of an aged piece of ivory. Instinctually, I knew she was Korean, like my mom; Korean, like me. No one was like me.

"Hi. We've been in the same homeroom class for the past three years, but we've never spoken, and…um…I thought today would be a good day to start. My name is Stacy," she said matter-of-factly, and held out her hand.

I stared at it, a little confused. No one just came up to me to talk. It wasn't what normal people did. Automatically I thought that either something was wrong with her, or something was up. "I'm Grace," I said, still eyeing her hand, trying to figure out whether or not I'd accept it, or hedge my bets and keep my hands to myself.

Hand still extended, she smiled. "I know."

I didn't know what possessed me to do it; it seemed like I was being friendly to a whole bunch of strangers this week, but I reached for her hand and shook it. She was eager to return my handshake, and smiled brightly at me. "So what classes do you have this year? I've got trig next, and then Spanish and open period," she jabbered, flowing into a conversation as smoothly as if we had been doing it for years.

"Um. I have French Four next, and then Calculus," I answered hesitantly. "I also have open period after that."

She seemed thrilled by that. "Ooh, that's great! Where do you go? I go to the cafeteria 'cuz my mom works there and I can get some lunch while it's still hot."

I couldn't imagine the food here tasting that much better while hot, but it would be a great concept…imagine that, hot cafeteria food. "I went to the library yesterday…"

She nodded her head, seeming to understand why I would choose isolation to food. "Maybe I'll join you today. Would that be alright?"

I shrugged my shoulders, half hoping that she'd make the same decision she had made yesterday. "Sure, why not?"

She beamed at me as if I had just given her a gift. "Thanks!"

An awkward silence began between us, but I didn't have much experience speaking with other girls, so I couldn't exactly start up a conversation with her about the things she'd probably be interested in, and she appeared to be trying to read my thoughts. The idea of that made me laugh. Loudly.

She stared at me, startled. "What's the punch line?"

"Er- I was thinking about something I had read yesterday." I improvised quickly.

She seemed to accept it, and was about to say something else when mercifully the bell rang to head to first period. Sighing, she waved at me. "I'll see you in the library, Grace!"

"Sure," I said back, and looked around as a couple of heads turned to stare at me.

I grabbed my backpack and headed out of the classroom towards Madame Hidani's class on the next floor. She was once again writing something on the board. From what I could see, it appeared to be the same assignment we had had yesterday. Obviously having only two out of twenty students turn in their assignments wasn't going to fly with Madame Hidani.

I ignored the stares of the other girls in the classroom. I ignored the way their eyes felt like they were burning holes into my skin, ignored the way they seemed ready to either ask me a million questions about Robert—I wondered if they even know his first name—or strangle me for having the audacity to share the same airspace as him. I focused on my desk and headed towards it. I'd be bombarded with questions, accusations, and insinuations soon enough. I might as well be comfortable while it happened.

Placing my bag on the floor beside the chair, I sat down and awaited the onslaught.

But it didn't come.

Instead, *he* did.

One minute the entire room was on edge, and the next, it was as though a wave of calm and serenity had washed over everyone, leaving them drenched and satiated. Everyone except me, that is, because I was irritated by the source of that calm. I watched as he was surrounded, like a wounded calf by starved lions. He was glowing amid their attentions and for some reason that annoyed me even more.

I had to turn away then. I couldn't watch the fawning and the cooing. But mostly, I couldn't have him see it on my face, or perhaps hear it in my thoughts if he were trying to do that, too. The way I was feeling was as close to jealousy as I wanted to allow, and there was no reason for me to be jealous; how could I lay any claim on someone I had known less than twenty-four hours? He was, to quote Graham, in a different league than I was: the league of the impossibly beautiful and otherworldly.

When the bell rang to announce the beginning of class, I switched into student mode. I listened to Madame Hidani give out instructions, basically a repeat of yesterday only with an emphasis on turning it in or failing the semester on the second day. I wondered if I was exempt from having to do the assignment, since I had turned a completed one in yesterday…even if I didn't actually do it. Not wanting to take any chances, I removed my binder from my bag and took out a sheet of filler paper. I reached for my pencil and started the process of identifying my paper.

But it already was covered in writing…and not my own.

I scanned over the words and realized who had written it, the elegant handwriting familiar. I turned my head to look at him and saw that he was staring at me, his eyes pleading. I looked back to my paper, the fluttery feeling in the pit of my stomach threatening to crack my hard exterior.

Grace, I apologize if you took what I said today in the parking lot the wrong way. I hadn't meant for it to offend you. I was referring to everyone else's minds being boring and predictable, and that that predictability would make them assume that yours was exactly the same, when that is the furthest thing from the truth.

I replayed the conversation in my head, trying to see where he was wrong, trying to find one thing to contradict his statement, but I heard the words clearly as though he had just uttered them and realized he was right. But did I want to admit that?

I grabbed my pencil and started writing on a blank line. *Why didn't you say so in the parking lot?* I looked at him, half expecting him to answer me verbally, but he looked at the paper on my desk, letting me know the answer was already there.

I wanted to, but you didn't exactly seem willing to listen. And I didn't want to tell you in front of everyone that was watching that I think they're all idiots and that you are phenomenal.

I put my pencil to paper and wrote. *Where did you go, then? Did you stay outside with the* idiots *while phenomenal me went inside to feel sorry for myself?* I stopped writing, realizing that I had just admitted to the hurt I had felt at his perceived insult. It was too late to erase it, as new text started appearing below mine.

I stayed outside because if I had followed, everyone else would have as well, and I did not want to proceed to upset you further. Your neighbor showed up just as you walked into the school, and he would have had to witness your pain. As would his girlfriend. But she *would have enjoyed it.*

I closed my eyes after I read those last two sentences. I squeezed them shut as tightly as I could, trying very hard to keep my emotions in check, keep the hurt from appearing in the form of tears that would announce to everyone just how affected I was by what Graham had done to me.

Grace. His voice was inside my head again. I turned to look at him and felt my breath catch as the force of just how beautiful he was hit me like a bullet train at full speed. My imagination went haywire as I pictured the two of us together; there was no justice in this world if someone like him ended up with someone like me.

The real injustice is that you don't see how extraordinary you are, Grace. You are beautiful; just because you don't fit the mold that is set here, that doesn't erase that fact. You're loyal, almost to a fault, and you've the amazing ability to humble yourself if it means that you'd make someone you care about happy. You're not trying to deceive anyone, which makes you far better than I truly am—I'm sorry for writing about your neighbor and his girlfriend. I didn't mean to hurt you. It is very painful for me to see you so upset, your thoughts so full of sorrow.

My head was shaking with incredulity as I gazed back at my paper, needing something that wasn't so immaculate to focus on. That he was calling me beautiful was surreal—I probably *was* beautiful in some Dali-esque, melting clock sort of way—but he hadn't really hurt me; it was my own insecurities that had done me in, as usual. He'd been the only bright point in my life these past two days.

I looked back over at him and saw that he had heard that last bit. He was smiling. And it took my breath away completely. My reaction seemed to please him even more and it reflected in his face. His eyes were shimmering. I stared mesmerized at the morning sunlight reflecting off of them, like golden jewels floating in a silver lake.

What are *you, Robert?*

And in an instant, liquid silver suddenly turned into cold, solid steel, causing me to pull back at the dramatic change. The difference in his mood was stark, dramatic. It felt like someone had suddenly removed the warmth of the sun. Madame Hidani voiced a "brrr", and quipped about missing warm winters in Hawai'i; I knew that I wasn't the only one to have felt the chill enter the room.

I tried to read his face, tried to mask the fear on mine, and wondered what it was that I had done to have caused this reaction. I couldn't think of anything. I opened my mind, trying in vain to *hear* him, but all I heard was silence, icy and lonely. He turned in his seat, his expression stony, and I could do nothing else but the same. I looked down at the piece of paper in front of me, staring at it, watching silently as one by one, tear drops warped the lines and the penciled words that were in my handwriting. The words they were in response to were no longer there.

WELCOME BACK

Tuesday ended as badly as Monday had started. Robert ignored me for the rest of French and all through Calculus. The snub didn't go unnoticed by the rest of the class, which only hurt more. "So much for promises from beautiful strangers," I muttered as I headed to the library for third period.

Stacy's promise to join me at the library didn't materialize either, and lunch was spent sitting in a corner of the cafeteria dealing with the stares I received for not only being the pawn in Graham's sick game of Sims, but now the reason why Robert was actively seeking to flirt with every single girl in the school, angering every guy in the place. He seemed like he was on a mission, going from one group of girls to the next, making them laugh, sigh, blush…

It continued in Theater during sixth period. Since we had both missed it yesterday, we were both assigned to different groups, each one having to memorize a segment of a play to be acted out the following week. While I was begrudgingly accepted into a group consisting of nothing but pimply faced boys, Robert had been assigned to Erica's group, which consisted of nothing but blonde haired, pink lip-glossed balls of estrogen—all ready and willing to play the damsel in distress to his Prince Charming. He refused to look at me, which pleased Erica just fine.

When the bell rang at the end of the day I knew I'd be walking home. I tugged my bag onto my back and completed the journey that I had taken every year since I was a freshman. As expected, neither Dad nor Janice was there. A note was attached to the refrigerator letting me know that they'd be busy packing up her things and moving them here for the next few days.

Resigned to being fairly alone, I climbed the stairs to my room and fell onto my bed facedown. Déjà vu all over again.

The rest of that week, and the following two, I suffered the same silence, the same stares, the same torment of watching his flirting, and the ever growing burn in my chest as the jealousy that I didn't want to feel, didn't want to admit to feeling, started to take over. It was a monster inside of me, its tentacles burrowing into me, taking root and sprouting new ones whose sole intent was to burrow even deeper, leaving no part of me untouched.

I didn't try again to hear his thoughts, but knew that he could probably hear mine just fine, if he was even bothering to listen, and he'd hear just how confused and hurt I was. It wasn't the same kind of hurt that I felt when I thought about Graham. It seemed to be deeper. But how could I feel something like that for someone I barely knew?

And how could I feel this way about someone…who wasn't even a *someone*? What was he? He could read minds, project his thoughts to other people, he could fix things with the touch of his hand, and make things appear and disappear just by thinking about it. He had the ability to attract people like flies, and he could fill a room with warmth or chill it with ice.

What *was* he?

I didn't think I'd ever get any answers, not with him avoiding me in the same manner that Graham was. He was unapproachable when he surrounded himself with all of those girls. They acted as shields against me, ready and willing to fend off any contact between the two of us, regardless of who initiated it. Although, any type of contact would have been initiated by me if I had any courage left in me to do so.

The only part of the day that was endurable was third period when I'd head to the library. Stacy, who hadn't shown up that first day, did the following day, and every day thereafter. We didn't talk much—well, truthfully *I* didn't talk much—but her presence—knowing that she chose to be there—was comforting in some strange way.

She was always cheerful when she'd find me at some obscure table in the back. She'd sit and open a book to read, ask me some off-the-wall question out of the blue to see if she could draw forth some kind of reaction, and then return back to her book when she saw that she wasn't going to be successful. When the bell rang for lunch, she always smiled and said she'd see me in homeroom the next morning. I didn't know if it could be classified as friendship but I knew that it wasn't loneliness either, and anything that wasn't adding to that was greatly appreciated.

The third Saturday after school started I decided to pass the time by helping Janice unpack the boxes that she had finally moved in, while packing other boxes of my mom's things at the same time. Seeing my father's joy was bittersweet, knowing that it was coming at the cost of seeing the reminders of my mom get shoved into a box to be packed away into the attic until I had a place of my own.

I didn't hold that against Janice because I knew that she would have preferred them to remain. But Dad wanted as clean and fresh a start with Janice as possible, afraid that her leaving and moving up north was always imminent at just the merest hint of her being an interloper in our little family.

After a couple of hours of dealing with dust and mothballs, I remembered that I had wanted to get to the library before it closed, so I left rest of the moving to Dad and Janice, grabbed my bicycle and started pedaling. I had forgotten to pick up my last paycheck after what had happened with Graham, as well as a few books I had on hold that I was sure had come in. More than anything else, though, I simply needed to be somewhere I wouldn't have to see the type of giddy affection that was starting to grate on my nerves at home.

I understood that Dad was extremely happy, and it felt good to see him laughing and smiling more often now. But I couldn't help but feel like the position of interloper that Janice had once filled was now occupied by me. They talked about the baby, about the future, about who was going to cook dinner; every single conversation revolved around their new family unit that I just didn't quite feel a part of. In just a few short weeks, my entire world had flipped on its axis and it felt as though I were to blame for it all.

Plus, I wasn't exactly looking forward to the role of big sister. I was going to be eighteen in a couple of months and off to college right after it was born. I wouldn't be around much, so it wasn't like we were going to bond or anything, and I just wasn't looking forward to having to share my dad with anyone else so soon after relenting to share him with Janice. I knew I had time to get used to the idea, and my telling Janice to stay with Dad was kind of my cue to start doing that now, but I just couldn't do it as quickly as anyone of us would have liked.

To top it off, it's not like the kid would look like me. We'd have the same dad, but Janice wasn't Korean like mom was, and so it would probably look like any other kid in Heath, and fit in that much more easily. Some people got all the breaks.

I was so absorbed in my thoughts, I didn't hear the car until I tasted the blood in my mouth. My eyes were staring at the asphalt of the street, my cheek kissing its cold blackness. I could see the yellow divider line disappearing away from me…and I could pick out little asphalt rocks that had come loose over years of wear and tear. I moved my eyes down as I caught the movement of something. It was the fingers on my left hand. I was wiggling them without realizing it. I could tell the fingernail on my index finger had been torn off, and it looked like part of the knuckle on my thumb had been eaten by a hungry cat.

I looked up, unable to move anything else but my eyes to see a pair of shoes walking towards me. They were nice looking shoes; brown, with black laces. The slacks that touched the tips of the tongues were gray wool, and whoever owned those shoes wore white socks underneath those slacks. This was definitely someone who didn't show his feet much if he was wearing white socks with these pants and shoes.

I tried to say something but instead, a racking cough took over and I felt the blood bubble out, tasting its metallic bite as it began to slip past my teeth and out of my mouth. The shoes backed away. I moved my left hand out towards them, trying to let whoever belonged to them see that I was okay. I just needed a little help. But they kept backing up and soon, the shoes were gone. I heard a crunching sound and then felt the pattering of rocks on my head and back. Some of it fell in front of my eyes. More asphalt. Whoever owned those nice brown shoes had just driven away, and left me bleeding on the road.

I tried to move my right arm, but found that nothing happened. I took a silent inventory of all the parts of me that I could move. My left

94

foot could twitch on command, and I could wiggle my toes in my sneakers. I slowly moved my head downwards to see how my legs looked—the effort made me breathless as I bit through the pain. It would have been comical had I not known that the awkward angle that my right leg was positioned in was a clear indication that it had been broken. My left leg looked fine except for a misshapen object that was sticking out of a hole near my thigh. It looked like part of the bicycle. At least, the paint colors looked like it belonged to the bicycle.

Everything was starting to hurt now, and I could feel the sting of my face as the cuts and scrapes there from whatever it was that happened started to bleed. I tested out my voice once more, hoping that I wouldn't start coughing again, hoping that someone would be able to hear me, hoping that I was in an area where someone could.

"Help." I croaked. It was barely audible. I took a deep breath and tried again. "Heeelp."

I heard nothing except my own ragged breathing. There seemed to be something pressing against my chest, and it was starting to hurt each time I took a breath. I used my left hand and tried to roll over a bit onto my back, perhaps easing the pressure that was ever building in my lungs, but a sickening crunch, followed by a shot of immense pain down my right side cause me to land hard back on my face and stomach. The coughing started again, and with each racking movement, pain coursed through my body and blood spewed from my lips and nose.

This was it, I realized. I would die on the road, alone. A victim of…what? A hit and run? I didn't know, and probably wouldn't either. Instead of futilely trying to figure that part out, I sighed and pictured the faces of the people that had been important in my life, even if only for brief periods—it's what's supposed to happen when you're dying after all, right?.

I saw my dad's face, smiling and happy, his hands placed over a flat stomach that was holding his future child. He was looking up at Janice, love and contentment in his eyes. The vision from this morning at breakfast summed up their relationship quite well. At least he wouldn't be alone. I'd have hated that.

I saw the faces of my favorite teachers, their smiles and their

95

encouragement had always been just enough to keep me on the right track, knowing that without it, I'd have never been able to get as far as I had, never have the motivation to keep on going.

Strangely, I saw the face of Stacy. Though we barely knew each other, she had provided a rare comfort. That one hour every day was like a vacation from the rest of the world. And, though I appreciated it while she was there, I hadn't realized that I was truly grateful for it, for not having to endure an entire day absolutely alone. I was only sorry that I wasn't able to tell her so.

I saw Graham, his green eyes full of warmth and laughter, singing along, very poorly, to a Jim Croce song that was playing on his dad's stereo in the basement of their house. He had pulled me up to dance, causing me to look like an epileptic marionette, not stopping until I was laughing and singing along with him. It had been the first week of summer, just a few months ago.

The image became blurry then, and I blinked back the tears that had formed at the sweet memory that now only meant something to me. I would not cry anymore for him, and definitely not while I lay dying. It might have happened a little too late, but I realized that I finally deserved to be happy, too, and I knew what could make me very happy… And then the face that I hadn't expected, but so wanted to see appeared in my mind.

Silver eyes, no longer the cold steel that they had been in my dreams, but liquid, sparkling in a face so heart achingly beautiful the tears finally broke free and started flowing. He was holding my hand again, and I felt so light, the pressure that was crushing me seemed to just float away. Time was running out, I decided.

I felt suddenly sad that I wouldn't be able to spend the rest of my days staring into his eyes, or hearing his voice in my head. Whatever I had done to drive him away from me, I regretted more than anything else I had ever done or said. I had only wanted to know him, because in defiance of reason and logic, I had already come to care for him so deeply.

Robert's smile filled my head, and I could feel nothing but warmth flow through me as I smiled back because that smile, I could

96

feel, made him happy. I closed my eyes and sighed. There was no pain now, just warmth and contentment.

I waited for whatever it was that would come and take me away. The angels, the trumpets, the light; whatever it was that was supposed to be coming could do so at any time. I was ready.

HERO

The journey to the other side was taking a while. I knew I hadn't gotten lost, so where was everyone? Wasn't there supposed to be rejoicing and dancing and hoopla? Shouldn't I see faces of people I had lost—people that were waiting for me to arrive?

And then I heard it.

Laughter.

A very familiar laugh, one that I hadn't heard in nearly a month; the one that had haunted the moments in my dreams where I couldn't ignore the way my heart had felt. Why was he here, waiting with me for my…erm…ride?

You're not dead, Gee.

Not dead? What was I, if not dead? And why was he in my head?

We're waiting for the ambulance to arrive. The police are here, as well as your father. I'm in your head because I don't think your dad is quite comfortable with the idea of me talking to you when he's not sure just who exactly I am.

I could hear the random sounds of a police radio, and the different conversations occurring around me, and I knew he was right. But why was *he* here? He had made it a point to avoid me in school. Everything that he had said to me about no one being able to hurt me anymore had been a lie. He had promised that I'd never be hurt or made a fool of again; simply believing that had made me one, and proved him to be a liar. The acknowledgement of that caused me to stiffen, and in that moment I felt all of the pain that had been blocked from my mind. I opened my eyes. I screamed.

"Grace?" a strained voice cried. Dad! "Grace, it's okay, honey, the ambulance will be here very soon. Just hold on, okay?"

He squeezed me, and I could have sworn that even my hair hurt when he did that. I moaned, gritting my teeth, trying to keep from screaming again because his reaction wasn't making me feel any better.

I started to focus on the chaos that surrounded me then. It felt like I was in a Christmas light bulb. Everything outside of a small peripheral area was dark, but immediately around me, it was bright, with flickering blue and red lights. I could see several police officers directly in front of me standing near something on the ground that looked like some abstract art piece, beautiful in its deformity. Next to it was my book bag, positioned almost intentionally to demonstrate the contrasting textures of hard and soft, metal and cloth, warm and cold.

There was a third police officer standing to the left of me. He was speaking with someone I couldn't see. A spotlight that had been directed towards me was blinding his face to me. His? How was I so sure that this person was a he?

It came before I even realized it—the need to be certain. *Robert?*

And then the figure turned away from the officer and walked towards me, bending down out of the light so I could see his face. I felt my heart lurch forward, like it wanted to jump out of my chest and into his. And dammit, that hurt! I grimaced, and the concern on his face became the most beautiful thing I had ever seen. Genuine emotion, real, and right in front of me; his steel eyes were no more.

"I'm here, Gee," he said softly, reaching out to hold my left hand.

I looked at it, cradled in his, and then looked back up at him, confused. The wound that had been on my knuckle was gone, the nails on my fingers were all there. *You did this?*

He nodded his head, covering my hand with his, as if to hide it from my view. *You were bleeding very heavily; your heartbeat was very weak. I had to stop your internal bleeding...and some of your other injuries healed as a result.*

Internal bleeding? Other injuries? Healed? If I was healed, why in the world was I in so much pain?

You're not healed completely. You have more damage than I

could treat before the police arrived. Your right arm is broken in two places, and your wrist is shattered. Your left thigh was impaled by part of the handlebars on the bike, but it missed the bone--your right leg is broken in three places. You had tears in your liver and spleen. There's going to be some very nasty bruises on your face, but I was able to get the asphalt out, and I think I made your nose straighter.

I wasn't about to ask him how he had done these things, or why. I was just thankful he was here.

Dad, unaware of the unspoken conversation occurring between the two of us, grabbed my hand out of Robert's and started telling me what happened, his voice tormented and shaky. "You were hit by a car, Grace. A hit and run from what the police know so far. If Robert here hadn't been riding his bike down this way, I don't know what-" his voice broke, and he took a few deep breaths, trying to regain his composure. "Robert here found you and called 911."

"He saved my life," I whispered.

My dad, unable to hold back his emotions, nodded and started crying over me, sobbing like a grown man would in the presence of other grown men: reserved and silent with only singular tears and raspy, shaking breaths. I looked at the police officers surrounding us, their faces anxious, impatient to start asking me questions about what had happened, what I remembered.

The pain in my leg was beginning to increase, and I squirmed from the pressure of it as it crawled up to my abdomen. *Where* was that ambulance? I was looking very forward to being a pain-killer junkie with the way my body was feeling at the moment.

I removed my hand from Dad's grip, and reached for Robert—I completely ignored the grunt of displeasure from Dad—believing he would be able to help ease my pain, if only through the comfort of being able to touch him. Why had he begun to mean so much to me in such a short span of time? Why could he affect me the way no one else could? Even Graham?

Would you believe I ask myself the same questions? He grabbed my hand, held it once more between his and the pain lifted away from my body, like the removal of a suffocating blanket. I sighed.

100

How did you find me?

His face suddenly became pinched. I could see the memory in his head, hear it as though it were my own. He had heard me call out for help. He had heard it from very far away, and his face was riddled with confusion. He could hear my cry for help, but he couldn't hear my thoughts—he could sense that I wasn't nearby.

And...he was with someone else. He tried to distort the vision now, making everything fuzzy, as his voice told her of an urgent thing he just realized he had to do. He told her he'd call her later that evening. She made a pouty, whiny sound, but relented. She reached for his hand, and he held it, then kissed it. "Thank you for understanding, Erica," his voice said, his tone admiring, almost reverent.

I removed my hand from his, cutting off the vision I knew I could only see because we were touching. The pain slowly started returning, but it was coupled with a different kind of pain. One I was all too familiar with. But before it could take hold of me again, he placed his hands on my face, holding me immobile, and looked into my eyes.

He was in the parking lot, calling a cab for Erica on his cell phone, and then he was on his motorcycle, racing towards the sound of my thoughts. He was panicked, his palms sweaty for the first time in...centuries? He listened for my whimpers, my moans when my thoughts became too cloudy from pain. He found me, sprawled on the pavement, lying on my chest. He could only see my back at first. My right arm was twisted out behind me, my shoulder dislocated. The mangled remains of my bicycle lay partially between my feet.

He jumped off of his bike, letting it fall to the ground behind him as he rushed towards me, stopping as the smell of blood slapped him in the face. He uttered a foreign word I couldn't recognize, and then knelt in front of me, running his hands down my left side, looking at me.

But what I saw through his eyes wasn't me. At least, it wasn't me with skin. He was looking beneath it, looking at the shattered bones, the shards of which had pierced my lungs. He was looking at the torn internal organs that were leaking fluids into my body, slowly draining away the life force within me. He was looking at my heart, watching its beat slow down as it struggled to keep up.

He knew I was in a terrible amount of pain, and reached for my hand. He was taking the pain away from me, easing the stress and strain on my heart so he could further assess the damage done to my body. He looked at my face, into my eyes, and I smiled. A great glow from within him seemed to blind my vision of everything. It gave off an incredible heat, and I was afraid that if it continued, I'd burst into flames.

He placed his free hand onto my abdomen, breathing slowly, concentrating. He could *feel* bones mending, tears closing, blood absorbing. He looked at my leg wound where the handlebar of the bicycle was protruding. He wanted to remove it. He fought with himself over it. A battle of good angel vs. better angel raged forth on his shoulder. The angel won.

He left it, took his cell phone out of his pocket and dialed 911. He knelt there with me as he explained where we were, listened to the dispatcher who told him that the police would be on their way, and then hung up to call my dad. He could see my dad's face in my thoughts, see the last images I had had of him. He had called 911 to save my life, but he had called my dad to save *him*.

Slowly, Robert removed his hands from my face, and reached again for my hand. I let him hold it. Once again, I was in awe. Whatever his reasons for being with Erica tonight, they weren't more important than finding me and saving my family. I didn't know why, but for right now, that was more than anything I could have ever asked for from him.

"Grace, the ambulance is coming," Dad said softly, looking at the approaching red flashing lights.

In a blur of activity, I was examined, rolled to one side then the other as I was placed on some incredibly uncomfortable board; my neck was cocooned in a brace, an IV was shoved into my arm, and when I was asked if I was in any pain, I answered yes, because that wonderful voice that was in my head offering me words of comfort told me to. I was hoisted up onto a gurney and then rolled into the back of the ambulance where the paramedic whose nametag read Foley began his barrage of questioning about my injuries, where and what hurt, how much I weighed, how old I was, and so on.

I realized why Robert had told me to tell the paramedics that I had been in pain when I started to feel the pressure on my body again. He wouldn't be able to ride with me in the ambulance: that privilege belonged to my dad.

I'll be right behind the ambulance. The voice in my head said, and I felt an overwhelming sense of relief at those words. I didn't know just how desperate I had been to hear them until he had *said* them.

As soon as the ambulance doors were closed and we were headed towards the hospital, Dad started the interrogation. "So, is he the *friend* that gave you that shirt? How'd you meet him? What's his last name? How well do you know him?"

I knew I had to get this out of the way as quickly as possible, so I gave him the quickest and shortest answers I could. "Yes, school, Bellegarde, well enough."

He had a grim line on his face and I didn't exactly like what that meant because for some reason, I knew that it had nothing to do with my injuries or the hit and run. He had placed his elbows on his knees, one hand over the other, resting under his chin. I could hear the old cog wheels turning in his head, and wondered what it was that was causing him to look that way.

As if he knew what I was thinking, he looked at me and sighed. "Baby, I'm very grateful for what this Robert kid did for you tonight, but there's something about him that bothers me. I can't put my finger on it, but I don't feel comfortable with the idea of you and him-"

"Dad, can we not talk about this right now?"

The pain medication that they had injected into the IV was finally starting to work its magic all over my body. I felt very dizzy and lightheaded, my eyelids felt weighted down. I knew that any minute now I'd be asleep, but I needed to be sure that when I woke up, Robert would be there to answer my questions.

"Dad. D-don't send Robert away, okay?" I pleaded. I knew I sounded desperate, but in all reality, I was. I wasn't sure how long this moment of friendship with Robert would last and I had to make sure that no one around me did anything to speed up this timeline. "He's my friend, Dad, and I need him in my life right now."

Dad's face didn't seem to show any weakening in whatever opinion he had formed about Robert, but he nodded. "I owe him a great deal for what he did tonight, Grace. At the very least, I can allow him to stay with us at the hospital while you're checked over."

One down. One to go.

Robert? I send my thoughts out, directing them towards him, wondering if he could hear me over the sounds of the siren and the motorcycle combined.

I could hear your thoughts in the middle of a rock concert, Gee. Don't worry, I'm not leaving you. I'll be there when you wake up. I promise.

I sighed contentedly, and let the drugs take over my consciousness, pulling me down into the peaceful darkness.

ADMISSION

Some people have very vivid dreams, with bright colors, smells, tastes, and the ability to feel everything; others have dreams that are very mild and meaningless, flat, colorless. Some don't dream at all. I used to be one of the latter. Used to because the nightmare changed all of that.

I saw in extreme slow motion how my body bent and twisted after being hit. All sounds were magnified, intensified by the void of anything else but the vision in my dreams. I heard my bones crunching and cracking as I landed on my right side like a swan diving elephant. I could hear my screams, my moans, my grunts, and my haggard breathing. I could hear the blood bubbling up and out of me. I could hear it splash onto the asphalt. I heard the crunching of the asphalt under nice, expensive brown leather shoes, and the sounds of tires leaving me behind, the little tick-tick-tick sound of rocks that had come loose from the asphalt falling all around me.

But I didn't hear what hit me. I didn't hear tires screeching, or the crash of my body against the hood or side of any vehicle. There was nothing there that would prove that I had been hit from behind by a vehicle other than the fact that I had heard it leave. It was black silence.

And the nightmare only reinforced that fact by altering these unknown details ever so slightly so that it was always different, always unexpected, always terrifying. The only constants were the feeling of pain, abandonment…and death. Not the proverbial death of passing and release. Oh no, not for my mind. Death, the supernatural bringer of the cessation of life, had his black hand on mine, and wasn't letting go. *I won't leave you.*

I woke up drenched in sweat.

The hospital gown that loosely covered my body was soaked

with perspiration, the sheets beneath me as well. My eyes were staring at a stained and water damaged ceiling. It was as though the moisture from my body had radiated upwards and collected there, my own personal genetic graffiti.

I focused on the sounds around me. Beeping. The whoosh of the air conditioner. Footsteps in a hallway. Snoring? I turned towards that sound and saw Dad asleep in a chair next to the hospital bed. The lines that had been etched on his face from worry and concern for me were gone and I could see the remnants of the young man that had married my mom so many years ago.

My eyes looked away from him, now desperate to find the face that had promised to be there, the face that had been in my nightmare: the face of death. But how could he have taken on the face of death when he had saved my life?

I rationalized it as him representing all of the little deaths that I had suffered over the years, from the loss of my mom, to the loss of my self-esteem, the loss of my friendship and love with Graham, and even the loss of whatever type of relationship I had with *him*. All of them profound in how they had shaped me, shaped the way I now viewed this life that I had almost lost.

No, he wasn't death, but he wasn't here either. And it hurt. It hurt so much, I felt the inward pull of my body as it tried to protect itself, but nothing could do that. The pain medication dripping into my IV line wasn't going to protect me from this kind of pain. Nothing could, except him.

And then, as if out of a dream, the door to my hospital room opened and he was there. The sound that came out of my throat when I saw him was resembled nothing comprehendible; it was garbled and pathetic, but it did everything to let him know that I was relieved, ecstatic, and thankful that he hadn't chosen to leave me after all.

I went to get something to eat. You were still asleep, and your dad was here. I didn't think you'd wake up so soon.

I smiled, content to feel and hear this intrusion in my mind because it meant that he really was here. I extended my left hand towards him, realizing that my right arm and hand were completely encased in plaster and immobile at my side. He looked at it, almost unsure it seemed as to whether or not he wanted to touch me. I withdrew it, not wanting him to have to do so out of fear of hurting my feelings.

He looked over at Dad, saw that he was still asleep, and then seemed to make a decision, nodding to himself before coming to sit beside me on the hospital bed. He took my hand and placed it in one of his, while the other one reached up to cup my cheek.

How are you feeling?

Despite being broken, bruised, and battered in a billion places, I was feeling quite great at the moment. And he knew it, too. Whether or not he knew that it was mostly due to his presence, I didn't know, but I couldn't stop the ever growing feeling of warmth that was filling me up just by having him by my side.

Thank you for staying. I wanted him to know that I was truly grateful for him doing that for me. *Thank you for showing me the truth about tonight. All of it.* I wasn't going to ask him about Erica. I had no right to. Not after what he had done for me.

He looked at me, and seemed to be struggling with himself. I braced myself for whatever the outcome of this battle was.

I would have stayed even if you hadn't asked me to. It was...painful not being able to talk to you these past few weeks.

I stiffened—an automatic reaction to the doubt I felt at his words. *How was it painful for you? You're the one who shut me out, Robert. You're the one who deliberately went out of your way to ignore me. And I certainly didn't see you suffering when you were around Becca and Erica.* Especially *Erica. It might have been* painful *for you, but it was hell for me.*

Robert looked stricken. *Grace, I'm deeply sorry for being the cause of so much of your pain. When you asked me what I was, I had to pull away from you. It wasn't because I didn't want to tell you, that I don't want to tell you. It was because I cannot. Your safety is far more important to me than you knowing the truth. Gee, can I--can I tell you...tell you why I was with Erica?*

I looked at him, hurt and anger burning their accusations into my face. If I could have done so, I would have folded my arms over my chest to emphasize just how upset I was. But the need to know the truth was too overwhelming. I nodded, the sadness creeping in.

I was with her because I needed to know more about what happened with Graham to have caused him to hurt you so much. His mind is full of so many jumbled thoughts, one right after another, as though he were deliberately trying to forget something. I needed to know the truth. I already know from your own memories what happened. But what about him?

Call it my need to know more about you, and know what kind of person could cut you in such a way because I don't want to be that person. You've been occupying my thoughts so often lately. I was overwhelmed by this need to know more about you, and that need--it ensnared me, trapped me in my thoughts of you. And it is a prison of my own making. I don't deny that, and I will suffer it gladly if you will accept me back into your life.

I nodded, understanding how he felt, this need to know more. It was a hunger in both of us. But all I had done to drive him away was ask the question that he would have asked about me had the situations been reversed. What *was* he? And would I ever find out? How could I feel so strongly for someone and not know who he was beyond his name?

I looked at him, knowing he had heard the thoughts run through my mind, and feared that I had once again sent him silently screaming for the hills…too *afraid* to tell me more.

His *silence* was deafening.

Finally, his voice came.

Gee, the things you have seen, the things I have shown you, they're just hints at who I am, what I am, but they don't scratch the surface of the truth. I have kept you ignorant because knowing who and what I am is dangerous for your kind, but especially for you. However, I do not think that we can continue our friendship without you knowing more about me. I cannot tell you everything, but it must be your choice to want to know more. You must ask me to tell you.

I nodded my head, willing to hear anything he had to say to me at the moment, as long as it meant he'd stay with me, his hand holding mine, my face, his eyes staring into my own. He heard these thoughts and smiled. His thumb caressed my cheek, sending ribbons of heat shooting out of my body.

And then, the images started coming.

My mind was filled with the dancing colors of fire: Reds, oranges, yellows, whites, and blues. In the middle of the fire stood a woman, battered and bruised, her belly heavy with child; she was calling out in a language I couldn't understand. She had one bloody hand outstretched to an unseen being, her other hand lay on her stomach, the clothing underneath tattered and torn, seemingly trying to protect it from the licking flames.

From some dark corner, the object of her attention made a low, guttural sound, and then appeared, walking calmly through the flames. No, not walking; stalking. It was a large creature, hairy, almost wolf-like in appearance. Its ears were extremely large, tilting and turning towards any sound that it deemed worthy of notice. Its snout was long, coming to a rounded point at its nose, but its jaw didn't end near the apex of its eyes like most canines. It continued up towards its ears, allowing its mouth to open a full one-hundred-eighty degrees, as was demonstrated when it let out a fierce, snapping bark at the woman.

The woman took a few steps back, but quickly stepped forward again when she felt the lick of flames at her back. She had nowhere to go, and whatever decision she had come to, whatever agreement she had made with this creature was now a done deal. She closed her eyes and started saying something to herself in a strange, yet familiar language. The sound of the crackling flames seemed to become muted, the popping of wood ceased to fill my ears, as this woman's voice suddenly became the focal point of the vision. She wasn't talking, so much as she was singing, her voice a strange mixture of joy and sadness. "Quoniam angelis suis mandabit de te ut custodiant te in omnibus viis tuis…"

She had both hands on her belly, cradling it as she sang her melancholy song, her eyes closed and her body swaying softly. Her song slowly reached its crescendo when the attack came. The creature lunged at her throat, cutting off her song with a tremendous snarl. It

109

could snap her neck off in one motion, but it appeared to be hesitating, almost reluctant. But the hesitation lasted no more than an instant, and soon, the woman lay limp on the ground, her eyes sparkling with unshed tears that reflected the light from the flames around her, flames that appeared to be pleased with the sacrifice.

Quickly, the creature moved towards the woman's belly. Horrified, I watched as its mouth opened wide, as if to swallow the stomach whole, but instead, it appeared to be gnawing. Frantically, almost desperately, it carefully chewed a hole in the now dead woman's abdomen; a monster in every sense.

As its teeth continued their mission, I witnessed the transformation. Like a snake molting from its old skin, so, too did the creature. Fur fell, like rain sheeting off of a roof, revealing the pearl sheen of skin the color of moonlight. The back of this monster was not what I expected. It was smooth, lithe…feminine. Its head became smaller, fur falling away to reveal hair, long and blacker than a starless sky. Paw ended limbs became long, sinuous arms, topped with hands so small and graceful, it seemed almost farcical.

Those hands reached into the woman's belly now, and removed the precious child that had been protected there, revealed by the monster's teeth, and now cradled by her arms. She held the infant to her chest, cooing to it, comforting it as if she could erase from its earliest memories the death of its mother at the hands of the one whom now embraced it.

And then the monster spoke, in a language that was very familiar to me, in a voice that was so beautiful and melodious, I wanted to cry. *"Ne pleurez pas, mon fils. La vie est maintenant pour toujours la vôtre. La mort ne vous touchera jamais. Do not cry, my son. Life is now yours, forever. Death shall never touch you."*

She rose, holding the baby to her breast, and walked away from the flames as it finally claimed its prize.

Scenes of a young man in a small village filled my head then; his beautiful dark hair and silver eyes contrasting with the bright greens and blues of the surrounding fauna and sky. His angelic face smiling as he walked towards a woman who stood in the doorway of a little mud cottage, her belly large with child, her long, dark hair blowing in the cool breeze.

She held her arms out as he walked into them; he knelt down, hugging her belly and kissing it fondly. She patted his head tenderly, pulling him inside with her. *"It is time,"* she told him in heavily accented English, and he nodded, quickly gathering things from all corners of the little one room cottage. The woman walked over to a bed in the far corner of the room and began to undress.

She lay down on the quilt and placed her hands over her naked belly. The young man came to her then, his arms containing a clay bowl, some linen cloths, water in a pitcher, and what looked like the head of an axe. The woman took the linen cloths and placed them beneath her, spreading them out as if to protect the quilt underneath.

The young man poured the water into the bowl and placed it onto the table beside the bed, a reserved linen cloth lay next to it. He climbed up on the bed then beside her, handing her the axe head as he did so. She took it and opened her mouth. As it had in her other form, her mouth hinged open one-hundred-eighty degrees, and she placed the axe head between her teeth, clamping down tightly.

Her hands then moved to her belly, her fingers slowly rubbing up and down the dark line that stretched from her navel to the dark apex beneath it, as her fingernails turned into long, blood red claws. Suddenly, she was ripping her abdomen open, a fierce, primal scream tearing from her throat, the axe head collapsing a bit under the pressure of her teeth.

The young man, patiently waiting beside the woman, was splattered with the thick, black blood that spurted from the self-inflicted wound. He watched as the woman struggled with pulling open her abdomen. It seemed as though her belly was fighting with her, trying to close up on itself, and she was desperately trying to keep it open. The young man placed his hand on her arm, and with a final pull, she had her stomach flayed open, a shudder running through her body as she continued to ooze dark, viscous liquid onto the cloths beneath her.

From some unseen source, the young man pulled out a knife, and started to work on the womb, slicing its delicate tissue open with

111

much too much skill for someone his age. Dropping the knife to the side of him, he reached in and pulled out a tiny, blood covered newborn. While still holding onto the baby, he leapt off of the bed with the grace of a cat, and landed next to the bowl of water. He dipped the adjacent cloth into it and proceeded to wipe down the squirming child. Satisfied that it was clean enough to join its mother, he placed it at her breast.

Quickly, he went back to the woman's now empty abdomen, removing the hands that seemed frozen in place, and pushed the gaping wounds closed with nimble hands. He bent his head down and kissed the wound, blowing on it softly, humming a familiar tune. The sun was going down, the room was darkening, and still he hummed. The mewling cries from the infant had long since died down.

The darkness took over the room, and suddenly I was surrounded by the unnatural brightness of the hospital's fluorescent lighting. I could still hear the tune being hummed in my head as I stared into Robert's eyes, seeing his questioning gaze, knowing what he was thinking right then because he asked me without saying a word.

You were showing me your birth…and the birth of your…sister? You really do have a sister?

He nodded once.

A-are you human?

He shook his head. He dropped his hand from my face then, and tried to remove his other hand from mine. I held on like my life depended on it.

He stared down at my hand, my knuckles turning white with the force of my attempt to hold him prisoner at my side. *Why aren't you trying to run away from me? Didn't you get it? I'm not human. Hell, I'm not even some fictional monster that you've read about.*

Why should I be running away from you? I've seen worse things in a Scorsese movie. And as for not being some fictional monster, I would never think that, Robert. I've read a lot of books, and there are only so many things you could be, but I doubt any of them are monsters.

He cocked his head to the side, amused. *Well please then, Grace, do enlighten me as to what those things might be so that I can*

112

narrow it down for you.

Biting my lip, I wondered what I had gotten myself into. The last time we had had a conversation similar to this one, he had pulled back, and avoided me like the plague. I had to tread carefully.

Well, it's obvious you're not a vampire, and you don't smell like you're a zombie because I imagine they smell pretty rank and you always smell so wonderful. You might be a werewolf, since I've never seen you after a full moon. Is that it? Are you a werewolf?

He rolled his eyes.

Okay, so not a werewolf. What about a kelpie?

He started laughing. Loudly, the robust sound waking up Dad.

"Grace, you're awake. Oh, thank God." He got up quickly and gave me a once over, making sure that nothing had changed about me while I had been unconscious. "Are you feeling okay? Do you need anything? Something to drink? Eat?"

"I am kind of hungry. I haven't eaten since breakfast," I told him, remembering my last meal.

Dad looked over at Robert, "Would you like something, too?"

"A coke sounds good," he answered. Dad nodded, and looked back at me. "How about I get you a burger and fries from the cafeteria?"

I grinned and my stomach growled at the mere mention of greasy fries. "That sounds great, Dad. Ooh, and get me a coke, too. Please!"

"Two cokes and food. Coming up," he agreed. He hesitated a bit, looking between Robert and be before finally turning around and leaving. Watching how slowly he moved, how his shoulders slouched down, I couldn't help but worry about him.

Robert waited until the door had closed, then started laughing again. "Kelpie? Do I look a horse to you?"

I turned my head to look at him and blushed, my thoughts brought back to our little discussion. "You know, it's not like I said merman or something. You said it wasn't a fictional character that I had read about, but I'd bet that you thought I wasn't that well-read."

He laughed again. "I know you're intelligent, Grace. I was

expecting merman, vampire, even Frankenstein. But Kelpie threw me off. Not many people know about them. That and I think I should be insulted."

I shrugged. "So not Kelpie, not werewolf, not vampire, not merman, and not Frankenstein, right? At least that narrows down the list. There's still X-Men, swamp thing, and my personal favorite, David Copperfield. He's not human either."

His eyes were watering, he was laughing so much. "I can assure you that David Copperfield is very much human, albeit in a loose sense of the term. And while the X-Men idea would be interesting, I'm much cooler than Wolverine and Cyclops combined. Oh, and the swamp thing? Do I look that messy? That's just as bad as the Kelpie!"

His laughter was infectious, and I began to laugh with him. He looked at me, his smile bright and full, and—there really was no other word in the dictionary to describe it—perfect, and what I saw was so stunning, so brilliant, I gasped. His face seemed to radiate light; it fanned around him like a halo, bright and warm and promising, a corona of light that turned his features ethereal and divine. Not a Kelpie. Not a vampire. Not a mutant comic book character or some human magician. What he was, in that very moment, what he'd been in every moment since I had first laid eyes on him, was an angel.

He stopped laughing then, hearing my thoughts, knowing what conclusion I had come to, hearing what he was in my eyes, in my heart. His silence, coupled with the look on his face scared me for one endless second. *Is that what you are, Robert? Are you an angel?*

Slowly, so slow I nearly doubted the movement, he brought his hand to my face again, caressing it gently, and stared deeply into my eyes. It was his way of warning me. He was about to share something very intimate with me. It would border on the impossible, the improbable, and the irrational.

I knew I would never be the same person after all that had happened in just these few, short weeks, but what he was about to share with me was going to be completely life altering and wholly unbelievable. I could see it in his eyes.

He leaned in to press his forehead against mine, my mind ready and willing to accept whatever it was he wanted to fill it with. I did not expect what came.

There were no visions of past events, horrifically fascinating, terrifyingly intriguing, or otherwise. There were no frightening memories of blood and broken bones, of death and dying.

Instead, I saw my face as he saw it, as it was in that moment. Trusting, and…happy. The purple bruises that covered my face were not enough to disguise the blush in my cheek as—still with my eyes closed—I saw him lift his hand away from the side of my face to brush my lips with the back of his fingers.

I could see my lips part as I drew in a breath, saw my exhalation as the sigh came when he touched my bottom lip with the pad of his thumb. I could see myself bring my bottom lip inwards, to taste the spot that he had touched, letting it fall back out in yet another sigh when I realized that I could almost imagine what it would feel like with his lips on mine.

Impossible, improbable, irrational.

Kind of like everything that's happened so far. When he lifted his face to kiss my forehead, I counted…counted the seconds, counted the minutes, counted the heartbeats until his lips left my skin. And then I counted how long it took before I stopped feeling their burn. I gave up when I realized that I'd probably feel it until I took my last breath. It felt as though everything he did, every touch, every whisper, every thought was permanently burned into my mind. And, I knew that for as long as I lived, I would never want it any other way.

BEGINNINGS

I hadn't realized that my eyes were closed again until I opened them to see the mercury of his. I had always used liquid to describe the way they looked when they were this color, but never had I been this close to his face to see that I had been more correct than I thought. The shimmer of his irises looked like actual molten silver rolling around in a bowl, the pupil merely floating on its gilt surface.

He was so close I could count his eyelashes, see that while they were the blue black of his hair, the ends were ash gray, and seemed to have multiple tips like the plume of a feather. I needed to touch his face, but he held my left hand now, tighter than I had when he had tried to remove it. Without thinking, I moved my right hand towards his face, and touched it softly with my fingers. Just the side of his face, his temple, his cheek, but it felt so good. I wanted to cup his face like he did mine, but the plaster of the cast was in the way.

I turned my head to look at my right arm, and then quickly returned to look at Robert. "I can move my hand and arm," I said, alarmed, and raised and lowered it as if to prove the point. "I'm not supposed to be able to do that, am I?"

His smile was sheepish. "It's not like you didn't know that my touch could heal you."

Well, I had known that. But he had worked his little healing thing on me before, and my bones hadn't healed so quickly. "Why did it happen so fast this time?" I was nervous, wondering how I was going to explain this to the doctors, or to Dad.

"It was because I've pleased you," he answered proudly. "The human body seems to respond much better to healing when it feels sated, pleasured in some way."

I blushed, because feeling pleased was an understatement when describing how my heart raced, and how things were fluttering in my

116

stomach at the moment. I started to gather up the courage to say that perhaps I needed more healing when suddenly Robert was no longer next to me on the bed, but rather, sitting on the chair that Dad had been sleeping in. I looked at him questioningly, almost dejectedly, when the door opened and Dad walked in with a tray of food, the doctor right behind him.

Dad looked at my face, flushed most likely, and then looked at Robert, whose face only showed concern for me as the doctor began pulling, twisting, bending, and poking me, seeing how my injuries were healing.

"Grace, are you feeling okay? You look like you might have a fever," he said, putting the food and drinks down onto the little rolling table next to the bed and placing his hand on my forehead. He pulled it back quickly. "Jesus, you're burning up! Doc, she's got a fever!"

I'm sure the doctor had already come to that conclusion after man-handling me, but just to placate him, he pulled out an object that looked like a reflex hammer with a ball at the end and rolled it across my forehead and down my neck. After glancing at its reading, he looked at me and said, "It looks like you have a nice little fever, dear. We're going to get you some Tylenol to try and bring it down, okay?"

I nodded, not too concerned about the fever at all. Not with my own little miracle sitting just three feet away from me.

Dad, on the other hand, wasn't going to accept just Tylenol as the solution. "Don't you think you should see what's causing the fever? She might have an infection! We have Tylenol at home. She's in a hospital, for crissakes! Don't you have stuff here that's stronger? Faster? If all you're going to give her is Tylenol, I could go home and get some right now so that I won't have to see the $25 charge for two pills."

I sat there, gaping. Dad wasn't always the most patient, but I had never seen him act like this before. To hear him go off on the doctor was scary.

You just saw my birth, and you think THIS *is scary?*

I looked at Robert sitting peacefully in his chair and frowned. He wasn't helping. "Dad, it's okay. Tylenol is fine. It's probably just stress or something."

He looked at me and shook his head, not accepting that as enough. "Look, baby, I already lost your mom and I came pretty damn close to losing you tonight. I know how these things work. One minute you're fine, and the next, you've got a fever, and then you're gone. I won't let that happen." He was gripping my shoulders, the strain and terror on his face was hard to stomach.

"Dad, this isn't like mom. I was hit by a car, but I'm fine. A few broken bones, some bruises, but I'm fine. It's going to be okay, Dad." I tried to reassure him.

Robert stood up and placed his hand on Dad's shoulder. It appeared to be a comforting gesture, but I knew what Robert was doing before he had even raised his hand. He had told me silently, warning me not to interfere. In an instant, Dad collapsed, Robert catching him under his arms.

The doctor rushed quickly to see to him, checking his vital signs while pressing the nurse call button on the side of the bed. Soon, the room was filled with people who were not interested in how I was feeling at all, fever or no fever. Instead, Dad was taken to a room of his own to be treated for exhaustion and dehydration caused by stress.

You're good. I looked at Robert and his smile told me he agreed.

As soon as everyone else had cleared out of the room, Robert returned to the edge of the bed. As much as I wanted him to hold me again—and I so wanted him to hold me again—he had yet to answer my question…one of many. But, before that, I wanted an answer to a very simple question.

"Did you cause me to have a fever?"

The smile on his face couldn't have been any more smug. "Yes."

"Why?"

He reached out and grabbed my hand, brought it to his face. "So that I could be alone with you."

My heart started racing, but then he let go of my hand and reached for the rolling table, pulling it between us and grabbing his

118

coke.

"You've got questions that I have the answers to, and I didn't want to answer them while your father was here, so I had to give him something to get worked up over. It only took a little nudging on my part with his emotions—and your fever—but as soon as he hit that pivotal point, I knew I could easily have him pass out without causing any suspicion." He sounded like some war strategist. It might have sounded so simple to him, but to me it was all too complex. The what-ifs would have driven me crazy before a single step had been taken.

I watched as he opened the bottle and took a long swig. "Now, you had some questions?"

I had to blink a few times before I remembered what it was that I wanted to ask. "You never answered my first question. Are you an angel?"

He knew what I was going to ask, knew what I wanted to know, and his answer was well prepared, almost rehearsed. "Yes, although what I am differs depending on which country you're in. Aren't you going to eat?" He gestured towards the food on the tray, the burger and fries that Dad had gotten for me now semi-cold, the grease congealing before our eyes.

I shook my head at the food, too busy digesting what he had just confirmed for me. An angel—I was actually friends with an angel—was sitting on my bed and talking to me and...drinking a soda in front of me. It was all too surreal. Gathering my thoughts back up I looked at him and took a deep breath—probably the last one I'd be able to take if he smiled at me again—and began. "You showed me your...*birth*...but the woman who took you away and called you her son killed your mother. Why?"

I had started with one of the most difficult questions, I know, but if we could get through that one, asking the rest would be a lot easier. I waited patiently for him to respond. After what seemed like an eternity of listening to the two of us breathe, he started.

"The woman that you saw carrying me in her womb was not my mother. She was a vessel, an incubator, what would be called a surrogate in today's time. My mother, the monster that you saw attack

119

her, was doing her a kindness. I know it's hard to understand, what with such visible violence and seeming cruelty, but the fate that awaited that woman for bearing me was far worse.

"Her name was Hanina. She was a farm worker in the fields owned by my mother. She was loyal, devoted because she knew what my mother was, knew that the blessings of God would be upon her for being obedient and kind.

" She had been married for several years to a very cruel man. He had beaten her after she failed to become pregnant with a child within a month of being wed, and beat her every month following for seven years. She never told anyone. She endured the beatings, endured his rage against her body, and rage against her female flesh. She had vowed to God that she would be a dutiful wife, and so she was in everything except bearing him his heir."

"Why didn't your mother know about what was happening to Hanina? Couldn't she read her mind? Read the mind of her husband?" I asked, not understanding why she did use her gift.

"My mother has always been particular about the minds she delves into. After centuries of seeing the sick and depraved thoughts that humans were capable of having, she simply stopped altogether unless it was absolutely necessary."

I nodded, knowing that if I had the ability to look into the mind of someone like Mr. Branke, I'd need to boil my brain in vinegar. "Sorry about interrupting. Please continue," I said.

His lips formed a grim line at my thoughts, but went on, "After one particularly bad beating, she was late to the fields. Hanina's husband had told my mother that she was probably sick, being bellyful. My mother went to Hanina's hut to see for herself, having known that Hanina would never be late just because she was with child. She found Hanina lying on the ground, barely breathing, her weak heart sending out the drumbeats to call forth the archangels who would carry her home. My mother, never having been attached to a human before, recognized the loyalty that Hanina had shown, and asked her what would she like most in the world before she was to join God.

"Hanina said, quite simply, 'to have a child is all I want'. My mother didn't understand this. Hadn't Hanina's husband just told her that she was pregnant? But my mother could tell that Hanina was no more pregnant than she was as soon as she touched her womb. She could also feel the many other wounds that she'd endured, hear her body's tale in the song that her blood beat out. She was so loyal, so devoted to God, husband, and to my mother that she had endured in silence the misery that her marriage truly was. It angered my mother. She became enraged.

"She summoned Hanina's husband to the hut where she demanded he answer for his crimes. He spat at the two of them, called them horrible names, and cursed them with the very name of God on his lips. Hanina had been cursed—there was nothing that could be done for her now. But Hanina's husband had dared to curse one of God's angels. His curse became an invisible noose around his neck and he choked on it. His dying thoughts were that my mother was a witch and that he'd see her in Hell. It was one of the last times she ever listened to a human's thoughts.

"Hanina was now doomed, but my mother, feeling it her duty to see that she be allowed at least her dying wish after failing to keep her safe, blessed her barren womb with a child. This was a compromise between angel and human; that Hanina would carry in her a child that my mother could not.

"Hanina spent the next nine months living very happily. Her hands never left her belly, and she never cowered at what was growing beneath them, even when I started to talk to her in her dreams. She saw through me the death that was her husband's curse. But never did she stop loving me inside of her. She would sing to me the psalms, and tell me of the joys I would experience as God would surely bless me for being her salvation.

"The moment of reckoning finally came one night when a fire broke out in the fields. My mother didn't need the crops to survive—it was a trivial thing, that farm—but she had chosen to live as peaceful and human-like a life as she could, and she knew that simply letting it burn would destroy what peace she could find amongst humanity, so she went to fight the fire alongside her servants.

"Hanina had smelled the smoke from her hut, and ever loyal, she went to try and fight the fire, too. She did not know that the fire had been intentionally set by those who wanted to harm her for what they believed had led to her widowhood and the perceived bastard inside her belly.

"They beat her, raped her, and were preparing to set her body on fire when my mother appeared. My mother's gift, her unique ability is to change forms, any form she wishes, and so she changed into the creature that is most comfortable for her—that of the she-wolf—so that she could hunt down the ones who had tried to destroy her child.

She killed all of them and relished it, but by then it was nearly too late. The flames were nearly upon Hanina, the air around her being sucked away like a vacuum—no human would be able to survive that. Hanina asked my mother to kill her quickly, mercifully, so that no suffering and no harm would come to me.

"You asked why my mother killed Hanina. The answer is, because my birth required her death. Had she not taken it, I would have in a very violent and unforgivable way. Without truly realizing it, my mother's blessing was fulfilling the curse that Hanina's husband had made."

Robert paused. He seemed to be going over something in his mind, and I wished that I could hear the thoughts running through there just as easily as he could mine. Finally, he started again.

"Hanina's death heralded my beginning, while my birth heralded her end. But it also brought with it the end to my mother's time on earth as she had known it. The farm workers had seen her change. They had seen her walk through fire to kill Hanina, seen her rip me out of Hanina's womb, seen far too much and my mother knew she had to leave. But, she couldn't leave all of those people with the knowledge that they now possessed.

"My mother did something that night that she's never forgiven herself for. She descended upon the people like a plague, killing them all as quickly and as mercifully as possible. She had no other recourse. Her secret was now my secret, too, and she had to protect it. The farmers' deaths were blamed on the fire, and no one could find fault in

122

that excuse since crop fires spread very quickly, and usually every single slave was sent to try and put the fires out by their masters.

"My mother killed all of them because of me. Her desire to reward a servant and to have a child cost the lives of over a hundred people. So much death—right from the beginning—all caused because of my birth. My mother says that because of that, I was blessed with my ability to heal, to atone for the sacrifices made so that I could survive."

When he stopped, I took a moment to process all of the information that he had shared with me. That he would trust me with all of this, knowing what price it had cost so many, was intimidating and...terrifying. Would he kill me the same way his mother had killed all of her servants? Could he?

My thoughts caused his eyes to widen, his face to grow pale. No. Of course he couldn't. He was no killer.

He closed his eyes quickly before I could continue to study their reaction and reached for my neck, his hands caressing my shoulders, my throat. He pressed his forehead against mine once more, our two minds touching in more ways than one.

Impossible.

BLIND

I was able to leave the hospital after only two days. The doctors were amazed at how remarkable my recovery had been. Walking with the aid of crutches? Able to grasp things with my right hand? It was all attributed to my youth and stubbornness, the doctor told Dad, and prescribed me pain medication "for later".

I was wheeled out to the car by a nurse who had requested a double shift just so she could stare at Robert for a little while longer. He said the thoughts she had about him were borderline criminal. But, he obliged her as much as possible. He allowed her to stare at him holding my hand, whispering in my ear, kissing my forehead, kissing my palm. I had no problem with that.

Those chaste kisses though had a way of healing the injuries that were the most visible. My left leg's puncture wound had completely closed and the bruises on my face were a faded yellow around my eyes. I left the hospital the victim of a hit and run but I looked in better condition than Dad did—although I was still confined to the casts. The night he spent asleep in a hospital room of his own had done him some good, but his concern over me, coupled with the fact that the police were nowhere near close to figuring out who had hit me, was taking its toll on him.

Janice came to pick the both of us up, spending as much time fawning over Dad as she did me. It felt nice, I had to admit, having that maternal attention directed towards me after being without it for so long. She also acted as a buffer between Dad and Robert, whom Dad had decided was spending way too much time with me for someone I had just met in school less than a month ago.

She kept him occupied while Robert helped me into the back of the little SUV, and then distracted him even further when he kissed the top of my head before telling me that he'd see me at my house before shutting the door. When we arrived home she suggested that Robert, who had beat us there on his motorcycle, help carry me inside the house so that I wouldn't need to use the awkward crutches to hop up the porch steps.

Then, just before Dad was about to object, she pretended to get dizzy so he would focus his attention on her. I only found out about the fakery afterwards when Dad was helping Janice up the stairs to their room. Robert had propped up my useless casted leg onto a pillow on the couch, and then sat beside me, guiding me to lean back against him.

He patted my hair, rubbed my shoulders, and shared his thoughts with me. I had begun to appreciate this part, when we were communicating like this, our two minds touching each other; it felt like my mind was overcome with a strange sense of peace, all my previous annoyance at such a thing a distant memory. We were still in this position when Janice and Dad came back down the stairs twenty minutes later to discuss lunch.

Robert immediately offered to help make it with Janice, and left me with one thought before leaving for the kitchen. *He cares about you. Almost as much as I do.*

Dad sat down near my propped up foot, touching the toes that peeked out from the cast, and sighed. "How are you feeling, kiddo?"

"I'm fine, Dad. More than fine, actually," I said honestly. "I'm not in pain, I'm not being forced to eat vile hospital food, and I don't have to be poked and prodded anymore. I'm great!"

Dad nodded, somewhat convinced, but it appeared as though something was weighing on his mind. Oh, to be able to read his mind so that I would know what to say when he finally said it!

He patted my good foot, sighing once more. "Grace, Graham is coming over in a few minutes. He wanted to see how you were doing. He heard about the accident and is very worried."

I didn't know what to say. The cynical part of me said he was coming over to see the freak in a cast. The hopeful part of me said he was coming over to say how sorry he was for hurting me, and that he wanted to be friends again, and more, if that's what I wanted.

I wasn't going to play the surprised fool at that admission. I had

125

genuinely loved Graham, and still did. The seventeen-year-old girl I was felt thrilled at the idea of him possibly realizing how close he came to losing me and wanting to never take me for granted again.

I quickly went over in my head what I was going to say if he were to indeed express any type of remorse, twirling my fingers around each other in an effort to calm my nerves. There was a knock on the door and I took a deep breath while Dad got up and answered it. I could feel the nervousness in me vibrate up and down my body, and a pained, pinched feeling started to bubble in my heart; the memories of that Monday just one month ago was still fresh and new, much to my disappointment.

Dad walked into the living room followed by someone. I looked up from my fidgeting fingers to smile at Graham, rather than grimace like I wanted to, but it wasn't Graham who stood behind my father. It was a girl. One that I had never seen before, but whose face was so familiar I would have had to have been blind to not know who she was.

"Um, Grace, this is Lark Bellegarde. She says she's Robert's sister. Their mother sent her over here to see if she could fetch him," Dad said to me while staring in awe at the beautiful girl standing next to him. If ever a face could be used to illustrate the definition of angelic, hers was it. If she smiled, I would have had no doubt that I'd hear music in my ears. This was the same girl whose birth Robert had aided in his vision, I realized.

In that flash of recognition, she hissed at me. It wasn't audible. It was in my mind. She could read and project thoughts like Robert could. Of course she could! The look on her face was cold, contemptuous. She was no fan of mine. *Join the club.*

She blinked, shocked it seemed by my reaction. It was then that I noticed her eyes, and what looked like a strange bundle of sticks she carried in her hand. Lark, the angel's sister, was blind!

I may be blind, human, but I can still see, and my powers are limitless in comparison to your weak, human self.

Though the voice itself was musical, her anger was shockingly cold. It was like with every word she thought, along with it she sent a dagger of ice. It hurt, and she knew it, even if she couldn't see the

126

reaction on my face.

Robert appeared suddenly, having felt the encounter between his sister and me, not only *hearing* it. His eyes were steel again, cold. Lark's face was smug. Dad stood next to Lark, oblivious to what was happening, that the two of them were having an argument completely in silence; an argument about me.

As if realizing that they had an audience, Lark fell back into character with ease, and delivered her lines. "Rob, Mom wants you home now. There're two weddings this week and she needs you to help with set-up."

Rob's entire posture changed then. He nodded stiffly and came over to me on the couch, kneeling down so he could speak to me on eye level. "I'll be back as soon as I can, but it won't be for a few days. You'll have to make do with your dad's cooking, but I did leave you with the best canned soup and tuna sandwich in the history of soup and sandwich combos," he smiled at me and then leaned forward and kissed my forehead.

I looked into his eyes, seeing the hard metal soften slightly. *Why are you leaving? Truth.*

I cannot tell you that right now. Just know that I'll be back in no more than a couple of days.

Will you really come back? I hated that I sounded so desperate.

I promise I will be back as soon as I can. He brought my hand to his lips and kissed each fingertip. I felt each and every single one all the way to the bottoms of my feet. My fingers felt so sensitive, I thought I could feel the lines on his lips and the pulse that beat beneath them.

He stood up and winked at me, called out his goodbyes to Janice, thanked Dad, and dragged Lark out of the house. It happened so quickly that Janice had barely walked out of the kitchen when I heard Robert's motorcycle speed off. Dad was muttering something to himself about kisses and boundaries when there was another knock at the door.

He turned around and went to answer it. I was still glowing when Graham walked in, my father trailing behind, still mumbling under his breath. Graham looked at me on the couch, my limbs in casts, propped up on pillows, and his features became incredibly anguished. He walked gingerly towards me, as though merely moving the air around me would hurt me, and then knelt in front of me.

"Oh God, Grace, I didn't know. I didn't know until just a few minutes ago." He looked at my leg in its cast, not knowing that it was completely healed underneath, and with his lip trembling, put his head down onto my lap. "I'm so sorry, Grace-" his voice stumbled, and for a brief second, I could see the little boy who had cried when he saw what remained of his whale in front of me. "I'm so sorry for hurting you. You didn't have anyone to turn to and I'm so sorry; I'm such a jerk."

This was it. This was what I had been waiting for. This was what I had hoped he'd do. And yet…it didn't feel as good as I had thought it would. Perhaps it was because I couldn't stand to see him hurting, too—I never could—and here he was in obvious pain. Perhaps it was because I knew that while his grief and remorse were real, my injuries were not.

Sighing, I placed my hand on his head, the act familiar and comforting. He sighed, knowing that soon I'd be playing with his hair and telling him that he'd score a lot more girlfriends if he'd stop using so much gel. Only this time I wouldn't say anything at all.

And that quickly, with just those few words of remorse from him, we fell back into our old routine, as if the betrayal, the heartache had never even happened. Perhaps I was an idiot for it, but this was Graham. Nothing could erase the history between us.

Soon, Janice was asking him if he wanted to stay for lunch, since we were obviously missing our previous guest. He agreed and took the spot next to me that Robert had occupied. It bothered me—how deeply my heart had been broken, how miserable I had felt, and how easily all had been seemingly forgiven and forgotten by him. I felt cheated somehow—I expected so much more from this—but accepted that for now, this was better than the alternative.

Graham stayed until dinner, when his mother came to visit with a tray of vegetarian lasagna in her hands. He said he'd be over in the morning before school to see how I was doing, and then they left. Dad hadn't said a word until it was time for bed and I was trying to hop up the stairs with his help; pretending that I couldn't walk was going to be tedious.

"Grace, how do you feel about Graham coming back into your life now that you have Robert in it as well?"

I didn't answer until we were at my bedroom door.

"I don't know. I never—not in a million years—thought I'd be the girl with two guys in my life, two guys that I care about a lot. Up until a few hours ago, I was still amazed that I had even one."

Dad opened my door and helped me into my room. I gasped. It. Was. Clean!! Janice must have done this; I wondered what she thought of my disorderly room...and where exactly she had hid everything. Dad helped me hop to the bed and then went to grab me a pair of boxers and a tank top. He sat down on the bed next to me then, getting ready for what appeared to be a long talk.

Eyeing the clothes he had laid out, I decided that I could wait to change. This looked important.

"Grace, how much do you care about these boys?" he asked me.

"I care about them both a great deal, Dad." I said shyly, looking down at some invisible speck on the floor to avoid having to look into his face while answering. I knew that he'd hear the truth in my tone.

He took a hold of my right hand, cast and all, and sighed. "I was afraid of that. You realize what you're starting here, right? Two guys caring about the same girl—that girl caring about both of them?"

I nodded, understanding the point he was trying to make; but I also knew some facts that he didn't. "Dad, Graham and I are going to be nothing but friends. He has a girlfriend, they're 'serious', and no matter how close I may come to dying, he's never going to look at me the way he looks at her."

Dad put his hand under my chin and lifted my face up to look into my eyes, his features soft and warm. "That's his loss, Grace. But...you wish he would, right?"

I didn't know what to say to that. Part of me did want him to look at me the way he looked at Erica. It would be foolish to lie, especially since it wasn't that long ago that I had wanted that so very badly that when it became clear it would never happen, it crushed me. But there was that other part of me that knew when Robert looked at me, nothing could ever match the fire that burned inside of me. And I knew that I was more than willing to burn forever.

"I don't know what I want from Graham, Dad. Right now, his friendship is more than I expected, and I'll take what I can get if it means having him in my life again."

Dad seemed displeased by that answer, the aging lines returning to his forehead and mouth. "He hurt you pretty badly, Grace. I think if school hadn't started, you'd still be in your room-" he held my face in both of his hands like he did when I was a little girl "-and I just don't want you going down this road a second time, only to get hurt all over again. By *either* of them."

I raised my hands to cover his and squeezed his fingers, faking a wince as I did so to hide the fact that my arm wasn't broken after all, and kissed his cheek. "Dad, you know me so well, and yet you don't give me the credit I deserve."

He patted my thigh and kissed the top of head before standing to leave. He walked to my doorway and then turned around. "Grace, you've been the one constant in my life since your mother died. Always kind hearted, always generous and genuine. I always give you the credit you deserve. I just think that you might not be aware of your own heart, not where love is concerned. Love can make you blind to a lot of things, but most especially to what you really want and what's good for you." And then he was gone.

I thought about what he meant when he said that love makes us blind to what we really want. I knew what I wanted; I wanted love.

BODYGUARD

Restless nights don't make for very pleasant mornings. Sleeping in useless casts was beginning to get on my nerves. Dressing in clothes that were too small to get around the casts on my arm and leg, or too big to be any more useful than having a towel draped over my body was ranking a close second to not being able to go to the bathroom without having it be announced by my hopping to and from.

Janice made breakfast the morning after I came home while Dad helped me downstairs. I didn't know how long I'd be able to keep the charade of my broken limbs going, but it wouldn't be for long if the irritation didn't let up soon.

I sat down to a meal of scrambled eggs and bacon while Dad read the paper. The story of the hit and run was all over the front page. The mystery vehicle, the mystery driver, my injuries, and the hero were all there in black and white. It was difficult to swallow my eggs as the severity of the accident was described in detail in twelve point font.

Robert's face was prominently displayed next to my junior year photo—I gagged at the blatant juxtaposition—right beneath the headline. There was a back story about his family on another page; I reminded myself to read it when Dad was done. I already knew more than anyone with a press badge would be able to dig up, but it would be interesting to know what exactly the media knew about him and his family.

There was a knock at the back door, and as though there had never been a change, never an absence of him in my life, Graham walked through the door and smiled at me. And pathetic me couldn't help it—I smiled back. That rush of happiness that I had always gotten when he smiled filled me up. It instantly got on my nerves, too. Well that was certainly different.

He sat down in the empty chair next to me and started eating from my plate, again falling back into routine. Perhaps I was so thin

131

because I had never been able to finish a meal when he was around… I snatched a piece of bacon out of his hand, frowning at his need to steal food from an injured *friend*. "Hey!" he protested, reaching for the strip of meat in my hand.

"That's my bacon. Get your own." I barked, pulling my hand back. I laughed when he reached over to Dad's plate and grabbed the last one there. Dad was oblivious, too caught up in whatever it was that he was reading.

"Did you know that Robert's family is extremely wealthy, and apparently very philanthropic? Evidently they've donated money to the hospital and the firehouse for purchase of more ambulances and the hiring of new paramedics," Dad said from behind the paper, his hand reaching towards his now empty plate, feeling around for the bacon that was now digesting in Graham's bottomless stomach.

The paper bent down—Dad glared at Graham. "Don't your parents feed you?"

Graham smiled again. "Only enough to make it here." Then he laughed. "I've got to get going. I have to pick up Erica." He turned to face me, as if to see my reaction.

He got one. It was a scowl. A genuine, bona fide scowl.

He didn't like it, I could tell, but I didn't care. Erica was going to be a point of contention between the two of us until we were able to discuss her privately. Even then, I was sure that we'd butt heads about her. He just wasn't aware why…yet.

"Go on then. I'll see you around," I told him, my voice not exactly hiding my annoyance. He lightly punched my shoulder. Just like nothing had ever happened.

"Use the front door, Graham," Dad muttered from behind his paper again.

Graham nodded and started walking out of the kitchen. The doorbell rang then, and Janice went to answer it. She sure fell into the housewife role fast, I noticed.

My head lifted when I heard the commotion. It wasn't so much the shouting that suddenly made me forget about my cast on my leg and bolt out of my chair—hobbling like some demented horse towards the

132

front door—but the sound of something heavy falling, and groaning that did. I raced out of the kitchen and stared at the scene that lay before me in the hallway fronting the entryway.

Graham—six-foot tall, football star Graham—was on the floor writhing in pain. A very manly pain. Standing over him, in all her five-foot-four-inch glory, was Stacy. My third period companion was wearing a very satisfied smirk on her face.

"Serves you right for being here, you jerk," she spat.

Janice was holding her hand to her mouth, trying to hide her laughter. "You appear to have a bodyguard, Grace," she whispered to before leaving me to deal with what had happened.

Stacy looked up at me, her face filled with concern as she took in my casts, and pointed to Graham who was still rolling on the floor. "This pathetic waste of skin here needed a little lesson on how to treat a lady."

She smiled as he flinched when she started walking towards me. "Since you're in no condition to do it, I thought I'd lend you a hand. Or foot." She looked me up and down, assessing the visible damage for herself. "How are you feeling? I didn't know you were home until I read the story in the paper this morning, and I had to come and see if you were okay."

This was the most she'd ever spoken to me at one time, and I was amazed at how much I enjoyed listening to it. "I'm fine, actually. I'll be able to go back to school in a couple of weeks."

The groans coming from the door grew louder and I sighed. The bigger they are, the harder it is to pick up their egos. "I know you meant well, Stacy, but we're going to have to help Graham up. He came over yesterday and apologized for everything he did, and I forgave him. We're working things out…sorta."

She looked at me, shocked. "You're a lot better person than I am." She walked back towards Graham, and muttered, "Must be the non-Korean half."

Together, Stacy with amazing strength for her size, and me with…erm…amusement, helped Graham to a sitting position. His face was red. I don't know if it was from embarrassment or pain, but I couldn't help but feel a little bit satisfied in it. I owed Stacy now. Friendship for life was the least I could offer her.

"Graham, are you okay?" I asked, trying very hard to keep the corners of my mouth from curling up.

While waiting for his response, I caught a movement out of the corner of my eye. Dad had poked his head out of the kitchen to see for himself what Janice had probably already described. Seeing Graham on the floor, and Stacy standing next to him, her petite frame tense from her anger and frustration seemed to please him. He flashed me a thumbs up and then disappeared.

"Wh-ugh-why did you k-ki-kick me?" Graham finally wheezed.

Stacy shrugged her shoulders as she replied, "You deserved it. And I don't like you. And you hurt my friend. And there are a lot of other reasons, but the only one that matters right now is because I knew it would feel good to do it."

I had to admit, those were pretty good reasons. Especially the one about him hurting her friend…me. I was quite pleased about that one. "Graham, are you okay?" I asked again, this time not fighting down the smile that filled half of my face.

"I guess I deserved that…I'm okay, Grace. Just need a minute," he panted.

Stacy rolled her eyes. "You've already had five."

I laughed at that one. Graham didn't, and it didn't bother me one bit. "Come on, Graham. You need to get up now. Your girlfriend isn't going to be very understanding of the fact that you were late because you were at my house."

"It's the peroxide…" Stacy mumbled, coming forward to help me lift Graham to his feet.

Graham took a deep breath and tried his best to regain his composure. "I'll come by after practice to see how you're doing, okay? That is, if you don't mind the company." He looked warily at Stacy, who was smiling. Like a cat would at a mouse. A very kickable mouse.

"I don't mind, Graham. I'll see you later. Have fun at school," I said as he limped out of the house.

Stacy watched him shuffle towards his house and shook her

head. "That guy is no good. He acts like a complete ass and thinks he's God's gift to women. I've seen what that is, and he doesn't even come close." She gave me another once over. "So I know the newspaper account. Do you mind if I hear it from the horse's mouth?" She asked, cutting to the chase.

"What do you want to know?" I replied, hobbling over to the couch, the casts suddenly feeling very heavy with the burden of their lie.

She helped me as I tried to sit down and then sat on the coffee table. A very *un*-Korean thing to do, that's for sure. I didn't remember much about my mother's culture, but I knew you didn't sit on tables in other people's houses.

"I wanted to know what happened. I mean, stuff like this doesn't just happen, you know? And whoever did this is still out there. Maybe if you told me, I could be on the lookout." She smiled, my own personal bodyguard.

I laughed as the image of her shoving people out of my way while I was walking up and down the hallways of our school popped into my head. She seemed to know what I was thinking because she started laughing, too. It felt unbelievably comfortable, sitting here sharing a private joke with her, and I thought to myself that I could definitely get used to it.

Sobering up to the reality of what she wanted to hear, however, I began telling her the details of what had led up to, and what had happened immediately after the accident. When I got to the part about the brown shoes, she stopped me.

"Did you say he was wearing brown shoes and black laces?" She asked me, her eyes wide…alarmed.

I nodded my head. "Yes. They were pretty expensive shoes, too. It looked like he polished them or something. Not even a scuff or scratch mark were on them. I should know. I got a pretty damn close-up view of them."

Stacy's jaw stuck out, while an idea seemed to be bouncing around in her head, trying to find the correct slot to fall into. "Heath's not a big town. I'm sure it'd be quite easy for the police department to find someone with fancy brown shoes and black laces who owns a car with front end damage. I didn't read about the shoes in the paper though, so at least the guy doesn't know that he can be identified."

I wondered then if she were right. And if she had spent way too much time watching or reading crime dramas. "The police only really have bits and pieces of what happened. I wasn't able to give a full statement while in the hospital because my dad had to be hospitalized, too, so he couldn't give his permission for them to talk to me. That pretty much means whatever the paper has...it's not what I gave to the cops."

Stacy pondered what I had said before looking at her watch. "I gotta get going before I'm late for school. I think I'll stop by after Tae Kwon Do class and see how you're doing. I'm really glad you're okay, Grace, just so you know. I was really worried about you. Thank you for telling me all of this."

I thought back to when I had been lying on the road, when I had seen the faces of all the people I cared about pass before my eyes, and I remembered that she had been there among them. It had surprised me then, but I understood that she was a part of my life that had made me happy. It brought a little normalcy to the life that I had always felt was so dismally abnormal, I'd never find a place for myself in it other than as the freakish oddity.

I gave her a genuine smile. "Thank you for coming, Stacy. It means a lot. Really."

She smiled back and then gave me an awkward hug; awkward not only because I wasn't expecting it, and because I hugged her back, but because she wasn't expecting me to. If the huge grin on her face was any indication, I'd have to say that she was very pleased.

I'd be lying if I said I wasn't pleased as well.

SOLILOQUY

Sitting at home after Dad had gone to work, and with Janice upstairs cleaning out the spare room left me with a lot of time to think about what had happened these past days. In an instant, my life had changed. I went from being whole yet wholly missing to being broken, and completely found. The hit and run had altered my world again, shifted everything and this time, the world was upside down and I was right side up.

I was now someone worth fighting for, someone worth saving. The feeling was incredible. I had the overwhelming urge to burst into song, some cheesy musical number that included my off-beat dancing; I settled for the Time Warp.

That was how Janice found me; hysterical in my newfound joy, putting my hands on my hips—completely unabashed—pulling my knees in tight, and absolutely not showing any signs of a broken right leg or injured left one. I froze, seeing her face, the reaction, and knowing that I'd have to think of an explanation really quickly before she started suspecting me of faking my injuries.

I started to speak, the words ready to leave my mouth, when she began laughing at me. "Oh my goodness, those must be fantastic pain killers they have you on, Grace. Your dancing was hilarious!" She was laughing so hysterically, I almost felt offended. Almost. It's hard to feel offended when you know you look absolutely ridiculous.

I knew not to look a gift horse in the mouth, so I agreed with her on the pain killers comment and then sat down, still feeling giddy but cautious now that I knew I had an audience who wasn't quite willing to remain upstairs. I was feeling like my old self, just…happier. There was no other way to describe it. I was actually happier after being mowed down by a car than I was when I had been sitting on top of one, ready to spill my guts. The irony nearly sent me into another round of laughter because who really thinks it's better to have been in a hit and run?

I looked at the casts on my leg and arm. I knew that underneath them, my limbs were perfectly fine. But what if they weren't? What if Robert didn't have the ability to heal anyone? What if he didn't have the acute hearing he did? Where would I be now?

The answer was simple. I'd be dead.

It was a reality that was difficult to accept. Even if someone had found me on the road shortly after being hit, I knew that the injures that Robert had healed before help arrived were not so easily repaired after as long a wait as we'd had for the ambulance. Time would have been my death sentence just as easily as the hit and run would have.

But Robert had heard me. He had heard my cry for help, as weak as it was, and came for me. I hadn't questioned why…and really hadn't gotten much of an explanation on the how. I had been so relieved, so incredibly happy that he had found me, and that he was there, talking to me and holding my hand that I didn't think about what his reasons were for coming in the first place. I knew he trusted me. I knew that more than I knew anything else at the moment, and that helped me to push aside any other thought that was nagging in my mind.

I didn't realize I had fallen asleep until I heard the doorbell ring. I sat up, noticing that I had been sleeping on the couch, covered by some hideous looking blanket, and made an attempt to stand. I was incredibly dizzy for some reason and nearly toppled over onto the coffee table. Janice, who had been on her way to answer the door saw me and rushed to help me back to a sitting position, calling out "Come in!!" to whomever it was standing on the other side of that damn bell.

Janice was putting my feet back up onto the couch and covering them with that ugly blanket when a small cough alerted us to the guest who had allowed himself into the house at her request. It was Mr. Branke, the Octopus. He had a manila envelope in one hand, a bunch of flowers in the other.

"Good afternoon, Miss Shelley. I came by to drop off your class assignments and bring you these." He handed both the flowers and the envelope to me, smiling widely, causing him to resemble a hyena circling what it thought was a wounded calf. I took the envelope and the flowers as quickly as I could, snatching them out of his hands so fast, flower petals showered onto the floor.

"Um. Thank you," I said, trying—but failing miserably—to smile. Showing any type of affection was the wrong thing to do because as soon as he saw the corners of my mouth twitch up, even in strained measure, Mr. Branke sat down next to my feet and started to pat them beneath the blanket. My attempt to be polite had been received as an invitation of familiarity that was far too intimate for anyone…especially between a teacher and a student. I cringed, looking at those chubby, sausage like fingers fiddle over the blanket on my feet.

Janice—thank God for Janice—seemed to notice my discomfort. "Excuse me, Mr…" she paused for him to tell her his name.

"Branke. August Branke. I'm Grace's biology teacher," he replied, smiling. Like a crocodile.

"Yes, well, Mr. Branke, Grace has been through a great deal, as you know, and she needs her rest. I will tell her father that you stopped by with her homework, and-" she looked at the quivering pile of weeds in my hands "-the *lovely* flowers. So if you don't mind, let me see you out." She waved her arm towards the door, in case he needed a visual as well as verbal cue that it was time for him to leave.

He stood up, taking the hint as well as anyone would, and nodded at me. "I hope to see you back in school soon, Grace."

I nodded back, but couldn't muster up enough to smile.

Janice walked with him towards the door, and I threw the flowers he had brought me onto the ground. The manila envelope—now *that* I opened. Inside were assignments from all of my classes: those that I had missed, and those that I would miss for the next two weeks that I had been ordered to stay home.

The assignments from French class were typical translation and description worksheets. Mrs. Hoppbaker from Calculus had us working on polar coordinates, while Mr. Branke wanted me to study up on the cellular structure of the human pituitary gland for a test we were having that Friday I'd be returning. *Well sure thing, Mr. Branke, I'll just whip out my trusty ol' Guide to the Pituitary Gland right now!*

Mrs. Muniz in English Lit had chosen Edgar Alan Poe as the author of the semester and required us to choose a few poems to dissect in essay form, in no less than twenty pages, to be turned in at the end of the semester. I hadn't expected Poe. Last year's copy of the fourth year syllabus hadn't really contained any poetry in the book list, and I had never been a fan of Poe's woeful and dreary prose about love lost. But then again, that was before I had lost love myself.

I had a new perspective on things, on life. I made a mental note to check out a few of Poe's collective works from the library as soon as I could.

Sixth period theatre was going to pose a problem for me with regards to the class assignments because I wasn't able to be there; I couldn't rehearse any lines, which also meant I couldn't act them out either, not that I was complaining about such a thing, of course. But, when I looked for the sixth period assignment list, there was none.

I held the manila envelope upside down and shook it. A little slip of paper the same color as the envelope fell out and floated onto the floor. I bent to pick it up and saw that it was a note. It read, "*Your study partner for sixth period Dramatic Arts has been randomly chosen and will be by later this afternoon to provide you with your study material and assignment requirements.*"

I tried to remember who was in sixth period to see what the odds were that I'd be paired up with someone who couldn't stand me. I knew that Erica was in my class, as well as a few of her blondemates. I wouldn't have much of a problem with the pimply boys, whose names I somehow remembered as Chad, Dwayne, and Shawn, or Chips, Dip, and Salsa as they preferred to call themselves. I did enjoy being in their group the previous week. They weren't as critical as I had feared, and Friday's performance had earned us a solid B+.

There were a few other people I couldn't quite remember who seemed innocuous, and then there was Robert. Who would his partner be? Surely I wouldn't be so fortunate that I'd get him as my partner. Besides, he'd said he'd be gone for a few days, which meant there was no way he'd be coming over today.

I sighed and hoped that I'd be partnered with either Chips, Dip, or Salsa. When Janice went to answer the doorbell that rang again fifteen minutes later, I swore never to hope for anything again; I'd just be let down.

Following Janice into the living room was Erica. Janice had no idea who she was, so she seemed cheerful that more people were coming to visit me. I could see that Erica was also very glad to be visiting me, wrapped up on our old, ugly couch in an even uglier and probably older blanket.

"Would you like something to drink, Erica?" Janice asked, looking very happy that I had another girl come to visit. "I have to get started on dinner, so it's no problem for me to get you anything. What about you, Grace? Are you hungry?"

Erica and I glared at each other as we both responded "No thank you."

Janice shrugged her shoulders and left, still beaming that, by all appearances, my social life was starting to look more and more normal.

Erica was the first to speak as soon as Janice was out of earshot. "I see the rumors are true, you did go and get yourself hit by some car. Honestly though, if you think this little plan is going to get Graham back into your life, you're sadly mistaken."

I fought the urge to deny her hidden accusation. She wouldn't have believed it anyway. "Why are you here, Erica?"

She looked around the living room, taking in the sparse furnishings and smirked. "You and I were partnered up to write and perform a solilo-something, and since I'm too busy with Graham to really have anything to do with it, I brought it over for you to write up. I'll just pick up my lines later and then we'll perform them next Friday if you show up. If you don't, I'll still get an A, so please…take your time."

She removed a bunch of papers from an obnoxiously large purse and tossed them onto the coffee table. "Those are the requirements. I don't know what it says, just that I sure as hell wasn't going to be writing that stuff out. I *have* a life." She put her hands on her hips, her tapping left foot sticking out from beneath a very impractical September-in-Ohio full length slip dress, and waited for me to pick up

141

what looked like half a ream of paper.

Curiosity getting the better of me, I hefted it onto my lap and started going over the requirements and the examples given, which made up the bulk of the packet. It seemed pretty cut and dry with the exception of one thing: the soliloquy I would read would be written by Erica, while she would read one that I had written especially for her. The part that made my stomach churn with apprehension and doubt however was that we weren't allowed to see the other's work until the day of our recital next week. As if it couldn't get any worse…

I looked at her, wondering if she even comprehended what this meant. Did she even understand what a soliloquy was? I looked at her, remembering her struggle to pronounce "*dormant*" that first day back at school, and shook my head. Of course she didn't.

"What? You're not going to write it?" she asked, a look of panic crossing her face.

"Erica, we have to write soliloquies for the other person. I will write yours and you'll write mine." I explained.

She stared at me, her face a completely empty slate. "What do you mean, I have to write yours. Your what?"

"My soliloquy. It's a type of dialogue where we speak to ourselves. I have to write yours, and you have to write mine," I said, exasperated. "We-have-to-write-them-for-each-o-ther."

She nodded her head, her face running through several emotions, finally landing on glee. Her eyes actually twinkled. It would have been beautiful if I didn't notice the sinister grin that accompanied it. "I get it. And we have to read what each other wrote, right? No matter what?"

I grimaced. I knew exactly where this was going, and so did she. "Yes."

Satisfied with my answer, she turned and headed towards the door. "I'll try not to be too honest," she called over her shoulder before leaving.

It was then that I knew she had known what the assignment had entailed the entire time, and had merely wanted to hear me say it out loud. There was no going back now. But, would I be able to be kind to her? Or, would I write what I felt, what I knew to be the truth?

I knew that she'd do her worst, be as absolutely cruel as possible with me, and I had to brace myself for that. I had to expect Graham to be the focus of her writing, because that was where she knew she could hurt me the most. I had no control over what she had planned for me, but I could control how I responded to it. I wasn't going to go to pieces over this. I had just survived a hit and run, right? Erica would be a piece of cake!

Solid in my assessment, I called for Janice to bring me a pen and my binder from my backpack. I wasn't sure when Graham or Stacy would get off their respective practices, so I had to get as many of the thoughts that I had running through my mind jotted down so that I wouldn't forget them.

I wrote until the pen's ink started skipping, which required that I get up and find one that wouldn't. I wrote until my hand started cramping, and then realized that was because I was gripping the pen too tightly. I wrote until the sun started going down and I needed to flip on a light.

I was so engrossed in the free flow of thoughts to paper, I almost didn't notice when Graham, a sub sandwich firmly wedged between his lips, a giant cup of Coke in his hand, and stinking of sweat and grass, plopped down next to me. It was his stink that gave me enough warning to close my binder before he could see what I had been working on.

"Ugh, you reek," I complained, falling back into our old routine like a foot falling into an old shoe. He proceeded to shake his head, spraying me with sweat, and we both convulsed into laughter. I couldn't know if he felt as comfortable as I did, but I hoped he did, even though a part of me told me not to. Especially when the words that were written beneath my hand seemed to be screaming to be found out.

FIGHT

When Stacy arrived, Graham had already finished his sandwich, his coke, some pot roast that Janice had made for dinner, and a bowl of ice cream. She commented that his side of the couch seemed to be dipping disproportionately to mine, and she was right. I'm sure I could have placed a bowling ball in my lap and it would have swiftly rolled to his side due to the sharp incline. He, naturally, took this as Stacy calling him fat.

"And that's what you are, lard-boy. Now move. I want to sit next to Grace and ask her about something important," she said contemptuously, her hands on her hips and a menacing gleam flickering in her eyes. She looked intimidating, dressed in her black and white uniform, hair pulled back into a tight ponytail, perspiration shining on her face. I admired her, and envied her.

Graham, however, didn't seem all that intimidated, or envious. He looked annoyed. I could smell a fight coming, and while normally I'd want to be as far away from it as possible, the idea of witnessing these two go at it intrigued me.

"Who the hell made you queen, huh?" he mocked.

Stacy smirked. "I'm sorry. Did you want that title for yourself, Princess?"

Graham's face grew rigid. "I'm not leaving. This has been my spot since forever so you can find yourself someplace else to sit. Grace might be your friend now, but she's been my *best* friend for my entire life."

Stacy looked smug then. "You mean your entire life up until you started dating Erica Hamilton behind her back and dumped her in the middle of your street, right? Your *best* friend."

With what sounded like a herniated snarl, Graham stood up. His sudden movement sent me jerking back into the armrest of the couch

144

while Stacy assumed an anticipatory stance, her face suddenly calm, her features feline, suiting her quick and lithe motions.

"You need to get out of my face, little girl. Grace and I worked things out. Bring it up one more time and I'll shove that belt down your throat."

I had never seen Graham so angry before. He was fuming, every part of his face red, from his eyes to his ears. I looked at Stacy to see if she was as worried as I. Of course she wasn't. She didn't know Graham, so any change in his mood was new to her and absolutely meaningless.

"Try it, Princess. I'm sure you're just dying to prove how macho you are, considering that you weren't even the one who saved her life," she jeered, her weight shifting from one foot to the other as she awaited his response.

Graham's face turned a very brilliant shade of purple at Stacy's taunting and I watched as he lunged, his hands reaching forward, fingers outstretched, ready. "NO!" I cried out, but didn't know who I was directing it to, because his reaction set Stacy in motion, and like a cat swerving to avoid a spray of water, she agilely stepped around him, his momentum causing him to plunge headfirst into Dad's recliner. Stacy was quickly behind him, turning the recliner's handle and causing it to lean back into a horizontal position which, coupled with Graham's weight and continued momentum, resulted in him being flipped over, landing on his face behind the chair.

It happened so quickly, I wasn't sure if it had happened at all. Then Janice appeared, her face full of concern…for the chair.

Graham groaned on the floor. "That's the second time today you had me on the floor."

Stacy shrugged her shoulders. "I was being nice. Piss me off and I'll make sure you never leave that floor again." She stepped around the coffee table and then took his place on the sofa by my feet. "So, how was your day?"

I stared, my mouth open, my eyes wide at the calm, serene expression that was on her face. She just felled an angry footballer nearly twice her size who had charged at her in a fit of rage, and she didn't even have a hair out of place. "Are you some kind of super woman?" I managed to get out while looking back and forth between her and Graham, who was still on the floor, probably trying to figure out how to salvage his pride.

She laughed at me, at my surprise. "I'm just used to being picked on and attacked by guys twice my size. I have five brothers, six uncles, and a dad who runs the do jang, my Tae Kwon Do school. Graham pissed off doesn't scare me at all. You want to see me scared? Make my mom mad!"

It was easy to laugh with Stacy, I realized, as I started laughing, too. I hadn't realized that life was much bigger and broader than the little world I had built around my relationship with Graham. Again, I felt a strange bit of gratitude for the hit and run, because without it, I wasn't sure if my relationship with Stacy would have progressed past the library meetings we had. I remembered the image that I had conjured up that morning about her as my bodyguard, remembering how comical it had seemed then. Not so, anymore. She had a skill that made her definitely capable of filling that imaginary role. It was something that I admired greatly, desperately. Suddenly, I had an idea.

"Um, Stacy, do you think it would be too late for *me* to start learning Tae Kwon Do?"

Her mouth dropped open, obviously shocked at my question. "No, Grace. I think it's about time you started learning!"

I smiled. "How much are the classes? I want to start as soon as I get these stupid casts off. What do I need, when can I start? How tough is it?" I was excited now.

Her eyes closed as she concentrated on something. "I think I could probably get you the family discount, and you can borrow most of my stuff. I have a lot of doboks that might fit you. They're long on me, but they should be just right on you, and you'll get your first tti when you start." She clapped her hands together. "Oooh! I get to teach you! I just remembered that my dad asked me to teach the beginners class! You'll be my student!"

Suddenly, I wasn't so excited. "Um…you're going to be my teacher?"

146

I saw the corners of her mouth turn down as her mood darkened at my question. "Yeah. Why? You don't want to be taught by a *girl*?"

Realizing that just how quickly and easily I could end up on the floor next to Graham, I shook my head. "Oh no. It'll be great. Yeah." I tried to sound cheerful. I even managed a toothy grin.

It seemed enough because she grabbed my binder and reached in to tear out a sheet of paper. "I'm going to write the directions to get to-" she stopped when she saw what I had been writing. She turned to look at me, her face a mixture of shock and mirth. "You have Mr. Danielson." Her voice sounded affected. "The second verbal assignments are always soliloquies. Hmm…and *this* one looks like it's going to be great…fun…is she writing yours as well?"

I nodded my head, and then tipped my head towards Graham's prone body, hoping she'd get the hint that he was in the dark about that little fact. "She's going to have a great deal of enjoyment at my expense come next Friday."

Stacy smiled. "I think you will as well, just going by these little notes you have here. I might consider cutting class and sneaking it just to watch. And hey! You're coming back to school next week, eh?"

It again took me by surprise how pleased it made me feel to know that someone actually cared about me coming back to school. Part of me wondered where she had been three years ago, but I knew now that I wouldn't have been able to appreciate her friendship then.

"Yeah, I'll be coming back to school next week Friday. I think the doctor will let me go once he sees that I can manage pretty well. It doesn't even feel like I've got broken bones!" I giggled nervously at that last bit.

Stacy looked over at Graham still lying on the floor, not moving. I looked, too, wondering what her reasons for staring at him were. "So I read that the new guy, Robert, he saved your life?"

"He happened to be heading that way towards his family's property when he saw me on the road," I said, repeating the same story for her as I had to my dad, a police officer who had gotten into trouble for asking without my dad present, the multiple doctors who had come to see me, and the three nurses who had all wanted to get as close to

147

Robert as his clothes would allow.

Stacy nodded her head, still staring at Graham. "I heard he rode behind the ambulance all the way to the hospital, and stayed until you came home."

I looked back at Graham while I answered her, "Yeah. He was great. He stayed with me in the room the whole time." I could see Graham's hand clench into a fist when I said this, though I couldn't see his face because it was obscured by the chair. I was starting to figure out what Stacy was up to. I wasn't so sure I wanted to travel down this road.

Stacy, on the other hand, wanted to stick to her map. "So are you two, you know, *dating*?"

I looked at her, unable to answer, because I didn't know. "I think—I think that we're really, really good friends," was all I could come up with. We were more than that—the secrets that Robert had shared with me went beyond anything simple friendship could allow—but as much as I liked Stacy, I wasn't sure that I was ready to go into details about how he made me feel. And most certainly, I wasn't willing to admit to anything with Graham less than five feet away from me.

"Well, he's something else, I'll say that much, Grace. He's handsome, his family's rich from what I've read, and now he's a hero. You'd be pretty stupid not to try and snatch him up before one of the other girls at Heath do. They're like vultures who vomit on their food so others don't get their beaks in it," she said, suddenly staring at her fingernails, as if they were the most important things in the world.

I looked over to the floor to see if Graham was still clenching his fists at his side, but he wasn't there. He was standing directly in front of the coffee table, his eyes very focused, intent. I wasn't sure what to make of it. Maybe he'd hit his head a little too hard on the ground, because his eyes seemed glazed over.

"Are you?" he asked, "Are you going to *snatch* him up?"

"Why, Graham?" I asked in return, knowing I didn't want to hear the answer. "Why does it matter?"

He looked at his feet then, unable to look at me when he

148

answered, "You said you were in love with me. You can't be interested in someone else so soon."

Stacy scoffed while I stuttered.

"Aww. Is the princess jealous?" she mocked.

I started to take a more adult approach. And then I threw that out of the window and stepped more in line with Stacy. "You tossed me aside, like garbage, Graham, for Erica Hamilton. *Erica Hamilton*: The biggest witch in the school. You told her things about me, about my life that are *private*. *My* secrets, *my* pain, *my* suffering, and you told them to her to make yourself look like some kind of saint, martyring yourself for my sake, so that Grace the SuperFreak could have at least one friend in Heath.

"You left me broken and hurt, and you *lied* to me about NC Prep! You knew you weren't going and you still lied to me! I told you that I was in love with you because it was true. But you know what else is true? You don't love me the same way that I love you. With you, love is a trophy that comes in different sizes, and you're always trying to get the biggest one out there. Mine wasn't the biggest, or the shiniest. For me, love is a ribbon. It doesn't matter what color or size it is, as long as I can pin it to my heart.

"I love you, Graham, so much it hurts me to realize that you do, too, and then know that it's just not enough for me after everything you've done." I didn't realize I had started crying. I felt a tissue being pressed into my hand, felt a comforting hand at my back, and saw the face of someone I had wanted to love me back for so long truly see me for the first time.

Stacy grabbed my hands, using another tissue to pat my now puffy eyes, and said softly. "Do you feel better now that you've finally told him how you really feel?"

I nodded, believing in it. "Graham, I told you that I forgive you, and I do. I *do*. But I think that you've got to understand that you lost the right to decide who I can and cannot be interested in the minute you decided that Erica was worth more than our entire friendship."

Graham's face looked...somber. He nodded his head, but said nothing. He turned towards the door.

"Graham…" I started, not wanting him to leave, but he held up his hand to stop me.

"Grace, you're very right and you're also very wrong. I need to go; I've got to think about a few things-" he paused and looked at me with a pained expression in his eyes before turning away quickly "-I cannot talk to you about them right now. And not with *her* here, either. I'll call you," he said, almost to the door more so than to me, and then he was gone. Part of me feared that I had just given Erica fresh material for my soliloquy.

"I say good riddance," Stacy said flatly, again staring at her nails.

"He's been my best friend since we were babies…" I whispered, the hurt from his leaving had come back to crowd my chest. It wasn't alone and was fighting with the other emotions there now. The little war going on inside of me made me feel as though I was drowning.

"Yes, and then he tossed your friendship out the window as soon as he saw that he had to deal with the emotional repercussions of it. Some friend," Stacy replied. "You're better off knowing how he really feels, Grace. Lifetime friendship or not, if he cannot love you the way you want and deserve because he's too busy loving himself, you're just wasting your time."

I knew she was right. I knew that she had had Graham figured out the minute she had met him, while I was still trying to see him through my own self-imposed, rose colored prison. I just kept believing that there was more to him than what he was showing, saying…doing. I had to have hope for him, because even if my heart now beat for someone else, it didn't mean it didn't still ache for what it had once wanted. And now my heart was confused.

What kind of love did it want? The kind that I knew very well, but that had betrayed me as soon as it made itself known? The kind that was unknown and impossible because it was felt for something that was too amazing, too incredible to exist? Or the kind that settles for what it can get, scavenging on the scraps tossed out to it because it knows it won't get better?

I shook my head as Dad's words from the night before came

back to me. Sometimes parents suck…especially when they're right.

FAMILY

Stacy left shortly after Graham did. Neither of us had realized the time until Dad had walked in, apologizing for being so late for dinner. He waved at Stacy, kissed me on the top of my head, and walked straight into the kitchen, disappearing to enjoy his dinner with Janice.

She apologized before leaving for what her instigations had caused. She seemed truly remorseful, having seen the hurt on my face and the change in my demeanor, but I tried to reassure her that she had helped me to realize a few things that I might not have done otherwise. Besides, I told her, she was going to be my teacher soon, and I'd have to learn to get used to her beating me up in some fashion. She had laughed at that, and gave me another hug. This time, it wasn't so awkward.

I considered going to bed right away, feeling so drained after all that had happened, but I needed to take a shower. I was feeling quite grossed out by my own stench, especially what was coming from the casts. I couldn't solve that problem any time soon without being declared a medical miracle and then being turned into some science experiment, so I focused instead on cleaning the rest of me.

I hopped up the stairs to my bedroom and grabbed the pair of cut off sweats that Janice had loaned me after hearing me complain about my boxers being too small to fit over the cast, as well as a tank top, and some underwear, and hopped into the shower. Kept on the hamper that was in there were two black trash bags and four large rubber bands that were used to prevent the casts from getting wet. An ingenious idea of Dad's, I had to say.

Getting into the shower after sealing off my casts, I wondered what would Erica write, what Graham would tell her when he called her tonight, and when I'd see Robert again. What would he say when he learned that I was going to start learning Tae Kwon Do? What would he think when he saw my memories of the past few days with Graham? Would he even come back at all?

That last question scared me; I wasn't even sure that he would come back. All of that arguing with Graham about my affections for someone other than him and there was a chance that Robert might not even return, much less return how I felt about him. I couldn't drive that thought out of my mind. Not even when I got soap in my eyes and it burned so much I thought I'd be permanently blind from it.

When the water ran cold I knew it was time to get out. I shook the right side of my body, trying to get as much water off before stepping out of the shower, and dried myself quickly—the cold water was jump starting the freezing process early.

After dressing in a rush, I hobbled over to my room, my teeth already chattering. I silently cursed Janice and her pregnancy hormones taking control of the thermostat—she swore she was hot even when there was frost on the windows. Dad said nothing, just kept on adding layer after layer of clothing until he could barely sit down, his movements restricted by the thick padding.

I closed my bedroom door and nearly ran to my bed, I was so cold. The comforter on top was frigid, and I knew it would be a while before it started to do its job and offer me some comfort. I could feel the pull of sleep dragging me under as my eyes closed in defeat, the cold accelerating my fall into slumber. And the voice that had filled my dreams since the hit and run was there again…

Are you cold?

I shivered, but not from the cold.

Do you want me to warm you?

I nodded, my teeth biting into the blanket because I was already warm—the voice was fire incarnate. I started to dream. Endless ribbons were flowing all around me, weaving through my legs, around my arms, and through my hair; I was becoming the fabric of my own dreams. The ribbons were closing in on me, pulling tighter and tighter as the mesh grew smaller and smaller. I soon became aware that there had been only one ribbon. Its span had wrapped around me completely, imprisoning me, like a mummy about to be sealed forever in my silken sarcophagus.

153

I could see one length of the ribbon flowing out past me, its end lost in the horizon of a starless sky. The other end was coiled in a pile by my feet. The end that that was lost to me was being pulled by some unseen force. I felt myself topple, and then I was falling. I unraveled like a yoyo, and then bounced back up like one, too. Up and down, the invisible end of the ribbon was tugging, back and forth—it was a battle for what lay in its confines but why?

Two emerald green beacons flashed at me from the faraway darkness, and I knew who was on that end—I called out his name to stop. He couldn't do this to me awake and also in my dreams! It wasn't right! It wasn't fair!

The other end of the ribbon had run out of slack, and started tugging at me. The force on that end was stronger, more determined, like there was more to lose if it let go. I could feel the tension in the ribbon. I could smell it, taste it; it was potent and strong. And then both ends began their pulling. Both ends pulling for their own reasons, one end cold, with icicles forming on its edges, the other end hot, glowing with its internal heat.

I reached for the warmth when my arms were free, the tugging snapping, shredding threads here and there, weakening the ribbon as the struggle for dominance grew more desperate. And then suddenly I was falling. The ribbon had been severed, one end whole, the other frayed and torn. I was falling, not from the sky, but from the earth. I remembered believing that my world had been thrown off its axis, but this was different; I was right side up, while the world was upside down. I was falling…up.

No. Not falling—floating.

I opened my eyes—his name came out in a sigh because I knew the fire had me. "Robert…"

He smiled at me, his arms cradling me to him; my arms were around his neck and my head leaning against his chest as I held him to me just as securely. Perhaps even more so. We were…we were flying! And we were surrounded, it seemed, by wisps of smoke, gray mixed with white tufts: My angel on a cloud.

I looked down and saw the lights of homes and street lamps

twinkling like upside down stars, as if to make up for those that were missing from the sky. And in the cold, starless night, I felt nothing but warmth. I felt no fear of falling, I felt no chill. I was safe with him no matter where we were heading. If nothing else, I was sure of that much.

I watched him, his face serene, his smile satisfied. He was content. In his arms, I felt more than that. I felt—no, I knew without an ounce of doubt in my soul—there was no one who had ever been closer to heaven than I was right then.

I knew it by the way my blood warmed when he pressed his lips against my hair in a reassuring way. I knew it by the way my skin sang when he pressed his mouth against my ear and whispered in French how glad he was that he had been able to steal away sooner than he had originally thought. I knew it by the way it felt as though I would simply float higher if he were to let me go.

When I saw his liquid eyes rippling like a disturbed pool of molten metal, I knew that he could hear my thoughts and it pleased him. He pulled me closer to him, I held on tighter, and neither of us felt satisfied, my human frailty and his divine strength finding no compromise in such an awkward and unyielding position. I finally asked him where we were headed when he started his descent. The gray wisps around us slowly dissipated, and then we were on the ground, his landing so smooth I only realized it when my sock-covered feet curled over cold gravel.

I looked around at the familiar surroundings and knew we were at his family's retreat; a large white tent had been set up on the greens while the gazebo had been decorated with flowers and gauze. There had been a wedding here recently, I surmised, but the guests had long gone, and the bride and groom were off celebrating their first night as husband and wife together somewhere.

The remnants of the celebrations were chaotic, but recorded completely the quick progression and celebration of two individual lives joining together and starting out as one all in the happenings of a single day. The gazebo was calm and serene, where the vows till forever were given. The table where bride and groom had been central figures still contained two champagne flutes; both still half full of the now flat golden liquid, lipstick smeared on the lip of one of them.

All of it was symbolic, in a way, of how things were now with Robert and I. In one day, we'd gone from virtual strangers to tied for life. His secret, which he had shared so willingly, was now mine, and would be until the day I died.

There had been no cake and no gauze, no band playing big band standards, no flower girls asleep on someone's lap, and definitely no champagne.

But there was chili.

I laughed. Yes. There had been chili.

"Why did you bring me here, Robert?" I asked finally, feeling suddenly melancholy as I acknowledged that the circumstances would not allow for any more similarities.

He sensed my mood before he'd heard my thoughts. He grabbed my hand and pulled me towards the center of the tent. "I brought you here because I wanted you to meet my family."

I jerked my head around quickly, wondering if I had missed something. There was no one here but us. I looked up at him, puzzled. "Are they going to show up? Are we meeting them here so late?"

He laughed. "They're already here. Watch. Pay attention. Do. Not. Blink."

I frowned. I had been paying attention. When he pointed towards the bride and groom's table, I took in the glasses of champagne once again, the flowers that had been scattered on the tablecloth in a rush to start dancing, and the tiny stains of food and drink that made for a marvelous harlequin overlay on the bright white linen. I blinked as suddenly, instantly, magically there were no glasses. As if they had disappeared. The only evidence that they had even been there were the rings of moisture they had left on the tablecloth.

I walked awkwardly over to touch the two circles, to reassure myself that those, at least, were real. I was an inch away from feeling the cool moisture on my fingertips when a light, sweetly fragranced breeze rushed around me, touching me gracefully as though someone were hugging me, causing me to jerk back; and then the damask cloth was gone, leaving a bare table in its place.

I whipped around to stare at Robert. He was laughing, the corners of his eyes crinkled in amusement. I must have looked pretty funny as a partially immobilized, soon-to-be heart attack victim because all around me, the tables that had once been covered in dishes and cloths, flowers and napkins, were all bare, and my eyes kept growing wider, my jaw dropped lower, my heartbeat growing far more irregular.

"Oh." I turned around and saw no movement, just things disappearing. "How…?"

I watched, dumbstruck, as one by one, the tables were removed in the blink of an eye. No. Faster! In the time it takes most people to blink in astonishment, the entire floor had been cleared of tables, linens, and service. I tried to see if anything had been missed, but nothing had. Not even a grain of rice lay on the portable flooring beneath my feet. It was as if nothing had been here, and the wedding had never taken place.

All that remained were the tent and the floor because in that moment, the lights under the tent and those in the gravel parking lot went out.

It was nearly black as pitch and I felt the slight trembling of fear creep up in me as the realization hit that I was very alone. Robert had disappeared when the lights went out and now, abandoned in the darkness, I was more afraid than I had ever been in my life.

"Robert?" my shaky voice called out, the cold of the September night becoming more apparent in my loneliness.

"Look up," he said softly from behind me, but rather than obey, I turned towards the direction of his voice. He wasn't there.

He chuckled. "Look up, Gee. Trust me."

So I did.

And the sky suddenly appeared, the starlight bursting out from nothing, like someone had just thrown diamonds across the black velvet night. "Oh!" I gasped, in awe of something so simple, yet so beautiful. It felt as though he, himself, had given me the sky for my keeping.

"It's so beautiful," I sighed. "You never see the stars like that at home; the street lights kind of turn everything yellow. I think I could look at this all night…" Awestruck, I just stared upwards, completely content in the quiet magic of a starlit sky.

I could say the same thing.

I blinked, and looked around again. He was standing by a small table that had been set up near the gazebo. I hadn't noticed it before, but as he had in the visions he had shared with me that first day, Robert was now giving off a very visible…glow. It was a pale golden light, soft and comforting.

"You're a glow-in-the-dark Robert," I mused.

"I'm also a mood glow-in-the-dark Robert. Our colors change with how we're feeling."

I hobbled towards him and saw with my own eyes that he was right. Whatever his mood was before, it had changed, and the once golden glow was now a brilliant white. "So what are you feeling now?"

He reached out his hand to me, and pulled me very quickly into his arms. "I'm feeling blissfully happy."

"Why?" I asked, my tone hesitant but hopeful as I landed squarely against his rock solid chest, my cast making a solid thunking sound as it hit him.

"I'm happy because you know my secrets, you know what I am, and you have not once asked me to do something that goes beyond the human limits. Quite honestly, you haven't asked me for anything.

"You're perfectly content to stare at the stars, happy with me showing you the sky, as if I had just gifted you with jewels. Like I said, you're *very* different from the other girls. It's an amazing thing, and that makes me happy," he said, pushing back a lock of hair from my face.

"Oh." I tried to mask my disappointment. He was happy because I was *different*? That did nothing for my ego. Or, it would have done nothing for my ego, had I had one to begin with.

He sighed, a little exasperated. "I thought we'd been through this already. Different doesn't mean bad, Grace."

I looked at him. Could he really be so obtuse? His glow changed from white to green, and his arms loosened around me. "Are you annoyed now?"

How did you guess?

"Because if I had to pick a color that would personify annoyance to me, it'd be green." I replied

Why do you think I'm obtuse?

I cocked my head to the side. "Now I *know* you're obtuse." I straightened my head out and then shook it, amazed that he could read my mind, yet could not figure out what I was feeling.

Well, enlighten me. Be my Yoda.

I stepped out from the circle of his arms and held my own out, my right arm stiff in its cast. "I was hoping that this—what I am, who I am, the fact that I'm here—would be what made your glow...white. Instead, it's because I'm 'different'. Whether different is a good or bad thing isn't the problem. I know I'm different. It's a fact that's been pointed out to me every single day of my life. But when you say that you're happy right now *because* I'm different, well...that doesn't make me feel all that great about myself. Especially when the last thing I ever wanted to be was *different*."

Robert reached for me again and slowly pulled me back into the circle of his embrace. "Silly girl. You're so much more than different. And there is much more that I'm happy about than just your differences.

"Yes, I'm happy that you are here. More than mere human words—in any language—can express. And yes, I'm exceptionally grateful that you are who you are, and that you are a part of my life. But, when I said that I'm happy you're different than those other girls, a great deal of that has to do with my family who can, and will, appreciate you so much because of it." He kissed my forehead then and turned me around.

I choked on whatever it was I was going to say. Then, I gasped.

Standing before me was the most beautiful woman I had ever seen. And she was also eerily familiar. Her face was pure porcelain, smooth and perfect. Her long, black hair was braided and pulled over her shoulder, the end unencumbered by any type of hairband, and yet the braid held. Her thin, graceful hands reached forward, an offering of welcome. "Hello, Grace." Her voice was soft, melodic. "My name is Ameila. I am N'Uriel—excuse me—I am *Robert's* mother."

I placed my hand in hers, lulled, almost enchanted by her voice and beauty. And as it had with Robert, the instant my skin touched hers, my mind was flooded with her thoughts.

Though she had been intrigued to see me, she had also been unsure of what type of person I would be. She had no faith in human girls, no faith in their honesty or their hearts. Time had only made them worse, more self-centered and superficial. She had tolerated so many previous indiscretions by her son, so many faithless, useless girls. She had expected me to be the same: Beautiful and empty, like an expertly wrapped gift box. She was surprised to truly see that my features were plain, and my affections were sincere.

"I'm very pleased to meet you, Mrs. Bellegarde." I told her, my voice squeaky and nervous. I meant the words, but still felt fearful that she'd think I was lying.

"Please, call me Ameila. I am no more a married woman than you are, my dear," she laughed, her voice sounding like notes plucked off a harp in rising and falling harmonies and melodies.

She stepped aside then so that I could meet the other member of this trio of Bellegardes. But we had already met. And her face was still cold.

"H-h-hello, Lark," I stumbled, unable to contain the shakiness in my voice.

"I'm not going to kill you, so quit acting like it," came her biting reply.

Robert's body stiffened behind me and I almost choked when she smiled and I saw fangs.

Ameila released a deep growl of admonishment, her daughter's name sounding sharp and dangerous when tossed out so angrily.

The fangs quickly retreated, and I blinked, as if to wipe away the vision from my eyes.

Scared, are you? You should be.

Her voice echoed through my head and I knew that Robert had heard it too because I was soon stumbling back, no longer supported by him; he was in front of me, hissing at his sister like some deranged cobra, one hand braced against my front, the other clenched in a fist at his side.

"Oh come off it, Rob. I was just playing with the girl. Really, if she's going to be your girlfriend, she's going to have to develop a spine. Far better she grow one from dealing with me than discover she has none when the time comes," she said out loud, a smirk teasing the corner of her beautiful mouth.

I wanted to pay attention to the part where she said I needed to develop a spine but the necessity of one was the furthest thing from my mind because when Lark said "your girlfriend", my ears began to buzz with such intensity, I nearly took off floating all on my own. But, in an instant, self-consciousness took a firm hold of me and tied me down. Robert was responding.

"Who or what I date is none of your concern, Lark. She's in no more danger than any of the others were, and I trust you'll do nothing to prove me wrong."

In that moment, I remembered something from the thoughts his mother passed into my mind: All of his "*previous indiscretions*" and "*so many useless girls*". How many had there been? And if I was so different, why would I be in the same boat as all of the "*others*"?

The familiar feeling of complete and utter inadequacy rolled over me as I realized that I wasn't different at all. Despite my claims of wanting just that, it hurt to know that I truly was exactly the same, and I'd end up exactly the same. And what did that mean exactly? He wasn't with them, so that could only mean one thing...

Impossible, improbable, irrational. It truly was.

Lark snorted. "I don't have to do anything, brother, for your reputation precedes you." She nodded towards me, and Robert turned to look at me.

He could see the hurt and confusion written on my face, but made no move to comfort me—he knew there was nothing he could say to make me feel any differently at the moment. His mother's words had condemned him and his own had been the writ that made it official.

Ameila came to stand between us, knowing what both of us were thinking, and knowing that she had been the catalyst to the growing canyon between her son and I.

"Robert, I have a gift for Grace in the gazebo. Could you please go and get it?" she asked, more a suggestion than a request. It seemed ridiculous, this semblance of privacy knowing that he would still be able to hear us, hear our thoughts, but the gesture comforted me somehow.

"Grace, I know that what I said has upset you. It wasn't mea— no. It *was* meant to upset you. I'm concerned for you and though I adore my son with as much love as a mother can give, I cannot deny his faults," she said as she watched him leave while taking my hand and leading me to a familiar bench.

I sat down next to her, trying to grasp what she was saying to me while also trying to understand what had already been said that could not be taken back. I looked at Ameila and felt immediately awkward. It was easy to do so when someone so beautiful was looking at you the way she was looking at me.

"Ameila, I know you're concerned for your son, that you're worried that I'll expose him…that I'll take advantage of his secret. I won't. I can't. There's not much that I can guarantee about anything, especially to an angel, but I can do that. You don't have to pretend to be concerned for me," I said carefully, trying very hard to not think about anything but the fact that I meant those words.

She brought my hand to her heart. "Oh dear. You poor, poor child. I forget how much you don't know." She shook her head as if the thought that I was so woefully ignorant was a tragedy in and of itself. She looked at me, her eyes full of both amusement and sadness. How incredible to be able to feel both without any confliction.

"Grace, you don't understand. I cannot be dishonest with you. No angel can. With a few exceptions, we are bound by our laws to be honest. When I said that I was concerned about you, I meant it," Ameila said, smiling sadly and patting my cheek.

"Why would you be concerned about me? You don't even know me. Robert doesn't even know me." That statement couldn't be any more truthful, I told myself, leaning my head into my free hand, my elbow resting on my knee. It all seemed so crazy.

The beautiful woman sitting next to me patted my hand still enclosed within her own. "You sweet girl. You seem to be under the misconception that angels are bound to the same rules and laws as you humans. We are not. Robert knows more about you than you could dream; we all do. Our minds are open to each other, and what he sees in you, we do as well, just as what we see, so, too does he.

"He's so hungry for information about you that he has delved unbelievably deep into your mind; he knows your entire life, from beginning to present; even the memories your mind isn't capable of recalling due to age, time, and…trauma are known to him. You intrigue him, Grace, and after seeing your life in his eyes, I admit you intrigue me, too. It is because of this that I cannot accept him wanting to be with you; it would hurt you too greatly when the time came where he'd find himself bored with you, as he has with so many others.

"I have seen the broken hearts that he has left behind, Grace, and while I have understood all of them, and have even hoped for them on occasion, I cannot say that I would feel unmoved if the same thing were to happen to you. You are different, as my son says, and in the ways that truly matter. It gives me hope, but it also causes me to fear greatly for your welfare. You've already suffered tragic losses in your life—the depth of emotions I feel and see in you that you possess for my son; to lose him would be like nothing else you've ever experienced, and I fear that you would no longer be the same person when that time came."

Listening to her speak, I felt the sadness within me seep out, like a stain on my heart. She did not want me to be with her son because she was certain that he'd hurt me in some devastatingly painful way. That she would care enough about me to want to prevent that, that maternal sense of protection that she displayed was enough to cause me to lose my hold on my emotions.

Oh great, now you're going to use the waterworks? Please. Like he hasn't seen that a thousand times. Lark's voice was in my head, icy in its mocking.

The great part about losing control over your emotions is that when someone angers you, even if they are an angel, you can no longer be held responsible for your words and actions. And the moment I had heard Lark's voice intruding into my head, I knew that if I did not say something, I'd regret it for the rest of my life.

Well? Are you going to sit there and think about saying

something, or are you actually going to do it? Fickle, idiotic humans; Always believing yourselves to be so superior because you're human, and yet still wanting to be like us and the others. It's pathetic.

I couldn't have stopped the words from leaving my mouth if I had wanted to. But I didn't want to…

"How difficult it must be for you Lark, to always know that even with your *'limitless'* powers, you're still just as imperfect and flawed in your world as you are in mine."

Her sightless eyes showed no reaction to my statement. Her face was like stone. Even her mind did not lash out with the venom that I expected and braced myself for.

The reaction that I had to my own words, on the other hand, I had not braced myself for, had not expected. I felt ashamed and ever the hypocrite. So much for not being held responsible for your actions; I was now my own judge, jury, and executioner.

"I…I'm sorry, Lark. That was wrong. I shouldn't have said that, shouldn't have thought it," I apologized, staring at the ground, not knowing if she was even there anymore, much less listening.

As corny as it may sound, I suddenly heard angels singing. It was a curious thing, with two voices that were similar in so many ways. I knew immediately that one was a distinct alto, the other a soprano. The song they were singing was charismatic, lively. It almost sounded like…laughter!

And so it was, but not the laughter coming from two different voices. No, it wouldn't be something as simple as that. I listened very carefully, focusing on the similarities, and realized that the voices belonged to the same person. And that person was singing in my head, her thoughts—a duet in my mind singing of regret and folly. It was an amazing feat, and I couldn't help but be awed by that.

"You have an amazing gift, Lark," I whispered, my eyes stinging at the threat of tears. I did not want to cry in front of her but knowing that she'd hear my thoughts as soon as they formed, I almost felt like it was pointless to even fight it.

I was right. You humans are fickle. One minute you're picking on what you perceive to be a disability, and the next, you're apologizing

164

and crying as though you've crushed my poor, fragile self-esteem. News flash, honey; I'm an angel, not a flower. You're not going to cause me to wilt by pointing your spotlight on my flaws.

I turned to look at Ameila who I knew had heard every single word her daughter had said, and was surprised to see not a grim expression, but a pleased one.

"You have impressed her," she said to me, smiling. "Few humans ever do."

Well. I had impressed Lark, the ice angel. I felt much better.

The duet filled my head again.

Don't think that I like you any more now than I did five minutes ago.

Oh of course not. I knew better than to be hopeful. Especially after...

I turned my head towards the gazebo, knowing that Robert would still be there. Whatever his mother had placed there for me had long since been found. He was merely waiting for some sign that it was okay to approach us, and I didn't want to be the one to give it.

Ameila, however, thought it was time that we did discuss this because she focused her gaze in the same direction and Robert's head picked up, nodded, and then he was walking towards us at a very slow pace.

His mother turned to me, let go of my hand, and placed both of hers on my face. She began to fill my mind with the images that Robert was seeing in his. All of them contained images of my face.

"Whatever his intentions are for you, Grace, I do know that he cares for you a great deal. I cannot say for certain that they are as intense as those you feel for him, and unfortunately there is nothing you can do to prevent how you feel about Robert. No human can. You naturally feel a compulsion to be around us, a strong desire, one could say, to be with us, in so many ways. It is what keeps us from being too scrutinized for our subtle differences. You would ignore anything— believe anything just to be with us."

I sat there, stunned. Was that it? Were my feelings merely the side effects of being near an honest to goodness angel? A contact high?

I had been emotionally destabilized by Graham, had my home life physically altered by the presence of not one, but two new individuals coming into it, and had made a mortal enemy without ever having met or interacted with her simply by existing. My entire life had changed in just the prologue of my senior year. It would make sense that I'd be even more susceptible to the unnatural charms of one hormonal angel.

"So is that what you think this all is for me then? My human reaction to Robert being an angel?

"Grace, I know that you're far different from any human girl that Robert's ever known. You're certainly the first that he's ever wanted us to meet. I'm just not sure if you're truly capable of feeling for Robert what you'd feel for one of your own kind if he weren't what he was," Ameila sighed, her shoulders hunched down as her words flowed out in the answer that I had asked for, but didn't really want.

"And, Robert's past is what it is. He's lived a very long life— and he hasn't done so alone. I have seen the strongest of minds succumb to the charms of my son. He is, after all, an angel. It isn't his gift, of course—just who he is."

I nodded my head, not wanting to accept that she thought I had the mind of a lemming, eager and willing to follow the pack—I could see where Robert got his obtuseness from. Wanting to change the direction of this conversation before it brought me even more down, I asked, "So these gifts—every angel has them?"

Ameila's lips pursed. "Each angel possesses a strength that is beneficial to all of us as a whole. Think of it as a body part. Each one of us could be an arm, a leg, an ear. Separate, we have our own, individual purpose. Together, we're one body. There are some things we all can do, like change the way someone feels, alter their moods with our own, alter the way the weather behaves. You already know that we can rearrange the natural way of things—your hair for example—and move things without touching them at all. You humans call it telekinesis; we call it laziness.

"And then there are the strengths that are ours and ours alone. Some are purely physical. I'm aware that Robert has shown you that I can change forms. This is my ability, what I contribute to my kind as well as yours. Robert's, as you now know, is healing. It's the mental abilities, however…those we can share.

"There are those of us who can see the futures of each mortal walking this earth because the future is a living, breathing entity, much like you humans. And, because of our ability to share our thoughts so freely without a care, when one knows, all can know if we want them to. We will all know when someone will die, when someone will become sick, when someone will become hurt if the beginning of the chain chooses to send forth this knowledge. This constant influx of information might seem daunting and overwhelming to you, but for us, it is merely a blip, taking up only a fragment, a fraction of our minds.

"We're also very strong. We never get sick—our bodies are not human, though we look it—we have hearts and we have lungs; we eat, but we don't need to follow the same human rituals as you do. Our hearts will keep on beating without oxygen or sustenance because we're not alive as a result of their existence. We are alive because of our destinies."

Ameila paused then, her face growing very serious as she looked over at Robert still standing in the gazebo. She looked at her son with what can only be described as motherly concern, the silent thought that mingled within her head, whether she was sharing them or not, creating a crease in her otherwise perfect brow. She took a deep breath and sighed, patting my hand before continuing, "But destiny…destiny is no living, breathing thing either. It does not change with the tide. It isn't shaped by emotions or actions. It has been set in stone from the moment life itself has existed. The destinies of those not yet born have already been laid out."

I tried to digest all of this new information as Ameila continued to pat my hand, knowing that I was feeling incredibly overwhelmed by the tide of revelations and secrets that had washed into my mind—not just this night—but over the past few days. Sensing that we weren't alone anymore, I looked up from Ameila's face and saw that Robert was standing in front of me, a small box in his hand. I blanched at the angry expression that ironed into his face the harsh lines of confusion. Even then, he was so beautiful it made my heart sprint towards an unseen finish line. He glared at his mother as he handed her the small box, which she then handed to me.

I took it, thanking her softly, and opened it. Inside was a…rock. "Um…thanks," I mumbled, the confusion clear in my tone and on my face.

"It's a piece of the Parthenon. Robert told me that your mother had an extreme fondness for Greek mythology—I thought that you would appreciate something that came from a time when it was more than just myth," Ameila explained, smiling as she picked up the rock. "Robert and Lark say I'm terrible at giving gifts; I think too much about it, they both tell me. If you don't like it, please just let me know."

I snatched the rock from her fingers, afraid to offend her, and actually appreciating the sentiment behind her choice. "I like it. Really. I didn't understand it at first, but now that I do… Thank you, Ameila." I gave her my brightest smile, hoping it appeared sincere. I wasn't lying. I just wasn't sure that I would feel the same way after tonight.

I placed the rock back into the box and closed the lid carefully. Searching for a pocket to place the box in, I looked down at my clothes and blushed, embarrassed at my state of undress. Why hadn't I realized that I'd been in my pajamas this entire time? "Um…I'd like to go home now," I said as I stood up, feeling extremely self-conscious

When Robert offered me his hand so that he could lift me into his arms, I stepped back. "And I'd like Lark to be the one to take me home."

He flinched. Actually flinched, as though I had hurt him, like such a thing were possible. Of course I had hurt him, I realized. I'd hurt his pride. Grace the SuperFreak was rejecting him.

He stiffened, his eyes, cold steel, were angry. "If that's what you wish to think."

And in an instant, he was gone.

Ameila sighed, her face pained. "I will talk to him. He is upset at his sister and I for interfering. We never have before, and for all his time here on this earth, he doesn't understand why.

"Thank you, Grace, for allowing us this visit. I should like to speak to you again sometime, situations permitting, of course." She

168

kissed my cheek and disappeared, leaving so quickly, she might have never been there at all.

"Lark?" I called out; I did not know where she had disappeared to, or if she was even there. I just knew that if she wasn't, I'd have a very long walk home. In my boxers.

As if that would happen.

Suddenly she was there, appearing as if out of nowhere, and I began to sputter like a mad person.

It was unnerving, and she knew it.

And she liked it.

I took a few deep breaths to calm myself. "Lark, could you take me home? I-I know I should have asked you first before I told Robert that you would, but I…" The words seemed to fail me.

Lark's face lit up, then. I caught my breath—her smile, coupled with her now blazing white glow would have lit up a ballroom. Instead, it illuminated the two of us: Me with a face so sad and drawn I'm sure even Tragedy would tell me I was a downer, while Lark's face could only be called ethereal and breathtaking.

Another musical duet—the sound of her laughter—filled my head, but this time I could actually see her amusement. "I guess I should tell you now that I owe you, Grace. You've given me far more entertainment in one night than I've had witness to in decades. No one has ever turned my brother down for anything. It's not…normal for you humans to do so; you're always so easily charmed that we could tell you to walk off of a cliff and you'd do so. And, apparently, Robert doesn't take rejection very well. I think he's had this coming for a long time and I'm glad that it was you that did it."

I didn't know what to say to that. I didn't know what to say to anything, really. I could feel the exhaustion wearing down on me as the seconds ticked by and knew that if I didn't lie down soon, I'd be pass out on the bench. Everything else was secondary.

I looked at Lark—her unseeing eyes seeing far more than they let on were pointed directly at me. "Are you ready?" she asked, her foot tapping with impatience. My human thought process was too slow for her.

I nodded my head. She came towards me with her arms outstretched, and I shrank back. "Wh-what are you doing?" I asked, backing away from her even as she came closer.

"You wanted me to take you home, right?" she said, her tone bored.

"Well…yes, but I was thinking that perhaps you came in a car or something," I mumbled as her hands got closer to my arms.

She stopped then and placed one hand on her hip, while pointing towards her face with the other. "Do you see these eyes? I know that I can. I can see what I look like through your eyes. Tell me what department of motor vehicles office is going to allow me to even apply, much less take the test with eyes like these?"

And she was right, of course. Her nearly colorless, sightless eyes were obvious. Even more so in her beautiful face.

"So, how are you going to take me home?"

She smirked. "How did Robert get you here?"

Oh.

"Oh. What? Did you think he was the only one who could fly without wings?" She laughed again. "I see there are a lot of things that Robert didn't explain to you."

"It's kind of hard to explain thousands of years of information in a day," I muttered.

"That is true, but you'd think that'd he at least tell you some of the basics. Instead he went all theatrical on you—trying to get you so frightened, you'd cling to him. Typical male."

I thought about that for a bit. "Well, could *you* tell me the things that hc didn't?"

Her face looked thoughtful. She approached me, and very quickly, before I could retreat, scooped me up in her arms. "I'll tell you as much as you want to know that I can." And she pushed off with her feet, launching us into the sky…and we were sailing.

THE CALL

The awkward feeling of being carried by Lark kept me from talking for a few minutes, despite the flood of questions that was threatening to breach the levies of my self-control. She carried me in a way that made it feel like I were a pile of dirty laundry. She didn't want me to drop, but at the same time, she didn't want me to touch her either. And, much like with Robert, we were surrounded by what looked like smoke. It almost looked like our feet were on fire, and at any moment, bright orange and yellow flames would start licking at my legs.

"Why the smoke?" I asked finally, starting my inquisition.

"Well, we're kind of conspicuous—two people just indiscriminately flying around—so this helps to hide us when we travel this way. It's sort of like angel camouflage."

I nodded, understanding the need to remain unseen. Now that the first question was out of the way, I couldn't stop the current that had been pent up too long. Instead, I just let the first question to fall out next have its chance to be heard. "What kind of special abilities do you have?"

"Well, you know how my mother was talking about how our minds are always open, and connected? That we can always hear each other?" I nodded as she continued, "Well, she wasn't exactly telling the truth. She wasn't lying, of course. You already know about that rule. It is true, our minds are all connected, but for most of us, we have to be near each other in order to hear each other's thoughts.

"I, on the other hand, don't need to be near anyone. I can hear the thoughts of anyone, anywhere." She had a smug look on her face, as though she were proving it right now by listening in on someone she probably shouldn't.

"Whose thoughts are you listening to now?" I asked, curious.

She gave me a wicked grin. "The President of the United States.

He's playing a game of Battleship online by himself and is mad that he's losing."

I couldn't contain the loud snort of laughter that burst out of my mouth. She couldn't lie, so I had no reason to doubt her, which made the whole image in my mind just that much more comical.

"What else do you want to know? I know that can't be your only question," she said, trying to control the corners of her twitching mouth.

"What are some of the things you can't do?"

"Hmm…well, the list is pretty long. How long do you plan on living again?" She raised a solitary eyebrow and looked at me—well, it looked like she was looking at me—and smiled slyly.

I looked to the side, her sightless, yet seeing eyes giving me the creeps. "I'll live for as long as it takes to learn everything about Robert I can."

The smile on Lark's face grew wider. I assumed it was because she was looking forward to a lot more occasions where I'd be turning her brother down for one thing or another. "Okay then, let's see…we're not allowed to tell anyone about who or what we are without a good reason. It's pretty self-explanatory why, but the good reasons part is kind of confusing. Some things that I'd never figure to be a good enough reason turns out to be perfectly fine. It's all circumstantial, basically.

"We're not allowed to lie. We physically cannot do it—the consequences against us are instantaneous and…severe. We're not allowed to take a human life without just cause. The punishment for that can be very severe. But as with the lying, for the most part it is physically impossible for us to do it."

We swayed to the side a bit—a flock of birds passing us as though we didn't exist—and Lark smiled a knowing, semi-amused smile. "Just for your own future reference, animals don't see us. Dogs, cats, wild ferocious lions—we simply don't exist as far as they're concerned. There are some of us who can *speak* to them, but for the most part, we're just an aberration of space. It was be explained in the bible, if you've ever read it, that God gave man dominion over the earth,

172

blah-blah-blah. Long story short, we're air to them."

She watched the birds sail through the sky, and sighed, continuing with her list. "We're not allowed to use our powers for personal benefits outside of what we need. We don't live hand to mouth, of course, because that wouldn't be believable for society. They see us—so beautiful and graceful in comparison to you—and they can't believe that we're poor or uneducated.

"For whatever reason, you humans seem to think that beauty and intelligence go hand in hand, so we fill the roles that society and humanity dictates we belong in. It is the easiest way to blend in, and we don't fight it. Besides, the money we get as a result can be far more attractive to you humans than any innate charming ability we possess.

"No angel can break our laws without judgment from the Seraphim, and punishment from the Thrones-"

"Seraphim? Thrones?" I knew I sounded confused because I genuinely was. "You have punishment thrones?"

"The Seraphim are the elders, some of the oldest of our kind who hand down judgments either for or against our actions, while the Thrones…they're the angels who actually dole out the punishments to the condemned that are handed down by the Seraphim. When one of the rules are broken, and a sentence has been handed down, they are the ones who carry out that sentence," she explained, her eyes shimmering like iridescent glass—cold and hard with an ethereal light that had no explanation…no source.

She closed them, realizing that I had been staring, and gave me a half-smile. "Now, where was I? Oh yes, there can be no interfering in the destiny of a human. We can see the destinies of most people, and sometimes, our nature dares us to interfere, to help or punish as we would see fit. But, the majority of us are not Seraphim, nor Thrones, and for good reason. If you want to know, most of us are your typical, push you out of the way of a moving vehicle type guardian angel.

"What else? Oh! We're not allowed to harm wing-bringers-"

"What are wing-bringers?" I interrupted, the name sparking an immediate interest in me.

"Yes, Robert didn't tell you about that either, did he?" She shook her head. "A wing-bringer is someone who is the catalyst to the rebirth of an angel, meaning they are the person who triggers the growth of an angel's wings. Call it puberty for angels."

I looked at her, shocked. There really were winged angels? After seeing all three of them without wings, I had assumed that they were merely symbolic, or a part of the mythology that was told to throw humans off of the truth.

She shook her head again. "Just because you don't see them on us, that doesn't mean we don't have them. Well...Robert and I don't have them. We haven't met our wing-bringers yet. That reminds me of another one of the rules; we're not allowed to show our wings in public. Even in flight, most of the winged ones don't use them. They're merely decorative, from what many have told me, and bear no real purpose when it comes to flying."

"So why the significance of the wing-bringer, if the wings aren't all that important?" I asked.

She turned her head to look at me, her face very serious then. "Wings are extremely important. We cannot get into Heaven without them."

I looked at her in shock. "But, you're angels! Isn't that where you belong? Isn't that where you live?" The few stories and the pictures that I knew all told a different story entirely compared to the confusing one that was now being laid brick by brick in my mind.

"Grace, toss your preconceived notions about those naked, harp playing sissies you've seen painted on church ceilings out of the window. Angels are born on earth, just like humans, and live on earth until such time that we're deemed worthy to enter Heaven. But—and I want this to be perfectly clear to you—we do not live there. Simply being an angel doesn't mean that we're automatically granted access—it is not our dream to end up there like you humans do. You should know above all things that there are no guarantees in life. That rings true for human and angel alike.

"Robert is over fifteen-hundred years old. He hasn't even seen a feather pop up, much less a complete set of wings. He knows his destiny is to ascend and answer the call. It is all of our destinies. We're just not sure when exactly that will be and what it will be. I've only been around for five hundred years; that's practically an infant when you compare me to some of the others. I might have to wait a millennia before I even get an idea as to what my call will lead me to, and even then, only after I meet my wing-bringer and the circumstances are right."

I felt breathless at all of the information that she was revealing to me—so many secrets and yet, I knew that this wasn't even the tip of the iceberg—there was so much I still wanted to know. "So, this wing-bringer...what exactly does he or she do—how do they *bring* wings?"

She seemed to contemplate that for a bit. "You know, I don't know. It's not something that is written down as an exact science. Wing-bringers have been human lovers, human enemies, complete strangers, newborns, the aged and the infirm. The belief amongst some of the elders is that there must be a great pull of emotions for the wing-bringer in order to trigger the change.

"For example, love is a very powerful emotion, but rage and jealousy can often times be more so. Mother's wing-bringer was a man whom she thought she was in love with. She thought he loved her too, but unfortunately, he was in love with another woman. When she found out that he had been wed to her in secret, she became incensed, and nearly killed him in a fit of jealousy and rage. Her anger triggered her change."

After meeting her, and talking to her, it was difficult for me to picture Ameila as anything but serene—despite what I had already seen from Robert—so the idea that she could become so angry that her body suddenly sprouted wings just went beyond the scope of my imagination. I looked down at the darkness below us and asked the one question that begged the loudest for an answer, "What's 'the call'?"

Lark was silent for the first time since we had started our flight. I didn't know if I had asked the wrong question or not, but remembering how Robert had reacted when I had asked him what he was that second day, I feared I had once again over-stepped my bounds.

"You did no such thing. Stop being such a ninny," she snapped, annoyance dressing every word. "You're right—I'm annoyed. I'm

175

merely trying to think of a way to explain it. I don't exactly get to reveal these kinds of things to people on an everyday basis, so I'm trying to find a way to do so without using terms that you'd just ask me about immediately afterwards."

"Oh. Okay then. Sorry."

She clicked her tongue in disapproval. "Alright, so you wanted to know what 'the call' is. You know now that the change brings an angel's wings…but it also acts like a switch that turns on a sort of internal speaker. It is through that speaker that we hear the call. It is what every angel lives for; it's why we're born. In short, it is our destiny.

"You probably know about archangels, especially if you've gone to a church-" she felt me shake my head and sighed "-okay, you didn't go to church, but I won't doubt that your knowledge on archangels is fairly limited to what human minds were allowed to remember. The archangels are the quintessential examples of what the call is. They live only for their duty. Their duty is the call. They do not do anything else but answer it. They have all made sacrifices, leaving behind their soul mates, their wing-bringers, their children, in order to fulfill their duty to it. They are the standard that many of us hold ourselves to. They are the angel equivalent to workaholics.

"Without the call, many of us just wander aimlessly, no objective, no goal; we're all just waiting for the call. To put it simply, it gives us a sense of purpose beyond what this human life offers. There are those who have no problem with their lives on Earth, of course. Those who are content to be farmers, teachers…even politicians, and have no problem waiting for the call, willing and hoping it would take its time even though they know that their destiny involves them receiving it."

The idea of angels as politicians caused me to bubble up with laughter again. "How can an angel be a politician? They cannot lie, and yet by running as a human being, they are, in fact, lying. It's incredibly ironic."

Lark nodded her head, understanding the point I was trying to make. "You have to remember that the only boxes any person checks

176

when they run for office usually revolve around whether they're male or female, a citizen or not, what their race and ethnicities are, and how old they happen to be. There are no 'human' and 'inhuman' boxes to check, and any documents that are required can easily be obtained."

I choked on my laughter. "So how many angels put down born in five hundred A.D.?"

She grimaced at that. "There is a loophole around lying when it comes to protecting our identities. We can say we're any age we want to be, and give any name we want to give, if it ensures that our secret is kept safe."

I couldn't help myself. The laughter just kept coming out of me as more and more, I realized that Lark had been right in telling me to throw out all of my preconceived and terribly misinformed notions on what angels were. They were beautiful, but they sure weren't perfect, nor were they honest either. It was all very enlightening.

"I'm glad you're amused," she remarked with sarcasm, her body stiff, her smile now gone. "It's difficult to do that, you know. Tell a lie, even if we're allowed to. It's physically painful. Robert, for example, has to tell everyone that he's eighteen, when you already know he's not. Every time he says he's eighteen, it's like he's branding a big L on his chest. He's been telling people that his name is Robert for so long, he's used to that sting of a lie, but his real name is N'Uriel."

I remembered Ameila using that name first, then correcting it when she was speaking to me about him. "I thought N'Uriel was his middle name." I started feeling the stirrings of sadness as that conversation started to come back to me, but quickly shook it off. I was not going to allow myself to take away anything from this moment.

"He was born N'Uriel. No last name. That came much later, along with the Robert."

"So why the change?" I asked. "I kind of like it. It's different." Like me.

"N'Uriel became Robert during the Crusades, when names that sounded too Moorish or too much like a Saracen were an automatic death sentence. It wasn't his life that he and my mother were fearful for, but rather the exposure that trying to kill him would have brought;

and, during a time when even the most devout were questioning whether or not God existed, our presence would have been seen as an evil omen, rather than as a blessing. There was also the matter of having to destroy the witnesses.

"I know you are aware of what happened after Robert's birth, what my mother had to do. You know now that what she did was against the rules. She believed she had just cause, of course. She was, after all, protecting her child. What could warrant more justification than that?

"The Seraphim, however, were angry. She had killed over a hundred innocents to protect what they thought was an infant that had been ill-conceived. There was a great uproar among them, and they began to gather. It is rare when they all come together to discuss a punishment, and they all wait until each one has arrived before coming to a uniform decision, so when the rumblings started that all who sit above were gathering, everyone knew that it was very, very bad.

"The Seraphim have their own calls that they have to fulfill, and so it took over one thousand years before the verdict was handed down; it came with such great pomp and circumstance, you'd think she were being promoted.

"Stripped of her wings, they said. She would be banished to the human world, average, normal, powerless. It had been unanimous. The decision would include us, and that made the punishment all the more terrifying. But then the Seraphim discovered what my mother had protected all those centuries ago. They discovered what Robert was. No longer an infant, but a young man; strong, vibrant, and gifted. He was a healer, and his birth was…extraordinary. His destiny was laid out for all eyes to see, and to be the one who banished him and his mother? That was unforgivable.

"They had no other recourse but to pardon my mother for her crimes. But, the pardon was a one-time deal, and had my mother not changed how we all lived, we'd all be dead. My mother no longer read the humans' minds. She didn't come to aid those she knew were in trouble—she only answered her call. We stopped being farmers, and lived simply as a wealthy widow with two children. It kept her from having servants, employees…anyone whom she might become attached to. She ceased living…she just existed so that we would."

I tried to figure out what had made Robert so special that his existence was enough to save his mother and sister's lives. I also tried to grasp the concept that an angel could somehow die.

"Oh, we die, Grace. We're immortal, not invincible. There are a few ways that an angel can die; the most common is by becoming human. We don't choose it…well, most don't anyway. Usually it is a sentence that we're handed when we commit a crime that goes beyond redemption," Lark said softly, her voice hinting at something I was afraid to touch on.

She sighed, her mood changing. She was displaying a muted orange glow now. I could only assume it expressed sorrow or sadness, just going by the way the lines on her face appeared out of nowhere, defining her emotions like nothing else could.

"Angels die…someone I loved very dearly was sentenced to a human life here. He made mistakes, horrible, terrible mistakes, and this was seen by the Seraphim as a complete and total rejection of our way of life. So they sentenced him to a human life on earth.

"To you humans, it's nothing. You're born and raised for this life. You find what you're good at, or learn the skill sets to be good at it, and then you do it. For an angel who is born with powers that are limitless, no requirement for the things that humans need due to biology, it is a shock to the system. Many of us have no marketable skills without our powers. It's easy to be a farmer when you can change into a swarm of bees and pollinate your own crop, or be a stock market analyst when you can see the future. But when you suddenly lose all of those abilities, you might as well jump into the river with an anvil tied to your leg.

"And…for an angel to see a former angel grow old and die— there is nothing in this life for me that can compare to that pain."

For a moment, I realized how similar we were. We both had the knowledge, the experience of seeing someone we loved very dearly die. We both felt the emptiness inside of us, and it hurt us both still, although hers could be centuries old.

"Who was it—the angel that was turned human?" My voice was very soft and affected…rough with sorrow for the two of us and our losses.

She remained silent. I had gone too far.

"I'm sorry for overstepping my bounds, Lark. I didn't mean to offend or hurt you," I told her while looking away, trying not to see the overwhelming sadness on her face that I could feel coming from the chill her body gave off.

She nodded her head and I knew that my time for questioning was over. I had already learned a great deal from her—much more than I had from Robert—although the information that he had shown me was very personal while hers was more general. It spoke a great deal about the differences between our relationships.

I had to remind myself, of course, that where Robert had intended on taking our relationship was not running in sync to what I had hoped. He knew he was going to leave me if his wings came. His family knew. That I would most likely be merely a temporary stop on whatever journey he was taking towards his "call" was painful to acknowledge, but also very infuriating. I was merely a distraction on his way to wherever it was he was heading, and I did not like it at all.

But I also had to admit to myself that I still wanted it. I still wanted that short amount of time with him, even if being with me was merely something to pass the time. As hurt as I was knowing that our lives couldn't be joined forever like he had made me believe, I still wanted it, fake or not, because at least with him, I was more than just Grace. I was someone to trust, to care about.

I was so lost in my concessions that I did not realize that we were in my bedroom. How had Lark gotten me in without banging my head against the frame or sill?

Skill.

She set my feet on the floor and I quickly sat on my bed, the overwhelming need for sleep battling with my desire to apologize to Robert, to tell him I'm okay with whatever he wanted, as long as it included me.

Silly human. To sell yourself so short—it reeks of desperation.

180

Guys don't like that. Play hard to get. It works a lot better on angels than it does on humans, especially if you have the ability to keep us out of your thoughts.

I looked at Lark with droopy eyes. "But I don't know how to do that; I don't know how to keep you out of my thoughts."

Lark shrugged her shoulders. She wasn't going to argue with me about something that she thought was ridiculous to begin with.

You go to sleep, Grace. Thank you again for the fun. I do have to say that talking to you about all of this was quite cathartic. I might have to do it again. Maybe.

I nodded my head, vaguely aware of lying down on my bed and pulling the covers up to my chin. I opened my eyes and started to tell her thanks for bringing me home but she was gone. As if she had never been there. As if nothing had even happened that night. I could only hope that someone else would think so, as well.

BREAK A LEG

I didn't hear from Robert again after that night in the park. I wish I could have said that I didn't notice his absence. It wouldn't have been hard to believe. Both Stacy and Graham made it their life's mission to spend as much time with me as possible, and whether that was to actually spend time with me or to intentionally get on each other's nerves, I don't think I'll ever know.

Graham was always there in the morning to see how I was doing, and to grab a plate of breakfast...or three. We still hadn't spoken about what was said in my living room, and I was quite content to let him continue to stew over it if it meant that when the conversations finally did happen, it'd be one that he didn't walk away from.

Stacy had taken to calling just before she left for school to see how I was doing, and they both always arrived immediately after their practices, leaving way after dinner to head home after spending the evening with me. Dad complained that Graham ate enough for half a basketball team, while Janice complained that Stacy could out eat Graham after a full twelve course meal. I just knew both seemed eager to talk to me alone, but never got the chance to because the other one was there.

I spent a great deal of the next week putting together Erica's soliloquy. During the afternoons before Graham and Stacy dropped by, I would ask Janice to take me to the library. I attempted to do some research for my poetry essay, but I always wound up looking for anything I could about angels, finding mostly artwork and a few random scriptures. What I did find important, I jotted down in a notebook alongside my essay research, and reminded myself to look at it later.

I completed the home and class work assignments that Mr. Branke had brought over on that last Thursday night before returning to school, while Stacy and Graham argued about the baseball game that

182

was on television. I never questioned Graham whether Erica knew that he had been spending so much time at my home. If he wasn't willing to bring her up, neither would I. But I knew that come Friday afternoon, something was going to change between Graham and I for good, and it would all be based on a five minute dialogue.

With all of the distractions, all of the diversions, all of the conversations about sports, politics, school, my postponed Tae Kwon Do lessons, and all of the refereeing between Graham and Stacy, nothing could keep my mind off of my angel and where he was, what he was doing, and if he was listening to my thoughts about him. But mostly, I worried that he wasn't.

When I woke up on Friday morning I felt extremely conflicted. I wasn't sure if I was ready for what lay ahead. The intense scrutiny would start almost immediately, and I didn't know how to prepare myself for it. In small doses, it was tolerable. I'd dealt with it my entire life. But this was going to be different. This was going to be my first day all over again. I needed to feel confident, but the only thing that did that was an angel, and he wasn't speaking to me.

After spending an obscene amount of time in the shower trying to see if my entire being could wash down the drain like the soap did, I finally made my way downstairs where breakfast and an anxious Dad would be waiting for me. I saw him look up from his paper when I entered the kitchen and he smiled at me, very pleased that I had made it out of the bathroom with all of my skin intact, albeit far more wrinkled than usual.

I was seated for no more than thirty seconds when Janice had a plate piled high with scrambled eggs and sausage in front of me, a "you're going to eat everything or else" warning glued to her face. Swallowing whatever remark I was foolish enough to even form in my throat, I reached for the glass of milk she placed next to my right elbow and took a deep gulp. I had already lost one battle to a formidable opponent, and it wasn't even six thirty yet. How was I going to win the war of Friday if I started out with a loss to a pregnant woman?

I picked up the fork that she handed me and glumly ate the eggs, all the while wondering how I'd be getting to school today. As if he had read my mind, Dad put his paper down. "So, is Graham picking you up or am I going to have to play chauffer?"

I put a forkful of eggs into my mouth to give myself some time to think. I hadn't asked Graham if he was going to pick me up because I knew that he'd be picking up Erica and that would just be extremely uncomfortable for all of us. And, if I had to be honest with myself, I was still holding out hope that outside, behind Janice's little SUV, there'd be a monstrous black motorcycle and rider waiting for me.

The absurdity of the image of me in my casts on the back of the motorcycle quickly killed my hope, however. Dad wasn't going to let me get on the back of some two wheeled death machine when I still looked like the victim of a four wheeled one. I swallowed my eggs and smiled. "I think you'll be playing chauffer, Dad."

He smiled back, pleased with that idea. I hadn't really thought much about how he had reacted to the accident once we came home from the hospital, but I knew that he'd tried to be a lot more attentive, almost to the point of getting on my nerves. He seemed to be trying very hard to not miss a single thing, and I found that to be very comforting. I reached my hand out to pat his as it rested on his coffee mug.

He looked over his paper again, his eyes full of warmth and happiness. "Thank you, Grace."

After I had completed the herculean task of finishing the food that Janice had placed in front of me, I pulled her aside. "Janice, do you think you have anything that might fit me, so that I don't have to go to school in sweat pants?"

She seemed shocked that I would ask such a thing, but I knew that the perpetual sixteen-year-old girl in her that exists purely for the sake of all things makeover quickly took over, and she was dragging me upstairs, calling out to Dad to "stay downstairs" because it was "girl time". We headed towards the room she shared with Dad, and for a brief moment, I couldn't move. This was the room that my dad had shared with my mom. To go in with Janice seemed like a small betrayal.

I tried to take in a few slow, deep breaths, but instead it seemed

184

like they were more quick gulps of tainted air. Knowing that I couldn't stall any longer, I finally stepped in, grateful that Janice had not noticed my hesitation; she was too busy digging through her side of the closet for what she mumbled was the "perfect skirt" that had a "perfect cut" and was the "perfect color". I was certain that I had enough flaws to cancel out the perfection without trying, so I simply let her go on and on about perfect clothes that went with perfect shoes, and needed the perfect accessories.

When she emerged from her closet looking like a sale mad shopper at a doorbuster sale, I almost ran out screaming. She had a gleam in her eye that you only saw in serial killers, sharks, and kids who got perfect scores on the SATs. I was terrified of that look, but remembering that I had asked for it, I just gritted my teeth and pretended that this was simply my getting ready for battle. I was heading to war, and I needed to look the part.

I didn't dare look in the mirror while Janice stripped, dressed, and primped me until I felt I'd actually shine like a newly waxed car. It was only afterwards, when she stepped to the side so that I could see my reflection in the large dresser mirror that I nearly fell over.

Janice had dressed me in a charcoal gray wool skirt that flared open around my knees just enough to give it some shape. Above that, she had put on me a white, three-quarter-sleeve collared shirt with satin pinstripes. It had a ruffled trim edging the hem where it buttoned up with tiny little black buttons, and was dressed up with a wide dark gray belt. Around my neck, she had placed a simple cameo choker with black ribbon. My hair had been pulled back into a neat ponytail.

I still looked like me. Only more put together. I smiled at my reflection, feeling like a complete and utter idiot and knowing that this was the last thing I should have done, but also knowing that it was too late to change now.

I quickly hobbled into my room to put on the left side of my favorite pair of boots and then went downstairs to shock Dad out of his Dockers.

Noticing that he wasn't in the kitchen, I went into the living room, but found that he wasn't there either. I suddenly heard the horn of his car honk and knew that he'd already started the car and was waiting for me outside.

Janice appeared then with my backpack in her hand. "I hope you have a great day back, Grace, and break a leg during your dialogue today."

I let out a sort of strangled laugh. "I think I already did that part." The overwhelming feeling to hug her suddenly took over me, and I reached out my arms to grab her quickly. She didn't let me go that easily.

"I'm very, very glad that you are in my life, Grace."

In that moment, I knew that I could say it back and mean it. "I'm glad that you're in my life, too, Janice."

It was enough for the both of us, but even if it weren't, the impatient honking of a familiar horn signaled that it was time for me to go. With my bag slung over one shoulder, I reached for the crutches that were had been conspicuously placed near the door. I had hobbled, hopped, and simply walked all throughout the house without using them once since coming home, and I certainly didn't want to start now. But the illusion of a cast was not as believable without the addition of them so I placed the butts under my arms and lurched out of the door in that familiar and awkward gait one associates with them.

Dad had pulled the car out of the garage and the front passenger door was open, waiting for me. Trying to be as graceful as possible in Janice's skirt and blouse, I tottered to the car, quickly trying to figure out how to get into it without falling flat on my face. I contemplated tossing the crutches into the car and then casually climbing in but with my luck, I'd probably cnd up taking out a window or two. I also wasn't sure if I could sit down in the seat properly in a skirt while holding onto the crutches at the same time, so doing that first and then pulling the crutches in behind me was also out of the question.

As I approached the car door, I realized I'd have to simply ask Dad for help. "Dad could you-" The movement in the car killed off whatever it was I had planned to say. The rear passenger door opened and in a fraction of a second, it was like I'd stepped out of reality and into a dream because Robert was there, his hand at my elbow, slowly

186

removing the crutch from beneath my arm, smiling and looking down at me with his shimmering eyes.

"You look beautiful," he said softly, and I couldn't do anything but stare, my mouth gaping open, my heart beating fiercely in my chest; my mind was yearning to hear his voice again, only in a more intimate way, in the way it had grown accustomed to and now missed dearly.

I've missed you, too.

I beamed. I knew it from the way he looked at me, his smile a mixture of amusement and pleasure, to the way Dad groaned loudly from the driver's seat, annoyed and disappointed.

"Okay, let's get you inside before your dad changes his mind about taking me along and leaves me stranded." He said it loudly enough that so that Dad could hear him, even though I knew that he could probably get to school faster than we could in the car. Incredibly, my smile grew wider.

I held onto his hand as I lowered myself into the passenger seat, allowing him to remove the other crutch and place my right leg into the car. The cast prevented me from bending it, so it just sort of stuck out at an awkward angle, causing me to lean uncomfortably to one side. Robert quickly reached for the seat release to push it all the way back, immediately allowing me to sit more comfortably.

When he pulled my seatbelt across my chest and snapped it into place, I caught a whiff of his angelic scent and had to bite my tongue to keep from groaning—it smelled so…heavenly. And the hell of it was that I could do nothing about it. Not while Dad was sitting right next to me, his eyes glaring in response to Robert's forwardness. Not while I was so unsure of where exactly Robert and I stood. I just bit my tongue harder, and stared straight ahead of me, not moving or breathing until Robert had closed my door and wedged himself into the seat behind me, his leg room severely amputated by my seat's new position.

As soon as the car started moving, I rolled my window down and took in a great gulp of air. The crispness of the September morning was enough to clear my head. I looked at Dad, his face serious, his hands gripped tight on the steering wheel, and wondered why he was so tense.

He doesn't like me hanging around. Ever since he discovered that you were capable of liking guys...and that they like you back, his paternal instincts have kicked in and he's becoming very protective over your virtue.

I snorted at that, but turned it into a cough when I saw Dad look at me suspiciously from the corner of his eye. "I think I swallowed a bug," I improvised quickly. I looked into the side view mirror to see Robert's reflection staring back, his head cocked to one side as though he were puzzled.

I waited for him to tell me what he was thinking but I was met with only silence. He continued to stare at me during the twenty minute ride through traffic, his face growing more and more confused the closer we got to school. I didn't understand what kept him from telling me what was wrong, and that only caused me to worry as well.

When Dad pulled up into Heath High's parking lot, I nearly bolted out of the car, desperate to know what was so wrong. Dad's hand on mine was the only reason I didn't.

"Grace, I hope—I know you'll have a good day at school. But, if it gets too overwhelming, have the office call me." He patted my hand, like he used to when I was a little girl. I stared at that hand, suddenly wondering what I was doing. I wasn't ready to go back to school! I wasn't ready to be stared at again, to hear the whispered comments that were never meant to be quiet, or feel the chilly bite of cold shoulders. I definitely wasn't ready to do my soliloquy. All I wanted to do in that moment was crawl into my dad's lap and pretend I was seven years old again.

But, a warm hand on my shoulder brought me back to seventeen. I turned to look at Robert and despite the concerned look on his face, I suddenly felt my confidence return to me, as well as a few other feelings I probably shouldn't be having.

Robert's face suddenly lit up like a Christmas tree. *I can hear you again!*

He helped me out of the car, handing me the crutches while filling me on everything that I had apparently been missing in the car. Or, more importantly, what he'd been missing. Apparently it was a lot.

188

Immediately after my phony coughing fit, Robert had lost all ability to read my thoughts, and the growing silence in my head had confused him.

But what confused me even more was when I called out to you, you did not hear me. It was as if my thoughts were absorbed by the emptiness, and there was no trace that I had even been there.

I waved to Dad as he pulled away, his face tight, muttering something about boys and guns. I smiled, mildly pleased that this was new for both of us, and turned to face Robert, my mind beginning to run through what I had been thinking about that he hadn't heard. The reality that the only thing I had been thinking about was what was causing the concern to etch lines on his angelic face seemed to upset him more than it did bring relief.

My concern about his inability to read my thoughts kept me from noticing the stares from dozens of pairs of eyes, or the whispers hidden behind hands and folders. It wasn't until Robert and I started walking towards the school that I realized that no one was talking. I could only guess what was more shocking: my coming to school so soon after being hit by a car, my wearing something other than a pair of jeans and a ratty t-shirt, or my walking side by side with Robert, my book bag on his shoulder, his eyes gazing down at me.

Of course, everyone at school already knew about how he had been the one to find me and call 911. His reputation as a hero had already been firmly cemented as a Heath High legend. His stock had gone up as a result, and I could see it in the eyes of every guy and girl there. He had won everyone over without using an ounce of charm by saving *my* life, and the irony in that was almost too much to take.

Out of nowhere, a short, raven headed girl came flying towards us, her face positively glowing with excitement and happiness. She crashed into me, hugging me fiercely, sending my crutches clattering to the ground and my arms around her for support. "I'm *so* glad you're here! And oh my God, you look great! TGIF for sure!"

As soon as she loosened her hold on me, Robert had my crutches back under my arms, not wanting to weaken the charade that we both knew I was playing. "Thanks, Stacy," I mumbled, too shocked by the display of affection made so publicly, and with such a captive audience at that. I tried to take a step forward, but found my knees were knocking so bad, I was sure that my left one would be covered with a very large bruise from the cast on my right.

Stacy snatched my book bag off of Robert's shoulder, and looked at him. "Well, don't you think you should help her out? Some hero you are. Holding her book bag really isn't worthy of that title. I'm doing it right now, and no one's decided to have *my* baby." She stared at all of the girls who looked like they'd be willing to do much more than have Robert's child. Some of them looked very eager and willing to take my place, even if that included also being hit by a car and left for dead. But, try as I might, I couldn't find fault in any of them because I was almost certain that my face had the same look on it.

Robert laughed, and Stacy took that as her cue to start walking. "So, today's the day, huh?"

I nodded, stepping-pulling-swinging myself forward, trying to match the rhythm of her pace while also trying to not fall flat on my face. I hopped up the steps to the school's main entrance quite easily, feeling very thankful that even though I knew the snide comments about me were being made, I did not hear a single one. No one dared say anything within earshot of Robert because doing so would cheapen his actions, and no one wanted to do that.

I almost felt smug, which was not a feeling I had ever truly felt in school…or ever. I didn't trust myself to allow it to happen now, though. I still had a long day ahead of me, and the most difficult part wouldn't begin until the day was nearly through. I took comfort in knowing that the first half of my day would at least have me with Stacy and Robert by my side.

As we walked to Mr. Frey's classroom, I suddenly remembered that Robert had homeroom with Becca, Erica's best friend. He would be able to read her mind and see if Erica had shared any information about what she'd written for me to say today. I was almost too nervous to ask when I realized that simply by thinking about it, I already had…technically.

Is that what you want me to do?

190

I hesitated before shaking my head slightly, knowing that as imperceptible as it would have been to anyone else, he would see it. I couldn't ask him to cheat for me. I had never cheated before. Add to that the fact that I had never asked Robert to use his abilities to help me in any way, and I wouldn't start now.

The bell rang and my nerves started twitching. I knew that for better or worse I was going to have to go through with this, but that didn't mean that my body was going to want to cooperate.

I saw Stacy walk into the classroom, my book bag still on her shoulder, and turned my face towards Robert's to thank him and tell him that we'd talk in first period. He placed a soft hand against my cheek, and I pressed it into his palm, grateful for the way it calmed me and made me forget—even if for only a moment—what it was that was troubling me.

"Thank you," I whispered. It was the only thing I could think of to say. There was a lot more that we needed to talk about, but at that moment I could only say those two words and be glad for their existence.

"No, thank you." He bent down and kissed the top of my head. It was such a small gesture, mundane in so many ways, and yet…it was enough. I turned around and stepped-pulled-swung myself towards the desk that Stacy was keeping free for me. I ignored the blatant gawking that seemed to come from everyone, including a far from asleep Mr. Frey, and carefully slid into the seat next to Stacy who took the crutches out of my hand before I could protest.

"Why do you need these anyway? I swear you'd get around a lot faster without these sticks." She leaned them up against her desk and pointed to my book bag by her feet. "Is *it* in there?"

I knew what *it* was, and nodded my head. "It isn't going to win me any Nobel Peace Prizes, but I won't be sued for libel either."

Stacy grimaced at that. "I wouldn't put it past her to try and do it anyway, or at least threaten you about it. She's been talking about hers for the past two days and I have no doubt that she's planning on making you into the school's pariah. I hope that you're ready for it."

Ready for what? I had already lived through an emotional and physical nightmare. What else was there left for her to do? The thought of losing Graham again floated around for a bit, but flew away when I came to the decision that whatever his choices were, I had nothing to do with them anymore.

"I've already experienced the role of Pariah. She can't do anything to me now that hasn't already been done. I'm ready for this to be over with. I'm ready." I knew that when I was handed my script and I took my place onstage, I'd know for sure if I were truly ready, but at that moment, there was nothing else that could be done, no preparations I could make, and no words to make me feel more confident. I was as ready as I'd ever be. My only question was whether or not the day would drag or fly by. It didn't matter to me either way.

When the bell rang for first period it dawned on me that my entire conversation with Stacy had been the main focus of everyone else in the classroom. We were the only ones who stood up when the bell rang, and the first ones out of the door; everyone else was trying to quickly cover up the fact that they'd been eavesdropping with nonsensical chatter, very loud scraping of chairs across the floor, and books being slammed on top of each other.

Stacy found it to be highly amusing. I cringed at the thought of more people knowing about what was coming. With every step-pull-swing of my body, I drew closer to a pivotal moment in what was turning out to be one very interesting senior year in high school.

cs

At exactly thirty minutes past one, I entered the auditorium that served as the classroom for sixth period theater. Robert had met me outside of English Lit, as he had with Biology, and carried my book bag while I did my best impersonation of a human pendulum.

As much as I knew he had wanted to talk with me about what had happened the night at the park, I couldn't deal with that and focus on what was coming at the same time. We sat silent throughout French class because he wasn't thrilled with not being able to talk about it. By the time Calculus was over, we'd come to an understanding that whatever there was to discuss would simply have to wait until the day was through and I had recovered, if necessary, from the damage that Erica's soliloquy was going to inflict on me.

The auditorium looked very empty when we arrived, our class sitting near the stage area, and Mr. Danielson standing onstage having a very animated discussion with another teacher about something I couldn't quite catch. Robert stiffened, which told me that he didn't like what he had heard, but wouldn't tell me what it was quite yet. I frowned, not liking the way his forehead creased up.

We sat down in the front row seats along with the rest of the class and waited for the bell to ring. I heard the door of the auditorium open up behind us, and tried to turn to see who it was, but Robert placed his hand on my chin and held my face immobile. The sound of dozens of feet stomping against the wood flooring of the auditorium caused my eyes to grow wide in my face, and my breathing to increase rapidly.

We had an audience, and from the sound of the buzzing coming from behind me, coupled with the nonstop rumble of feet, it was a large one. I kept trying to turn my face to see, my hands getting sweaty with panic, but Robert shook his head, his hand still holding my chin, his other hand gripping mine. *You don't need to see it to know it's there. Focus on what you have to do. I'm here. It's going to be fine.*

I looked into his eyes, seeing my reflection in them and realizing that I was showing more in my face than I ever could with just my mind, and that everyone could see just how I was feeling. Including Erica, who walked past us just then, her face wearing the same smug smile I had denied myself earlier this morning.

It was that smile that finally snapped me back into focus. Robert knew it, too. He let go of my chin, but continued to watch me.

"I'll be fine. I'm fine. I can do this." I reached for my book bag, which he had placed by his feet, and unzipped it. I grabbed the blue folder that held my soliloquy for Erica and pulled it out. Sticking the folder between my teeth, I reached for my crutches and stood up.

Robert pulled the folder out of my mouth, smiling. "I don't think she'll appreciate you getting spit all over her dialogue."

I shrugged my shoulders as I placed the cumbersome crutches

underneath my arms and then snatched the folder out of Robert's hand. "I don't think that really matters right now, do you? She's going to crucify me in front of all of these people, and she's going to enjoy every second of it. The only thing I have on my side is the truth, and that won't matter much to any of them." I motioned to the people behind me with the folder in my hand.

Robert grabbed my elbow, his rock solid strength effectively stopping me from moving. "You're wrong. You also have Stacy on your side. And Graham…" He motioned with his head at someone who was approaching us.

I hesitated to look, unsure if he'd grab my chin again to prevent me from seeing who it was that was headed directly for us. When I was positive that he wouldn't stop me, I turned my head to see Graham, a determined expression on his face.

What is he doing? I looked at Robert again, panic flooding into me.

He wants to know what's going on. He didn't know that you and Erica were in the same class. Or that I was as well.

Oh dear bananas. The last thing I needed was a confrontation between Robert and Graham. And in front of what was starting to look like half of the student body, too.

Taking a few deep breaths, I turned my body completely around to face Graham. "What are you doing here?"

He looked at Robert's hand on my elbow, and then back at me. "Erica told me that she had a thing today for her dramatics class. She didn't tell me that you were in the same class with her. She didn't tell me a lot about this class, actually," he said, glancing back at Robert, his eyes mere slits.

I was sick. Whatever it was that Erica had planned for today was going to hurt Graham, too, and she had meant for me to be the one to do it. I looked at Robert's face and his eyes were cold steel, his mouth a grim line. Both confirmed my suspicions. My head started spinning, and I could see the little black and white dots twinkling in front of my eyes, like snow on the television set; the precursor to the dreaded faint. How utterly appropriate.

Take some deep breaths, Gee.

It wasn't as though I wasn't trying. I was taking the deepest, slowest breaths I could, but the cold sweat that broken out on my forehead has also spread to my palms. Robert helped me to sit back down, while Graham grabbed my crutches. Both seemed too intent on making sure I didn't pass out to care about the other's presence at the moment, which suited me just fine.

I…needed something. I couldn't figure out what it was, but it was close. It was something that was so close, I could taste it. A warm hand still holding my elbow squeezed it gently, no iron grip needed to keep me from leaving anymore. He had said that I had Stacy and Graham on my side.

I looked at Graham and through the snowstorm of my vision, saw the concern on his face—and surprisingly, the hurt—and knew that Robert had been right. I thought back to Stacy's face this morning, and how she had helped me so much this past week, and knew that he was right about that, too. But was that it?

"What about you? Do I have you on my side, too?" I asked, my voice shaky, my eyes still unable to focus well.

"Never doubt it for a second."

And that was it. I had three people in my corner. Three more than I ever imagined I'd ever have.

Actually, you have one more.

I looked at Robert, confused. He pointed towards the back of the auditorium, where a bunch of girls were gathered, laughing and pointing at a group of guys sitting a few rows down. I didn't have to look for long before I saw who he was pointing at. She was the only one not laughing, though her face was just as beautiful, just as perfect, and her eyes were just as sightless though I knew now how deceiving that blindness truly was.

"What is she doing here?" I kept staring at her, waiting for some sign of friendliness, anything.

"She goes to school here, too, Gee. She's a sophomore."

I snorted. *A sophomore? She's over five hundred years old; the least she could have been was a junior!*

I turned to look at her again and knew she had heard me. Of course she had heard me. She knew what I was going to say before it even came out of my mouth.

Hate me? I looked at her.

She shook her head. *Why would I hate you? I said the exact same thing. If I'm incapable of appreciating irony after five hundred years, I don't deserve this inhuman existence.*

I breathed a sigh of relief. It felt good. It felt really, really good actually, knowing that I had all of them supporting me, even if Graham was the only one who didn't know what exactly was going on. It was enough.

Steady and sure, I stood up again, accepting my crutches from Graham, and my folder from Robert. I ignored the stares as I stepped-pulled-swung myself towards Erica. I ignored the whispers. I ignored everything except my destination.

She saw me approaching, her face full of amusement, and I decided to smile back. All the humor left her face at my unexpected reaction and that smug smile I had refused to place on my face this morning came back with a vengeance. "Here's your soliloquy." I handed her the blue folder, pleased that I had taken the route I did with it.

She looked at it as though it would infect her with something, but didn't open it. She bent down to reach into her large tote bag and pulled out a manila folder that contained a few sheets of loose paper. "Here is yours. Remember, no peeking until we're called up."

I felt my smug smile dip a bit, but pulled the corners of my mouth back up before she could notice anything. I was going to get through this, one way or another, no matter what she had written for me to say. "You, too."

I remained standing there while she walked away, the blue folder in her hand appearing to weigh her down. When Mr. Danielson announced that we were ready to begin, I found myself being ushered back into my seat by several sets of hands. I looked up to see both Robert and Chips, sans Dip and Salsa, standing by me. I made the assumption that they had been partnered together, and together, had

196

worked to get me away from Erica as quickly as possible once our folders were exchanged.

The first pair up on stage happened to be Dip and Salsa, which explained their absence, and each took humorous jabs at their nicknames—Dip announcing that he was lactose intolerant to himself, and Salsa saying that no one really likes a chunky dunk—as well as making light of their prowess with the ladies, which neither had. It was easy to see why the trio truly got along so well and I couldn't help but feel a bit envious of them for it.

Three more pairs went up before Robert and Chips had their turn. Robert lamented at how handsome he was, and how he'd fallen in love with himself, but still could do nothing but envy the utter awesomeness of a guy named Chips.

The giggles from the audience pleased Chips, whose grin would have been bright enough to forgo the use of the spotlight that seemed to be singeing his clothing right before our eyes. When it was his turn to speak, he spoke about his obsession with food, and how he had named everything he didn't want to eat "Robert" so that he'd have an incentive not to eat his new best friend in the whole wide world, his "BFFL".

That drew a series of loud guffaws from the two dips, as well as some pretty amused laughter from an unlikely, yet familiar source who less than an hour ago had been upset over his mere presence. And then, it was my turn.

FACE OFF

Erica glided up to the stage effortlessly. I took notice of her skintight, dark denim jeans and black boots, her olive green off the shoulder, low cut top with white camisole underneath, and admitted to myself that even dressed as casually as she was, she still outshined me in Janice's best. With Robert and Chips' help, I hopped onto the stage and nodded my readiness to Mr. Danielson, whose face looked as excited as a kid on Christmas.

This was what he had been waiting for. As I looked around the auditorium, the faces that I could make out despite the bright, blinding spotlight all held the same curiosity and excitement. They had all come to see a show. A show that Erica apparently promised them would be worth it. God help us if it wasn't. God help me if it was.

Because her last name alphabetically came before mine, she was given the opportunity to go first and get hers out of the way. She declined, deferring to me, and I could have sworn I saw purple stripes and a tail pop out from her face, her smile was so Cheshire cat-like.

I hobbled my way to the microphone standing dead center in the middle of the stage. There was a black music stand there to place our scripts on, which I did. I removed the crutches from underneath my arms, and bent down and placed them onto the stage floor. I didn't need them for this.

I opened up the manila folder and removed the three sheets of paper that contained my soliloquy. I closed my eyes.

You can do this.

I licked my lips that had gone painfully dry.

I'm here for you, Gee.

I counted to ten, then opened my lids and began reading the lines on the first page.

"I hate to look at myself in the mirror. Who am I to anyone but a stranger, even me? The three people in this world that know me don't even know the real me, and all that they do know just plain bores them to death. It would be different if I were attractive, or smart, or funny. Since I'm none of those, I simply exist in a world where I don't fit in.

"I look different from all of the other girls, and if *I* notice it, then of course they do, too. And if the girls are noticing how different I am, of course the boys are. I cannot even get my own best friend to take me out, and he's used to the way I look.

"But even my looks are something that people can get past. It's not like I'm the ugliest girl in the school. I guess I could be passable if I tried hard enough. Plus there's always plastic surgery to fix the things makeup can't.

"No. My looks, even my clothes can change. But the real me is where the problem is. The part of me that no one really knows, but they whisper about when they think I'm not listening. I know what they're saying.

"They say that I'm stupid for thinking that Graham loves me and wants to be with me. I probably am. He's one of the most popular guys in school while I'm just the freak, so how could we even make a friendship work? What do we have in common besides our addresses? And if I can't land him, what makes me think I'll land Robert Bellegarde? A guy like him can get any girl he wants. Shouldn't I have learned with Graham that if guys are nice to me, it's only because they feel sorry for me?

"Why is it that I never get just how desperate I really am? I've thrown myself at two guys now, and both have rejected me for someone else. I don't understand why I simply cannot give up like a normal person would.

"The answer is simple, of course. I'm *not* normal. That's the point I need to grasp that I just can't. Everyone else knows what kind of person I am, and I know what they think I'm capable of. I know by the way that they look at me that they wonder if I did it, if I was to blame for it.

"They all think I'm responsible for my mother's death; they all think I killed her. Maybe I did. Maybe *I* drove her to crash the car.

Maybe I was being such a brat that she simply couldn't take it anymore and decided that the best thing was to take out both of us. She always had a hard time controlling me, and everyone knew that I was a handful at that time. It's why none of those other girls would ever be my friend. It's why Graham was the only one who ever talked to me. It was why Dad was always out of town. I was difficult.

"No. I was more than difficult. I was a terror. A monster. I don't blame my mother for picturing eleven more years of living with me and thinking it was too much to deal with. I always made things much too difficult for everyone. Maybe I should have been drowned at birth. And there I go: Making it about me again. It's always about me.

"Why do I have to make it about me? Even now, talking to myself, it's about me! I should be talking about the country or poor, starving children in Africa, but all I can think about is myself! It's like I'm obsessed or something. I just don't get it. This is why people stare at me all the time, why no one wants to be my friend, why I'm always the butt of everyone's joke.

"I'm too self-involved. I'm too needy. I want too much from people. It's like I'm an emotional leech and I'm just looking for my next victim to feed off of. Perhaps…maybe it would have been better if I hadn't survived the hit and run. Maybe it wasn't even a hit and run. Maybe it was me being so needy, I threw myself in front of some poor guy's car. Maybe I was just trying to finish what my mother had started. Maybe…"

When that last word left my lips, and I heard my voice echo off of the walls, only then did I actually feel the trembling in my arms and legs, even through the casts. The casts! They were rattling against the music stand and the floor, and the sound was like one of Dad's antique word processors typing up a twenty page essay. It was the only sound in the entire auditorium once my voice stopped echoing.

I had done it. Spastic shaking and all, I had done it without stopping, without crying, without screaming out denials, and most importantly, I had done it without a single audience member saying anything. I couldn't see them, the lights were far too bright in my face, but I knew the faces that were the most important were not looking at me with the same disgust I felt for having said those words. They were looking at me with disgust for the person who had written them.

And that person was standing off to the side with a smile that would brighten even the darkest room plastered on her gleeful face. Cheshire cat indeed; she was the red queen and the cat all rolled into one. One great, big, sadistic, scepter carrying, red and purple smile with a tail.

"Well...thank you, Miss Shelley, for sailing through that...uninspired and absolutely predictable diatribe written by Miss Hamilton. I think that were it not for the person reading it, most of us would have walked out before the third line was ever uttered. You were the only redeeming thing about that piece, and I applaud you for sticking with it and completing it even though I'm certain that it disgusted you as much as it did the rest of us." Mr. Danielson stood up and ushered me off of the stage.

I clumsily sat down near the stairwell, numb and speechless, my crutches leaning up against the wall behind me while he gathered the sheets of paper that were still on the music stand and unceremoniously tore them in half lengthwise. The sound of the paper tearing, more so than the actual tearing itself, caused a few gasps to ripple across the auditorium. I turned around in disbelief, afraid that I had just embarrassed myself for nothing.

I watched as Erica walked out on to the stage, my blue folder in her hand, that evil smile still stretching from ear to ear, and stood in front of the microphone. Whatever her thoughts, the tearing of her three page ode to me wasn't enough to disturb them. She opened the folder and removed the two neatly typed sheets of paper that had been placed inside.

With utter confidence, a confidence I certainly hadn't possessed when I started, she placed those papers directly on top of the folder and placed that on top of the music stand. She seemed so comfortable, so at ease, and I knew it was because she had enjoyed the reaction of the audience, and more importantly, my own.

It had bolstered her. If I hadn't known who she was, what she was capable of, I would have thought her to be the most approachable person in the world. But I knew exactly what type of person she was, and she had demonstrated in black and white just what she was willing to do in order to get her way. What exactly she was trying to get, I wasn't quite sure yet, but I knew that after today I would definitely find out. She had already embarrassed me, and planted seeds of doubt amongst the people who had witnessed my reading. What else was left?

I heard someone cough, and realized that the no one had uttered a single sound other than the few gasps at the tearing of my script. Erica had herself a captive audience, and she liked that.

I held my breath as I saw her take a deep one to start. And then her voice began to read the words that I had agonized over for what had, at the time, seemed like a lifetime but now felt as though I had rushed through it instead.

"He loves me. There is no doubt that he loves me. The way he smiles at me, the way he listens to me and the things that I say; there couldn't be any more proof necessary to convince me that he feels so deeply for me.

"In my own little tea party of life, he is my ultimate guest; one who never needed an invitation, and who has always been and will always be welcome. He enjoys my crooked, funny little mixed up world. He accepts me for who I am, and that's an amazing, beautiful, incredible thing. But, most importantly, he sees behind the mask that so many people like me wear to protect our real selves.

"But, what if the me he knows isn't the real me? What if it's just another mask that I wear as well? Two masks, one underneath the other, both hiding the me underneath; Victor, Victoria, and Erica.

"Everyone sees the first mask. Cold. Mean. Angry. Beautiful Erica wears that mask very well. People fear me, rather than respect me. But, cracked, cold, mean, and angry, I still fit into this mask wearing world like a round peg in its equally round hole. And, as cracked as that mask is, it still doesn't let the second mask beneath it show through. No one knows what's under that except him.

"That second mask shows me off as someone softer, more vulnerable. He sees me as sweet, caring, and loving. He sees the part of me that could be kind. He's seen it be generous, and he's enjoyed it.

202

It's helped to justify so many of his actions; it made him believe that all of it was worth it. And even that mask, soft and sweet, giving and loving, has allowed me to be as much a part of everyone and everything as anyone would want. I'm just as accepted as anyone else.

"But underneath that mask, underneath everything that everyone thinks they know, is the real me; the person that they'd never expect—the person that they'll never, ever see.

"The cruel me, the evil me, the heartless me. To show the real me would mean losing everything that I've worked so hard to set up. I cannot show him, or anyone, to what lengths I would go to get my way. I cannot let him see to what lengths I'd go to get rid of something as insignificant as a dormouse. I cannot let him think that his love is wasted on me.

"But, what happens if I'm honest? What happens when I reveal that beneath the first mask of ice, and beneath the second mask of down, lays someone who wears no mask at all, but instead a hat. And that hat is of someone quite mad? Will he still be willing to sit down at this Mad Hatter's table and have tea? Will I be two masks too late? Can I set back my watch to a time before truth? What was it the Mad Hatter said? '…it's very easy to take more than nothing.' And that's exactly it, isn't it?

"I have given nothing, and have taken so much more. I've taken his trust, and I've given him back nothing but lies which only take more themselves. I've taken his love and I've given him back nothing but hurt in pretty little sugar coated packages. Mask one and two. So perhaps I simply remove the hat, and keep the masks on. He doesn't need to know.

"I can simply try to put more cracks in the first mask, and polish up the second. The person that he loves wouldn't be hurtful and spiteful. The person he loves wouldn't be cruel and hateful. He loves me, and I have to be that person, because the truth is that he loves everyone—if he can't love me, then that makes me different in a way all my own. There are no cakes or drinks that can change me so that I'll fit into that slot he has opened in his life for me. And, I can't sit at my own tea party alone, different, while the rest of the world's story goes on."

The confusion on Erica's face was plain. The lines between her brows threw off the smile she kept planted on her mouth. It was as if her face were comprised of two halves, but both seemed intent on losing to the inner struggle she seemed to be having with herself.

"Um, I don't get it, Mr. Danielson. I thought this was supposed to be about me, and not about some silly kid's story."

Mr. Danielson, who had sat down on the stage to listen to Erica's monologue, shook his head, himself seeming confused. The way he brushed his hand through his hair, and the sigh that came out of him seemed a far more passive reaction than the one that he had given after my reading, but could he be just as disappointed, too? Perhaps I wasn't plain enough?

"Miss Hamilton, I don't understand what exactly it is that you don't get. Is it perhaps the symbolism? Or could it be that you don't get why Miss Shelley wasn't as spiteful with her words as you were with yours?"

Erica's face morphed through a few different shades of red before finally settling on an irate sort of rouge. "She wasn't spiteful? Calling me cruel and evil and heartless isn't spiteful?"

"Miss Hamilton, do I need to remind you of some of the things that you had Miss Shelley here say? Most of which go beyond spite and border on absolute vindictiveness, I might add."

A murmur started traveling through the audience. It sounded like a soft hum, barely perceptible, what with the whistling of steam coming out of Erica's ears, but it grew louder. It could only have been my imagination, but the murmur started to take on a more tangible vibe. The louder it got, the clearer it became, and the words certainly had an effect on Erica. She stormed off of the stage as the chant of "Flunk Erica" echoed all around me.

I watched her, her shoulders hunched over, her face still confused, but her eyes now misted over with angry tears, and I couldn't help but feel a sort of sympathy towards her. Had I felt a bit more confident, I probably would have reached out my hand to her in truce, as a peace offering, or maybe just in support and understanding. Instead, having the taste of saying that I had killed my mother in my mouth caused me to feel far less confident, and far more disgusted with myself.

Flunk Erica? Flunk Grace for having had no backbone to stand up for my mother, for myself... Erica might have written that vile nastiness, but I read it. I put a voice to her words, gave them power and life, and the nausea that hadn't felt a need to make its appearance during my speech finally showed up at my acknowledgement of that.

Gee?

"Grace?"

I looked up to see two beautiful faces, two pairs of beautiful eyes, one green, the other silver, both filled with concern, and both for me. How could they be concerned for me after what I had just done?

Gee, you have done nothing wrong. Do not feel guilty and give Erica what she wants.

"Grace, I'm sorry about what Erica did. I didn't know that you were in the same class. She said that she had something planned for her partner, but I swear I didn't know it was you she was talking about. I-"

Robert's face was reassuring, while Graham looked so lost, his voice couldn't find its way back out of his mouth. He looked at Robert, and nodded. My eyes widened. Did Robert let Graham know about his secret?

No. He's come to a decision.

"Grace, I have to take care of something. Do you think you could wait here for me?"

I looked at Graham, his face hardened from the pain and anger he was feeling. I didn't like that face. It was the same face he had on when he told us we couldn't be friends anymore, and the dread in me started to pile up again, only this time I didn't have an old Buick's windshield to keep me propped up.

"I need to talk to Erica, Grace. I'll be back...I promise." He felt he had to reassure me. He knew what I was feeling. That wasn't expected.

"I'll be here."

He nodded his head at my own promise and stood up. I watched him walk away, this time with a lot less dread in my heart. Of course, this time, when I turned my head, there was another pair of eyes still on me, still gauging my emotions.

"How horrible was it? The thoughts in everyone's heads?" I knew he had no choice but to be honest with me, a painful perk I was glad for at the moment if only because I knew that I wouldn't be led into believing anything but the truth.

"You cannot begin to understand the deep level of sympathy that your fellow classmates feel for you. Odd though you are to them, none of them could have placed themselves in your shoes and felt they deserved it."

I felt the moisture build in my eyes, felt their weight cling to my lashes as they tried to cage in the tears, but their release was unstoppable, and they rushed out, free at last. "I don't understand how they could feel something like that for Grace the freak. What Erica wrote, a great deal of it is based on the truth. A lot of them *do* think that way, and I do often times blame myself for my mother's death because I know what happened…I just can't remember."

Robert's hand beneath my lower lashes, wiping away an errant tear, caused me to breathe in sharply. I bit my lip to keep from gasping at the intense burning sensation his skin had caused, and held my breath to try and slow down my racing heart. The emotions in me from the words I had uttered today felt so raw; he was affecting me differently than normal. That was the only thing I could blame this on.

The darkening metal of his eyes seemed to confirm my thoughts. He was hearing them just as clearly as if I had said them aloud, I already knew. "Grace, don't blame yourself for your mother's death. Her life had reached its intended end. You did not cause her death any more than you could have caused the deaths of everyone on the Titanic. This has been explained to you already." He reached for my hand, and gave it a reassuring squeeze.

I nodded my head in compliance. What else was there to do? It *had* been explained to me, although not in as much detail as I would have liked. Lark had told me just enough to keep me curious, and Robert had told me nothing at all, despite all of his admissions.

"It's just that what I said, as difficult as it was to say, it was as though she had been in my head, read some of my thoughts herself, and

206

just embellished them. Not all of them, but you know what I mean."

I couldn't look at him anymore. Not with the way I was feeling. Unbeknownst to either Erica or myself, we had written about each other's hidden selves, sides of us that we both perceived that no one had seen but were so wrong, for we had both seen it in each other. For her, the darkness she had kept hidden away; for me, the doubt and guilt I had tried to deny. How alike we both were, and how much that killed me to admit.

Again, the strange, insane feeling of needing to comfort her, wherever she was, crawled into my mind; I knew it was absolutely impossible for there to be anything between us now except animosity.

I looked up again when I saw Mr. Danielson squatting in front of me, a concerned puckering of his forehead masking what would have been a very pleasant face to look at had I even been remotely interested in doing so. "Grace, I think I should apologize for what happened here today. It was not my intention for any of this to occur."

I shrugged my shoulders. "You couldn't have known how far either of us were going to take it, Mr. Danielson."

"No, you're wrong, Grace. I should have known that the tension between you two would result in something like this. On her part at the very least but I didn't, and for that I'm truly sorry. What she made you say…I cannot believe—I want you to know that there will be a suspension hearing on Monday regarding today's incident."

I shook my head, my eyes widening in shock. "If she deserves to be suspended, then so do I. We both took pot shots at each other, and none of them were because we were fooling around. I don't think it would be fair to punish her and not me when we both did the exact same thing."

He stared at me, his expression one of surprise. I knew what he was thinking; I must be weird to want to go down in flames alongside Erica Hamilton after what she did. Truth was I simply couldn't let her be punished for something I knew was going to happen and yet something that I had allowed myself to be a part of anyway.

"Mr. Danielson, whatever her punishment, I deserve the same."

He brought his lips inward, clenched between his teeth in a thin line of disapproval. "You're definitely not like everyone else, Grace Shelley. After everything you've been through recently, I half expected you to burst into tears during your soliloquy, but you kept yourself together. Whatever it is that Miss Hamilton seems to think you're incapable of acquiring, I don't doubt you'll have no problem of getting it-" he looked at Robert, who was still looking at me…I could feel it "-if you don't have it already."

The hand that was still holding mine squeezed it again. A silent confirmation. I had him. I knew this. But as what?

Mr. Danielson stood up. "I'm going to go and see if I can find Miss Hamilton to discuss what's going to happen. If you change your mind, do let me know on Monday, Grace. That gives you the whole weekend to think about it."

As he walked away, it dawned on me what it was that Erica had wanted. She had wanted the emotional outburst, the retaliatory actions in defense of me; she wanted the very thing that my own conscience would not allow, and she wanted it because she wanted to be the victim. She wanted to lessen the sympathies that might have been felt towards me so that her pain and suffering could take center stage and not be overshadowed by whatever it was that I had gone through. She was…jealous.

"Holy crap." I was in disbelief.

Robert looked just as stunned as I felt.

"Erica Hamilton is jealous because people feel sorry for me?" Even saying it couldn't make it sound any less ridiculous. "But why?"

Robert stroked my thumb with his and sighed. "She's never felt that before. She's never had people thinking that she's vulnerable, or that she could be the victim of anything or anyone other than herself. She puts up such a strong front, people are afraid of her, and the natural instinct in people is to feel everything *but* sympathy. They shy away from her with most emotions really, but the one thing she has never been able to experience is sympathy, because who can feel sympathy towards someone who feels no sympathy towards others?

"Who can genuinely feel sorry for her when her own actions bring about her problems? Like today, for example: She was expecting you to go after her, and you did, but you didn't attack her in the same manner that she did to you, and because it wasn't so blatant, so obvious to her, she couldn't quite see that everyone else noticed and felt only that justice had been served.

"The suspension would have just been icing on the cake for her. You did her a great disservice by telling Mr. Danielson to not punish her without punishing you as well. If, for whatever reason, he decides that both of you should be reprimanded, it'll only make her that much more angry, because you'll be the one who was wrongly disciplined in the eyes of the student body, and that's the last thing she wants. You can't be the victim anymore if she's going to be."

Oh how good that almost sounded. How good it sounded to not be a victim, not be a freak, not be anything else and just be Grace. How strange, and wonderful, and confusing, and fantastic. But I could also see how pathetic it was, to finally be the envy of someone and have it not be because of something I had achieved, but rather because of circumstances beyond my control. "She can't share anything, can she? Not even a role that no one really ever wants."

Robert sighed again. "Whether she can't or won't doesn't matter; she's already a victim."

I nodded, knowing exactly what he meant. "Yeah. Of herself."

SHIFT

The auditorium was completely empty by the time Graham returned. A janitor had already asked Robert and I to leave twice, but I had promised Graham that I would stay until he came back, and with my uncertainty about where exactly our relationship stood after the soliloquies, I did not want to take any chance at weakening what little I might have left in way of a friendship with him. Losing his friendship, even for that short blip of time, had altered my world in ways that I did not want to relive.

Robert was still holding my hand, squeezing it reassuringly whenever my mind would run through some thoughts that were painful or foolishly self-deprecating. We had not spoken once since the realization had hit me that Erica had become a victim of her own machinations. He could still hear my thoughts, but didn't try to force me to hear his. The awaited intrusion by Stacy or Lark never materialized, and I was as yet still so unsure of so many things that just sitting here together was enough.

"Grace."

Graham squatted in front of me, his face unmistakably upset. "Grace, I want you to know that I did not know about any of this. What Erica did, what she tried to do to you...we're done, Grace. It's over between Erica and me. God, I didn't know. I swear to you, I did not know..."

"Of course you didn't know, Graham. I didn't think that you did." I tried my best to reassure him, removing my hand from Robert's and placing it on his. "You couldn't have known just how much she hated me."

Shaking his head, he turned his hand over and gripped mine with fierce fingers. "I should have known. I should have realized when she was pleased that you and I were friends again that something was

210

up. She was so insistent that I end my friendship with you this summer—I stalled for as long as I could—and when I did, she was so happy, I didn't think about what it would mean…"

I looked at my friend. His heart was broken, his trust had been shattered, and his world had been turned upside down. If anyone understood what he felt, it was certainly me. "Graham, I'm sorry-"

Graham's shouting silenced me. "Would you stop trying to apologize, Grace? I'm the one who screwed up and brought her into our lives. If I could go back and do it over again, do it differently, I would; I didn't know she'd go all Fatal Attraction on us!"

I smirked. "I'll be sure to warn the neighborhood rabbits."

He didn't seem amused.

"Graham, I'm not worried about Erica anymore. I'm only worried about how you're feeling." I wriggled my fingers free from his tight grip, the blood rushing to them all at once, and placed them, tingling and numb all at the same time, on the side of his face. "I didn't want any of this to hurt you."

Robert stood up suddenly, his face a mixture of so many emotions I could only pick out the anger in his steel eyes and the sadness in the downturn of his mouth. "Grace, let's get you home. I'm sure Janice and your father are wondering how things went today."

I removed my hand from Graham's face, the tone of Robert's voice, and the sorrow and guilt in Graham's eyes both pulling at something inside of me that I didn't even know existed. I looked at Robert's awaiting hand and reached for it. He pulled me up quickly, effortlessly. "My crutches-"

Graham handed them to me, apparently having grabbed them the minute I had removed my hand from his face. I allowed him to place them under my arms, and heard him sigh sadly as he stepped away. "She wants him, you know."

My eyes jerked up. "What?"

He flicked his eyes over to Robert's face, as though expecting some sign of acknowledgement to his statement. "She told me so after I said we were through. She said she didn't care if we were over because she and Robert were meant for each other."

I felt a bubble of laughter climb its way up my throat. It burst out and echoed around the auditorium, proof of my incredulity and faith all at once. "I'm sorry. I'm not laughing at you, Graham, please believe me. I'm laughing at her saying she and Robert were meant for each other."

Robert's face was a veritable rock, while Graham's was a composite of confusion, anger, pain, and humor.

"Grace, let's go." Robert tugged at my hand.

"How are you going to get her home?" Graham asked, his arms now folded across his chest, his face wiped clean of everything except a hint of arrogance. "Her Dad dropped the two of you off from what I heard."

I was beginning to wonder that myself, as I waited for Robert to answer. His motioned his head towards the door of the auditorium, and I heard Graham groan. I didn't even have to turn my head to know who could elicit such a reaction from him.

"I've got practice in thirty minutes so you two had better hurry up," Stacy yelled before heading out the door, the end of her ponytail the last thing I saw as she disappeared from view.

I looked into Robert's eyes. Still steel—cold, unmoving. I didn't like that. "When did you arrange for Stacy to take us home?"

"Yesterday. She was the one who suggested I come with you this morning."

I couldn't stop the amused smile that turned the corners of my mouth upwards from appearing. Someone was either playing matchmaker or...she was really trying to get on Graham's nerves. Either way, I had a lot to be thankful for when it came to Stacy, my sudden friend.

"Will you be coming to the house, too?" I turned to ask Graham. He seemed to struggle with an answer before finally nodding in the affirmative. "Good. I'll see you there then." He walked away, the weight of all that he'd learned today making him appear shorter to me for some reason.

Once he was gone, I hobbled towards the steps that led off the stage; since no one other than Robert was watching anymore, I simply walked down, too tired and annoyed to keep up the charade of using the crutches. The fact that after an entire day of using them, my body had become used to the step-pull-swing rhythm had escaped me until I realized that I had a little strut going on.

"That's actually quite cute."

I glared at Robert, annoyed that he was as aware of my movement as he was of my mind at that moment. "Care to explain to me why you were so rude just a little while ago?" I could still see the anger that hardened his eyes, preventing that small joy I would get from seeing the liquid shimmer enter into my vision.

"Not really."

"Not really? What do you mean, 'not really'?" We walked side by side, my crutches dragging on the ground as I stared at him, not amused at all by his response.

"I mean not really. Right now, let's leave it at that, okay Gee?"

I stopped walking. "Uh-uh. I want to know why you acted the way you did around Graham. I know it wasn't because of anything that I was thinking, so it must have been because he thought something that you didn't like. So what was it? Did he call you a name? Was he lying about being sorry? What?"

Robert continued to walk away but his voice never left my side...erm, head. *If you're not in the car in two minutes, Stacy will leave you here.*

How beyond rude could one get? Changing the subject in my mind? Ugh, I had to admit that he had a point. Realizing that I had come to the end of my freedom from crutchless motion, I reverted back to the step-pull-swing repetition I had perfected throughout the day and managed to get to the front of the school before Stacy decided that I simply wasn't worth taking home anymore.

Stacy's car was a cute little thing with a front end that looked as though it were smiling at you. "It's a Neon." She proclaimed proudly as I approached, my face obviously screaming "what is it".

"My oldest brother's old car. He bought himself one of those cutesy little hybrids last year and gave this to me when I turned seventeen. Isn't she cute? I call her Lola."

"Lola? Why?" The voice came from inside of the vehicle.

"Because she looks like a Lola." Stacy stepped aside, and I gasped at the passenger in the front seat.

"Um. Hi-Lark."

Lark smiled, although her pale gray eyes—though blind and sightless—were focused elsewhere. I turned my head and allowed my eyes to follow her gaze and saw Graham getting into his Buick.

He seems to have weathered this storm quite well.

I shook my head, not out of disagreement, but simply at the sound of her melodic voice filling my head without ever uttering a word. Though I should have been used to it, it was still strange. My mind kept telling me that lips should be moving, eyes focused on me, in order for conversations to be had.

You'll get used to it.

I certainly hoped that there'd be cause to as I watched Robert open the rear passenger door for me. The creases on his face and the angry hardness in his eyes had eased a bit, but for all of that, he was still the most beautiful thing I had ever laid eyes on, and I prayed that I certainly did have the time and reason to get used to it.

☃

Stacy dropped us off in front of my house, her hands jittery with nervousness as she realized how late she was, and knowing how angry her father was going to be. "I cannot be late anymore. I'm a teacher now! He's so going to whoop my butt when I get there!"

With completely unnatural—well, unnatural for a normal person—quickness, Robert had me out of the backseat of Stacy's Neon and standing in my driveway. Whatever that must have looked like to Stacy, she said nothing except an almost indistinguishable exclamation of farewell and then signed it with the peeling sound of tires against asphalt.

Lark had been the first one out, almost before the car had even stopped moving. She now stood with her hand on the seat of Robert's motorcycle which was still parked behind Janice's little SUV; her face was holding a smirk of amusement on it that would have looked absolutely unnatural on anyone else other than her.

"She's going to break about eighty-three traffic laws in order to get to practice, only to find out it's been cancelled. That's going to be amusing to see. I think I'll watch."

I looked at her, confused. "Watch? How are you going to do that?"

Her smirk grew into a full blown smile. "Well, I could go there, of course, and simply stand outside and watch it all unfold. But I think I'll just view it from her eyes and the eyes of her brother who cancelled the practice so he could catch some one-on-one time with his new girlfriend."

My jaw popped open in shock. "You can do that?"

She turned her head to face me. The eerie look in her pale eyes caused a shiver to run up and down my spine. I didn't necessarily like it when she did that, knowing that she could actually see me, just through someone else's eyes.

"I told you that my ability isn't limited by distance. Besides, she's funny. I like the thoughts that run through her head. I'm surprised Robert hasn't shared some of them with you."

I didn't need to say that Robert wouldn't have shared that kind of information with me. She could hear both of our thoughts on the subject quite clearly. It made her smirk again.

"How odd. Usually, he's all about the showing off. I'm amazed he hasn't said anything. This is a first. So many firsts today. How amusing."

I looked up at Robert, who had remained silent throughout the entire exchange. The slight crinkle in the corner of his eyes belied the dour expression elsewhere on his face.

"Well," I said in a rather annoyed tone. "Since I'm obviously out of the loop, I think I'll take myself inside." I placed the crutches underneath my arms, back to pretending again, and headed towards the front door.

Robert kept pace with me, the amusement spreading from his eyes to the mouth. By the time we reached the porch, he looked ready to burst out with laughter, his beautiful eyes liquid again. It was annoying. It was amazing.

"I won't ask what's so funny; I probably wouldn't get the joke anyway. I just want to thank you for being there for me today, Robert. It…meant a great deal to me." I reached for the doorknob and turned it, pushing the door wide open as I entered the house.

Janice had apparently been listening for the door. She came out of the kitchen with a dish towel in her hands, an anxious look on her face. "So, how was the first day back?"

"She did very well."

I looked behind me at the voice who had answered before I had a chance to. Robert was closing the door behind the two of us. "Don't you have to take Lark home?" I asked, the annoyance edging out anything else I might have been feeling.

Robert shook his head. "She's got a ride."

"With who?" My lips were pulled in an aggravated purse.

"With a friend." *Leave it alone, Grace.*

Comprehension finally kicked into gear and I nodded. "Oh. Ok." I smiled, the act forced due to my sheepishness.

"So how did the soliloquy go?" Janice asked, sitting down on the sofa, her eyes soft with concern, sensing that not everything went well.

I maneuvered my way to the recliner and sat down, placing the crutches next to me. I looked up to see that Robert was standing next to the recliner, his hand placed protectively on my shoulder. "It went as well as could be expected," I answered her.

I could tell by the look on Janice's face that my half-hearted answer wasn't going to cut it in the convincement department. "What I mean is that I didn't pass out or anything and I didn't turn into a ball of nerves while onstage. In fact, I did pretty well, all things considering…"

Janice cocked one eyebrow up, that last line dragging her curiosity out. "All things considering what?"

"All things considering the fact that she hadn't had time to prepare onstage like the rest of us." Robert's interjected answer seemed

216

to please Janice, who I knew had been given explicit orders to retrieve as much information as possible from me by Dad. Strike while the iron is hot, he'd say. This iron was ice cold.

Wiping her hands on the towel again, Janice stood up. "Well, okay then. If you're still in one piece, and Robert's here to keep you company until James gets back, I think I'll go and finish up on dinner. I'm making meatloaf if you're interested in staying, Robert."

All of my annoyance had vanished as soon as Robert had saved me from having to discuss the gory details of this afternoon, and now looking into his divine face, I didn't want anything else but for him to stay. For dinner. For dessert. Forever.

"If you don't mind having another mouth to feed this evening, I'd love to," he smiled. Janice, much like every other woman who had ever come into contact with him, seemed an inch away from swooning. Swooning? Did women in the twenty-first century do that anymore? If they didn't, Janice was about to start a new trend.

"Well. Hmm. I don't mind at all. Okay." Janice's lack of anything else to say seemed to confuse her as much as it did me, but the semi-bored look on Robert's face spoke volumes. He was used to it, the addled minds of women who came in contact with the aura of his divinity...his charm.

Annoyance flooded right back into me as I realized that this wasn't the first time that a female authority figure had behaved this way around him. How many mothers, step-mothers...grandmothers of the girls he'd dated in his long life had reacted in this exact same manner, even when propriety demanded exactly the opposite? I shook the thought out of my head. It wasn't right of me to expect anything of someone who'd been around far longer than some countries have existed.

I burst out laughing at the absurdity of that thought. That ridiculousness of it all was simply too much! I covered my mouth quickly, my self-consciousness kicking into gear, and looked around at my audience.

Fortunately, Janice had already retreated back to the kitchen, so all I was left with was the steely eyed stare of my angel. "You have to admit, that's pretty funny."

He shrugged. "I think the absurdity lies in your inability to realize that the reactions of everyone else bore me, and that your reactions are the only ones that interest me."

Remembering Lark's amusement at my treatment of her brother, I couldn't help but smile. "You don't take rejection well."

"I've never had to deal with it before. Lark was right. It's completely detestable. I'll have to remember to not do anything to make you reject me again." He sat in the spot that Janice had vacated, placing his hand on my casted knee, and searched my face. "Are you ready to talk about it? About what happened that night? Your head is full of so many questions, and I want to answer them, all of them if I can."

I shook my head. "Graham's supposed to be coming over, remember? I don't think he'd want to hear about my insecurities stemming from your many, many…many girlfriends."

He leaned in, bringing his face dangerously close to mine. "I'm not worried about Graham. I'm more concerned about us; where do we stand, Gee?"

My stomach did an Olympic qualifying somersault at the sound of him saying the words "us" and "we". Looking into those shimmering eyes, seeing that incredibly beautiful smile, inhaling the intoxicating fragrance of divinity that was absolutely unnatural and, ironically, very, very sinful, I should have been willing to give him whatever it was that he wanted. Heaven knew that I wanted to… "I think where we stand is on the precipice of a very good friendship…as long as you stop calling me Gee."

He pulled away from me, the frustration written clearly on his face. "That's not exactly making me feel better."

I smiled. "Well, it's a good thing that this isn't about you then, isn't it?"

He returned my smile. "A very good thing, because if it were, I'd have to start questioning whether or not I truly am what I've been brought up to believe. This is very disconcerting, not having any sway over you."

"Oh, you still have sway, just not as much as you'd like, or are used to." I put my hand over his, wondering how that felt, having his fingers sandwiched between my plastered limbs.

"I wouldn't know; I can't feel anything."

I started to remove my hand, that statement having caught me off guard. He quickly placed his other hand on top, holding me firmly in place. I looked at my hand, now sandwiched between his, feeling the heat radiate through the still shell. "I...I don't understand."

"Don't pull away every time you don't understand something, Grace. There are a lot of things about me you'll never understand, and if all you want from me is friendship, even that won't survive your constant retreats."

"Well then start explaining, because I'm feeling very confused here," I bit out, my patience wearing thin underneath the weight of my annoyance.

He grunted, a sly grin spreading on his face. "I thought you didn't want to discuss anything because Graham was coming over."

I rolled my eyes. "And I thought you weren't worried about him. Please, tell me what you mean when you say that you can't feel anything." I slowly removed my hand from beneath his and placed it against his cheek. "You can't feel this?"

He shook his head. "I can see how it feels through your eyes; you feel my warmth, the smoothness of my cheek, the way your hand gets hotter just by touching my skin, but I can't feel it myself, only through you, and even then, it's merely a reflection of your own emotions. It's one of the many things that separates us from humans."

"But you've never said anything before. All this time, I thought..." I couldn't finish the sentence. I didn't know how.

"I don't need to physically feel anything when I can appreciate how it feels to someone else," he said quickly, covering my hand on his face with his, "Isn't it better that I can see how you feel when you touch me...and I touch you, and enjoy that for what it is worth?"

"No. It isn't better. It's tragic. To not be able to feel the touch of another person is one of the saddest things I've ever heard. And it's also disturbing, if you want to know the truth. All of the times you touched me, you really weren't. I know it wasn't, but I can't help but feel like it was all a lie." I pulled away from him, but he prevented me from extricating my hand from his face.

Robert shook his head again. "Every time I held your hand, touched your face, kissed your hair, I could feel it from you, through you. It is enough for me. I cannot ask for anything more than that, Grace, especially considering all that I am and all that I have available to me. That would be selfish of me—to want something so much—just to be able to feel your softness, or your warmth."

"I don't understand. You're an angel. What kind of sick, twisted joke is it that angels can't feel anything?" I scoffed.

A sad smile formed on Robert's lips…lips that had never felt a kiss, and never would. "Grace, I *can* feel. That's what I'm trying to tell you—I feel everything through humans. Empathy and sympathy are things many humans say they feel, but those are things that we *must* feel. It is a part of who we are. It helps us to understand those that we're supposed to help or punish. Without it, what good are we? What good is our purpose here if we are incapable of truly understanding its value amongst your kind?"

"So you're telling me that you're okay with this? You're okay with knowing that the only way you can feel is through someone else's thoughts?" I was in disbelief that someone could accept such limitations.

"What else can I be but okay with it? I've had over fifteen hundred years to get used to it, Grace. It's not as though I just discovered this little tidbit yesterday." His voice seemed agitated. His beautiful mouth turned down in a slight frown, the corners hinting at a full grimace. "I won't lie and say that I wouldn't love to be able to feel the sun's warmth on my face, or grass between my toes, or any other cliché that comes along that you humans take for granted. Of course I would love that. To have my own memory, instead of someone else's would be a gift! But I'm not going to get upset or angry because I can't."

His eyes were steel again. I knew he was upset. I seemed to be very good at doing that: Working his angelic emotions towards absolute human sentimental levels.

He laced his fingers with mine, and looked ready to say something else, but the sound of the doorbell ringing stopped him. Or maybe he had stopped just a second beforehand, having already known who was out there and what they were preparing to do.

Janice came back out of the kitchen, the seemingly obligatory kitchen towel between her hands. "I'll get that. You two stay put." She walked towards the front door, opening it with a wide arc. "I was wondering when you'd smell dinner cooking! Come in!"

She came leading a dripping wet Graham behind her. He was soaked from the rain I had not realized had started to fall, and he still had that hard expression on his face that he'd had when he left the auditorium. He took one look at Robert and his expression became even sterner.

"Let me go and get you a towel, Graham." Janice was staring at the drops of water that were pooling on the floor beneath Graham. I could see that it was bothering her. When she returned with an old towel for him, Graham thanked her roughly. His mood wasn't about to give way for any sort of politeness for Janice. Or Robert, by the way he was glaring at him.

"So what took you so long?" I asked, trying to bring his focus to me. "I could have sworn you left before I did."

"I was planning to, but I forgot that I had practice today. I stayed for as long as necessary, then came here. Fortunately the rain kept us from stinking."

I agreed. "I, for one, am definitely glad for that. You always seem to stink something fierce after football practice." I wrinkled my nose to emphasize the word "stink".

He smiled, his dark mood lifting ever so slightly. "Well, now that I'm here, I want to talk about what happened today-" he glanced at Robert again, shifting his gaze downward to our hands still intertwined, "-alone."

Robert's grip loosened, and he removed his hand from mine. He stood up, and sighed. "I think I know when my presence is no longer required." He turned to look at me, and smiled sadly. "I'll talk to you later, Grace."

I watched, dumbfounded as he quietly left. Why were things always so hot and cold when it came to his reactions? And he was telling *me* to not pull away? I shook my head, the disbelief and the slow growing burn of disappointment in my chest fighting for a place to take hold. I looked at Graham, hoping that something in his face would give me cause to stop it.

I saw the smug smile, and the thoughts that caused them written clearly on his face; the disbelief turned into anger in an instant.

"Why did you do that?" I demanded. "What gives you the right to act like that, to come into my house and make demands like that?"

The smug smile did not leave his face, but some of the gleam from his eyes did. "I'm your friend, Grace, and I care about what happens to you."

"Sure. Now. A few weeks ago, you couldn't have cared less about what happened to me."

"That's not true. It's just that-"

"-you cared more for Erica. She was definitely worth it, wasn't she?" I knew I shouldn't have said it, but I did, and I didn't regret it.

"She wasn't worth it. You know that," he replied softly. His head hung down with obvious regret.

My head bobbed once in agreement with him. "You threw our entire friendship away because of her, and she ended up hurting you because of me anyway. And, try as I might, I can't help but feel badly because of it. But that doesn't mean that I'm going to sit by and let you be rude to my friends, Graham."

"Didn't you hear me earlier today, Grace? Erica's got her sights set on getting him. She told me about their date the night you were hit by that car. She told me about her date with him last night. Don't you see, Grace? He's just as attracted to her as I was. The only difference between the two of us is that I care enough about you to stop seeing her."

"Wait. What was that about him going out on a date with her last night?" My heart sank so hard, so fast, I was sure that he'd heard it hit the ground. My doubts came, one by one, rushing around me like a

222

mob shouting their thoughts.

"They went to the movies last night. She had told me that she had to prepare for today and that we couldn't go out, but she was out with him. And it's not the first time either. Don't you see? He's going to hurt you just like I did. I don't want you to go through that again, Grace."

I couldn't help the snort that came out of me. "You don't want me to go through that again? Convenient, isn't it? Being able to just fall into the role of savior and protector after being the villain? You know, Graham, all of this might actually mean something to me if you hadn't been the reason why I needed Robert's friendship in the first place." I stood up, struggling a bit with the rocking motion of the recliner, and glowered at him.

"And just so you know, he told me about that first date. Unlike you, he could see through Erica, and merely went out with her to find out what she had planned for me."

"Is that what he told you? And you believe him?" He grabbed my arm, his grip strong and possessive.

I yanked myself away from him angrily. "Yes, I believe him. He wouldn't lie to me, Graham." Of course he wouldn't lie to me. He couldn't. He had told me the truth, before I had even known that he was incapable of doing anything but. Whatever his reasons for seeing Erica again last night, they weren't because he was interested in her. All of the screaming doubts quieted and left me, leaving behind them a void that longed to be filled and everything seemed to shift inside of me.

I had admitted to myself that I wanted Robert in my life no matter what, in any capacity, but I had let the bitter doubts to remain, allowed them to rush out at the slightest provocation. But now I realized—understood really—that even though he was an angel, he wasn't perfect, and I had been measuring myself against that false perfection.

I looked at Graham, and I couldn't be mad at him. If he hadn't been so cruel to me, hadn't destroyed any and all hope I had had in him loving me the way that I loved him, I wouldn't have been able to appreciate the gift that was Robert.

But what of the love I had for Graham? For so long I had thought that what I felt was the pure emotion of being *in* love; I had hoped that what he felt for me was the same. Not only had he not been willing to return my affections, he had also alienated me from his life so completely, he had sent my heart spiraling to the ground, mortally wounding it…or so I thought.

Instead, it crashed right through the earth, only to emerge on the other side, stronger, vibrant, although disguised in many layers of self-doubt, and pessimism. His hurtful actions had saved me from spending a lifetime of not seeing what it was that I deserved.

"Thank you, Graham." I hugged him, so truly grateful for the gift he had unwittingly given me by breaking my heart.

"Huh? For what?" His voice sounded bewildered, but his arms wrapped around me, squeezing me tight.

I pulled away slightly to look up into his face. "For being my friend. For all the years of being my friend, and for the moments when you weren't. For caring about me, for being here now, with love in your heart, and for having concern about mine. You've helped me see things in a new light, Graham." I stood up on the tips of my toes and pressed my lips against his cheek. "I couldn't ask for a better friend."

"Uh…you're welcome?" Graham snorted at his own confusion, but sobered up quickly, his voice suddenly somber. "I *am* your friend, Grace. I regret every moment that I wasn't. I know that what I did…and what I didn't do isn't what a friend would've done, and I'm never going to forgive myself for that. I never betrayed your trust though, Grace. I never told Erica a single secret that you shared with me…and what I did tell her was stupid…I'm gonna try to make it up to you, Grace—forever it that's what it takes."

"I know, Graham. I know. And as my friend, please, I want you to promise me that you'll trust my judgment."

He pulled away, understanding what I was asking. Judging by the way his body stiffened, he didn't like it. "Graham, I don't want to hear your complaints. I just want your friendship and your trust here. I think after everything that's happened between us, I deserve to have that."

"You have my friendship, Grace, but I have to question your judgment. You trusted me and I crushed you, big time. You know this Robert guy for just a few weeks and you're ready to trust him the same way you did me. That scares me, Grace."

I sighed, and pulled Graham close again. "Please. Please, trust me, Graham. He's different. If I'm wrong, you have free reign to totally rub it in. I'll even let you do it with your lucky gym shorts on."

I felt his body shake with amusement. "I think that's a pretty good offer." He pulled away again, but this time, he was smiling. "Just give me fair warning though, when he screws up-"

"If," I interjected.

"Okay, *if* he screws up. I want enough time to practice my rubbing in." He winked, and then pulled me back into a very strong embrace.

Graham's return into my life was now complete. He'd shifted roles a bit, but his fit was even tighter and more perfect than it had been before. I was happy.

MIST

Happy was a relative thing. Graham had left after dinner, as usual, stopping only to ask me if I wanted to visit the cemetery with him on Saturday.

One of the few things that we had in common which bonded us closer than most friends was the fact that we had both lost someone we loved very much; while I'd visit mom's grave, he'd visit the grave of his grandmother who had died just a few short weeks before the car accident that had killed my mom.

I had told him that I'd call him when I woke up and let him know what my plans were. It was enough for him and he said he'd try to wake up early so that he'd be the one to answer the phone. I had to admit that I was definitely enjoying this new fit.

After I had taken a shower and said my goodnights to Dad and Janice downstairs, I climbed back up, not bothering with the pretense of needing the crutches, and prepared to go to bed. The events of the day had finally begun to weigh down on me and I felt emotionally and physically exhausted. The lure of the seductive mistress called sleep was so tempting, even the blatantly coordinated bedding that Janice had somehow managed to dress my bed and pillows in wasn't enough to keep me from collapsing in a heap atop it.

It seemed, though, that as soon as my eyes had shut, the alarm on my dresser was announcing the start of another day. Those nights were always the worst to wake up from. No dreams, and yet…no rest. I felt like a zombie who hadn't had its fill of internal organs.

I scooted on my butt to the foot of my bed and reached for the alarm clock. My fingers' memory knew exactly where to push to turn the beeping off, and the silence that followed was heavenly. I stretched my arms out, a yawn breaking free and pulling out the tail end of the sleep that had yet to be fulfilled.

226

As I tried to open my eyes to the blurry shape that was my clock, my gaze instead focused on an object that was sitting beside it that I knew had not been there when I went to bed. It was a square vase with a single flower in it. I didn't know what type of flower it was since it wasn't a rose or a daffodil, the only two flowers I could recognize on sight.

It had five angular petals, their edges wavy, like curled ribbon. The base of each petal was a soft white, with a heart of deep pink running down the center towards each tip. The pink looked freckled with the same soft shade of white, as well as creams and light browns, and the center of the blossom held several stem-like projections that contained lumpy shaped objects covered in yellow spheres of what I could only guess to be pollen.

It looked like a star; a freckled, pink and white star. Underneath the vase was a small envelope. Quickly, with nervous fingers I reached for it, plying my fingernail beneath the edge of the opening and pulling out the tiny card that lay within.

The card held the familiar handwriting that was far too beautiful to really come from anything other than something supernatural and divine. I touched the scrolled letters.

"A gift to your mother, because without her, you would not exist in this world. With great affection, your very good friend."

"Cheater," I muttered, and smiled. He wanted me to place the flower on mom's grave. It was the sweetest thing anyone had ever done for me, and I felt warmth rush to my cheeks, a blush caused by no one, seen by no one, and yet embarrassing all the same. I pressed my hands to my cheeks, as though to push the blood back down, and sighed. "Silly."

I put the card back in the envelope and placed it on the dresser. I had never brought flowers to mom's grave before, and I couldn't think of a reason why. Today would be the first time, and the fact that he'd been the one to give me cause enough to do it was strangely comforting.

I set that thought aside while I looked at my window. It wasn't open. I walked over to it, and tried to lift it up, but saw the lock was still in place. "I wonder how he did that." Surely he didn't come in through the front door? I remembered the vision Robert had shown me of him "calling" my pencil over to him. Could he have done that? Simply "told" my window to unlock and open?

I sat back down on the bed, and scooted across to the other side where the nightstand stood, a relic from Dad's days as a bachelor. I pulled open the large drawer and found the item in there that had seen minimal use since it was first brought in, its necessity viewed only by a hopeful father who had thought I'd have girlfriends calling at all hours, instead of the boy next door looking for someone to challenge to a burping contest.

I pulled the phone out of the drawer, and placed it in my lap. It was an old, rectangular corded model with large, backlit buttons on the receiver. I think at one point it had been white, but with time and age, it had turned into a muted yellowish gray; it looked sickly.

I picked up the receiver and started to dial…what? I didn't know Robert's phone number. I didn't even know if he had a phone. Or a house for that matter. Surely he must have some place he went to, right?

I placed the receiver back on the cradle and stared at the phone. How could I not know what his phone number was, and yet know all of this other information about him that was so personal and private? It seemed so lopsided; I couldn't do anything but sit and frown at my total ignorance.

Suddenly a thought popped into my head that seemed so ridiculously simple, I felt like a total idiot for about three seconds. Of course! I may not have a phone number to reach him, but I had something better. I had Lark!

I focused on the single thought of Lark's name. Her ability to hear any thought, see any vision from unlimited distances was my key to getting through to Robert. I concentrated on getting her to hear me through the countless voices I was sure she was currently listening to. I felt like a statue, I was so still, but my mind was in motion, racing through endless nothing in hopes that somewhere, I'd find what I was searching for.

It wasn't long before I heard her voice in my head, like a song

228

that had been written just for me. *I'm glad you've finally figured out how to do it. I was getting close to thinking you were simple or something.*

I sighed in relief. It had worked! *Lark! It worked! Wow, this is amazing!*

Yes. Amazing. Great. You're looking for my brother I take it?

Ridiculously, I nodded my head. *I realized that I don't have a phone number to reach him. Or an address. I-I wasn't sure if you guys actually had a place to live or...*

I could hear the tone in her melody change. It lowered, the mood somewhat darker. *Or what? Did you think we were homeless, Grace? Or that we lived on some fluffy white cloud while playing harps and eating cream cheese? I'm sorry if my brother was rude in not giving you his number or bringing you to our home, but don't assume that simply because you don't see it, it doesn't exist. Especially knowing now what walks among you.*

The blush of embarrassment that crept across my face seemed to be screaming "I told you so!" because Lark did something that sounded a lot like laughter.

I'll tell Robert of your concerns--he'll be there in a minute or two. Open your window.

My eyes widened at her instructions. Did the necessity of unlocking my window mean that Robert actually *had* come through the front door while everyone was asleep? I got off of the bed quickly and did as I was instructed, not knowing whether I should lift it up. I sat back on the edge of the bed facing the window, and waited. I was thankful that the alarm clock on my dresser was a digital one so that I wouldn't have to hear the tick-tick of time creeping by while I waited.

By the time I started getting anxious and contemplated counting by Mississippis, I noticed the shadow blocking out the soft morning glow. It looked like a storm cloud had decided to take shape right outside of my window, and I frantically worked to raise the glass wall, hoping none of the neighbors would see, all the while specks of gray haze were flowing through the cracks between the window and the frame.

229

As I struggled to raise the window, the wall of gray cloud slowly entered my room, flowing all around like a fog, wrapping itself around the bed, the dresser, sliding across the walls, before enveloping me in a sweet mist. I could do nothing; I was so in awe of what I was witnessing—I didn't even breathe. The vapor began to solidify around me, slowly taking shape, curls of gray smoke turning into arms that were folded across my back, stray wisps that became hair of jet, and two liquid silver dew drops became the eyes that I could always see, even when my own were closed.

"You called?" he asked silkily.

I sputtered out an incoherent response and he laughed. Rather than attempt to answer him again, I placed my head against his shoulder and nodded, embarrassed and yet thankful. He could disappear into mist, he could fly, he could read minds. What was it that he couldn't do?

"I can't sneak into houses with vases and flowers." He laughed softly, pulling away from me and motioned with his head to the blossom that seemed to stand out on my bare dresser. "Do you like it?"

"Y-yes. It's beautiful. But how did you get it in here?"

"Well, your window *was* open last night. I simply locked it on my way out. I thought it was best."

"You locked it? Why?"

"So that once I was gone, I wouldn't be tempted to come back in. It was very difficult to leave; you looked so peaceful in your sleep, and it felt very comforting to see that. I didn't want to disturb you with my questions."

"You have questions?" I was shocked. He could read my mind. What would he need to ask me questions for?

"Grace, several times yesterday, your mind—it felt like you had turned your entire brain off—all I could hear were my own thoughts echoing around in there, as though I had walked into an empty hallway." He had that familiar pucker between his brows, the one that appeared when he was concerned about something.

"Really?" I stood there with my mouth open, probably looking like a paralyzed goldfish. "I didn't do anything different. At least, I don't think I did."

"Of course you didn't. You didn't realize any of it. You kept talking and going on about things, but when your mind would blink out, it felt very…odd. Like when a television loses audio feed, but the video is still going."

I didn't see what I had done differently, or what could have triggered the—for lack of a better term—blackouts that he'd had with my mind. "Do you have an idea why?"

"I have a few ideas, but all of my questions really have nothing to do with that."

"Oh. Well, what questions do you have for me, then?"

"Well, first, I would like to know what you are doing this evening."

"I don't know. I've never really planned my days out. No real social life, you know."

He smiled. "Well-" he pulled me to sit on the edge of the bed "-I was thinking that perhaps you would like to come with me to visit a friend of mine."

I cocked my head to the side. "Visit a friend with you? Who is it?"

"Someone very special to me, and someone who I know will be able to answer many of the questions that you might have yourself."

"O-kay…so what exactly should I wear to visit this friend of yours?"

He brought his hand to his chin and rubbed it, seeming to contemplate the answer to my question. "I think that you will need to wear something semi-formal."

I heard the air rush into my lungs as I gasped, and the thud of my jaw as it lowered as far as physics could allow. "S-s-semi-f-for-formal?"

"Yes. Is that going to be a problem?"

I made a guttural sound that was extremely unladylike. "Problem? I had to ask Janice for a skirt. I don't own anything besides old jeans and older t-shirts. The only semi-formal thing I ever owned was a dress I wore when I was seven to my mom's funeral. Besides, even if I had wanted or needed such things, we never had the money to buy them."

He sighed, a humble sound, and put his hand beneath my chin. "I will find you something suitable to wear, if you don't mind."

I shook my head. "I-I don't think I could accept it, it wouldn't be right. Perhaps you should visit this friend by yourself." The idea of Robert picking and choosing an outfit for me was mortifying. So much so, I'd rather skip an evening alone with Robert to prevent it from happening.

"Grace, you can accept my secrets, my horrors, and my friendship, but not a simple dress?" He had heard my thoughts, felt my embarrassment. "If you can go against the natural sway of my ability, then surely you can go against the sway of your own pride."

I looked at his face, from the amused lines surrounding his perfect mouth, to the burning silver fire in his eyes. For the first time since I had looked into them, I could see my reflection as he saw it. Not merely a biased vision through his thoughts, but who I was reflected in the mirrored depths that watched me with such an intense gaze.

I was stubborn and strong, and it could be seen in the way the morning sunlight glinted in my eyes, the way the lines in my lips deepened when I came to a decision, the way my cheeks grew red when the pride that forced me to bend to nothing else took a hold of me. And for a moment, though fleeting, I could see that indeed, I was different in a way that could be beautiful.

Robert's face brightened with an enormous smile. "And so you see the truth, finally." He leaned forward and kissed my hair. I could feel the smile still there on his lips as he spoke. "Grace, please. It would mean a great deal if you would come with me tonight. If it would make you feel better, I could ask Lark to get your dress instead. I may be older than her, but I'm fairly certain that she's got much better taste in clothing than I do."

The thought of Lark shopping for me scared me even more so than Robert. I shook my head. "No. If you want me to go so badly, then it should be in something you'd want me to wear. This is your friend, after all." I pulled my head away so that I could look at him.

232

"But—please, I'm begging you here—no ruffles."

His deep, beautiful laugh rang out and filled my room with its sweet sound. I tried to hush him, not wanting Dad or Janice to hear, but he only laughed louder. "Grace, Janice and your father are not here. I have not heard their thoughts since I've been here. Let me laugh as loudly as I like, because you have allowed me to sway you. I might be an angel after all!"

I took a moment to allow him his joy before asking, "They're not here?" That information was very shocking to me. Where would they have gone so early in the morning?

"While I was here yesterday, I noticed that Janice had been thinking about some tests she had to take this morning. She was worried because had she been younger, she wouldn't have had to take them. It causes her to worry about the baby."

I felt the heaviness of that small slice of reality settle on me. "Ugh, why is it always so up and down?" I sank even deeper into the mattress of the bed. "Can't I have at least one day of happiness without the world crashing down on me? A month ago I didn't even want Janice around, and now I'm worrying about her and the baby. It's like something is around my neck, Robert, and I can't breathe!"

"Grace, don't worry about Janice and the baby. They will be fine. She's healthy, and the baby is, too." Robert looked at me, his face a roadmap of concern, kindness, compassion, and caring. I felt the strong enclosure of his arms surround me, but it was his voice that gave me the greatest comfort. "There is nothing to worry about, trust me. I have it on good authority."

I smiled, and sighed in relief. I could trust him. I knew that more than anything else in this world.

Wrapping my arms around him and taking a deep breath, I marveled at the way the day was beginning. "It's not even seven o'clock and I'm ready to sleep in until Sunday. So, now that we've gone through my dramatic moment of the day, can I ask you where are we going tonight that requires me to be dressed so semi-formally?"

"Well, my friend-" the way he said *friend* seemed almost mocking "-I would like to take you to a wedding for the granddaughter of a friend of mine."

A wedding for the granddaughter of a friend? "How long have you known this friend?"

"I've known the family for nearly fifty years. Well, I should say that we've known the family for nearly fifty years. Lark and my mother will be there as well tonight."

"So will this meeting be like the last one? With secrets and revelations coming forward?" I asked playfully.

"There will be some surprises, yes. But we'll talk about that later. You have a day planned with Graham, and I don't want to ruin it." He eased away from me, my arms no match for his casual strength. "I will be back here at five, with your dress."

The word "dress" sent a cold chill down my spine. "Um—what color are you planning on getting this *dress* in?" The way I said "dress" made it sound like it was an expletive.

"I was thinking something in green. It would suit your coloring quite nicely. With no ruffles, of course."

I could find no fault in the color choice, and would have to trust that he'd choose something that didn't make me look like the frosting on a sickly looking cupcake. I couldn't do anything else.

"Fine. I wear a size two, just in case you were wondering. I'd hate for you to go to all this trouble only to purchase something that doesn't fit."

An amused grin spread across his face. "So you would be more concerned with the trouble I had gone through to get the dress, than if I brought you one that was a few sizes too big to fit or the connotations that could be made as a result?"

My lips pulled tight into a very concentrated frown. "It will be baggy on me anyway, so what's it being a few sizes too big going to do? Make sure it has some kind of tie in the back so that I can at least cinch it in a bit. I don't want to embarrass you too greatly in front of your friends."

He pulled me back into his embrace, squeezing me tightly, but gently. "Stop thinking so little of yourself. Did you not just see how beautiful you are? I will be showing you off tonight, in a dress that will

234

make you look like the treasure that you are, and there will be nothing that you can do, say, or wear that will embarrass me in front of my friends. Alright?" He kissed the top of my head again.

I nodded my head. He had done it again. "You're definitely an angel. You've gotten your way twice in less than an hour with the two things that I haven't been able to do since I was a child: wear a dress and feel good about myself. Only someone with divine powers could accomplish such a feat."

His laughter once again filled the room, and this time I let the sound fill me. I could afford that now, knowing that no one was going to come barging in with shock and accusations. It was such a wonderful feeling, I couldn't help but laugh with him.

The joy I felt at hearing our mixed laughter bouncing around the room, coupled with the warmth I felt, not just from the morning sun streaming through my window, but also from that place deep within me that appreciated the wonder that was happiness, melded to form a great bond around my quickly beating heart, turning it into something that I knew was strong, much stronger than I had ever imagined possible.

You are incredible.

And with a soft kiss on my forehead, and an even softer whisper of goodbye, he dematerialized into a faint mist again and slowly made his way out of my window. I watched as he disappeared, already missing the feel of his arms wrapped around me. Quickly, before I knew he was out of my mind's reach, I asked him one pressing question.

It's a stargazer lily, because now you have more than one reason to look up at the sky.

I couldn't help but smile. I hugged myself; the idea that he had put so much thought into something as simple as a flower just for me was overwhelming and surprising. Surely, I didn't deserve so much as this? Sighing, I reached for the phone once more and dialed Graham's number.

By the time Graham honked his horn, announcing that he was ready to leave, it was well past nine. As soon as I told him that Janice and Dad weren't home, all motivation to rush on over were gone for him since he knew that meant no hot breakfast would be waiting him in the kitchen. I was content with a bagel and some orange juice while he needed hulking amounts of everything.

I wrote a quick note to let Dad know where I would be, not wanting to have him come home to an empty house and not knowing where I was. I made sure to grab the vase that contained Robert's flower before heading out the door, opting not to take the crutches, and instead expound on the perceived wonders of painkillers. I was still feeling overwhelmed by Robert's gesture that did wonders to push me closer and closer to that edge where friendship ended and something else that I knew I wanted desperately began.

Graham eyed the solitary blossom with speculative eyes. "Where'd you get that?"

I placed the vase between my knees as I buckled my seat belt. "Robert brought it over this morning to place on Mom's grave."

He looked at me as though I had just told him that the world was rectangular in shape and was governed by two headed goats. "He brought them over this morning?"

"Yes. He said he wanted me to put this vase and flower on her grave, as a way of thanking her for giving birth to me." I enjoyed hearing the words come out of my lips. It solidified the sentiment, cemented it. I was even more pleased with Graham's reaction.

"Wow. Even I never thought of something like that. Score one for the new guy." The muttered statement went a long way to keeping the smile I had on my face.

We rode in near silence to the cemetery, the thought of where we were going and why heavy in both of our minds. Mount Calvary Catholic Cemetery was a few miles out of Heath in Newark. It was a simple cemetery that boasted no fancy entrance or signs. The sign that greeted visitors was quite rudimentary: Simple wooden planks were painted brown, while the name had been painted on with streaky white letters.

Mom used to bring me here when I was a little girl. There were many old civil war graves here, and we would play a game where we'd pick a headstone and create a story about the person's life. I was always saying things like how they were mythical creatures, or super heroes whose alter-egos had to die in order to protect their secret identities. She would always give them normal lives, but that they had made small, but significant impacts to the lives of those around them.

I remembered one particular headstone, where a mother and child had been buried together, their dates of death the same.

"Annaleigh and Katherine MacDonnell, died on June 12, 1890." Mom had read, her fingers touching the weathered engraving, lovingly tracing their indentations as we both knelt down on the damp grass. "Annaleigh was a beautiful woman who was the town's only teacher. She had a sister and two brothers, all of whom had reddish gold hair. She gave her daughter, Katherine the same hair color, although her eyes weren't blue like her mother's, but the chocolate brown that were the same color as her father's."

She took my hand and placed it on the almost imperceptible carving of a cherub above the names. "Annaleigh would have been a great mother, and Katherine would have been a beautiful, bright, and sweet natured girl had they survived past childbirth, but the angels came to take them to Heaven instead."

"Why, Mommy? Why did the angels take them to Heaven?"

A sad smile came over her face. "Because the plan God has for each of our lives isn't always the same plan we have for ourselves, Grace. Sometimes, our deaths have more of an impact than our births. It can inspire people to do great things, even greater than they would have had the deaths not happened at all."

She helped me to trace the wings on the cherub, and sighed. "The death of these people might have changed the world, Grace, so we sometimes have to look at death not as something sad, but as something to be glad for. Sometimes death changes our lives in ways we never expect. It can bring with it every emotion; we have to learn to recognize the ones that help us and the ones that hurt us. And we also have to be willing to accept that with everything else, death also brings with it love. That is why we must always be grateful and appreciate it, even if it brings some sadness with it."

She wiped a tear away from her eyes with her free hand. "I'm sorry baby. I'm making you all nervous and worried, aren't I? What do you think about Annaleigh and Katherine?"

In all my childish wisdom, I answered, "I think she was a super hero, and she didn't want her child to be taken away by evil mutants who wanted to turn her into a monster, so she ran away and pretended to die. I think that she put a doll in her coffin and she really ran off with a handsome hero who took her away to someplace safe forever and ever." I pointed down to the ground.

My mother brought me to her chest and hugged me very tightly. She kissed the top of my head and rocked me gently. "Your story is much better, baby. So much better than mine."

That was the last of our stories. We were coming home from that visit when we had the car accident, and other than that and waking up in the hospital, I remember very little from that night. Everyone said it was a miracle I had survived without any burns, because our car had been turned into a big, black hunk of metal, and my mother's body was burned beyond recognition.

I was brought back from my memories by the motion of the car coming to a halt. Graham put the car into park, and I looked out the window. There were elm trees surrounding us, with headstones scattered all around the green carpet of grass. It was such a beautiful place, despite the amount of sadness that overwhelmingly blanketed everything here.

With a sigh, I took a hold of Robert's vase and waited for Graham to open my door. He exited the car and walked around the front before opening my door and helping me out as I tried not to spill any water. The smell of freshly cut grass was so thick, I could actually taste it. Despite the morning growing late, I could also feel the moisture from the night, smell it on the trees, and even the headstones.

"I'm going to go and walk to Gran's marker. Will you be okay getting to your mom's?" Graham was already looking up a hill a few yards away where his grandmother's grave was located.

"Yeah, you go and do what you do. Mom's isn't that far away."

He nodded his head and started trudging through the soggy grass clippings. I turned to the area of flat grass that held the grave of my mother and headed towards the small granite block. Each step reminded me of the steps I had taken as a child on the day that she had been buried.

I could see my feet, dressed in white tights and black patent leather shoes, slogging through muddy grass as a somber Dad walked ahead of me, his head bowed down and his hands clasped behind his back. I could see the hem of my blue dress, swishing back and forth between my knees as I kept walking. I was biting the nail on my thumb, trying to occupy myself in some way because I didn't want to cry. Everyone else was crying. Some, like my mom's family from Korea, were sobbing very loudly and grabbing me into very rough hugs, speaking things that I couldn't quite understand very loudly into my face while rubbing their tear drenched cheeks against mine.

Dad was numb, and completely oblivious to my confusion and fear. Graham's parents, Richard and Iris, who had both genuinely liked Mom, came with Graham but wouldn't let him near me while I was being manhandled. Surrounded by so many people, so many relatives, I had never felt more alone and more scared.

Everyone kept whispering about the miracle that was my survival, only they all made it sound more like a crime. How had I survived with barely a scratch while my mother had to be mourned in a closed casket? Why had my mother crashed her car in the first place? Had I distracted her? The accusations that were in Erica's soliloquy weren't something she had just made up to rile me. While I had questioned myself of the very same things, these thoughts had been on the minds of so many people in town it was impossible to escape them, even after nearly eleven years.

When I came up to her headstone, the vase in my hand, I felt the rush of sadness that almost never happened during my visits here. I leaned down, slowly sitting on the damp ground, and placed Robert's vase next to the large granite rectangle that listed Mom's name, date of birth, and date of death. Beneath the two dates was the number 91, her favorite Psalm.

I kissed the simple marker and laid my cheek against it, tracing her name with my fingers. "Hi Mom." The cold granite felt amazingly comforting against my face, now covered in hot tears. "I have so much to tell you…it's incredible. It's like an entire lifetime has passed since I last came here, and so much has changed.

"I have a new friend. Her name is Stacy, and I could probably bet safely that she's the only other Korean girl in all of Heath. Her family runs the Tae Kwon Do school near the bakery and she teaches there. She's something else. She actually laid Graham flat without even touching him!"

I had to stop for a moment and think about how I was going to approach the subject of Robert. As silly as it was—knowing that mom had been dead for over ten years, and that I was talking to her headstone and not directly to her—I still felt awkward broaching the topic. I knew that it would have been the same had mom been alive and we were having this conversation at home in the living room.

"I-I've met someone. I know that the last time I was here, I told you that I was in love with Graham, and I was working up the courage to tell him. Well, I did, but it didn't exactly go the way that I had hoped. It didn't even go the way that I expected. But it's okay. Things are good between us, now. Better than good, actually. But I realized after all of that that I didn't know what being in love really was.

"I thought that what I was feeling for Graham was the kind of love that you talked about having with Dad. You know, the kind that made your heart seem like if it were removed from your chest, it would fly away because it beat so fast? I didn't really understand what that meant, didn't know just how deep and life changing that was until I met

240

Robert.

"Oh Mom, he's like something out of this world. It's as though I stepped off of the page that was my life and walked into a completely different book! He's kind, and sweet, and beautiful, and he cares about me. He might even love me, if I dare to stop being so self-conscious all the time. But Mom, more than that is the fact that I love him. I love him so much. It's like my world was in perpetual sleep mode, and then he came and made the sun rise, waking me up to a whole new world.

"I can't even begin to describe it. Just seeing his face when I close my eyes makes my heart seem ready to run away and join him, wherever he is. I have trouble keeping my thoughts straight around him sometimes, which is ironic, since he can read them. But he doesn't think I'm weird, or a freak, or anything like that. He actually sees me as beautiful, Mom. Me! He sees who I am, sees my memories, sees my mistakes, and he doesn't think any less of me. He couldn't tell me otherwise."

I reached down and pulled the pink and white flower out of the vase and stared at it. It still looked vibrant and healthy, as though it had been cut just seconds ago. Leave it to an angel to pluck the most perfect blossom that seemed like it would bloom forever.

"He gave me this flower to bring to you. Can you imagine how inadequate I felt, knowing that he brought you flowers before I had? Well…one flower, but you know what I mean. I guess I'll just have to bring you an entire bouquet now, huh? Oh Mom, I'm so happy…it's weird. Things were going downhill so fast. First with Graham, and then with Dad—did you know that he and Janice are having a baby? I felt so angry, like he was betraying you or something. I don't know why. You've been gone for so long, and I know that you'd want Dad to be happy—you wouldn't have wanted him to feel bad about finding that with someone else.

"And I understand all of that now; I understand how important being happy while we're here truly is, because I can appreciate it now. I can appreciate what it feels like to be happy—completely and fully happy—because of Graham, and Stacy, and Robert."

I put the flower back in its glass home, and returned to tracing the engravings. My finger was a lot wider than it was the first time I had done this, but my emotions were the same as I realized that I'd have to leave soon.

"I miss you, Mom. I miss you so much, and the only part that hurts me now is knowing that you can't share all of this with me. I don't know how the whole heaven and angels thing works, but I'm sure it's not like I can simply have Robert send you a message or anything.

"I just want you to know that I'm happy, Mom. I'm truly, truly happy. You don't have to worry too much about me, alright?"

I kissed the stone once more, my fingers tracing the nine and one, and began to recite the psalm that those numbers represented—a ritual mom and I had had after our cemetery visits. She loved to sing the psalms; some of my earliest memories of her were singing them while cooking, or cleaning. Some kids had "Mary Had A Little Lamb"; I had psalms 91 and 121.

This was how Graham found me, with my face pressed against now warm granite, my hand partially covering the lettering that marked this to be my mother's final resting place, and my voice, repeating the same few verses over and over again in a sing-song voice.

When I finished, my traditional good-bye to my mother complete, I looked up at him. And her.

"Lark! Wow, wh-what are you doing here?" I stared, stunned at the beautiful and ethereal being who could have been one of the very angels I had just sung about.

"I do etchings of the stones for art class." She pointed with her walking cane to a bag that was slung across Graham's chest, its canvas material stained with charcoal. "I've got a few good ones from what I could feel. A mother and child, a former civil war soldier, and I was in the middle of getting a rubbing of this woman who had the most unusual name when he came along."

I could do nothing for a while but gawk at her. Apparently Graham didn't think anything was unusual about a blind person doing charcoal rubbings of gravestones. Judging by the look on his face, he probably thought it was the coolest thing since power steering.

"Did you say you made a rubbing of a mother and child?"

242

Lark nodded and reached for the bag, lifting the flap that hung over the opening and then pulling out a leather folder. She counted two sheets and then pulled out the third. "Here it is. An Annaleigh and Katherine MacDonnell. I was intrigued by their joint date of death. It seemed that Annaleigh died in childbirth, and Katherine along with her. Very tragic."

I looked at the rubbing, my finger running along the empty space where the names had been engraved. "I remember them," I mumbled.

"You remember them? They died over a hundred years ago, Grace," Graham laughed.

I looked at him, feeling incredibly guilty for not having revealed that part of my life with him for some reason. "My mother and I used to come to the cemeteries when I was a little girl, and we'd make up stories about the people who were buried. Mom said that Annaleigh had been a teacher, and that Katherine had been her first child. I said that they were super heroes."

I waited for the laughter to come, but none did. Lark looked thoughtful. "I used to do that. I used to pretend that I had been friends or lovers of the people that had died, and that I was grieving over some great tragedy. I can't see the television so I'd just create my own soap operas in my head."

I looked at Graham, expecting something, anything to come out of him that sounded like a snort, a guffaw, a chuckle. Instead he just stared at Lark, his eyes wide, his mouth slightly open, as if wanting to say something but not knowing what. I realized that was what I must look like around Robert.

He's too far gone right now to think about anything worthwhile to say. All I hear in his head are the sounds of polish folk songs for some reason.

I blinked in shock. I didn't know if it was because Lark was sending her thoughts to me, or because I knew what she was hearing and why, and she didn't. *That's what his grandmother used to sing to him when he'd have nightmares.*

She looked surprised. *How odd that you'd know what he was*

thinking about, and understood it, while I couldn't. I suppose that's what comes of having known someone for so long.

I nodded my head once, making sure that Graham didn't take too much notice. "So, um, Lark, what name was it that you were rubbing when Graham found you?"

"It turned out to be his grandmother. Her name sounded so odd. 'Bronislawa' just doesn't seem like a name one would find in a cemetery in Ohio. I had to get a rubbing." She gave Graham a dazzling smile, and I could have sworn I saw his eyes cross.

"She was a very scary woman to everyone except Graham. To her, he was the sun, the moon, and all of the halogen bulbs in between," I pointed out. "She used to yell something at me all the time that I never understood, but Graham told me that she was scaring death away from me, to keep him from putting his hands around my throat. She frightened me so bad once, I was forbidden to go near her after that."

Lark's face was calm, but I could see in the way her mouth no longer appeared loose and carefree that something I said had upset her in some way. *Stupid superstitions.*

I understood the sentiment. Mom had said the same thing when she had heard what was being said. It had been Dad who no longer felt I should be around Graham's grandmother, and rather than argue with him about it, mom relented.

"Well, I asked Graham if he wouldn't mind dropping me off at the mall on your way home. I'm going to meet up with some friends and pick a few last minute things before tonight. It's only a few minutes away from here by car, and he said he didn't mind."

At the sound of his name, Graham's eyes refocused and he started blinking rapidly, his eyes dry from ogling Lark all this time. "Uh, yeah. I didn't think you'd mind, Grace, you know, since we're on this whole trusting friendship thing."

"Why would I mind, Graham? Lark is Robert's sister and like she said, it's only a few minutes away." As we walked towards the car, I had to suppress the smug smile that I could feel creeping up on me. The knowledge that people couldn't help but be affected by an angel's presence, and that Graham was more than affected while I had been able to resist somewhat was strangely satisfying. When it came to angels, Graham the football hero was bested by Grace the Superfreak.

"Why do people call you a freak?"

The sudden question sent both Graham's and my heads snapping in Lark's direction. Our faces both held shock and anger. I knew his anger stemmed from his built in need to defend me, but mine was at the fact that she had read my mind, and made no secret of it.

"Why are you even asking?" I looked at her. *Why don't you just pick through my memories and find out?*

"Yeah, why are you asking?"

Lark shrugged her shoulders. "I was just wondering. It seems to me that most of the kids here in Heath just needed someone to fill that slot in the yearbook, and your name was picked out of a hat or something. I was wondering why."

"Well, why don't you ask them why they call me a freak?" I snapped.

Lark raised an eyebrow, my challenge doing nothing but boring her. "I did. All I got were ridiculous comic book style explanations that had little to do with anything. You don't have tentacles coming out of your back, you're definitely not green, and you've no mutant powers or anything. I think the only thing freakish I've heard about you is the size of your forehead. Just a little too wide. Kind of Imax-y. Other than that, you're about as normal as they come."

Graham's posture changed then. His back straightened, and he pushed his shoulders back. I'd seen it a million times after he'd threaten to beat someone up for picking on me and they gave up. It was his peacock pose. "That's nothing new. I've been saying the same thing forever."

Lark rolled her eyes. *What's with you humans and your constant use of the term forever, as if you can comprehend it and all it entails?*

I could tell by the way the tone of her thoughts became dark that she was on the verge of anger. I grabbed Graham's arm and yanked him back into a stride, wanting to get into the car as quickly as possible. Lark's temper was unpredictable. She didn't just run your plain old hot and cold. She was celestially hot and cold. Solar winds hot, and dark side of the moon cold.

I get your point! Stop with the stupid metaphors already. I feel like you're describing some astrology project.

Graham started walking quickly, and I followed, keeping my eye on Lark, hoping she wouldn't ask the question out loud again. Heaven knew all she had to do was look in our heads to find out the answer. Why ask when our verbal answers might not add up to what our minds were thinking? Wasn't that counterproductive?

That's just it. How else am I to judge the integrity of a person if what comes out of their mouths isn't the same as what comes from their minds? You've placed a lot of trust in Graham, despite what he's done to you. I've seen how it's affected you. I can see the scars that your eyes cannot see, but can feel. She wore a grim line on her face that contradicted the softening of her translucent eyes.

And, I also see how much my brother cares for you. If Graham hurts you again, I fear for his safety. You don't understand how deeply my kind feels when we form an attachment to someone, Grace. It's like one of these trees here. Deep, long roots that dig and wrap themselves firmly into the soil; you humans become our soil. We grow because of you, we thrive because of you. If something poisons that soil, it poisons us. But, unlike these trees, we fight back.

My eyes blinked twice, understanding what she meant. Only, instead of roots, I saw a single ribbon.

I saw Lark's head nod. She saw the ribbon in my mind, too.

We were in Graham's Buick and turning left onto Hopewell Drive before Graham finally spoke. "Some people call Grace a freak because they don't understand how she could have survived the car wreck that killed her mom; no one has been able to explain it and I don't think anyone ever will. Others call her a freak because she's half-white, half-Korean. Now some people call her a freak because she survived the hit and run.

"No matter what their reasons, the truth is that Grace is called a freak because she's different, and you can't explain what makes her different. She just is."

I stared at him. It seemed like it hurt him to say those words, like they burned his throat to utter them. I watched as he rubbed the bottom of his eye with his thumb, and then wiped his thumb on his jeans, a dark, thin line forming where his finger touched the fabric. I bit my lip at the obvious difficulty he had with talking about how other people thought of me; He had been one of those people just a month ago, and he didn't like that.

"But if Grace is a freak, then so am I. I'm a jock who hangs around freaks instead of cheerleaders," he snorted.

From the back seat, Lark laughed. "Don't forget that now you're chauffeuring blind people, too. You're more of a freak than Grace is."

Graham nodded, his humor having returned. "That's true. I'm bringing down your stock, Grace. You'll never be homecoming queen now."

I joined in their amusement, the dark mood lifting from Lark, and the sadness from Graham seeming to fade away, if only for a moment.

It was amazing what truth could do for someone. Lark had heard nothing but pure honesty from Graham's mouth, the truth as we all knew it, mind reader and humans alike, and that had changed the way she viewed him now. I could see it by the way her eyes seemed a little less opaque; it was as if the fog of bitterness and anger that she kept around her—like some kind of shield from the dishonesty of people—had lifted just a bit.

I honestly thought he'd lie to me. He surprised me. Nothing surprises me. I might end up not liking it later, but for now, it's amusing.

My eyebrows raised in shock. Graham had taken Lark by surprise? *You can read minds, even the minds of those who can see the future, and you were surprised by Graham?*

I had discovered her weakness, and she didn't like it. But I did. I thoroughly enjoyed my moment, laughing loudly, without caring a bit if in that moment, I really did look like a freak. I didn't know when I'd get another opportunity, as sharp and quick witted as she was, not to mention the fact that she could probably re-break my leg and arm in less time than it took me to get half a blink out.

It looked like I'd get a reprieve when she leaned back into her seat, her arms folded across her chest, a slow smile creeping across her face. She was amused, too!

I looked out of the window and realized that we were pulling into the parking lot of the shopping center. "I don't think I've ever been in this mall."

"I don't think you've ever been in any mall." Graham snorted.

I resisted the urge to stick my tongue out at him—it felt much better to punch him in the arm instead. The "ouch" that followed was very satisfying.

When we pulled up to the curb fronting the mall, I saw that Lark had a small, pink cell phone pressed to her ear. As soon as the car had stopped, she was outside.

"I'll see you tonight, Grace. Thank you, Graham, for the ride— I'll see you in school on Monday! 'Ciao!'" She walked very quickly towards the entrance, practicing great restraint not to just blur into nothingness with the speed she was so used to. If you didn't know it, you'd never have guessed she was blind.

The mall was far behind us when Graham finally asked the question I knew had plagued him as soon as he'd heard Lark mention seeing me later this evening.

"I'm going to a wedding with Robert and his family," I answered, my tone making it clear that I wasn't interested in arguing about it.

I saw the muscles in his neck tighten a bit as he stuck his jaw out, the idea of my going out with Robert obviously not sitting well with him. Well, he could suck on rocks for all I care. It was my first official date with Robert, and nothing was going to ruin it.

Except for the dress. I groaned. Loudly.

"What's the matter? Realized I was still here?" Graham pouted. He actually pouted!

"I told Robert he could buy me a dress for the wedding."

It was Graham's turn to laugh this time. "You're letting him buy you a dress?"

I folded my arms across my chest. "Yes," I answered, indignantly.

"You're not afraid that he'll get you something that'll make you look—well let's face it, a lot of stuff will—make you look twelve?"

My lips did funny things as I pondered his question. "I told him no ruffles. Ugh—I don't know anything about dresses—I've never shopped for a dress, and all I know about them is that ruffles are hideous. Oh my God, what did I do? He's going to buy me something that looks like it belongs on a twelve year-old, isn't he?" The feeling of panic bubbled up underneath my skin as we pulled up in front of our house.

I looked at the watch on my wrist and realized that it was nearly twelve-thirty. I needed to eat something for lunch, and I also needed to lie down and try and calm my nerves. Graham helped me out of the car and walked with me to the front door. I saw that Janice's SUV—which had been gone when we had left—was now back in its spot in the driveway.

"Well, that's a nice distraction," I muttered. I could focus on how the doctor's appointment went, instead of the impending doom of wearing a dress.

Graham eyed me suspiciously. "You're actually going to wear it, aren't you?"

I nodded my head. It was either that or attend the wedding in jeans and my Jack Skellington shirt.

"I think you'll look beautiful," was his reply.

Surprise covered my face as I looked at him. "The last time you saw me in a dress was over ten years ago! How would you know whether or not I'd look 'beautiful', as if that were even a possibility?"

"You forget that yesterday, you were wearing a skirt, and a skirt is, I think, half a dress; you looked beautiful in it, so I'm gonna bet that if you looked beautiful in half a dress, you'll look twice as beautiful in a whole one," Graham said emphatically, his head nodding with every other word.

My chest felt warm as several feelings all piled in together to fill up my heart. They were all trying to get my attention, but the one I ignored was the melancholy that seemed ready to shout "Why now?"

I grabbed his hand and pulled him in for an awkward hug. His tall, athletic frame against my thin, moderately short one, hampered by stiff, plastered limbs made for an odd pairing, but we managed to make the embrace work. "Thank you, Graham. You really are a good friend."

"Of course I am. I know my talents." He pulled back, forcing my release, and opened the front door for me.

"Dad, Janice—I'm home!" I shouted. I stared at the little table that sat in the little hallway that was supposed to hold your keys, wallet—whatever it was one took when they had an active social life. I had nothing to place there, and that fact suddenly caught me off guard.

"Graham, remind me the next time we're near the mall that I need to get a purse," I said to him as we walked into the living room. Dad was sitting in his recliner, reading a very thick book—it had babies on the cover. "What are you reading Dad?"

He looked up over the pages and smiled at me. "Hey kiddo." He nodded to Graham. "Hey Graham, there're sandwiches in the kitchen." He waited until Graham had left us alone before he continued, "This is supposed to be the best baby book on the market, and since it's been so long since you've been in diapers, I thought I'd bone up on what to do. Did the weather hold up at the cemetery?"

I nodded. "It was a nice day. The ground was a little wet, but it always is this time of year." I sat down on the couch next to him, my face anxious for him to tell me how the appointment went. "So, where's Janice? How'd the doctor's visit go?"

He looked at me, puzzled.

I could have slapped myself. He hadn't told me about the doctor's appointment. Robert had, and not having much experience in the lying department left me at a loss for words to try and recover from the gaffe.

"Did Janice tell you about the appointment? I thought she had wanted to keep it private, what with the worries she's had and all. Oh well," he looked at the page he had been reading, committing it to

250

memory, and then put it down to focus on our conversation. "According to the obstetrician, the baby is doing very well. Janice is a little over thirteen weeks pregnant, and if she can make it three more weeks, then she'll be past the most dangerous point. This book says that we can find out if it's a boy or a girl by your birthday. Wouldn't that be a great present?" He was beaming.

I couldn't help but smile back. "Not to mention cheap!" The fact that my birthday fell on Christmas had always meant dual purpose presents, so the idea that he was referring to it specifically as my birthday felt good.

"So, tell me about your morning. What did you do besides visit Mom's grave?"

Did I have the courage to tell him? He'd find out sooner or later... "Well, Robert stopped by this morning—he brought over a flower for me to take to Mom's grave—and he asked me to go with him to a wedding for a family friend—the flower was really beautiful."

Dad's face held absolutely still, his expression frozen on his face. It was dismay. I didn't even know if he had taken a breath in the last few minutes, he seemed so distracted by what I had told him. I was ready to shout out for Janice to call 911 when he sighed, his shoulders slumping, and started speaking again.

"I guess I knew it was going to happen sooner or later, the two of you dating I mean."

I bit my lip, trying to figure out what exactly I could say to bring back the cheer he had had when reading about changing dirty diapers. Mostly though, I was trying to figure out how it was that he knew something like this would happen when I didn't.

"Is he going to pick you up, or are you going to be needing a ride to this wedding?"

My hands were gripping my knees very tightly, the plaster against plaster on my right side making it a bit easier to try and not focus on the next bit of information I had to share. "Um, Dad—he's coming to pick me up. He kind of has to, since he's bringing my dress."

"He's what?" Dad's eyes grew wide with shock. "He's bringing you a dress?"

I nodded, "He's buying it, actually, since I don't own anything even remotely dress-like."

And then I saw it. Saw something that I didn't expect to see on his face. He smiled. The corners of his eyes crinkled up, and in that moment, he looked very young. He was pleased, happy.

"He's actually getting you to wear a dress. Will wonders never cease."

I wanted to say that it was only because Robert was an angel, and had supernatural sway when it came to my reservations but I knew that wasn't true; and even if it were, Dad would have laughed at me, and agreed without knowing that I was being serious.

Instead, I simply shrugged my shoulders and threw his words back at him, "It was going to happen sooner or later."

Graham came out of the kitchen then, his hand wrapped around a massive submarine sandwich, his mouth full of food. And still, he managed to spout out a question.

"Did she tell you about the dress?"

I threw my hands up. "Really, is this as momentous an occasion as you two are making it out to be?"

The looks on their faces echoed the answer that my conscience had started screaming before the question had even left my lips. Yes, this was a momentous occasion. I was going on my first date, and I was doing it in a dress of all things. There wasn't anything more momentous that that. Not in the life of your average teenager. Unless, of course, you weren't average, and that first date happened to be with an angel…who could fly…and read minds.

PREPARATION

Graham had insisted on waiting for Robert to arrive. Dad seemed to think this was a great idea, and the two of them had no problem sitting on the sofa and watching one guy related movie after another for the next few hours while I tried to figure out what exactly I had to do to get ready.

I took a long shower, scrubbing my skin until it glowed red from all the friction. I shaved my left leg and my armpits, and even borrowed a pair of tweezers from Janice to trim the stray strands of hair that floated above my eyes. My eyebrows, thank goodness, were the only things on my face that I believe are perfect. No need for zealous plucking or shaping. They had just the right arch, thickness, and length, and I cannot believe I just said that.

In my boxers and tank top, I sat on my bed, waiting. I smelled like a fruit salad, having allowed Janice to drench me in some of her pastel body lotions and sprays. She even gave me a tube of lip gloss that, she said, "would look good with anything because it's sheer." I'd take her word for it because that was as far ahead as I'd allow her to get.

I knew I'd have to wear a little bit of makeup, but I just wasn't sure to what degree. That dress was becoming more and more of an irritant to me and it was mainly because I wouldn't know what it would look like until it was here. What color would it be? What length? I certainly hoped it wasn't short. I didn't want my casts to be the focus of conversation, and unfortunately, as useless as they were, I simply couldn't remove them either. Only two weeks had gone by since the accident and by all accounts, I shouldn't even be out of bed, much less walking around without crutches.

Robert's healing ability had saved my life, but it had also made me one big fraud as well, and that was weighing on my conscience.

I looked at the clock on my dresser and scowled. It felt like the clock was teasing me; I had no doubt that if it could, the numbers would scroll backwards, drawing out the tension for as long as possible in the hopes that I'd explode from being wound too tight. My fingers began a tapping rhythm against my leg, my impatience rapping out a beat that grew faster as each minute ticked by.

I had my window open, willing the sound of a motorcycle, car, bus—anything to announce Robert's arrival. I was beginning to feel the twinges of doubt that he'd even show up when I heard the doorbell ring. I rushed to the window to see if there was another vehicle outside, but I saw nothing.

"Stupid solicitors," I mumbled. I stared at my fingernails, deciding whether or not it would be acceptable to start chewing on them when I heard Dad call my name. I looked at the clock on my dresser. Five o'clock, on the nose. Of course he'd arrive exactly on time, just as he'd said.

Trying to look as uninterested and as calm as possible, I descended down the stairs and walked into the living room. Three male figures were standing there forming a triangle of male aggression. Graham had his arms folded against his chest, while Dad had one hand braced across his abdomen and the other was rubbing his chin, as though he were contemplating something of dire importance.

The apex of this unusual triad was a beautiful creature dressed all in black, his face serene, as though the tension that seemed to choke even me had no effect on him. He was holding up a garment bag in one hand, a large, separate store bag in the other. He knew I was coming down before I had even taken a single step out of my bedroom door, knew that I had been excited, knew that I was trying to keep all of my emotions reigned in. And he liked it.

"Hello, Grace."

My cheeks hurt, I was smiling so widely. "You're on time."

"I told you I'd be here at five. I hope you didn't doubt me," he said, smiling back.

Dad's cough and Graham's grunt reminded me that they were still in the room. "Is that the dress?"

He handed me the two bags, and nodded, "Your dress, a pair of matching sandals, and some extras to pick and choose at your discretion."

I eyed them warily. "Will I know how to put them all on?"

A voice from behind me answered, "I'll help you." Janice grabbed the bags out of my hands and nudged me towards the stairs, pulling me when my feet refused to budge. "Come on, let's get you dressed."

When I climbed up the first two steps, I turned to look behind me. The triad was now looking in my direction, watching me leave an awkward caterpillar. Would I return as a beautiful butterfly? Or would I return as the caterpillar version of James Gumb?

I swallowed my fear and apprehension and continued up the stairs. Janice was already in my room, the garment bag hanging up in the closet, the other bag's contents dumped out on my bed. I closed the door behind me, needing the few moments that doing so required to commit to what I was about to do.

Taking a deep breath, I walked over to Janice. Her face was lit with excitement. I could see that she was looking forward to this about as much as Dad wasn't. "Are you ready to see it?" she asked me.

I could do nothing else but nod, my voice simply not cooperating with me at the moment. I took another deep breath as I watched her pull the zipper of the garment bag down, and push the bag around and away from the material that lay within.

At first, it looked like a waterfall of shimmering moss had spilled from the bag. I took a few steps closer, curious at the strange color. Janice pulled the dress completely out of the bag and held it out so that I could see it better.

It was strapless, the front bust area covered in rough cut crystals that ran through every shade between a rich golden amber to deep chocolate browns, ranging from the size of a pea to that of a quarter. The crystals extended only a few inches down the bust, and where they ended, two streams of moss colored chiffon flowed down. The dress itself was constructed of satin in the same gray-green color. The shimmer of the satin and the delicate and flowing chiffon trailed to the floor; it wasn't a short dress. My first wish granted.

"Well, there's really nothing else to do but put it on," I sighed. It was definitely much prettier than I had expected. I took off my shirt and shorts, when a seemingly important question came into my head. "What kind of bra do I wear with this?"

"You wear a strapless bra or a bustier with a strapless dress," Janice answered me before recognition dawned on her. "Oh."

"Yeah. Oh. I don't have one of those." Of course I didn't have one. I'd never needed one.

Janice put the tip of her thumb between her lips, chewing on it as she thought about what could be done. "It would be completely inappropriate for him to have done it. He wouldn't have. He couldn't...but let's see if Robert has something that might work in this pile of packages."

She sat on the bed and contemplated each package that she'd emptied from the larger bag. "Ah-hah. I'll have to have a discussion with him about this—highly improper—so expensive, too..."

She grabbed a pale, opalescent pink box with black lettering and handed it to me. I looked at the elegant script that listed the name. I lifted the lid and gasped. I covered my mouth, and looked at Janice. Provocateur indeed! Amongst the tissue was something I had never thought I'd ever wear: a shiny, satin corset.

"H-how am I supposed to get this on?" I looked at Janice, terrified that I'd strangle myself with it.

She smiled. "I'm more concerned with how it was that Robert came about purchasing that for you, but that can be answered later. Let's get this on you. Come here."

She took the foreign-to-Grace device out of its box and proceeded to undo about eight hooks, then wrapped the corset around me, refastening the hooks in the front. She turned me around and pushed the garment up over my bra, then began to tighten the strings. When she had worked halfway down the back, she unhooked my bra. "You can take that off now, Grace."

I pulled the bra out from beneath the corset and then let the straps fall down my arms, all while Janice proceeded to strangle me from the chest down. "Oomph" I groaned as she pulled the strings as

256

tight as they could go without forcing me to bend over, and then tying them into what I hoped was an easily undone bow. I would want nothing getting between me and oxygen when I came home and could take this medieval torture device off.

Janice turned me around again, assessing the job she'd done, and raised her eyebrows in...surprise? Shock? "Wow. I'm going to have to ask Robert where he found this so that I can get one of these for myself."

Looking at the clock on my dresser, she quickly grabbed the dress and unzipped it. "Okay, you're going to have to sit down on the bed. I'll slip this over your feet, and then you'll stand and I'll pull it up."

I did exactly as she had instructed, allowing her to slide the smooth fabric over my legs. I stood and felt the fabric rush over my waist and the corset. I felt her pull the zipper up my back, tucking the corset strings in so as not to catch them, and then she stepped back to give me room to allow the material to fall around me. It was a perfect fit. Of course it was. He'd made sure of that.

Janice looked at the pile of boxes and bags on the bed and started rummaging through them. In one box she found a set of hair clips with jeweled dragonflies on them. In another, she found a pair of strappy bronze sandals that were exactly my size. She emptied out the contents of a small bag and discovered two small velvet boxes. One contained an amber pendant in the shape of a heart, while the other had amber drop earrings.

"I've got to say this much about your Robert. He's got incredible taste. He's spent an awful lot on you for one evening, Grace. I have to wonder what exactly it is he expects from you after all of this," she said, holding up the jewelry boxes to emphasize her point about cost.

"He doesn't expect anything of me," I told her, knowing that it was the truth far more than it was anything else. "And even if he does, he's not exactly going to be getting anything out of this other than perhaps extreme embarrassment and regret."

The clicking sound of Janice's tongue told me that I probably didn't know what I was talking about. I just didn't know which part. Sighing, she grabbed my brush from the dresser and began detangling my hair. In less time than in took to dress me, she had my hair pinned up in a French twist, loose strands tumbling out near my ears and down the back of my neck.

She took the necklace out of its box and fastened it to me, the pendant resting nicely against my chest. She took the earrings out and a surprised "oh" came out of her mouth. "They're clip-ons."

I looked at the jewelry in her hands and she was right. I didn't understand how Robert could have gotten everything else right but that. "I guess he didn't know that I have pierced ears," I mumbled.

Janice looked closely at me, her eyes scrutinizing something that I couldn't see without a mirror. "Um—your ears aren't pierced, Grace."

"What?" I quickly went around her and shoved my face into the mirror that sat above my dresser, zeroing in on the lobes that I had had pierced when I was only five, the little golden star earrings having never left them since. Only there were no golden stars. There were no holes. "How in the-" I kept turning my head to the left and the right, thinking that when I flipped back, there'd be a glint of gold there. Each time, I was disappointed.

He'd gotten it right after all. How had he known something about me that I didn't? And where were my earrings? I ground my teeth as this newfound information and lack thereof dug itself a nice hole in my mind, intent on settling in there until I found out the circumstances that led to this.

I sighed and grabbed the earrings from Janice, apparently amused and slightly alarmed that I had been oblivious to my lack of earring holes. I clipped the amber pieces to my ears, and reached for the sandals. Well…sandal, really. I wasn't going to be wearing the right one, after all. I put it on my foot and tried walking around. The slight heel on it cause me to limp as I took several steps around the room, but it wasn't uncomfortable, and I sent a little prayer of thanks his way for finding a pair of women's shoes that weren't created for the utter destruction of my feet.

Janice took a look at me and nodded her head a few times,

obviously thinking about what else was needed to complete the gift-wrapping she was doing to me. She went over to the dresser and picked up something that was definitely not mine and a little pot that also wasn't mine, and started unscrewing the lid off of it.

"I'm going to line your eyes, apply a bit of mascara, and then you'll wear the gloss. That'll be it. You don't need anything else," she said as she came toward me with the brush, wielding it like the tool that it was, only it looked more like a weapon to me. "Close your eyes, Grace."

I did as she instructed, and waited, feeling the soft, but firm strokes of what I could only guess was the brush going across the bottom of my eyelid. "Open your eyes." I did that as well, and she again came at me with another bristled weapon.

She applied the mascara to my lashes very slowly and carefully, apparently sensing my fear and distrust. "Honestly, I've never met someone so afraid of mascara before," I heard her mutter, while she returned the brush back to its innocuous tube that looked like a stranger on my dresser. Finally, she grabbed the tube of gloss and handed it to me.

"Okay, you're going to have to put this on yourself. It'll be the only thing you'll reapply, so you'll have to know how to do it without making it look too tacky."

I know the look I gave her would have been the exact same one I'd have shared had she just told me that I was going to have to perform a triple bypass on a hippopotamus, while tap dancing to the meowing cat Christmas CD that Dad owned. How did one make gloss not look tacky?

I learned that it was quite simple, really. The trick was to apply it to your top lip only, and then rub it into your bottom one. Janice went through this with me using baby steps, and while I might never get so dolled up again, I might actually get used to the gloss thing after she showed me how easy it was.

"Well, Grace. I can't say anything else but this. If your mother was half as beautiful as you look right now, I'm fairly certain your Dad was a very lucky man when he married her," Janice exclaimed, not a sound if insincerity in her voice as she stepped aside so that I could finally focus and take a look at myself.

"Thank you, Janice," I said, and glanced in the mirror. I was speechless. The girl who stared back at me in the mirror surely wasn't me! Was my hair really that rich of a brown? My eyes—did they look green or was that my imagination? The freckles that danced across my face looked as though they belonged there as the rose of a blush crept across my cheeks, drowning out any sign of imperfection. I couldn't believe it.

"That's not me," I whispered.

Janice chuckled. She reached for one more box and handed it to me. "This, I believe, is your wrap."

My what? I took the box from her and opened it up. Inside was a bundle of what looked like the same chiffon that flowed from the front of my dress. I took it out of its box and marveled as it tumbled to the floor, its ends weighted down with the same crystals from the front of the dress. I noticed that it wasn't a narrow strip of material, but rather wide, and multi-layered, causing it to be less sheer, but still giving off that subtle softness.

"Well, put it on," Janice told me, and helped as I did.

She ushered me towards the door, opening it before letting me out first, then rushing around me in the hallway so that she could be the first to come down the stairs, her intent very clear. She wanted to see the guys' reactions when I appeared.

Slowly, taking a deep breath with every other step, I made my way down the stairs and into the living room. Janice's arrival had disrupted whatever it was that the guys had been doing for the past hour, and all three were standing, their faces anxious as I took that last step down.

The first sound I heard was the intake of air, and then the groan, followed by the sigh.

Dad was the first one to approach me. Obviously this had all been pre-arranged because neither Graham nor Robert made any move to come forward. "Grace—wow. You look so beautiful." His eyes were damp, and I knew that if he let loose one single tear, I'd have

260

endured that heinous mascara torture for nothing because I'd wash it all away with the flood of mine.

"Thanks, Dad." I tried to sound rough, stiff, firm. My shaky voice wasn't going to let me win this round.

"I mean it, kiddo. You look incredible. That's some dress," he said, looking me up and down, and then hugging me fiercely—like a father would right before sending his only child off to war. It was bringing me closer to losing that battle with the tears.

"Okay Dad, you're going to have to let me go now," I whispered into his ear. He nodded, but didn't release his grip. Instead, it grew tighter. "Dad…?"

"Alright, alright. I'm letting go. Give an old man a break when he's watching his little girl grow up right before his eyes, will ya?"

He looked at Robert and sighed after he'd put enough distance between the two of us. "You got my baby into a dress, and you've got me digging up the waterworks here. I don't know whether to hug you or hit you."

Robert smiled. "I'd prefer the hug, but understand if you'd rather hit me."

Graham stepped forward then, his mouth a cavern of awe, his eyes wide.

"You said I'd look better in a whole dress. Are you going to take back your words?" I asked him, my hands on my hips, my feet braced for any biting comment he might make.

He shook his head, his jaw wagging as he did so. "You look incredible."

And that was it. He wasn't going to say anything else. I saw him glance at Robert and I knew why. He wasn't going to ruin this moment with any snide comments or off-handed remarks—no matter how much he wanted to make them—because he cared about my feelings.

Finally, it was Robert's turn. His eyes were filled with happiness as he held his hand out to me. I gladly took it. He raised my hand to his mouth and kissed my knuckles very softly, faintly. It was something that you only saw in period pieces on television or in the theater. And now, in my living room…but no one ever felt the fierce raging beat that my heart was pounding in my chest, or the breathless joy that flowed through me with each, soft caress.

"You are everything they've said and more," he said softly. *Radiant, spectacular, phenomenal, glorious—you've surpassed any expectation I might have had, and even more so I don't think I've ever, in all my years on this earth, been more stunned than I am right now.*

As unladylike and unattractive as it was to do, I couldn't stop my mouth from falling open at his admission. *Weren't you peeking? Looking in my or Janice's mind, looking for our reactions? What I looked like beforehand? Cheat?*

The look in his eyes told me that he had not. His surprise had been genuine. I was amazed. "How gentlemanly of you." I murmured, a secret smile faintly touching my lips.

Robert offered me his arm then, and looked at Dad. "I think our car is here. I will have Grace back by eleven, if that is alright with you, Mr. Shelley."

Dad's face was blank. For a first date, he'd probably had some sort of set curfew speech planned in his head, but he hadn't counted on Robert being one step ahead of him and setting one himself at the exact same hour that I would have had to been home had I actually had a social life. He grunted and then responded, "I think that is fine, although if Grace finds herself having a good time, I guess it would be alright if you were to bring her home by midnight."

I looked at Dad, and then at Robert. It was so quick, I would have missed it if I had blinked; he winked at me. "Thank you, Mr. Shelley. I appreciate and value your trust in my bringing your daughter back home safely."

This time, it was Dad's turn to wink at me, although when compared to Robert's, it looked more like half his face was falling asleep. "How could I not trust you with her safety, Robert? You saved her life. I think I can bend the rules just a little bit for that."

Graham, who had been quietly watching the exchange between the two threw his hands up and headed towards the kitchen. "I need something to eat."

Janice, who had also been standing quietly off to the side, suddenly made a squeaking sound. "I need to get my camera!"

"Oh no! Let's go, quick, before she takes a picture," I cried, tugging on Robert's arm, but he wasn't budging. I was too late. Janice had stashed her camera somewhere close by, probably in preparation for my escape.

"Not so fast, Grace! I just want two photos; One of you alone and then one with Robert."

"Aw Janice, you know photos of me never turn out right," I whined. I sounded like a bratty teenager, and I bit my lip to stop the nasal sound from coming out.

Janice shook her head, not swayed one bit. Whining never worked. "Come on. Let's get one of just you."

Robert took a few steps away from me, leaving me standing alone in the middle of the living room. Janice called my name and told me to smile. I tried.

"Hmm. This flash isn't working right. It came out too bright," Janice said, looking at the little screen on her camera that displayed the photo she had just taken.

"No, that's just me," I muttered, knowing full well that it was.

"Well, let's try one with you and Robert, then."

As if he had never left, Robert was at my side, his arm around my waist, his hand resting on my hip. He looked down at me, and I looked up at him. I didn't notice the flash, but I did hear the coo from Janice as she proclaimed her latest attempt at amateur photography a success.

"It's beautiful. It's like there's a halo of light around the two of you. Come look!"

I couldn't stop myself. There had never, ever been a photograph of me that hadn't come out ruined in some way. I was in absolute disbelief. But Janice was right. Her little screen held the photo that she had shot of Robert and I looking into each other's eyes. The connection between the two of us was obvious. One could even say that we looked in love. But what you couldn't ignore was the fact that we both seemed to glow. It gave the picture a very ethereal quality, and the irony was almost too much for me.

"Isn't it beautiful?" Janice proclaimed, and showed it to Dad, who nodded in agreement. "I'm going to definitely print this one up. Want to take one more?"

"Okay, let's go, Robert," I cried, and grabbed his hand, dragging him towards the door.

"Hold on, kiddo, you have to say goodbye to your old man, first," Dad called out.

I stopped moving and turned around, not really wanting to have to look into his face and see the tears that had been threatening to fall earlier. I was almost out of the house, tear free!

Dad pulled me into another fierce hug, oblivious to what the sudden motion was doing to my hair, or my dress. I was, too, but the feminine instinct that seemed to suddenly appear as soon as my hair or dress was threatened caused me pull back and utter words I never imagined I'd ever say. "Careful, Dad, you might mess my hair and dress up."

He sighed, and let me go. "You're right. Go on. Have fun. I won't wait up."

I kissed his cheek. "Thanks, Dad."

And in a flash, we were outside, standing in the driveway. It had happened so fast, I was almost certain that Dad probably still thought we were standing next to him.

Feeling amused by that thought, I looked at Robert, finally able to appreciate the way his liquid eyes shimmered and rippled like two silver pools. "So, how exactly are we going to get to this wedding?"

He raised his eyebrows and looked at the street, causing me to follow his gaze. A black car pulled up then. I didn't know what kind of car it was. All I knew was that it was shiny, black, sleek, and here. Someone stepped out of the driver's side and walked around it, deftly opening the rear passenger door, and waited for Robert and I to enter.

The driver wore an all-black suit, and he had a severe look to him. I looked at Robert again, the question already in my head.

"No. He's not one of my kind. He's just a very loyal friend."

I nodded and allowed him to lead me towards the car. He

helped me get my dress and my cast inside of the vehicle and climbed in after me, the door closing behind him. As we pulled away from my house, I took a good look at what we were riding in and, as it had been doing a lot these past few weeks, my jaw once again dropped in a dramatic fashion.

"Oh dear bananas, do you know what kind of car this is?" I looked at him, feeling immediately stupid because of course he knew what car this was.

Everyone knew what kind of car this was. It wasn't like a Mercedes or a BMW, two brands that had become quite common in certain areas of Heath. Oh no. One look at the solitary B in the emblem gave it away quite easily. These weren't common in Heath, much less the whole of Ohio. And I was now riding in one. "How fitting that we should be riding in a vehicle with wings in its logo," I murmured.

MIXED COMPANY

My knees were shaking so badly by the time we pulled into the road leading to the Bellegarde family retreat that I had to physically hold them still with my hands. I didn't know why I was so nervous, but a stray thought that had been floating around in my head hinted to me that tonight wasn't going to be a typical first date. Not that a typical first date included riding around in a vehicle that cost more than the average house in Heath was worth, with a bona fide angel to boot, but because I simply did not know what to expect.

I had no experience when it came to dating, but I knew that tonight wasn't going to be your average dinner and a movie kind of evening. We were going to a wedding for the granddaughter of someone that Robert had known when they were young. This meant that this person knew that something was different about him, and probably knew a great deal more about him than I did.

Aside from his family and others of his kind, I had held the thought that I was the only other person who knew what he was like a badge of honor, a rare and special prize that was mine and mine alone. To know that I was just one of several felt like I was being robbed of something, even though whatever it was could never be as tangible and real as what I felt every time Robert looked at me.

And he was looking at me now, his eyes full of humor, as though he knew something that I did not. But, of course he did. He always would. That was one of the many prices one had to pay when they befriended something as wonderful and magical as an angel.

"I know you hear my thoughts. Just come out and say whatever it is that you're thinking," I told him, not exactly thrilled that he hadn't done so yet.

"I don't know what exactly to think," he replied, although judging by the way he was smiling, he had already thought of a lot. "I

266

will say that I'm getting closer and closer to figuring out how you manage to keep me from reading your thoughts."

My eyes grew large in surprise. "Really? How?"

"I'll let you know when I'm certain. Until then, I have a question I'd like to ask you.

I held my breath, and waited.

"I was wondering if you'd like me to remove your casts."

The air came out of me slowly, as though I were deflating. I nodded my head before really thinking about the consequences, and then decided that I simply didn't care what the consequences were. Oh to have freedom of movement! I twisted my body around in the seat, pulled up the hem of the dress and laid my leg in his lap. I pointed to it with my casted hand, "Can you start with that."

He laughed. "I can always feel your annoyance when you think about them, but I'm going to have to put them back on before I bring you home. I'm just taking them off for tonight."

"So my freedom will turn into a prison again at midnight. All I need is a pumpkin and some mice and I'm all set," I responded.

"And what shall I turn into when the clock strikes twelve?" he asked, his eyes twinkling at me in the darkness of the car as his hands skimmed my toes peeking out from the footed part of the cast.

"Nothing. There is no midnight when it comes to you," I breathed. Or, rather, I didn't, because right then I felt a strange tingle run up the back of my leg, as though someone had drawn a line running from my ankle to my thigh with a feather. "Oh!" I squirmed, the sensation was so...odd.

I looked at Robert's hands, and saw that he was tapping the cast at the base of my heel. Only, the tapping was very, very fast, the movement nearly imperceptible. I only noticed it because I could feel it. The cast was great at enhancing the vibrations the tapping created. And then he stopped. I inhaled, the rush of air filling my lugs to near bursting, and then I blew it all out in a gasp of shock when he lifted the cast off of my leg in one piece, although split open along the back, the front looking like it had been hinged.

"H-h-how'd you do that?"

"A magician never reveals his secrets." He waggled his eyebrows at me, and smiled.

"Ugh, what is that smell?!" My nose wrinkled up as the pungent odor assailed my senses.

He laughed. "That's coming from you."

I scoffed, offended, "It is not!"

He pointed to my leg, which was looking rather sickly pale, and…grotesquely hairy, and smiled. "I'm afraid it is. The cast has done wonders to make your leg a breeding ground of odor causing bacteria."

I realized he was right. Offended and offensive. Great. What a way to start off a first date. Embarrassed, I groaned. "What am I going to do? I can't go to the wedding smelling and looking like road kill!"

"Shh. Don't worry. Let me take care of it," he whispered, and held my foot in his hands.

I stared in muted shock as he brought my foot to his mouth, holding it steady when I tried to jerk it away. He exhaled on it, sending a shiver up my leg and straight to that part of my stomach that made funny little leaps every time he touched me or looked at me in a certain way, only this time, my stomach didn't just take a tiny leap, it did a triple jump, landing somewhere in my chest next to my rapidly beating heart.

I remembered him doing the same thing on my hand after I had burned it that first day after we'd met, and the blisters had just disappeared. But what could that same ability do to a dank, swampy leg? That was abysmally hairy?

I felt the strange tingling start at the very tip of my smallest toe. It was like a fly was sitting there, and then it was walking across the span of my toes, each tiny footstep leaving permanent prints on my skin that pulsed and throbbed in ever widening circles.

I watched, awestruck as my leg started to change in color, the pale, moist skin turning from nearly translucent to a far more normal pinkish beige. I felt my eyes ratchet even wider as I watched the patches of hair seem to retreat back into my skin. I looked back into his face, "Wha-how?"

He smiled, and pulled the edge of my dress down, covering my now cast free, and strangely sweet smelling leg. He reached for my arm and repeated the rapid tapping on my elbow. When it, too, had been split open, the same awful smell assailed my nose. As he had with my foot, Robert brought my hand up to his mouth and exhaled on it.

I started to pull my hand away, wanting to bring my arm right to my face, to witness the change as closely as possible, but he tightened his grip on my hand. I watched him as he brought my hand back to his mouth, and he kissed the tips of my fingers. He placed my hand on his cheek and sighed. "I think you feel things better through your right hand than you do with your left. It's more sensitive."

I couldn't respond. I hadn't been able to discern any real difference between the way my right hand felt in comparison to my left. And, in all honesty, it didn't matter which hand was doing it; I could only feel the hammering of my heart and the gymnastic stunts my stomach was performing whenever I was touching Robert, or he was touching me.

He chuckled at my thoughts, and I looked away, embarrassed as always. An awkward silence followed, and remained there, heavy, until the car finally stopped moving, and the passenger side door opened. After he placed my casts on the floor, he stepped out of the car. He turned around and held his hand out to me.

It was then that I realized I only had one shoe on.

"Robert, I-" he held up his hand, stopping my obvious announcement.

The front passenger side door opened and shut very quickly, only being slowed down by the physics of the door itself, and not by the individual opening it. Then Robert was on one knee in front of me, placing the other sandal on my bare foot.

"How—what—where—when?" I stuttered, feeling absolutely foolish but unable to stop myself as my eyes flicked from the sandal to his face, and back.

"You forgot who and why," he teased. When he was satisfied that the sandal was buckled securely, he pulled me out of the car. "Ready, Cinderella?"

Just as it had been when we'd last been here, there was a large

269

tent filled with lights that sat over fully set tables and chairs. This time, however, there were strips of shimmering bronze fabric running down the tables and tied to the chairs, like ribbons adorning a present.

The flower arrangements on each table were large glass trees that held dark orange and bright pink blossoms; crystal drops were dangling from each branch. There appeared to be bright pink boxes at each place setting, their bows looking like bronze firecracker explosions, and I didn't think that after tonight I'd ever want to sit at a table that didn't have the very same centerpiece or place setting.

Shaking his head at my thoughts, Robert pulled me towards a smaller tent set up near the gazebo. It, too, had been decorated in bronze, pink, and orange, with crystals dangling everywhere. There were chairs set up facing the gazebo, and I assumed that's where the wedding would be taking place.

The majority of the seats had been filled, but Robert wasn't taking me to sit down. He was taking me towards someone. The murmurs of acknowledgement and excitement couldn't be missed as we passed row after row, stopping at the first one where one chair had been removed to allow for a deceptively frail looking woman and her wheelchair.

She looked up from her conversation with the woman next to her and smiled, the creases around her startling blue eyes deepening with her obvious joy at seeing Robert. "Robbie! I was wondering if you'd get here in time! And at last I get to meet your Grace!" She looked at me, her eyes full of warmth and welcome. "I've seen your face so many times, but I must say that his thoughts don't do you any justice."

I smiled at her compliment, not wanting to tell her that all the images in his mind were of the normal, everyday me. The Grace standing in front of her was an anomaly, but she didn't need to know that.

Robert bent down on one knee and took the woman's hand, which seemed so small and fragile in his, I was afraid he'd break it. He raised it to his lips and kissed it reverently. He looked into her eyes and grinned, then looked at me. "Grace, this is Eloise MacInherney. She's the friend whose granddaughter is getting married tonight."

"It's nice to meet you, Mrs. MacInherney," I said.

"Oh pish, it's Ellie to you and everyone else who matters," she replied, waving her hand at my formality. "I'm so glad you could come tonight. It's always good to be around family and friends."

I looked around at the guests in attendance and realized, oddly, that no one looked familiar. Heath wasn't exactly a small town, but with so many people here I thought I'd at least see one person that I'd recognize. Instead the faces belonged to strangers. With the exception of two who were standing off to the side, conspicuous as always.

Lark and Ameila both nodded at me and smiled. Lark, beautiful in an ivory gown, looked amused, while Ameila, who resembled a rare jewel in her blood red dress that pooled on the floor beneath her feet, looked concerned although I probably only noticed that because I had seen the same looks on their faces before. While no longer concerned as much about Lark's opinion of me, considering the great leaps we'd made since our first meeting, the way Ameila seemed to stare at me with a mixture of pity, sadness, and concern made me feel wholly inadequate.

Lark, having heard my thoughts, turned to look at her mother. Ameila made no show in trying to hide her emotions, and that seemed to upset Lark, who shook her head and started stomping towards us, her feet leaving distinct and deep impressions in the grass behind her.

"Lark is on the warpath," Ellie remarked.

Robert didn't need to turn around and look for himself to see that she was right, but he did so anyway. He then looked at me, and shook his head. "Mother's not upset about you and I being here, Grace. Someone else is here that she did not expect to arrive."

I didn't understand. Who could be here that would upset Ameila?

Ellie shook her head as well. "Sam. It's got to be Sam."

Sam? "Who's Sam?" I asked, obviously out of the loop and not liking it.

Larks voice behind me answered, "Sam is sort of like our adopted brother, and a pain in the a-"

"Lark!" Robert hissed, cutting her off.

271

Lark smiled. "He's also Robert's best friend, and a complete piece of sh-"

"LARK!"

Sighing, Lark walked away. *I don't need to say it for it to be true.*

I couldn't help but giggle at that, and then tried desperately to stop myself when I saw the look in Robert's face.

"Sam's not that bad of a lot, really," Ellie said, her eyes misty from trying to fight the humor herself. "He's just a bit rough around the edges. Like a cookie. A salty, slightly over baked cookie, but still, you know what it's supposed to be, and with enough milk, you might even be able to enjoy it."

Tucking my lips between my teeth to keep from bursting out into full blown laughter, I nodded my head. It was the only response I risked giving, not wanting to take the chance that anything more would release the floodgates, and I'd be unable to control myself. And in front of so many strangers.

Someone in a long, fuchsia dress tapped Ellie on her shoulder and whispered something in her ear. She nodded, and raised her hand in some sort of signal. I tried to look at who it was she was signaling, but in the same time it took me to think about the action, I was no longer near her, but in a seat somewhere in the back, Robert sitting serenely next to me, his hand holding mine.

"What was that?" I asked, the sudden change of scenery causing my heart to race in surprise.

"The ceremony is about to start," he answered, and patted my hand.

A voice so incredibly lovely began singing what would later be described as "the most romantic of all arias", and the procession of bridesmaids and groomsmen began. The woman who had been wearing the fuchsia dress appeared to have been the maid of honor, as she was the last to appear before the bride.

She was dressed in a very simple spaghetti strap dress that was made to resemble a mermaid's shape. She had a soft, gauzy veil over her hair that was held in place by a very whimsical tiara made of pearls and fuchsia and orange crystals. It stood out dramatically against her dark hair, but did not look out of place.

She was smiling, looking at the man who waited for her in the gazebo ahead. He wore a black tuxedo with—I snorted—bright orange high-top sneakers. This was obviously a couple who enjoyed life, and liked to have fun.

It was only then that I noticed who was walking her down the aisle. I mouthed his name, my shock keeping me from doing anything else. The murmurs of awe and praise in the bride and her escort were travelling up and down the aisles, and no one seemed to find fault in the arrangement.

"Beautiful, isn't she?" a voice next to me asked.

I turned to stare into a pair of golden eyes that sat in one of the most handsome faces I'd ever seen. He had hair the same golden color, and it traveled in waves past his shoulders. He wore it loose, although it didn't seem to be threatening to do anything but look perfect. His smile was comforting, his lips curled up in an amused smile.

I knew he was an angel, too. There was simply no other explanation for his perfection, and no sense in denying it. "Yes, she is."

He nodded. "She looks just like her grandmother did all those many years ago. They possess the same spirit, you know—fiery and determined. It's no wonder that Rob's taken it upon himself to walk her down the aisle. It's like looking back some fifty, sixty years."

I turned to watch Rob place a kiss on the bride's cheek just before placing her hand in the groom's. He hesitated, almost like a reluctant father would, but then the transfer was complete and he was taking a seat. But it wasn't next to me.

"I'm sure he and Ellie never thought all those years ago that they'd be sitting here, attending a wedding together."

I shifted myself around to stare once again into the stranger's tawny eyes, suddenly feeling very uncomfortable. "Who are you, and how do you know so much about Ellie and Robert?"

He leaned back into his chair, his demeanor casual, relaxed, and answered with a knowing smile. "I'm Sam. And, little human girl, I know so much about Ellie and Rob because I was the one who introduced them. They really made a cute couple back then, but they weren't suited, him being an angel and all. But it's nice that they stayed friends, don't you think?"

I looked at him, unable to say anything. Smiling at my vocal paralysis, he continued. "I mean, imagine how hard it must have been, watching her marry someone else, have children, and…grow old. I can't imagine enduring that with someone I professed to love."

I looked down in my lap, staring at my fingers. The same fingers Robert had kissed not too long ago in the car, kissed in the same way he'd kissed Ellie's hand…

I lifted my head and looked again at Sam. "I think it's very romantic, actually; I think that he must trust and care for me a lot to go to all this trouble to bring me here to meet her and her family."

I turned my back to him and tried to watch the rest of the ceremony, wondering the whole time if what I had said was true. I could see Sam staring at me out of the corner of my eye, his expression confused, his mouth no longer curved into a smile. Good. I hope he was hearing Lark's thoughts about him, and I hope he was hearing the uncensored version.

When the officiate announced that the groom could now kiss the bride, a great whoop of joy filled the night and to my surprise, the bride dipped her groom, planting a very silly, yet loving kiss on his lips before shouting, "I've got you now!" Everyone around me laughed. Well…almost everyone.

Sam's face was still. It was like the joy that was flowing through the tent was just passing around him instead of being absorbed like it was with everyone else. I couldn't understand how he could simply ignore the immense amount of affection that was radiating out, like he was numb to emotion as well as physical feeling.

"Are you ready for the reception, Grace?"

I turned to see Robert standing next to me, the row of seats now completely empty save for me and, I turned to look at Sam…he was gone! I looked up at Robert, wondering if he'd seen his brother sitting next to me, heard our conversation. So many questions were in my mind, in my eyes, and the only one that he answered was the only one that I really wanted to know.

"Grace, please understand that I was never in love with Eloise. I loved her, of course I did. She was electus patronus; it's our duty to-"

"Electus what-us? What are you talking about?" I interrupted.

"The electus patronus are the chosen guardians, those of certain families that have been selected to protect our identities, ease our way in your human world. Those whom are here today have a family history that is about as long and old as this country, but they are merely the finger in the hand of those who seek to keep our secrets safe. They are, in essence, our human family."

"And Ellie was—is—an electus patronus," I said, rather than asked, because he had already stated so.

"Yes," he replied, "She's been one since she was eighteen. I met her for the first time on her nineteenth birthday, when mother, Lark, and I returned from a trip to Europe. She was new, and sweet, and vivacious. And, she knew everything that a human can learn about us so there were no secrets to keep, which made talking to her easy. She made it easy to love her.

"But love isn't a guarantee to happiness. Obviously we weren't suited, and definitely not destined. She was looking for a complete future for herself, one that included marriage, and children, and housewarming parties. I couldn't offer those things to her, whether I wanted to or not, because those things are reserved for a special kind of love—the kind for hearts that are destined for each other, that have room inside of them for more than ambition and duty. I tried to say that I wanted all of the same things that she did, but I couldn't. I cannot lie.

"But, Ellie wasn't angry, or hurt. She was devoted to her role as protector, committed, but she wanted a family, too. She never questioned my decision to end our relationship, and, as she told me after the birth of her daughter, she was thankful to me for not being able to lie to her about what I wanted and give her a fool's hope."

I was, too. I was incredibly, insanely, intensely glad.

He sat down next to me, chuckling as he did so, and motioned towards the larger tent where the guests were all seated, the celebratory atmosphere quite evident. "Everyone in there is either electus patronus or one of my kind. We are all tied together by birth, by blood, by right, by duty, and most importantly, by faith.

"You are the only one here who isn't one of my kind or one of theirs and they all know it. One of the reasons why I brought you here was because you mean a great deal to me, and I wanted everyone here to know that."

"Including Ellie?" I asked.

"*Especially* Ellie. But, more importantly, I wanted *you* to know that. By bringing you here, I'm bringing you into *my* world. I've told you some secrets, but this one involves more than just me, Grace. Your knowing about this lets them know that I trust you enough to have put not just my entire life, but theirs as well in your hands. You're safe here."

The enormity of his trust in me made me speechless. His secret wasn't just *his* secret to me anymore. It was one that was shared by many, only they knew much, much more than I did. What else did they know? Did they like the fact that I now knew about them? And more importantly, was I deserving of that trust?

And then, as if I were struck by lightning, the dawning of a simple truth hit me. "You brought me here to protect me."

THE FUDGESICLE AND DAFFODIL EXPERIMENT

He smiled, glad for my revelation. "Yes. Until you had been introduced to everyone, you'd always be considered a threat."

"But why?"

"Because, quite simply, you mean more to me than just a moment of physical feeling. You've touched my existence in a way that very few have, and you know that we angels are emotional beings—the slightest switch in how we feel can result in either incredible creation or great destruction. You don't know to what extent our strength and our abilities go-"

"Because you haven't told me," I interjected.

"Well, true, I haven't. You only know bits and pieces about us, and I apologize for the neglect in that area. I owe you so much more in the way of being forthcoming, and I will be. But that is for later. Tonight is about other things."

I couldn't help but ask, "What other things?"

"It has a lot to do with Ellie, and you especially. I wanted a human's advice about you, advice I could trust, because I don't understand your mind, your thoughts. You think differently from everyone else, and I'm not talking about opinions and morals. I'm talking about the actual way you think. You're a lot like us in some ways, because you actually compartmentalize your thoughts, put things in their own individual areas while thinking; you think about many things all at once, which is fascinating to find in a human.

"It's also why you're able to hide your thoughts. I figured it out while Sam was talking to you. You were thinking about so many things already, and when he told you about Ellie, it was like your mind had split into four corners. The emotional, rational, logical, and cynical parts of your brain were warring with each other; it's like you have a mental referee who separated them, and the empty space that lay in between was all that I could see and hear." Robert looked at me with amazement shining in his eyes, and I felt almost like some kind of science experiment that just won a ribbon at a fair.

"But, if you can't see or hear anything, how do you know that's how it is?" I asked, skeptical, but then again, I couldn't see in my own head the same things he did. My memories were all in 2D while he could see everything in 4D.

Robert's smug smile left me breathless as he answered my question, "I think it's because you're beginning to trust me. Either that or I've started recognizing the signs, and can find a way to cling onto a thought in your mind until you've designated a place for it to go."

"Robert," I started, "I'm not sure I understand…"

The smug smile became sweet, and spread across his face. "Let's try a little experiment. We'll start with something simple. I'll give you two subjects, and I want to you think about both of them and then I want you to think about something else, anything."

I nodded my head, and closed my eyes, preparing myself for whatever it was that he'd throw my way. "Think about…fudgesicles and daffodils."

I wanted to say something about the ridiculousness of those two items combined, but chose not to. Instead, I thought about the frozen, fudge-flavored treats and the bright yellow flowers that were prevalent in Ohio—I thought about how much damage a melted fudgesicle could do to the dress that Robert had bought, and how out of place a bouquet of daffodils would look placed next to the sticky stain. I pictured trying to get someone to dry clean the stain out and being told it cost more than my lab for Biology. Thinking of Biology made me picture Mr. Branke's face, and I suddenly felt ill.

"Grace?"

"Hmm?" I murmured, and realized that Robert was actually shaking me. I opened my eyes and took in the gleeful expression on his face.

"You did it!" Robert cheered, pride beaming from his smile. "That was amazing! At first, all I could see was the fudgesicle in your mind. The flowers appeared next, but then the two started to blend, and

278

things started getting darker; your mind had gone completely blank—as though it had tuned out completely—but I knew that it hadn't, because your face was so intense. And then it looked…well, positively green."

"Oh, I was thinking about Mr. Branke, and Biology class," my voice croaked, the nausea slowly creeping back into me by the mere mentioning of his name.

I saw liquid eyes turn solid as he understood the change in my mood. "He makes all of the girls uncomfortable. You're not alone in your opinion of him."

I gave a shrug. "It's not like that makes it any less creepy. Anyway, can we not talk about Mr. Branke, or school, or anything else right now?" I eyed the waiters coming out to serve dinner under the large tent and my stomach growled. Loudly.

He laughed and nodded his understanding. "Come, hungry one. Let's feed you before the dancing begins. We can talk more afterwards." He pulled me up and started leading me towards the intoxicating smell of food!

Thankfully, seating assignments were taken very seriously by angel and electus patronus alike—apparently the whole honesty thing kept anyone from taking someone else's spot—so our seats were still free when we sat down next to Lark and Ameila. I was introduced to several of the individuals on the table with us, amazed at who was and who wasn't an angel. It appeared that the electus patronus were all beautiful as well, their only give away being how they reacted to the heat of their dinner and the chill of their drinks.

One person in particular whom I had been told was an angel visiting from France was exceptionally beautiful, even for an angel, with silvery hair that had been braided into glistening ropes that were piled high atop of her head, swooping down in elegant arabesques that framed her extraordinary face.

She had alabaster skin—so perfect and flawless it was almost transparent—and her lips were stained strawberry pink, lush and always lifted up in a smile. What was most striking, however, was the color of her eyes. I had seen the silver of Robert's, and now the gold of Sam's, but for the first time, I took in the glorious sparkle of violet eyes.

They were filled with amusement as she took in my examination of her, and I felt myself flush in embarrassment at having been caught staring.

Her hand graced mine lightly, the briefest of touches, before she turned away to speak to the individual on her opposite side. I watched her for a few moments more, mesmerized by her, by everything there was about her. The way her laughter made her head toss back with careless beauty, the way her hands moved in such an animated way as she spoke that they demanded almost as much attention as her lilting voice did. She appeared so young, so youthful and yet she had an air about her that seemed older and wiser than even Ameila, who looked— in human years anyway—several years older.

"Do angels age?" I asked Robert when I could finally tear my eyes away from the silver-haired goddess.

Robert reached for my hand under the table and squeezed it, a jolt of energy and feeling turning my stomach inside out and sending my heart into a race to keep up with the wishes I silently made as I waited for him to answer.

"We can if we want to. I don't have to look like this; I could look much older if I wished, but I've found this age to be much easier to live with—humans are more amenable to youth I've found. Why do you ask?"

I flicked my eyes at the different faces that surrounded us, angel and human alike, avoiding the one next to me and whispered, "I didn't know…your mother can change forms, so I thought the reason she looked old enough to be your mother was because of that. I took it for granted that the rest of you would look young as well."

"It's ok. You're not the first person to ask that question, and you definitely won't be the last. Ahh, here comes our server." He smiled and squeezed my hand again, then released it when the food arrived. I groaned when I saw the paltry amount of food on my plate. My stomach was growling for super-sized something—anything—and instead it appeared that all I'd be eating for dinner was your basic micro-diet sized morsels.

I eyed everyone else on the table, all too deeply invested in their own mental conversations to really notice the expanse of bare plates in front of them. Oh, they were eating, but there could have been raw slugs on their plates and they wouldn't have noticed, too engrossed in discussing electus patronus type things most likely—things that I was still woefully ignorant about. Even Robert was heavy occupied in a silent conversation with his family. I could tell simply by how they were leaning in towards each other, their eyes flitting from one to the other like glowing silver fireflies.

I ate in silence, suddenly feeling far more out of place here than I ever had in school. Sure, I looked like they did, dressed to the nines in an expensive gown, shoes, jewelry. But I was just playing a role after all, while this was their life.

I was very limited when it came to my knowledge about angels; all I knew was what I had been told, and since the few angels that I knew had made it quite clear that all of my preconceived notions were false, what I did know to be true was pretty sparse, and could never compare to what the electus patronus knew.

Suddenly curious, I wanted to know what exactly they did know. If there was ever a better time to get as much information about angels from a human perspective, now would be it. And, I knew just who to ask. That was one reason why I had been brought here after all, right? Not feeling the need to excuse myself, since no one seemed to be paying attention anyway, I stood up and started looking for the person who would have answers to my questions.

It wasn't that difficult to find her. She was the only one there in a wheelchair, her white hair piled beautifully on her head in a bun that resembled a very large, round, iced cinnamon roll.

"Ellie?" I said softly, not really wanting to disturb her as she sat away from everyone else, watching her granddaughter and new grandson-in-law as they shared a private conversation.

She turned her head around and smiled when she saw me. "Ah, Grace, come-" she patted a chair that was next to her "-sit down and let's have a chat, shall we?"

I did as she asked, quite pleased that she seemed as interested in talking as I was.

"You see my Hannah over there?" she motioned towards the bride. "She's the tenth generation of MacInherney to be an electus patronus. Her grandfather would be so proud."

I looked at her face intently, watching it grow a little sad, her eyes growing a bit glassy with newly formed tears that begged to fall. She wiped them away as she began to speak. "Lawrence, my husband, well, he was the only one of his siblings who had passed the test, you see, and when we had our only child, Olivia, we were very disappointed when she announced to us that she didn't even want to take the test. She said she didn't believe in the existence of God anymore, and that there was no reason to believe in his servants if there was no God.

"That nearly killed my Lawrence, it did. He was not the same man after that. We electus patronus are nothing if not faithful, so the loss of faith among us can be very heartbreaking."

I raised my hand a bit, needing her to answer something. "What test?"

She laughed at her omission. "Oh dear, you don't know? The test, well, it's pretty straightforward. We're asked what the worst thing that we've done is. Do you see how simple it is? How absolutely simple?"

I nodded. Of course it was perfect in its simplicity. When one had the ability to run through your entire life in a matter of seconds, view your every deed, good and bad, and then asked you what the worst thing you've ever done was, any answer that was a lie would be denounced on the spot.

"The mind is an amazing thing, Grace. When we form a memory, the first imprint that burns itself into our mind, the image that is created before we can form an opinion about it, well…that remains forever; that's the true memory. Over time, we see it as something different because age and perception blurs the lines a bit, even changes it completely, but when the time comes for the test, we *have* to see things clearly, see things the way that they're supposed to be and not how we want them to be, otherwise we'll give the wrong answer."

"Do you mind if I ask you what your answer was?" I asked anxiously.

"Why, of course I don't mind. I might be a little vain, and maybe even a little prideful, but not so much that I cannot admit to doing something very, very wrong and without any real justification whatsoever.

"Quite frankly, dear, I only wanted to follow in my parents' and my siblings' footsteps because I foolishly wanted to marry an angel. I told them something completely different, of course, because I didn't want them to hound me with talk of duty and obligation, but the truth was there in my head, clear as day.

"I lied about so many things during those days. Oh, I was terrible back then, a regular little hellion! When it finally came time for the test, I was surprised that my family would be there—that had never happened before—and I knew when I opened my mouth to answer that the worst thing that I had ever done was hurt them with my lies. I broke their hearts, but I also redeemed myself by being honest about it," Ellie sighed, a wistful look in her eyes.

"That must have burned one heck of a memory into your mind," I quipped and she clapped her hands, laughing loudly with little care to who heard or saw. I envied her that freedom.

"Oh, Grace. You've got wit. That's good. It's hard to find true wit in your generation. Too many smart mouths, not enough smart minds."

"Thank you," I said, smiling awkwardly at her compliment. "Do you mind if I ask you a few more questions?" I asked, my voice pleading, not wanting to miss this opportunity now that I knew she was so willing to share.

Ellie patted my knee and laughed softly. "Dearest Grace, ask me anything. I may not suffer pain like our sweet angels when they lie, but my conscience pricks when I do, so if you have any fears about that, don't worry about it."

I swallowed that bit of information and quickly ran down my mental list of questions I wanted—no, needed—answers to. There were so many, but the first one came up rather quickly, and I was ashamed at its existence, since it had not even been a thought until Sam had planted its seed during the ceremony.

"Are you still in love with Robert?" my voice was crisp, the hidden message in my tone was clear.

Ellie tittered. "Oh dear, I loved him, but I was never *in* love with Robert. He is lovely, I won't ever deny that, but he and I would have never suited."

I recalled Sam having said so, but pressed further, "What do you mean, you 'would have never suited'?"

"Quite simply, my life was moving forward, and his was stuck in the fifth century," she answered. "I wanted to get married, have children, have a home. Robbie couldn't give me those things. He wanted to make me happy, but he simply couldn't give me what I wanted. So, I found my future with someone else, and I haven't regretted it once."

I studied her smile and saw that it hinted at sadness, despite her claim of having no regret. "Has it been hard, growing old and watching him not age a single day even though he could if he wanted?"

She nodded, her chin quivering a bit. "I don't want you to think it's because I wish to be with him. Rather, it's because I know that there will be so much that I'll miss. I wouldn't even be here today if not for Robbie. He saved my life."

I reached for her hand and patted it, knowing exactly how she felt. "He saved mine, too."

She looked at me, her blue eyes gazing at me with such intensity, I wanted to look away, but I didn't. "Sweet child, I meant that he saved my life for one day. I've got a get out of jail free card, and it's only good for this one night."

I didn't understand what she meant by that, and told her so. She removed her hand from beneath mine, only to place hers on top. "Grace, by this time tomorrow, I shall be with my Lord, and I'll have gone knowing that I was able to see my granddaughter marry her prince charming. That was all that I had ever asked for in life, and it was Robbie that made sure it would happen. He's a miracle. A walking miracle, that boy is."

"I still don't understand, Ellie. What did Robert do?"

"He postponed my death, Grace. I don't know how he did it,

and I thought I knew why-" she motioned to her granddaughter, who was now in the middle of what seemed like a shrimp eating contest with several bridesmaids and her new husband "-but seeing you, seeing how Robbie looks at you, I see that I was wrong. He's very taken with you, you know."

I blushed at that. It was definitely something that I could see myself being comfortable with. "So he's told me."

"Cherish that, Grace. When an angel looks at a human that way, it's forever. Angels look perfect, but they're incomplete."

My confusion at what she said must have amused her because she gave me a knowing smile which made her eyes twinkle with mischief.

"Now then, those can't be the only questions you have to ask. Please. Ask me anything. It's the least I can do to repay Robbie for allowing me this one night," she said sweetly, her smile no longer tinged with sadness.

I inhaled deeply, and asked her the first of what would compile the longest list of questions in the history of the world. Or at least, that's how I looked at it. "What exactly are the angels' secrets that need guarding?"

Ellie looked at me and smiled. "You mean other than the fact that not only do they exist, but that they live amongst us like normal people?"

If I hadn't known she was a human, I would have sworn she was an angelic mind reader she was so spot-on with that reply.

"Well, I'm sure you've already figured out one major one; the angels aren't perfect. Imagine the uproar in the church if it were to be found out that not only were angels singing in rock bands, or were standing up in front of congress, but they were also somewhat promiscuous?" she winked.

"Why? Why are they like that?" I leaned towards her, not wanting to miss a single word of her answer. I felt like a starving child, snatching at the bread crumbs that Ellie was handing out.

She held out her hands, examining them for a moment, then reached out and held mine. "Because of this. Did anyone explain to you about the differences between a juvenile angel and those that have ascended?"

I racked my mind through all of the things that I had been told, by Robert, by Ameila, by Lark…two things stood out. "I want to say that the juveniles don't have wings…and haven't received the call."

"Yes. But it is also because they cannot feel anything…physical," and she could tell by my reaction that I was aware of that, too. She continued, "Juvenile angels are such extraordinary creatures, with unbelievable strength and ability, but their one weakness is that they cannot feel joy and pleasure the way the ascended can, the way we can, and it deprives them of that emotion. So, they proceed to induce that feeling by giving it to someone else-"

I nodded my head, remembering what Robert had told me about feeling his touch through my mind, as opposed to through his own skin. The thought was still unsettling.

"-And that feeling can be very addictive. It can be like a drug to some juveniles, male and female alike. They crave it, how it makes their bodies feel, how it makes their minds suddenly free of thought. The ascended, they have a purpose. The juveniles, well…they don't, other than to wait for the call."

I didn't know my jaw had been open until she had released one of my hands and pushed my chin up, effectively closing my mouth. Was Robert one of those…addicts? My eyes, which I was fairly certain were at max capacity with regards to how wide they could be, suddenly found an extra millimeter or two to open at the thought. Surely he'd never tell me, because I had never asked, but was he?

"Oh Grace, I know what you're thinking, and while Robert may have appreciated being with women and appreciated their thoughts about him, he certainly never became like some of the others," Ellie said, patting my hand, trying to comfort me.

"How can you be so sure?" I asked, not feeling comforted at all.

She stopped the patting, and removed her hands from me, her smile gone, "Because he told me." She was offended.

Of course she would be. Angels couldn't lie. If he had told her, it was the truth, and irrefutable. "I'm sorry. I should have remembered."

She sighed, "I understand why you are so doubtful, Grace. You grew up in a world where things like angels didn't exist, and truth and honesty are dead virtues that belong to no one. But, I do hope that you now see that neither is true.

"I don't envy you, having to be pulled into this world without knowing anything about it, and having so much of this burden of truth be placed on your head. But, I guarantee you that it will be worth it. Robbie is special. Even among his kind," she said, smiling while looking past me.

I felt the gentle hand upon my shoulder and looked up into his eyes. Of course they were his eyes. It could only be him standing next to me, and I knew Ellie was right. It will be worth it.

"How are you two beautiful ladies doing?" he asked, but only looking at me.

"Haven't you been needling around in our heads, Robbie?" Ellie laughed, "Did you come to make sure that I didn't chase young Grace here off, or did you come here to ask one of us to dance?"

He laughed, his eyes twinkling. "Ellie, if you don't mind, I'd like to take Grace for a spin around the floor first."

She waved her hand as if to dismiss us. "Go on, have fun! I'm no good at these new dances anyway. Too much oomph, not enough cha cha."

Robert's laugh grew louder, his perfect teeth shining bright white, his whole body shaking with his amusement. "There'll never be enough cha cha for you, Ellie." He bent down and kissed the hand that she offered to him. "I shall return for a dance with the second most beautiful woman here, so please save one for me."

I had to admit, Robert did know how to win over the ladies. I could feel mine, but I was thoroughly impressed when I saw Ellie's blush creep up her neck and slowly bloom across her cheeks. It was apparent that it had been a while since someone had made her feel— well…like a school girl. And who better to do that than someone who had known her when she *was* just a school girl?

Leading me onto the temporary dance floor that was crowded

287

with party guests, Robert swung me out, then with a sharp tug pulled me back in, causing me to spin into a very tight embrace, one hand holding mine clasped against my heart, the other placed at the small of my back, my free hand falling naturally onto his shoulder. "I know you haven't had much fun so far this evening," he whispered into my ear, "but I do plan on making sure that the rest of it is pleasant, if not thoroughly enjoyable."

"Robert, it doesn't matter what we do. If I'm with you, it's already enjoyable," I promised. I rested my head against his chest, listening to the beating of his heart, and wondered what exactly was beneath the skin and bones that caused that beautiful rhythm.

It's my heart. It is the same as yours.

I shook my head. *No it isn't. Your heart has beaten for fifteen hundred years—and will continue to beat for at least another fifteen hundred—while mine will be lucky to beat for as long as Ellie's has.*

He kissed my hair and then pressed his cheek against my head. *I will see to it that it beats for as long as possible.*

I smiled. Of course he would. *This is nice.*

What is?

This, my first dance...our first dance. I think I expected it to be awkward and clumsy, and instead it feels like I've been doing this for as long as you have.

I could feel his body shake slightly as he laughed.

I lifted my head from his chest, looking at his amused face. *Why are you laughing?*

I think I was expecting the same thing.

My mouth opened in a mock gasp. *So little faith in my dancing abilities?*

He smiled. *More like so little faith in* my *ability to cover up the fact that I had so little faith in your dancing abilities. That, and I wasn't so sure I'd be able to heal my feet. You've got big feet; I should know, I bought the shoes you're wearing tonight.*

I laughed and then shrieked as he spun us around very quickly. *Stop! You're going to make me dizzy!* I started laughing hysterically as he spun us faster, my head falling back, my hair coming loose of its pins.

He slowed and soon, we were simply rocking in a slow, gentle motion. *I thought I was making you dizzy.*

Giggling, I nodded my head before placing it back on his chest. "I think that no matter what you were doing, you'd make me dizzy," that last bit coming out in a breathy gasp.

Resting his chin on my head, he sighed. *I know what you mean.*

I felt my hand creep up to his neck, my fingers searching for the pulse point there that would echo the beat I heard in his chest. *You mean you make yourself dizzy, too?*

He laughed softly. *You silly girl. I meant that you leave me feeling very dizzy, too. It's a rather odd sensation; I'm sure that I'm going to need to feel it often in order to truly understand it.*

I felt his pulse quicken and that small piece of knowledge made me feel breathless indeed.

How strange. It's the opposite with me. When I'm not around you that is when I feel breathless. I liken it to being a fish, and you are my water. When I'm not around you, I feel as though I cannot breathe. And you have to understand the irony in that because I've never in my entire existence ever needed to.

I lifted my head up off of his chest again and searched his face. Confusion, amazement, and humor at what he had just revealed to me could be seen plainly. What I had to search for was hidden in his eyes. He looked frightened.

Robert placed his hand at the back of my head and pressed it back down to his chest, sighing wryly. *I am afraid. I don't understand the feeling, but it is there. I have never felt it before, and it is exhilarating and strange and confusing all at the same time. I have always seen fear in the minds of other people, but I have never been able to understand it because it is a foreign emotion to me, and because of that, I couldn't actually* feel *it. Does that make sense to you?*

I nodded, understanding it completely. He was supposed to be the epitome of empathy, and yet he couldn't empathize with the fearful because he had never been fearful himself. What did he have to be fearful of?

I don't know. So much of this is new to me. I brought you into my world thinking that I'd be changing your life, when the opposite is true; you have been changing mine in ways that time has never been able to. I can read and study the world and all of its inhabitants...but you've made me feel things that I didn't know I had it in me to feel. It's...strange.

I smiled. I was now the normal one, the one who was used to feeling something as trivial as fear, and he was the weird one. I felt his body shake once more with laughter and I sighed with contentment.

The hand that had been pressed against the back of my head lowered itself to the small of my back once again, and he pressed there, bringing me closer, embracing me in that moment of understanding. I nestled my face closer to his neck, wanting to smell his skin, lose myself in the scent and feel of him as we swayed slowly to the beat of music I couldn't hear because his voice was in my mind...and it was the only sound I ever wanted to hear again.

STRANGE HAPPENINGS

Bliss is always short lived. I read that on a fortune cookie once. I didn't think that would ever apply to me, since bliss wasn't exactly a feeling that *I* was familiar with, but dancing in Robert's arms proved to be as blissful as things could get at the moment, and like that tiny scrap of grease soaked paper predicted, it was short lived.

"May I cut in, brother?" a smooth, silky voice asked behind me, and I stiffened as recognition hit.

Robert eased his hold on me, nudging me to turn around, which I did. Slowly. Hesitatingly.

"Sam! I don't see why not. I did promise Ellie to dance with her next," Robert replied.

I did not want to go. I looked at their faces and knew that both of them knew that I did not want to. But neither of them had the nerve to refuse. Stupid angel etiquette.

"Fine, let's dance," I muttered.

Sam took my hand and placed it on his shoulder; he grabbed my other hand and raised it up, then started twirling us in large circles, his feet moving fairly quickly, and mine stumbling to keep up. He smiled brilliantly, and I was certain that anyone else would have looked at that smile and thought it the most beautiful sight they had ever seen, but to me, he looked like a shark. His teeth were gleaming, and sharp, and I would have bet money that had he opened his mouth, I'd have seen rows and rows of teeth on the ready right behind the ones up front.

I wanted to introduce him to Erica. They were both predatory creatures. Perhaps the larger shark would eat the smaller shark, and then the larger shark would get a serious case of indigestion and change his diet. I liked that idea. My smile reflected it.

He seemed to take that as a welcoming sign, and began talking. "I wanted to apologize for my lack of tact earlier. I shouldn't have been so forthcoming with information about Rob and Ellie's relationship. That was for the two of them to tell, not I."

I nodded my head, gritting my teeth as I did so, because I wasn't buying it for a second. I thought he knew it, too, until he started talking again.

"You don't—your mind isn't—you're a very quiet girl," he finally uttered, his expression one of confusion. I knew my face mirrored the exact same confusion because he continued, "I guess I can see why you fascinate Rob so. Your head is so empty of thoughts, it must seem like a sanctuary for him. It's…quiet in there."

My eyes grew wide as I recognized the signs. Sam couldn't hear my thoughts! He was trying, but he kept falling into the void, the "*empty ring*" in my mind when my thoughts had gone into their own corners! I felt absolutely giddy at the thought. Not wanting him to think I was a total idiot though, I concentrated on clearing my head of any thoughts completely.

I must have focused more energy in looking like I was concentrating than actually concentrating because soon, I was shaking with the vibrations from Sam's laughter. It was annoying.

"You are definitely an interesting girl." The way he said "*interesting*" sounded very insulting.

I tried not to look as exasperated as I felt, and realizing that it was practically impossible, I gave up. "Why am I an *interesting* girl?"

The smile on his face turned wry. "You just are. I wouldn't have ever expected you to be the type that Rob would choose, but you are definitely unique in your own way."

"How can someone *just be* interesting? Something has to make someone interesting. Like, being funny, smart, witty, or talented at something," I responded.

He shrugged his shoulders. "You're interesting because you are."

"And you, Sam, are absolutely *un*-interesting. For an angel, you are quite boring."

Again, he started laughing, throwing his head back and allowing his voice to carry out. And yet it was unremarkable. How is it that

292

someone so beautiful could be so...blah?

Not wanting to turn this into a who was more interesting contest, I decided to change the subject. "So, you're Robert's adopted brother. How? He's never mentioned you before."

"In your world, he would be known as my protégé, my pupil if you will. In ours, I'm his big brother. It is a title of familiarity, and so joins us, binds us to each other in the way that blood can't," he answered.

I thought about that for a bit. It seemed a bit ridiculous that the title alone would be enough to make them brothers. But the fact that an angel couldn't lie could not be ignored either. He had said that Robert was his brother. Lark and Robert had as well. "So, you're a part of the Robert package then?"

He nodded, smiling as he understood what I meant. "Yes. I am."

There was nothing for it. I was going to have to get used to the idea of Sam if I had any hope of Robert getting used to the idea of me. "Well then, Sam, I'm Grace. Nice to meet you," I took a step back and held out my hand.

Laughing once more, he took it and shook it, forcefully. "Pleased to make your acquaintance, Grace."

Unsure now how to proceed after such a sterile greeting, we both stared at each other in the middle of the dance floor while bodies moved around us in an organized jumble of limbs, skirts, and the occasional coattail. He smiled, seemingly pleased at how utterly confounded I was. "Would you like to continue our dance?" he asked, and smiled again when he knew that I would answer in the negative.

I started to walk away, the need to bathe on the forefront of my mind, when a strong, yet gentle set of hands pulled me into an unnatural spin, away from Sam, away from the crowd, and away from the dance floor. I saw a blur of black in my movement, felt the back of my hand scrape against something rough, but couldn't see who it was that had decided to be my savior until a few moments after I was allowed to sit down and hold my head still.

"Lark!" I wheezed. It was very difficult to focus on anything other than my feet, but I knew it was her by the color of her dress. "Aren't you supposed to wear a darker color than the bride?" I muttered, not exactly pleased with her near nausea inducing antics.

She snorted. "Like I'm supposed to take fashion advice from someone who needed her boyfriend to pick out her dress?"

I shook my head. "He's not my boyfriend."

That seemed to surprise Lark, because instead of her usual snort, she…she did nothing.

"I don't know what he is. I don't know what we are," I sighed.

"But isn't this a date? I could have sworn I kept hearing that in his head." Lark seemed puzzled. "You know, none of his other girlfriends ever seemed to have any doubt as to where their relationships stood with Robert. I think perhaps you should ask him what you two are."

I groaned. It was a very loud groan. Sheepish, too. "He asked me that yesterday."

"And…"

I looked at her, and then glanced away quickly when I started speaking, ashamed. "I told him that we were good friends."

As if it were a trend to start laughing at me, Lark did just that. "Oh Grace, you are an idiot. Robert cares a great deal for you, and he already views you as his girlfriend. *You're* the one who labeled yourself. Or, should I say you're the one who failed to label yourself."

I scowled at her. I knew that I'd end up with one permanent crease in my forehead as a result, and I'd gladly name it Lark to remind me who put it there, because I had no other expression at my disposal to use.

She laughed again. "Don't get angry, Grace. Look, if it makes you feel better, you're the first person that Robert's ever introduced to the whole family."

I looked at her quizzically. "What do you mean, the whole family? You mean you, your mother, and Sam? Meeting you and your mother—okay, meeting your mother was nice—you and I obviously worked our way around our first meeting—but trying to make me feel better by saying that I'm the first person to meet Sam almost sounds like

294

an insult."

I should have kept my mouth shut, because Lark starting laughing once again. She gripped her sides, as though it would somehow help contain her laughter. Fat chance. I waited impatiently before finally allowing some of her humor creep into me.

"I see that smile, Grace Shelley," she teased. She came towards me, and instinctually I flinched. "Oh please, haven't you learned to trust me yet?" Without appearing to have moved at all, she was by my side, her arm wrapped around my waist, squeezing me like a girlfriend would. "You know what? I've met every single girl that Robert's ever dallied with, dated, flirted with, and so on. But with the exception of Ellie, who already knew our secret, he's never told anyone of the others what he was. He's never dared.

"And yes, he's never brought any of them to meet Sam either, who, for some ridiculous notion, he loves like an actual brother, so you should feel honored, rather than disgusted. But—I totally support your disgust, and will stand side by side with you in disgustdom. Together, we shall rule with absolute disgustation!"

It was my turn to laugh loudly, understanding now why one needs to hold onto their sides while doing so. It took a moment before I was able to speak, but when I started it was with a slightly less amused tone, "I don't get it, Lark. Sam is beautiful, the vision that I would have had pop into my head when asked what I thought an angel would have looked like before I met your brother…"

"So why does he give you the creeps?" Lark finished.

I nodded, "Yeah! Why?"

"Unfortunately I can't answer that question for you. Only he can. But, Sam received the call over two millennia ago, so he's rarely ever around, which means you'll probably only see him during special occasions. Be glad for it. The human sense of time is much slower than ours. For you, a month is like a day for us."

I stared at Lark, my face totally deadpanned. "That's it? That's all I get?"

She shrugged her shoulders. "What? You act as though I can read minds or something."

I did it before I could stop myself. I knew I shouldn't have done it, but it happened, and in the split second that it took for me to swing my arm back a bit and punch Lark in the arm, much like I had Graham, much like I had even Stacy, I had brought the entire wedding party to a standstill.

Lark's face was one of shock. The exact same expression was on every face that had turned to stare at the two of us, human and angel alike. I looked at her, my lip trembling, and sagged in relief as I realized that she knew that I had not done it because I had wanted to hurt her.

"I think I'm actually flattered that you regard our relationship with such ease and familiarity," she said, a strained smile on her face. "How is your hand?"

I shrugged, "My hand? It's fi—holy crap!"

My hand looked like it should hurt. No. It looked like it should be completely numb and dead, hanging off of my arm, useless. It was completely covered in purplish bruises, the pinky looking distorted a bit, and the nail on my index finger was missing. "What the hell happened to my hand?" I shrieked, panic bubbling up within me.

A gasp erupted among the crowd, and I didn't know if it was because of what I had done to Lark, or because of how my hand looked. I looked at her face, trying to see if this was completely normal. She was stoic, inspecting my hand with surgical precision, turning it by minute degrees, her eyes moving so quickly I felt dizzy just watching her. I shook my head and knew that if my hand didn't hurt, and if she wasn't shocked by the way it looked, then the crowd that had now surrounded us were doing so because I had probably committed some heinous crime and were about to descend upon me like some angelic plague.

I heard a loud whoosh, and in one astounding moment, the crowd of people that had seemed so heavenly and menacing at the same time parted, ironically, like the red sea. But they soon gathered once again, converging upon me like a swarm of beautiful bees. Only when they were close could I see that it wasn't anger or fear that they were feeling, but rather curiosity. Of course they were curious. I was the oddity, after all.

I really was a superfreak. I had just punched someone who could kill me before anyone would have noticed. "Oh, I'm such an idiot." I mumbled, resting my head in my free hand.

"You're not an idiot, Grace," the soft voice that I had wanted to hear—but at the same time didn't—whispered in my ear. He brushed my hair out of my face, and forced me to look at him. "Your human instincts might be a novelty to some of those who are here in normal situations, but knowing what you know, and yet seeing that you still did...*that*—it is very interesting to them, especially the electus patronus who would never dream of doing such a thing."

He took my hand away from Lark, who was still examining the myriad of hues ranging from one shade of blue to the deepest purple. "The pattern is interesting, isn't it? Like a honeycomb. Fascinating..."

He nodded, and splayed my fingers, wincing as he did so. Robert's head jerked up as his face turned towards me. "You didn't scream," he gasped. The crowd surrounding us murmured their shock.

I stared at him. "Was I supposed to? I will if it'll make you feel better." I opened my mouth, practicing the motions I would use to produce one.

A pair of identical creases formed at the corners of his eyebrows, framing a deeper indentation between them. "With bruising like this, you should be experiencing extreme pain, Grace. Look at your hand." He dangled my hand in front of me like a carrot, waiting for the horse of shock to lead me forward towards recognition.

"It doesn't hurt," I said simply.

His mouth took on the shape of a beautiful grimace. He groaned when he heard my thoughts. And he groaned when he realized that I knew he wasn't pleased. Well, it did look beautiful!

"Grace, do you understand how seriously strange this is?" Robert snapped.

The tone in his voice caused me to shrink back a bit, pulling my hand with me. "Strange is a relative term, don't you think? I mean, I'm standing in the middle of a wedding party for people who work for mythical creatures that aren't even supposed to exist. I've been hit by a car and left for dead, yet here I am, alive and well-"

"With a purple hand," Robert held my wrist back up, as if to emphasize his point.

I snatched it back and continued, "-*alive and well* and in a dress. In my world, that last fact is the epitome of strange. It beats a purple hand any day of the week, so no, I don't understand how strange that is because right now, the only thing that seems strange to *me* is why you're just staring at it instead of healing it."

I heard a few murmurs of approval in the audience that surrounded us, and I waited, dangling my hand in his face this time. "Are you going to help me out, or do I have to ask your Mom to do it? I know she can heal a little, and if I'm not screaming in pain, it can't be that bad."

"Maybe he forgot how?" a voice I recognized as Sam's said quietly.

Perhaps it was because it was Sam that had said it, perhaps it was because it was said in front of so many people, but I began to feel quite guilty in making Robert the object of ridicule when it was my own foolishness that had caused me to be in this mess in the first place. I looked up at him, not wanting to see embarrassment, or hurt in his eyes—or worse…nothing at all. Instead, they were liquid, flowing, and he was smiling.

I snap at you and you're concerned about how I'm feeling. I don't think I deserve to have you in my life, Grace, but I'm ever grateful for it.

I held my hand out to him, nicely this time. "Could you fix my hand, please?" I held my breath as he kissed it, starting at the tips of my fingers, and moving to the grape-like objects that could only be my knuckles. He turned my hand over and blew into my palm. His warm breath caused me to shiver, and I thought that to be a strange reaction. *Strange indeed.*

He closed my hand, and I watched amazed as the colors seemed to wash away, like paint, from my hand. It was like looking at a kaleidoscope, the changing shapes, patterns, and colors swirling beneath my skin. When the last of the purple had finally faded away, an

298

eruption of applause surrounded us. The grins and praise from everyone around us were a testament to the gift that he possessed.

I looked at Robert, sure that he'd be pleased with the reaction of the crowd, but instead, he looked upset. Panicky even. "Robert, what's wrong?"

He pulled me to him, and dragged me towards something. Or was it someone? No. It was both. It was a wheelchair.

"Ellie, Grace and I have to leave now. I came to tell you goodbye, but before that, I wanted to tell you that you have impacted my life in so many ways. You were my first true human friend. You have given me something that I couldn't have been able to gain on my own, and I will always be grateful to have known an incredible person like you."

He got down on both knees, leaned in and kissed her. I turned away, the moment being too private for me to witness. He was saying goodbye to her, and I knew what that meant. Whatever it was that they needed to share now, I couldn't take that away from them with my feelings of jealousy or inadequacy. I would have hated myself for it.

It was only when I felt Robert's hand squeeze mine did I turn around to say my own farewell. And the tears that I did not know were there, did not expect, suddenly started to spill over. "Thank you, Ellie, for taking care of Robert all this time." I didn't know what else to say.

She reached her arms up for me, and I went into them, allowing her to embrace me, comfort me. If I did not know that she was looking forward to her fate, I would have found the situation to be quite ironic, but I knew better. Instead, I felt the selfish sadness that I would never get to hear the thousands of stories of her time with Robert that I knew she had stored in her sharp mind.

"Thank you, Grace, for ensuring me that Robert has finally found his home," she whispered into my ear, her voice so soft, I strained to hear it, but knew that even if I had not, each word had somehow burned itself into my mind, the imprint of the first memory as she had called it.

She kissed my forehead, like a grandmother would, and then let me go. She looked at Robert, who was still kneeling on the ground, and smiled, "So Sam's taking me home?"

He nodded, smiling sadly. "Yes. You don't have anything to worry about tonight."

She nodded, her face peaceful. "That's good. I'm done with worrying. Especially about you. You be happy, Robbie. And you take care of this one. She's special. I can tell just by looking at her."

When she winked at me, I couldn't help but smile and wink back. It was exactly what she wanted, and she beamed at me, her blue eyes twinkling like sapphire stars in her face. "Goodbye, Grace. May life always bring you unexpected happiness."

Puzzled, I asked her why.

She waved as Robert pulled me away, her voice trailing behind me, "Because that's exactly what love is dear."

I continued to stare back at her, even as Robert pulled me away, until I could no longer see her face among the crowd. I wanted to yank my hand free and run back to her, to ask her more questions, to be there when her time came…to do something other than walk away knowing that I would never see her again.

As we approached the gravel parking lot, Robert's pace slowed. He searched among the cars for the one that had brought us here, and, finding it, tapped on the glass. A movement could be seen in the front cab, and I realized that the driver had fallen asleep.

"Why didn't he come and join the party?" I asked, shocked that he could have been left out intentionally.

Robert smiled knowingly, "Because he used to date Hannah, and that would have been quite awkward, don't you think?"

I nodded my head. "Quite."

The driver, who I later learned was named Thomas, emerged from the driver's side door and opened the rear passenger side door for us. I thanked him and slid in, muttering to myself about how unnecessary it was, having someone else open the door for you when you had two—no—four perfectly useful hands that could have done it themselves.

As soon as the door was shut and the driver was inside, we were moving, leaving. To me, it felt like we were running away. I didn't like that. I had been doing that for too long now, and I knew that the problems only followed you where you went.

"Robert, why did we have to leave?" I looked at the clock on the dashboard console, noticing that it read fifteen minutes after ten. "We still have over an hour…"

His face looked so composed, I thought I'd get some feedback that would have helped to lead the way to answering some of the remaining questions that I had. Instead, what I got was, "Thank you for your input, Captain Obvious."

I looked at him, annoyed at his lame attempt at sarcasm. So annoyed, I didn't even stop myself as the reflex response I was so used to uttering whenever Graham had attempted the same thing simply came out.

"You're quite welcome, General No Shit."

Judging by the intake of his breath, I knew that was the last thing he had been expecting of me, which meant that my mind had blocked itself off again, leaving him in the lurch. Either that or he was in some corner with the mangled remains of some other thoughts that I hadn't really been concentrating on too much. I was in the winning corner. And I wasn't backing down.

"I don't think that's very ladylike language," he said, his voice flat, his eyes cold steel.

I folded my arms across my chest, ready for this match. "I don't care if it's ladylike or not. I was provoked by someone who isn't acting like a gentleman so I don't think it's necessary for me to act like a lady."

"I am indeed a gentleman!"

"It's certainly not gentlemanly to drag your date out of a wedding reception before she's had a chance to say goodbye to the bride and groom. It's also rude and just plain selfish, so I suggest you correct your own behavior before you start chastising me about mine. And another thing, it's not angelic behavior either," I huffed, and folded my arms across my chest, angry and hurt that he had cut my evening short without explaining why.

He glared at me, his eyes turning harder with each breath that passed between us. "What you know about what is and isn't angelic behavior wouldn't even fill one chapter of an encyclopedia that expands the entire history of this world."

"And whose fault would that be, eh Mr. 'I can't tell you'? It's okay though, because encyclopedias come in disk form now and there is only *one* of those," I said in retort. And it felt good. *Damn* good.

He glowered at me, but I wasn't budging.

"Why did we leave?" I demanded.

Silence.

"Thomas? Could you turn the car around, please? I'd like to go back to the wedding," I said loudly, all the while keeping my eyes glued to Robert's.

"Mr. Bellegarde?" came the hesitant voice from the driver's seat.

Though he didn't say anything, I knew that he had *said* something to the driver because we did not turn around. We sped up instead.

I cannot believe that you are ruining this evening for me.

That seemed to soften the hardness in his eyes. His rigid posture relaxed, even if only infinitesimally. It was a start.

Why did we leave so early, Robert? What was so awful?

He sighed and ran his fingers through his hair. I watched as they made little paths through the black strands, and my fingers itched to trace those paths. Even as angry as I was, he still affected me so profoundly; I had to double my efforts to focus on why I was so upset otherwise I'd be just another one of those love sick twits who fawned over him in French class.

I heard it. I knew what sound it was because it was the only sound in the entire car. It was the only sound that would have made me forget for a moment that I was angry at him for taking me away so early.

It was a chuckle.

"Grace, sometimes I think your mind is simply not equipped to handle all you put it through."

I glared at him. "Insulting my mind isn't exactly going to win you any points with me, Robert."

He sighed, laughed once more, and then sighed again. He

leaned forward and grabbed a hold of my hand. Crap, I'd forgotten to keep them out of his reach. He laughed this time.

"Grace, I'm sorry that we left the party early. If it makes you feel better, then please know that I have known Hannah since she was born, and the last thing she had on her mind was our leaving without telling her goodbye."

I tugged at my hand, but it wasn't budging. "It doesn't matter now, does it? We're not going back." I felt my lower lip stick out involuntarily.

"No, we're not going back," he said softly, scooting closer to me, his movements slow so that I could see it happening.

I scooted away, "Are you taking me home then?"

It was like a game of scoot tag. He scooted. "I'm taking you to my home."

He was going to win the game, because I couldn't move. "What do you mean, you're taking me to your home?"

He moved as close to me as he dared, and that was pretty darn close, before he answered my question. "I mean, I'm taking you to see my home. You had expressed some doubt as to whether or not one existed, did you not?"

I huffed, "Yeah! To your sister!" How had he known?

"Angel," he said, as if that were an answer to all of my silent accusations.

I turned my head, not wanting to look into his eyes, not wanting to see the hypnotizing ripples that were ever present in those liquid pools that only existed when he was happy. I'd lose my train of thought if I took even one look. I knew it as sure as I knew my name.

Hearing my thoughts, I felt him scoot away, letting go of my hand as he did so. Only when I felt it was safe to turn my face did I do so. His face was less than an inch away from mine.

Gotcha.

The full impact of silver—liquid fire, hot and flowing hit me hard in that place in your belly that doesn't exist for food, but for something else entirely. It exists solely to possess the feeling that it barely held in check right then. I don't know what it was. I don't think

303

it has a name. I only know that it was there, familiar yet not, and it felt like it was boiling, ready to spill over at any moment. I knew it was messing with my breathing, because I was getting dizzy, and I didn't think I'd be able to remember how to breathe normally until he was at a safer distance.

"Robert, you—you're too close. You need to give me some space," I panted.

He shook his head, but did move back a bit. I whispered my thanks, and took a deep breath, luxuriating in it, and feeling saddened by it at the same time. Robert frowned in confusion. "What's the matter, Grace?"

"I don't know how to explain it. Can't you figure out by reading my thoughts?"

"If you can't figure out your own thoughts, how am I supposed to?"

I sighed, knowing that he was right. I turned my head and looked out of the car window, absentmindedly reaching for him with my hand. I had just rejected his nearness, and yet I still needed to feel him, feel he was there in some physical way, no matter how confusing it may have seemed. He accepted my hand, accepted me lacing my fingers through his, and accepted my sigh of contentment as the car slowed down and turned into a driveway that was lined on both sides by large rock walls.

It was unusual, to say the least. Most homes here had wooden fences, if they were fenced in at all, but that wasn't what made the rock wall stand out. It was the color of the rocks that did. In the darkness, I could still tell that they were a bright white, like the color of new snow. "Are they painted?" I asked, not taking my eyes off of the gleaming white expanse that bordered the car now on both sides. They were tall. I wasn't good at measuring by sight, but I wouldn't doubt that they stood taller than I did at five-seven".

"No, they're not painted. And they're six and a half feet tall," Robert's voice said, answering my unasked question.

I turned to look out the front of the vehicle to see where we were headed, and to see if the white walls would ever end. I laughed so loud,

304

I startled the poor driver, his response causing the car to jerk to a stop.

Where the walls ended, there stood two statues. Of angels blowing on trumpets. Wearing togas.

"Are you kidding me?" I knew my laughter was growing louder, and at any second, I was sure I'd throw in a snort or two, but the irony was too much for me to deal with. As we pulled past the statues, and apparently a wrought iron gate that I had not seen, I wiped away the tears that had come with my spontaneous laughter. "*Why* do you have angel statues in front of your gate?"

He was smiling, amused that I had found the situation humorous. "Too obvious?"

I nodded, trying now to contain the rampant giggles that had taken over my body.

"Well, it's the fact that it's so obvious that works to our advantage. Aside from a few subtle differences, we don't look much different from humans, nor do we behave much differently either. We're basically hiding in plain sight," he said, his voice sounding very self-satisfied, as though it were some great coup to look the way he did.

"You do know that the differences that you have are far from subtle," I started, looking him over to catalogue just the few obvious ones I could spot right away. "For one thing, your eyes are not human in the slightest. No one's eyes look like yours. Then there's your face. It's perfect. Nothing is too this or that. Everything is proportionate, symmetrical.

"There's the way your voice seems to put everyone around them into a trance. I know you're not doing it on purpose. You just…do it. Lark calls it your charm. When I talk, people want to cover their ears and run away screaming, but with you, they'd jump off a bridge in their grandmother's underwear if you said it would be an interesting sight to see."

He smiled at that last bit, and then pressed his hand to my mouth, "Shh. We're here."

The car had stopped in front of a large, white home. There was a simple, dark blue door in an overly large frame. It was flanked by two wrought iron sconces that were brightly lit. Robert waited until the driver had put the car in park, and then opened the door, not wanting to wait for the driver to do so himself. He was still holding my hand, and was pulling me across the seat until I was outside, my sandaled feet landing on concrete pavers that crisscrossed beneath them.

I took my time looking at the house. It was a two story, with two large bay windows in front, one on each side of the front door. The windows on the second floor had what looked like dark blue shutters framing the paned windows, with the window directly over the door being the only one without. I counted them, for some reason, noting that one window seemed out of place, as it extended over what could be a garage?

Robert tugged on my hand. "Don't you want to see what it looks like on the inside?

I shook my head, suddenly feeling very nervous.

He looked at me, perplexed. "Why?"

"Because we're alone," I said shyly.

That seemed to please him a great deal, because he dazzled me with a brilliant smile. "You have my promise that I will behave like an absolute gentleman, Grace."

And, knowing that he was telling the truth, I gladly accepted the hand that he then offered me as he led me into the house with the blue door.

SHORTCOMINGS

My tour of Robert's house had been conducted as though I were a potential buyer, and he an agent looking to earn himself a very hefty commission. He waxed poetic about everything, from the floors to the ceilings; even the switches for the lights were praised. We ended the tour in the kitchen, and I was thoroughly impressed with it; it seemed larger than the entire lower half of my house.

"This is exactly the size of kitchen that I think one would need in order to feed Graham," I joked, knowing that even the school cafeteria was probably no match for his penchant for eating. "What do you think?" I turned to Robert and waited for his response.

He wasn't there. "Robert? Where'd you go?"

I walked through a narrow hallway that I assumed was the butler's pantry, and ended up in the dining room. I ignored the furnishings in the room, having already seen them through the living room, and proceeded there. "Robert?"

I stood in the middle of the Bellegarde living room, surrounded by white sofas and glass tables, and couldn't help but shake my head at the impracticality of it. "Robert, where did you go?" I called out again. I looked at the digital clock that glowed in the silver box that I recognized as the cable box, and gasped.

"Robert! I have exactly three minutes to get home! Get down here, now!!" I shouted.

When the digital seven turned into an eight, I bolted for the front door, throwing it open when I got there, and ran outside. I didn't know where I was going. All I knew was that I was two minutes away from being in serious trouble, and I would be heading there on foot.

I ran for the gate, hopping on one foot as I took my sandals off. I threw them through the bars, hiked the skirt of the dress up, and started climbing. I was nearly to the top when my hands were pried off. "What?"

A pair of arms wrapped around my waist, and the ground was getting further and further away. And then, all I could see were trees. I squirmed frantically, my arms searching, my hands clawing. "Robert?"

"Would it be anyone else?"

I sighed and relaxed. Then I screamed, because I was falling. "Roberrrrrrt!"

With a loud "umph", I landed in his arms. Instinctively, I clamped onto him, my arms locking around his neck, my face pressed tightly against his chest. "Sorry. I needed a better grip on you and you were squirming too much," he murmured into my ear. I could feel his lips against the soft hairs there, and knew, just knew that he was smiling.

"I think my heart fell out somewhere over your driveway," I muttered into his shirt. He laughed quietly, nuzzling my hair as he did so.

Neither of us spoke for a bit after that; the only sound I could hear was the rush of wind around us as we travelled at an immense speed. When he finally spoke, he laughed quietly, nuzzling my hair as he did so. "Almost there."

I was about to ask what he meant when I realized that we were no longer moving. He placed my feet on the ground, unwrapped my arms from his neck, and placed my sandals in my hands. He gave me a once over, and then turned me around. We were standing at the front door of my house.

"How fast were we going?" I gasped.

"Fast. Very fast. Now open the door before you turn me into a liar." He placed a hand on my hair, then removed it very quickly.

I opened the door, turning to look behind me as I did so, but there was no one there.

"Robert?" I whispered.

Get inside of the house!

"Coward!" I hissed. But, I listened, taking one more look behind me, and then closing the door.

308

"Grace, is that you?" I heard being called out. So much for not waiting up.

"Yes, Dad, it's me."

I heard the springs of the recliner give way, and turned to see Dad standing in his robe by the bottom of the stairs. "Well, you're home at twelve on the dot. That Robert is very…punctual."

I smiled sheepishly. "Yes. Yes he is."

"So where is he? He didn't just drop you off and leave, did he?"

I shook my head, unable to get my tongue to cooperate and actually form the words that I knew were a lie.

Dad looked at my face, then looked at the door. "So what happened to him? You didn't punch him, did you?"

I started laughing, the sound coming out in hysterical gasps, and quickly covered my mouth with my hand. My right hand. My right, cast-less hand that was supposed to be broken.

"Your cast is missing!" Dad shouted, his finger pointing at the very obvious lack of plaster on my arm. "Why is it off of your arm?"

I tried to think of some good excuse, but my mouth moved before my brain kicked into gear. "Robert took it off." Seeing his shocked face, I quickly added, "It's perfectly fine, Dad. See? I can use it, it doesn't hurt or anything. I think the x-rays were wrong and they put the casts on me prematurely." I bent my arm and wiggled my fingers in front of him, as if that would be enough to convince him.

Dad's face was a very distinct shade of pinkish red. I would look up the name of the color later and find out it was called puce. "He took it off? With what?"

That one left me stumped. I opened my mouth to say something, anything other than the truth, and yet it still came out, "With his fingers." Why could I *not* tell a lie? I gritted my teeth, unwilling to say another word, no matter what was asked of me.

"Grace Anne Shelley, this isn't time for jokes. Did you let him cut that cast off of your arm?"

I shook my head, forcing my jaw to stay shut.

"I'm going to get to the bottom of this, Grace. This is very serious. If your arm is still broken-"

"But it's not!" I protested, once again wiggling my arm around to demonstrate that it wasn't.

He shook his head and pointed to the stairs. "Go upstairs. I'm making an appointment in the morning to see your doctor and finding out for myself."

I didn't bother trying to tell him that tomorrow would be Sunday. I simply did as I was told, and silently cursed Robert for leaving me to fend for myself after avoiding my questions at the same time. I wanted to stomp my feet, but I didn't want to wake Janice up. I wanted to do a lot of things, but I simply opened my bedroom door and walked in, closing it behind me.

The soft glow of the moon allowed me just enough light to make my way around the room. I tossed the sandals that were still in my hand—the hand that would probably get me grounded because it wasn't surrounded in plaster—onto the ground next to the bed and walked over to my dresser. I pulled out a pair of boxers and a tank top and threw those onto the bed behind me. I sat at the foot of my bed, and looked into the mirror.

"Gaaaah!" I croaked.

The soft white glow wasn't coming from the moon. It was coming from the person who was sitting on my bed, and who looked a bit too comfortable for my taste. I jumped off of the mattress, turning around and backing into my dresser, my heart pounding in my chest. I looked at my window. It was still shut. "How did you get in here?" I hissed.

He pointed to the window.

I looked at it again. This time I could see that it was slightly ajar. "Did you do that misting thing?" I whispered, my breath coming out in short bursts.

He nodded, and then smiled. *Why are you whispering?*

"Because I don't want my dad to hear!" I whispered angrily. "Why are you in here?"

I wanted to apologize.

"Couldn't it have waited until tomorrow?" When he shook his head, I added, "or at least until I've changed my clothes?"

310

He lifted his eyebrows, the look on his face unmistakable.

"I'm going to go and change in the bathroom," I muttered.

I left him sitting on my bed, being careful not to open my door too widely. I closed it and crept to the bathroom. After shutting the door and turning on the light, I took a good look at my reflection.

My hair looked immaculate. Not a single hair out of place. I remembered that he had touched my head, and sighed. He had tried to make me look as presentable as possible, knowing that Dad was there waiting for me. He also knew that his presence when Dad discovered my cast was missing would not have helped out in the least.

Darn.

He had left me alone on my doorstep to protect me. "Ugh. Too perfect," I muttered to myself. "Too damn perfect."

Deciding that stalling in the bathroom would not exactly be a good idea, I started to change. It was a struggle to get the zipper in the back of the dress down, but I managed to pull it down just enough where the dress would come down with a few tugs.

Once I had won the battle of the zipper, I was able to quickly change. I removed the jewelry and, after brushing my teeth and washing my face, I hurried back to my room. I closed the door softly, and turned around to face Robert.

He smiled at my scowl. *You look beautiful angry. And I am sorry.*

My jaw dropped. "Don't try to butter me up, Robert. I'm not in the mood." I dumped the corset and dress into his lap, and then bent down to pick up the sandals that I had tossed on the ground, and placed those in his lap as well.

I then sat at the foot of the bed, crossed my legs, and faced him. "Okay. No more running away, Robert. Are you going to answer my questions?"

Yes.

"All of them?"

Yes.

Satisfied, I relaxed. "Why did we leave the reception early?"

I felt uncomfortable.

311

"You felt uncomfortable? Why?"

Because I didn't want an audience watching me; I don't like having people see what I can do for others.

I could feel my face wrinkle up in confusion. "But why? You've got a gift, Robert! It's like Ellie said; you're special even among your own kind."

My healing ability may be viewed as a gift to you, Grace, but to me, it's almost like a curse.

I stared at him, my mind uncomprehending what he had just said. It didn't make sense to me that the ability to heal someone could somehow be a bad thing.

I can't heal everyone, Grace, and I don't know who it is that I can and cannot heal until I try.

"But you healed me. You did it three times. Are you saying that there might be a time when you won't be able to?"

His eyes looked stark. *I hope I never have to find out.*

"But that might happen."

He nodded his head, a sudden sadness blanketing his face.

I looked down at my hands in my lap. "And is that why you feel it's a curse? Because you might not be able to heal someone? Because if it is, it's a pretty silly reason."

You cannot begin to understand how immense the feeling of helplessness is, knowing that I have this amazing ability and not being able to use it to save a child, a parent, a friend for no reason other than it was their time.

The way he said friend made me think about Ellie. "You wanted to help keep Ellie alive…"

He nodded. *If I could have kept her alive for another century, I would have.*

I lifted my head up to look at him. "How did you keep her alive for tonight?"

I didn't. Someone else did.

"Who?" I asked. If there was someone else who could keep someone alive, even if it was for one more day, surely they'd know how to get around the whole "their time" issue.

312

I cannot tell you who it was.

"But you said you'd answer all of my questions." I gasped.

I cannot answer this one. I made a promise that I would not reveal who it was, and I cannot break that promise.

"Stupid angel etiquette…" I muttered.

I heard that.

"Good."

You have more questions.

I nodded. "What happened to my hand?"

I don't know.

"What do you mean, you don't know? Why did it look the way it did? And why didn't it hurt?"

I don't know. I expected the bruising. You wouldn't have known what attacking us would do.

"I didn't attack Lark!" I protested, my hands clenched into fists that betrayed my words.

I know that. You were playing around. That was never in question. But, you did hit Lark, expecting to encounter the soft give of human flesh.

"But that's exactly what it felt like."

But it wasn't, Grace. How can I explain this to you so that you'll understand. When you touch us, you feel soft skin, warm and smooth, like yours. But it doesn't give like your skin does. It's stronger. Much, much stronger. The only thing I can compare it to is spider silk.

My head cocked to the side, because let's face it, that sounded ridiculous. "My hand won't end up looking like a big blueberry if I punch a spider web, Robert."

No, of course it wouldn't. But spider silk is the strongest natural fiber in the world. It is stronger than steel. But it is pliable, soft. My skin, the skin of every angel is like that. It's like a very intricately woven fabric made of spider silk. Your punch to Lark, however lighthearted, however soft, would be like you punching a steel beam.

I looked at him, incredulous. "But it didn't *feel* like that. That's what I don't understand."

He nodded. *I know that. It's not supposed to feel like you punched a steel beam. Just hurt like it. And yet-*

"I didn't feel anything."

He nodded again.

"Wow."

I know. I don't understand it, either. The way your bruising patterns were formed was quite different as well.

I remembered the way Lark had described it as looking like a honeycomb. I had had many scrapes and bruises as a kid, but never recalled having bruises that looked like that. "Should I have broken my hand?"

He shook his head. "You didn't use enough force. Had you done so, it would have been taken by everyone at the wedding as a sign of aggression towards us, and that probably wouldn't have gone over so well."

Well, that was good, at least.

What's next?

I brought my knees up and rested my chin on them, thinking about what else it was that I had wanted to know. "Why are you and Sam so close?"

He laughed, but the sound was almost hollow. *You don't like Sam.*

"I just don't feel comfortable around him. I don't know why. Lark said that he'd have to tell me what it is about him that does that. Is that his ability or something? Or is it because I'm allergic to jerks?"

His body rocked with muted laughter before a half-smile formed on his face. *You're not alone in your feelings, Grace. However, Sam's a mentor and a friend. He's more than a friend. He's my brother in every sense of the word except genetically. He's always been there, whether to offer advice, or just support when I've felt lost and impatient.*

"Because you haven't heard the call yet?"

A slight nod of his head and a sigh answered me.

"So Sam helps you deal with that?" I asked, not really wanting to like Sam for helping Robert understand what he was going through, but at the same time, glad that he had someone who he could turn to.

Friendship, between humans or angels, could mean the difference between depression and happiness, and I did not want to ever think of my angel feeling the way that I had when I had no one.

Yes, he helps me deal with it. And thank you, for at least trying to see him in a different light. Even Lark refuses to do that.

Well, score one for the human girl.

Robert laughed silently. *You're already way ahead of the game, Grace.*

I smiled, feeling oddly giddy at such an offbeat compliment. But what else was to be expected of me, right? Hadn't we just gotten through discussing the consequences of punching an angel? Conversations like this didn't happen with just anyone.

"When is Ellie supposed to go? Does her family know? "

Robert shook his head. *It will happen before the sun rises, but no, her family does not know. Her daughter will be informed through the normal human methods, and Hannah will find out as soon as Ellie has crossed over.*

I felt an overwhelming sense of sadness come over me. "Why can't Hannah know? She's supposed to be one of your protectors, right?"

Yes, but Ellie wanted it this way. She wanted Hannah to be able to enjoy her wedding night.

The snort that came out of me was one that was in disbelief. The tone with which Robert had said "wedding night" made it seem as though Hannah was a vir-

She is.

My mouth opened up rather widely, shocked that he'd know such a thing. "And just how do you know something like that?"

She told me.

I couldn't—could not—simply couldn't believe that someone would share that kind of information with another person. And with their grandmother's ex-boyfriend no less!

Robert chuckled. *Believe it or not, she did. People tend to view us as priests when they know what we are. It can get annoying--but we understand. Do you know what she calls me? What makes it easier for her to talk to me?*

"Robbie?" Why not, since her grandmother did.

She calls me Grandpa Bob.

A smirk formed on my lips and I couldn't help but begin to test it out. "Grandpa Bob. I think it has a nice ring to it. I might call you that from now on."

He rolled his eyes at my jest. *I think there are other things you could call me that would sound much more palatable.*

The things I'd love to call him were far too familiar and intimate for what we were at the moment. Just the idea alone was enough to make the blood flood my cheeks, a testament to my embarrassment. I had labeled our relationship, Lark had told me, and all the things that I would have liked to call him, refer to him as, have him call me in return—they were all impossible until I had made my decision about what it was that I wanted known. And I knew that I had to come to a decision about him, about Graham, about everything soon.

Then, remembering the last thing that had been on my mind before the desperate need to get home took over, I turned my body to face him. "Why did you leave me in the kitchen?"

He looked away towards the window, and I saw his jaw jut out in stubbornness. His white glow turned a stark purple.

"Robert, you said you'd answer all of my questions," I reminded him—as if he could forget. "I want to know. Please."

He turned his face to me, his eyes steel once again, cold and flat. *Because I brought you to my home, I brought you into my life, and you choose not to talk about a future with me, but instead speak of someone who broke your heart, and how* my *kitchen would make* him *happy.*

I was stunned. Dumbfounded, actually. "Of all the silly-" I stared mutely at him as the realization of what had just happened slapped me in the face. "Are you jealous, Robert?"

I don't know what I am. I have never felt this emotion before. I'm not enjoying it. Impossibly, his jaw jutted out even farther, the vein in his neck growing fat from the tension this new emotion was giving him. *I cannot help but be angry at you for causing it, Grace.*

I got on my knees and crawled on the bed towards him. I

316

watched him flinch as I reached for his hand, but he did not take it away when I clasped it in mine. He did not respond when I squeezed it either. "Robert, I did not mean hurt you or make you jealous by mentioning Graham. I-I thought you'd have realized by now. I mean, you can read my mind, after all…"

He did not look at me, instead focusing on some unseen thing outside of my window. I looked at the reflection of his glow that bounced off of the glass and sighed.

"I guess I hide my thoughts better than I thought," I mumbled. I took in the distance between the two of us, trying to determine if he'd have enough time to bolt before I could get closer. I crawled quickly, until my face was just a foot away from his. I could see that his eyes were cold and hard, frozen in his anger, but I could also see the hurt and confusion that he felt in them.

"Robert, I'm sorry that you feel so strange, but I'm not sorry that you're feeling it because of me," I whispered, my heart feeling a familiar twinge as I continued, "but even if you hadn't felt it, it would not change the way I feel about you."

His face was so still, his eyes unmoving. I waited for some kind of reaction, anything. After fifteen hundred years of mastering the art of secrecy, I knew that I wasn't going get anything out of him but silence. I had hurt him without recognizing it.

The expectations that I had subconsciously placed on him had been too high; I took for granted the fact that while he was an angel, he was also a man, with a heart and a mind, and I had hurt him when I had failed to realize that he had seen my thoughts, seen the images and the dreams that I'd had of a romantic future with Graham. How could he not have known—not have seen that those were images that I now looked back on—not with regret, but with gladness—because the future I pictured wasn't with Graham, but with him?

Meeting Ellie tonight had put a lot of things into perspective. I simply couldn't keep how I felt inside for fear of rejection anymore, especially not when there was a chance that I would not have as much time with Robert as I would like. He wouldn't be able to heal me one day, and he wouldn't be able to postpone my death if that's what was

317

my fate; I simply couldn't face my future if I didn't let go of my fears. So, with an all too eerie sense of déjà vu, I said the words to him that I had said less than two months ago to someone else, only this time, I wasn't hesitant, because this time—this time I knew, not in my heart, but in my soul that I had no reason for doubt.

"I love you, Robert. You don't have to say it back. I don't need to hear it. Saying it is enough right now. Saying it is the only thing that will make me feel better. I love you, I love you, I love you."

I placed my hand on his heart, and laid my head on his chest, not knowing what else to say or do. I listened to his breathing, his heart beating the same rhythm it had drummed for so long, and I heard the way my heart seemed to follow it, keeping pace as it sped up when I again thought those three words.

I looked down towards the foot of the bed, and I could see the faint reflection of the two of us in my mirror above the dresser. His glow, muted by his clothes, illuminated just enough of my face to show the glitter of tears that rested against the bridge of my nose, the glint moving ever so slightly with each ragged breath that I took.

I watched as the purple radiance lightened, turning into a deep orange. It reminded me of the crystals and flowers that had decorated the wedding reception, and I couldn't believe that it had only been a few hours ago that the two of us had been dancing, happy and content.

So involved in my thoughts was I that I didn't feel his arms wrap around me, or feel his hand stroke my hair. It was only when I heard his sigh, heard the intake of his breath through his chest, did I notice that I was no longer simply laying on him, but I was being embraced, comforted.

I'm sorry, Grace. I-

I lifted my head to gaze at him, "I don't need apologies, Robert, not for anything. Just…don't turn away from me. Okay?" His eyes were softer. Not exactly liquid, but not steel, and definitely not icy. It was enough for me. I laid my head back down on his chest and closed my eyes, sighing when he began stroking my hair again.

How disappointed you must be in me.

I shook my head. "I'm not disappointed in you. How could I

318

be? You're still here; you didn't leave."

He placed both hands on my head then, and lifted it to look at him again. *I don't know if I can give you everything you want, Grace. I don't know if I can be everything to you that you want me to be. Once I get my wings—once I get the call—I cannot guarantee you that I'll be able to remain here, be with you. There will come a time when I will have to leave...*

I smiled sadly in the darkness. "I'm seventeen, Robert. The only thing I want is to spend as much time with you as possible. The only thing I want you to be is you. I'm not foolish enough to think beyond today. Not anymore. You might have forever, but the only guarantee I have is right now, and that's all I need. That's why I don't want to waste any time worrying about what I didn't say, or what I want to say. Because I know...I know that you'll have to leave me someday, and that I only get now."

"That sounds very mature of you, Grace, and woefully ignorant," he groaned, speaking for the first time, "but I'm glad you feel that way." He brought my head to his, and kissed my hair before letting me go, wrapping his arms around me once more.

I snuggled into his embrace, content and relieved. And brave. "Can I ask you another question?"

He nodded, albeit tentatively.

"Why is it that you've never felt—that is to say—why now?" I thought the rest of my question, not exactly brave enough to articulate it any further than that.

"Why haven't I ever been jealous before? I don't know. Maybe it's because I've never had any real type of competition before. You're the only person who's ever been...a challenge. And I told you, Grace, I wanted you to see yourself in my home, and you brought him up instead. You pictured him in my home and not me. He fills your thoughts, and it's hard to be in your mind when it feels like I'm not even a part of them." I could feel the tension in his body and the pain that tainted his words, and I hated myself for being the cause.

"Robert, Graham has been a part of my life since we were in diapers. Whatever—wherever my life takes me, I think he'll always be a part of it. I've always known it-" I chewed the inside of my cheek as I processed what I had just said, a thought forming in my mind "-and I think, that is why it hurt so much when he rejected me; I knew he was supposed to be in my life. Maybe not in that way, the way that I thought I wanted at the time, but in some form, and having him simply not existing there at all was like a piece of me was missing."

I raised my head again so I could see his face, look into his eyes as I continued, "I know now—I know that he's supposed to be in my life, but as nothing more than my friend. I love him. I never stopped loving him, even when he broke my heart, but if he hadn't, I think I'd still be sitting at home, pining after him while he continued to date Erica behind my back."

Robert's face, which had seemed so pained just a few minutes ago, now bore a smug smile. He shifted his weight, rolling the two of us over so that we were both on our sides facing each other. *I think that you and I would have still ended up right here.* He lifted his hand to brush a strand of my hair behind my ear, his smile turning sweet. *Either way, I'm glad that Graham was too blind to see what it was that he was giving up by choosing Erica. If not, I wouldn't be able to do this-*

I held my breath, and refused to blink; he placed his hand on the bed to brace himself as he leaned towards me. Slowly, carefully, his lips—soft, warm, and perfect—found their way to mine. I want to say that it was magical, that I saw rainbows and fairy dust or something fantastic like that, but I couldn't. It was more. Much more.

It was as though the world has fallen down around us, and everything was frozen in ice. But I wasn't cold. I was blazing hot, the fire starting where our lips joined, where angel met mortal, and I could feel the flames flickering out towards the limbs that I was fighting with desperately to keep still, not wanting them to latch onto him, not wanting to seem out of control because at that moment, I would have given anything to be just that.

His lips weren't insistent. They weren't demanding and they weren't anything but soft and gentle. I pulled away then, because God help me if they ever chose to be. And, also, because I needed to breathe. I knew that the dizziness I felt wasn't for lack of oxygen, but rather because something had changed between us, as though finally admitting how I felt had made me more attuned to him in some way. Breathing was simply a distraction.

Robert laughed softly at my thoughts, but I could see by the way he was breathing that I wasn't the only one who had been affected. His chest was rising and falling quite rapidly, as though he had been breathless, too. *You think breathing is a distraction?*

"I think *you're* a distraction," I responded, trying to remember that breathing in meant I had to breathe out as well. "Breathing is...difficult at the moment."

He brushed the side of my face with the back of his hand, rounding the curve of my cheek slowly, stopping to touch my lips with his fingertips. *Breathing is a necessity for you humans, and if kissing you causes you to have difficulties, I might have to refrain from doing it again.*

I gasped at his thought. "It's not that difficult!"

The soft laughter that filled my room plus the hand that was still finding its way around my face, as if to map out each and every angle and curve did wonders to distract me; when he leaned in and formed his lips to mine once more, I was completely taken aback. This time, there was no preparation, no time to tell my body what to do. My hands flew to his neck, to his face, greedy for the feel of his skin, the texture of his hair, the cut of his clothes. I never understood why authors used the word "pawing" to describe the way hands would touch a body during intimate scenes until my hands were doing just that. It felt almost primal, the way I was reacting, and had I been anywhere else, I might have even growled. But I wasn't anywhere else. I was in my bedroom, on my bed, with Robert, and the door to my bedroom was slowly opening.

I braced myself for the onslaught of yelling that I knew would soon be filling the house again. Instead, I felt my face fall onto the comforter of my bed, my muffled voice covering my surprise at the warm yet empty void on my bed.

"Grace? Are you okay?" Janice called out softly. "I heard some noises in here. I wanted to make sure you were alright."

"Mmm-hmm." I mumbled, turning my head towards her just enough so that I could see the door out of the corner of a now exposed eye; I was hoping that there was nothing else for her to see other than me on my bed. Alone.

"Okay. I was just checking. You go back to bed. Good-night."

"Mmmm-mihhh."

I watched as she walked out, pulling the door closed behind her. As soon as I heard it click shut, I was up, looking for the familiar glow. Instead, I felt a tickling sensation near my feet. I looked down, but in the darkness I couldn't see anything. I knelt on the ground and looked under my bed but saw nothing. I stood up and looked at the window. It hadn't been opened any further, and I wasn't sure if he could mist that quickly, so with no other option left, I headed towards the closet. Slowly, I opened the door. "Robert?" I hissed.

Why are you looking in your closet?

I whipped around, my arms flailing around instinctually to lash out at the voice, and crashed into an angel shaped wall. "I've done this before," I muttered, mostly to myself between gasps.

The wall began to shake with quiet laughter as it wrapped itself around me and carried me back to my bed. "You laugh at me now. I was very embarrassed that first day."

I was intrigued.

Of course he was intrigued. I was *different*. Different can be interesting, but how long until *different* just becomes *boring*?

Robert smiled as he lowered me onto the comforter. *I don't know if I'll ever get bored with you. I'm not sure if I can.* He lay down next to me, the two of us resuming our previous positions of lying on our sides and facing each other. *You've made me feel things that I've never felt in all of my existence. I don't know how that is possible, but it is true nonetheless. But Grace, I want you to understand something. What you said to me, about loving me...I don't want you to say it to me again. It isn't because I don't want to hear it, but rather because I don't want you to say it without me being able to say it in return.*

My hand went to his mouth, as if it were pulled there, and began to trace the curve of his bottom lip. I stared at it, mesmerized as I tried

322

to reason with him. "Robert, I don't expect anything from you. I've already been told once that I expect too much from people, and I finally admit that is true. I expected way too much from Graham, from Dad, even from my Mom. And, I mean my goodness, how easy it would be to expect the world from you! But I can't. I won't. I won't ruin it by wanting anything more than what you have to offer me. This—this right here is more than I could have ever hoped for, and I'm going to relish this moment no matter what happens tomorrow."

When he kissed my finger, I closed my eyes. It was such a simple gesture, yet it was enough to warm my skin and send shockwaves down my arm. I opened my eyes when he started to share his thoughts again. *Grace, you sound like you're settling for what I can give you, rather than what you deserve.*

My fingers pressed against his lips, as though to silence his thoughts so that I could speak again. "I'm not settling. How can simply loving you and, knowing that for me that is enough be settling? I can't think of having done anything that would warrant me deserving you, so how can feeling this way about you be settling?"

Robert sighed and reached for me. He pulled me close to him, my face pressed up against his neck, my arms locked against his chest. He rested his chin on my head and started reciting something. I listened carefully, the words sounding so familiar…

And here, in thought, to thee—in thought that can alone. Ascend thy empire and so be a partner of thy throne. By winged fantasy, my embassy is given, till secrecy shall knowledge be in the environs of Heaven.

I felt the slow tugs of slumber creep on me as I replayed the words over and over in my head. Before I succumbed to the sweet lull of his voice, I made one last request. "Stay."

I was asleep before he could answer, but in my dreams I heard him reply *forever.*

GROUND RULES

The alarm was going off again. I don't know why I never turn that thing off. It's not as though this was the first time. Waking up at such an early hour on Sunday was just unforgiveable in the slacker's handbook. I groaned and tried to sit up to attack the heinous buzzing contraption, but a weight against my waist kept me still. I turned my head and met the full impact of two liquid silver eyes.

Good morning, sleepy head.

I never could grasp just how a morning could truly be good—well, good enough to greet anyway—until just then, when I knew that last night hadn't been a dream, and that he had listened. He had stayed. "Robert!" I whispered gleefully. I reached for him, but again, the weight on my waist held me down. I glanced down to see what it was and observed that it was his arm. "And I thought I was the one who had asked you to stay," I teased, my hand finding his on the side of my waist, lacing our fingers together.

You toss and turn a lot in your sleep, your dreams are so vivid and…violent. I was afraid you'd kick me out of the bed and then wake up and get mad at me for not staying. He smiled, and I knew that there had never been a more beautiful thing to wake up to than that smile, even if he was teasing me.

I giggled and then sighed when he leaned in and placed a soft kiss against the corner of my mouth. *Come on, sleeping beauty, it's time to get up. Your father will be ready to tear my head off in about half an hour before taking you to the hospital, and I have to make sure that I'm presentable.* He listened to my silent question and grinned. *He'll want to know why I'm still in my tux, and I can't tell him it's because I spent the night in your room.*

Grasping onto the seriousness of the situation, I sighed again. "Well, I guess you'd better let me get up then so I can get ready." His arm lifted and I sat up, the loss of the weight making me feel suddenly bereft. I climbed to the foot of the bed and reached over, slamming my hand against the droning buzz coming from the alarm and basked in the resulting silence. Feeling the need for urgency, I ransacked my drawers for a pair of jeans and a t-shirt. My first pair of jeans in weeks! The amount of satisfaction in that thought was immeasurable; at that moment, I didn't care if Dad grounded me for a month!

Clutching my clothes to my chest, I looked over at Robert, who was lying on my bed, one arm propping up his head, his other arm lazily toying with my comforter and I silently thanked Janice for seeing a need there and changing it. "I'm going to change in the bathroom."

He smiled, already knowing that was my plan. My head was clearer to him now. He could see beyond the fog and the void that my cluttered mind portrayed. And, I could feel him in there, too. *How odd.*

I wanted to know what that meant, but I needed to change and brush my teeth first. The idea of waking up with him in my bed and scaring him away with dragon breath was enough to get me moving at a pace that would rival his own. It was when I had closed the bathroom door and stared in the mirror that I could hear his laughing in my head.

I ignored it as I quickly changed my clothes, being very careful to avoid the mirror just in case he chose to not be so gentlemanly and take a peek. That was going to be difficult now that I had made myself aware of it, this whole privacy thing. I knew that if I made him promise to never do that, he'd be tied to it, but I had to admit to the small, minute, microscopic part of me that almost didn't want to. Almost.

I brushed my teeth. Twice. And I headed towards my room, crashing into Dad in the process. "Um. Morning Dad."

His eyes were still glazed over from sleep, and his hair looked as though he'd fallen asleep under one of those vacuum hair-cutting deals, but he was still shrewd enough to give me a once over, as though he knew something else was different about me. I was too cheerful this morning, I told myself. That's what it was.

"Morning, Grace," he replied gruffly. "I'm going to call the hospital and see if we can get your arm x-rayed early, so I suggest you get dressed and ready to leave by eight."

"But I-"

He held up his hand, "No buts, Grace. I'm going to get your arm back in that cast. I saw those x-rays, and there's no way that your arm would have healed this fast. Now go and get dressed."

"Dad, I'm already dressed," I pointed out.

Blinking a few times to clear his foggy vision, he finally noticed my jeans and t-shirt. Unfortunately, he also noticed that my jean clad right leg was conspicuously cast free. "Where's your cast?" he asked, his voice calm but hinting at the anger that was threatening just beneath the surface.

"My leg is fine Dad—there's no need for the cast-"

It was as if I had learned nothing from the night before. The puce shade was back, but when combined with his helter-skelter hair, and his glassy eyes, he looked terrifying. I backed away, fearful of him for the first time.

"Grace, I want you to get in your room, I want you to call Robert, and I want you to tell him to meet us here in thirty minutes. Is that clear?"

I nodded, and inched my way around him, quickly opening my bedroom door and shutting it, bracing myself against it. As soon as the sound of the latch could be heard, Robert had me in his arms, my face pressed against his shoulder, his hands at the small of my back and the back of my head, warm and comforting.

"Oh, I've made a mess of things," I groaned. "I've never seen him that angry before. What is he going to do?"

Robert's movements were a blur of speed as I was sitting in his lap on the bed before I had even gotten to the word "angry". He stroked my hair, his hands reassuring. *He'll yell at me, accuse me of not caring for your welfare after all the trust he's put in me, threaten me with bodily harm if I ever set foot near you again...the usual things a father says when he loves his daughter.*

The groaning didn't seem to cease. "He's completely overacting. I'm so sorry about all of this."

A finger beneath my chin forced my face to look up, and a soft smile urged me to relax. *You have nothing to be sorry about. If you had*

326

to spend all night in those things, you'd have had a much worse night
than it was. I'll deal with this. Don't worry, Grace. It'll work out.

I shook my head. How was this going to work out? How was
he going to convince my father that it was perfectly sane and safe for
him to have removed my casts without telling him how or why? And
even if he did, what were the odds that Dad would believe him? It
wasn't looking to good on this end.

A knock on my door jolted us apart, and when my door opened
before I had a chance to answer whoever it was on the other side, Robert
had disappeared and Janice was walking in. "I just wanted to see that
you were okay. See if I can't try and get James to see it a bit from your
side."

She sat down next to me, oblivious to the remnant of gray mist
creeping out of my window, and placed her hands on mine, squeezing
them and sighing, "How was your date? Did you have fun?"

"Yes, for the most part," I replied, once again unable to do
anything but be honest.

Janice's face was full of happiness, and I knew that she would
be understanding about the casts. "Will you really talk to Dad about my
casts? He doesn't want to see that I really am fine without them."

She lifted her hands from mine and reached for my arm. She
examined the length, looked at my elbow, watched my face as she bent
and straightened my arm. She made me flex my fingers, flex my arm,
make a fist. She was school nurse Janice and I was patient Grace, being
given the once over to see if I could go back outside and play.

"I think your arm is perfectly fine, Grace. I don't know how.
From what your father told me, it was a clean break, and that should
take at least six weeks to heal, never mind the dislocated shoulder. And
then we have your leg. I saw you walk to the bathroom this morning,
and there's no way that you should be able to walk if your leg were truly
as bad as it was made out to be. I don't know how or why, and right
now, I don't want to. I'll tell your dad what I think, and after that, it's in
the doctor's hands. I can only hope that Robert can somehow convince
your father not to kill him."

I burst out into hysterical giggles as I thought about how my hand had looked after my playful jab at Lark. I didn't want to imagine what Dad would look like if he intentionally hit Robert. Janice's face was reproachful at my fit of laughter, and I attempted to stem it, not wanting to lose her confidence in my side. I quickly tucked my lips between my teeth and pressed down hard, the pain and the resulting tears doing much to sober me up to the gravity of the situation.

When Janice stood up and left, I looked at the clock and saw that there was exactly ten minutes left before Robert would be standing on the doorstep, ringing that bell. He hadn't told me he'd be there in thirty minutes, but I knew that he'd heard Dad's orders and wouldn't do anything to cause me to get into any more trouble. I looked at the sunlight shining through my window, and saw the glint of amber reflected against the wall; I followed the reflection to its source. It was one of the crystals from the dress; it had apparently fallen off after I had removed the dress and dropped it in Robert's lap. I bent down to retrieve it and held it up into the light.

The colors that sparkled from within it reminded me of fire and gold all at once, bouncing out onto the walls, sending shards of light and flash into every corner. I twisted my hand, causing the crystal's ocher rainbow to move along the white walls, as though splashing it with the colors of the sunrise and sunset that you couldn't see without staring directly at the sun.

My gaze was drawn to the center of the crystal; my vision entranced by the sweet hum of the soft colors that swayed and bent in the light. Their hypnotic dance lulled me into such a state of repose; I could see flames leaping and dancing around a familiar woman holding tightly to a child. I could see the woman's tears, and I could see the abject fear on her face as the flames grew higher and hungrier, their tongues reaching towards them, smelling the sweetness of apprehension.

She turned to me and she reached her hand out, her dark eyes filled with hope, as though I were her salvation. I felt my arm rise, felt it reach out towards her, but she was too far away. I saw the way her eyes glossed over with unshed tears as the fire surrounded her, cutting off all means of escape, and I watched as the flames consumed her. I could not close my eyes until hers blinked in the recognition of death,

328

and the darkness that was there was replaced by amber gold.

It was then that I opened my eyes, not realizing that I had closed them, and noticed that the crystal seemed to have lost some of its sparkle. Yesterday's sun was definitely a fluke, I decided as I looked out of my window and saw that the clouds were rolling through, settling in for another rainy October morning. The sunlight that had warmed up the room and had helped the pretty bauble decorate my life with a bit of color was fading behind a gloomy Sunday morning. Sighing, I placed the crystal on the nightstand next to my bed and headed downstairs. My daydreaming had burned a few more minutes away, leaving me absolutely no time to be left alone with Dad while he plotted the dozens of ways he'd kill Robert.

As soon as my foot hit the bottom step, the doorbell rang. Dad, having forgone his usual routine of sitting at the kitchen table to read his paper and eat his breakfast, had instead placed a cup of coffee and a plate of toast on the coffee table. Alongside them were an unopened paper and a book on first aid. He sat in the recliner, waiting, a contemplative look on his face. I was tempted to ask if the book was for him or Robert, but kept my mouth shut. It just wouldn't do for me to start running off at the mouth.

Seeing that he wasn't going to get up and get the door, I went to answer it. I took a deep breath as I turned the handle on the knob. He was standing there in the same black jacket he had worn the first day that I had seen him. His hair was disheveled, but everything else about him was perfect. His smile was reassuring, and his eyes were full of promise and reassurance. Maybe there wouldn't be a need for the first aid book after all.

He looked at me, puzzled, and his eyes softened with humor. *Your father has a first aid book out?* I could feel him, feel him in my thoughts as he searched my memory for the image, and when he saw it, he smiled. *He truly does love you. You are very blessed, Grace.*

I gaped at him. My father was about to give him the third degree and here Robert was, praising the man. Too perfect.

He grinned and held his arm out to the side of me. "Ladies first."

I sighed. Even though it had been only a few minutes since I last heard him speak, hearing the words come out of his mouth reminded much I loved his voice. "You should do that more often," I prodded, "Just so I don't ever forget what it sounds like."

"I'll remember to from now on." His smile was playful, teasing despite the reason his presence was required.

Entering the living room, I reached for his hand. If Dad was going to give him the third degree, he'd do it while facing me, too. Robert intertwined his fingers with mine. It was the only thing either of us could do before the onslaught of Dad's anger was upon us.

He stood in front of the two of us, his arms folded across his chest tightly, as if he were holding them back, and his voice boomed out at Robert in an angry bark. "I want to know why you thought it would be a good idea to remove Grace's casts."

Robert answered the only way he knew how. Honestly. "Because she didn't need them anymore."

Of course Dad wasn't going to accept that answer, not from some kid, no matter what they did in order to save my life. "That's absolute crap and you know it. Do you know what kind of damage you could have caused because of your stupidity?"

I flinched at the insult, and started to speak when the crushing grip of Robert's hand, and a flurry of thoughts silenced me. "Mr. Shelley, I was wrong to have removed Grace's casts without your permission, or that of her doctor. I should have left them on until it was advisable by her physician to have them removed. If any harm has come to Grace as a result of my impetuousness, I will never forgive myself."

Dad opened his mouth to say something, and then shut it. He paced around for a bit, nodding to himself, then started to say something else, but changed his mind again. He did this twice more, looking like a confused goldfish, before finally speaking again.

"Robert, I'm taking Grace to the hospital to have her arm and leg re-x-rayed. If she's suffered any more damage to her breaks because of your foolishness, I will hold you personally and financially responsible. Until I know for sure that she'll be fine, I think it's best that the two of you don't see each other anymore."

"Dad!" I protested, "You can't do that! It was my choice! He wouldn't have removed the casts if I hadn't said I wanted him to!"

Robert again squeezed my hand. "It's okay, Grace. Your father is right. What's paramount here is your health and safety. Everything else can wait."

Traitor! I looked in Robert's eyes and simply could not understand when it was that he had decided to aid in Dad's complicity. *I'm fine. You know I'm fine. How can you do this?*

"Let's go, Grace. Get in the car," Dad ordered. I took one last look at Robert, his face sad, but his eyes still smiling, and then did as I was told.

Ꮳ

"See, James. I told you she was okay. You should have listened to me and we could have avoided this entire fiasco."

Janice was doing her best to reassure Dad that the doctors had been correct when one by one, they all concurred that my bones were not broken, and that I had healed in a remarkably fast amount of time, although that could have been contributed to my young age, as one doctor had put it. "She's going to be fine, James."

Dad shook his head for the four hundredth time that day—no exaggeration. It was nearly four in the afternoon and we'd seen four different doctors from two different shifts who all gave the same diagnosis regarding my breaks—or lack thereof. Sitting in Dad's car had taken an act of deception on Janice's part—a slight fib about being dizzy and nauseated by the hospital smell—but it was a step closer to getting away from the hospital. Without another doctor nearby to accost, Dad was finally coming to grips with the fact that my leg and arm weren't broken, and that Robert hadn't placed me in any type of danger.

Okay, so maybe not that last part. But Janice was wearing him down; I could see it on his face. "James, I don't see how many more times you have to be told that she's okay before you finally accept that she *is* okay."

Dad's hands were gripping the top of the steering wheel, his head resting on them. "You don't understand, Janice. You don't understand what this is like."

Janice's hand reached out to comfort him; she stroked his hair, and patted his shoulder. "Tell me then. Tell me so that I can understand, because I really want to. I'm sure Grace would, too." She turned her head to look at me in the backseat, and I nodded mutely, knowing that saying anything right now would simply set Dad off again, and I didn't know about Janice but I knew that I personally was quite done with being "that girl with the crazed father".

I'd be lucky if I were given an aspirin in this hospital again, much less treated for anything after what Dad had put the staff through today.

Dad lifted his head and I could see his reflection in the rearview mirror. His eyes rested on purple half-moons, the exhaustion written quite plainly in them. But there was also something else hidden behind them. Was it fear? I watched as he turned his head towards Janice, and spoke, not necessarily to her.

"You don't know what it's like. After Abby's accident, everyone kept wondering how anyone could have survived without a scratch or burn on them. The explosion took out a telephone pole that was twenty feet away; twenty feet away! And everyone kept looking at this little girl like she was either some kind of miracle or oddity.

"But people—people are fickle when it comes to what they like to talk about, what keeps them interested. The miracle of a child surviving a car accident just doesn't sound as exciting as a child causing the accident and surviving it when her mother didn't. Grace didn't remember anything, so the explanations were all based on speculations and assumptions.

"It doesn't matter if there's any truth to the story or not. What matters is what sounds more interesting. This has followed Grace her entire life, and she's suffered for it. I probably should have moved, rather than subject her to the constant scrutiny she's had to go through by some of the kids here, but I couldn't leave; Abby's buried here, and I simply couldn't leave because people were gossiping.

"And now this—don't you see what people will say? What they'll think? She's going to be ridiculed again, because for whatever reason, she's not healing like a normal person. Normal people get burned in fires. Normal people get hurt when they're thrown from vehicles. Normal people's bones don't heal in two weeks after being run over by a car."

Normal people don't date angels.

"James, you're being ridiculous. I'm sure that-"

Dad's anger silenced everything, even my breathing, as he raged. "I'm not being ridiculous! I'm the one who's raised her, seen the way she's been left out of everything. I'm the one who's had to comfort her when the birthday party invitations went to every girl in her class but her, when the kids would tease her because of how she looks; I was the one who watched her grow up with only one friend, and I was the one who watched when that friend left her, too. Don't tell me that what I've seen and what I know will happen is me being ridiculous, Janice!"

I sat stunned. The memories of my childhood had long since dulled to a mild irritation, but I never knew that they had affected Dad so profoundly. He had never indicated that he'd been distressed by it; I had always thought that he'd simply viewed it as a part of life. And to know that he was aware as to why, that brought our current situation into perspective. More than his fear that I would be hurting myself if my leg and arm were still broken, he was worried about how people would treat me. He was worried about my emotional wellbeing. I rubbed my fingers against my eyes, my tears acting as lubrication.

"Dad, it's okay. I don't care about what they say anymore." I looked at his face. The pain there added years to his age, and I needed to rid him of that. Rid him of the fear of my own pain and rejection. "I'm going to be fine, Dad. Really."

He shifted in the seat to face me, his mouth wore a small frown, and his hair—it was still a mess, but he was Dad. I could see myself in his face, see the parts of him that were shared with me, and I could see the parts that had been my mom's to keep. And now, those belonged to

Janice… "Dad, my life has never been better. I have friends—real friends who don't care about the accident, or what other people are saying behind my back, or any of that. They care about me—Robert cares about me. I'm not alone in this anymore, Dad. And neither are you. Janice is here with you, too."

He looked at Janice, and I could see as his face softened that he knew it, too. If I had had any doubts about Janice remaining, they were gone in that instant. There was definite love there between the two of them. I could see it. And after a moment, I could hear it as they pressed their heads together, whispering the words to each other. It was a scene that was familiar to me in most ways except for one, but I couldn't afford to be melancholy, not when I already had so much.

When the car started and we left the hospital parking lot, I stared out of the window. The ride home was a familiar one, and I easily slipped into a moment much like this one, where Dad and I were headed home from the hospital after being told that I was fine, just in shock. Dad hadn't yelled then, but then again, he didn't do much of anything. He had simply buckled me in and then drove home. At least this time, he had someone with him other than me.

As we pulled into the driveway, I could see a Stacy's Neon and Robert's motorcycle parked at the curb. Both were leaning against her car, talking and waiting. Stacy's face was anxious, while Robert's seemed pleased. I smiled at the thoughts he chose to share with me. Stacy had been caught wind of our date and wanted all of the details. Like a typical girlfriend would. It felt good.

As we all exited the vehicle, I could see the tenseness that had slightly retreated in Dad suddenly return. And it had brought some friends. "Robert, I would like to have a word with you and Grace inside. Stacy, please excuse us, but this has to be done in private."

Stacy nodded, her anxiousness replaced by confusion and curiosity. Janice wrapped an arm around her shoulders and said, more to me than to Dad, "I'll stay here with her while you go inside and talk."

As the three of us walked inside of the house, the flashes of memory stabbed at me—of walking into the house after mom had died— I shook my head at the darkness of the incomplete memory. The silence now was just as stark, just as bleak. I followed Dad into the living room, and sat on the couch as he sat in his recliner. Robert, having nowhere else to sit, sat next to me. Did he dare to hold my hand? Did I? As if to confirm that he'd dare anything, he reached for my hand and brought it to his mouth, placing a very soft kiss at the base of my knuckles, his eyes full of mischief.

"Ahem."

We both turned our heads; Dad's features were strangely aloof. I could feel my mouth grow slack as he began to talk, a slight smile on his face as he did so. "Robert, I wanted to let you know that you were right about Grace's injuries. She has healed completely, much to the surprise of the doctors that examined her today. I will admit when I'm wrong, and in this instance, I was. However, your taking of the matter into your hands was unacceptable and irresponsible, and there has to be consequences for your actions. For both of your actions."

Robert nodded while I simply gawked. "I understand, sir."

Dad rubbed his hands on his knees and continued, "Grace is grounded for the next two weeks. She won't be allowed to go anywhere, and she won't be allowed to have any friends over either. She's just started going back to school, and I think that the distractions that you pose to her wouldn't be conducive to her studies.

"Two weeks from now, you'll be allowed to see her every other day at the house, and you may take her out during the weekends, but she must be home by eleven, regardless of what the function. I will want to meet your parents, of course, and discuss what happened with them so that they can make the proper decisions regarding how they feel you should be punished. And I want a number where I can reach you should anything stupid like this happens again."

I started to say something, but Robert squeezed my hand, a warning. Instead, he spoke, "All of that sounds perfectly acceptable, reasonable, and just, sir. Mr. Shelly, if I may. I was wondering if it would be alright if I took Grace to and from school, so that she wouldn't have to walk or ride her bicycle there."

Dad brought a hand to his chin and rubbed it, contemplating the suggestion. "I guess that would be alright. Are you going to be doing so on that bike of yours out there?" he motioned with his head towards the door.

Robert's smile was cocky, but he shook his head. "If you'd prefer I pick her up in a car, I have one of those available as well. I simply ride the bike because it's cheap on gas."

The notion that Robert was thinking of economy on something that looked like it cost more than Dad's car did new was lost on Dad, as he appreciated any sign of frugality. "What kind of car do you own, Robert?"

I suddenly became the third wheel as Robert leaned forward to answer, "Well, since my eighteenth birthday just passed a couple of weeks ago, I received a car from my mother as a gift."

Intrigued, Dad leaned forward, too. "What was it?"

"A Charger, sir."

"What model year?"

"The latest one, sir."

Dad whistled. Dad never whistles. "That's a very nice gift. What made her choose that one? I would have thought that you'd prefer one of those European models."

Robert smiled. "Because it's an American car. Buy American, that's what we're encouraged to do, right?" His British accent never seemed more prominent than it did at that moment, when the word "American" passed through his lips. The tone was the same one he had every time he said the word "human"; it seemed like he was emphasizing the word to hint to us that he was different.

Whatever the reason, Dad seemed impressed by his answer, and they continued to discuss the virtues of American made vehicles while I sat silent and entertained myself by staring at my fingernails. Leaving a girl alone in her thoughts was dangerous as I wondered when it was that I had stopped chewing them, because for the first time in years, they looked healthy. Everything looked healthy. My skin this morning had looked pink and flushed, as opposed to the slightly dull and pallid it had always been. My eyes seemed brighter, my hair was, for lack of a better word, glossy, and my lips looked…like they had had their first kiss.

I brought my fingers to my lips and remembered how careful

that first kiss had been. I pressed my fingers against them a bit harder, remembering the second kiss and how less careful it had been, and how controlled Robert had been while I seemed a veritable mess. It didn't matter that he had the age and experience to be patient, and keep his emotions contained, while I was new to everything. I doubted that I'd ever have felt such an intense heat rushing through me with anyone else as I did with Robert.

"What's the matter, Grace? Are you feeling nauseated?"

Dad's question caught me off guard, and my hand dropped. "What?"

"You look a bit flushed, Grace. Perhaps you should lie down."

I looked from Dad to Robert, confusion written all over my face. Robert stood up, his eyes sparkling with humor, while Dad's was filled with concern. "I guess I will be leaving now, Mr. Shelley. Thank you, for allowing me to pick Grace up from school. I shall see you in the morning, Grace."

I watched as he left, unable to say anything. I finally whispered a soft "bye" after I heard the door close, knowing that he'd hear it, even if I barely did. It didn't take long before Stacy and Janice walked in, taking Robert's departure as their cue that all was clear. I didn't know what to say to either of them. Stacy wasn't even supposed to be here anymore, but she wasn't aware of that yet.

"So, I heard you're a free bird. No more broken wing, eh?" Stacy joked as she sat down next to me, filling up the void that Robert had left behind.

I nodded my head, and looked at Dad, waiting for him to tell her she had to leave, or explain the conditions of my grounding. He seemed to be waiting for me to do the same. Sighing and rolling my eyes, I turned to Stacy. "I'm kinda grounded, Stacy, and I can't have any friends over for the next two weeks so we're going to have to cut this visit short."

Ugh, it sounded like I was ten, and not two months shy of eighteen. I didn't understand the need of such a harsh punishment for doing nothing wrong. And hadn't Dad been the very one who said he didn't want people thinking I was weird? Surely healing and then being punished for it wasn't normal!

Stacy's face seemed crestfallen as she realized she had to leave. "Well, I guess I'll go then. I'll see you in homeroom tomorrow?"

"Yeah. I'll be there."

She bobbed her head, as if accepting that little piece of information was somehow some poor consolation prize to staying. I was overwhelmed by the amount of information that small gesture told me. She was genuinely disappointed that she couldn't spend time with me. I couldn't help but hug her then, the feelings of gratitude completely taking over and reducing me to a pile of chewed up emotion.

And, unsurprisingly, she returned the hug, squeezing me as tightly as she could because she wanted to.

When she left a few minutes later, I decided that it was about time I started making dinner again. I hadn't done so in almost two months, and I was sure that Janice could use the break. Seeing that she already had the fixings for meatloaf out, I got to work on mixing the meat, breadcrumbs, eggs, and seasoning. As I shaped the loaf on the pan, I had to admit that my life was also shaping out pretty well. Even if I was grounded for the next two weeks.

THREE

I had feared that the two weeks of being grounded would have dragged on forever, especially once the talk about how quickly I had healed began circulating around the school, but I hadn't thought about just how many hours a day I spent in classes—with Robert in half of them—or just how easy it was to simply head up to my room and find Robert sitting or lying on the bed, as if he'd always been there.

He'd always welcome me as though I had been away for hours rather than a few minutes, with strong arms, and kisses that were sweet and tender. But they were also hesitant, as though he were holding something back from me, and I wasn't sure what or why. I wasn't about to complain though. Sweet kisses from Robert, no matter how contained, were far more than I had ever expected, and certainly had no cause to think I deserved them.

I was also surprised at how comfortable I was with having him staying with me in my room, falling asleep with his arms around me, his heart beat and his steady breathing lulling me to sleep each night. I'd always wake up with his arm across my waist, a vise keeping me from lashing out in my sleep. "One day, you're going to have to tell me what I'm dreaming about that causes me to be so rough with you," I had told him after the fourth time I had woken up to feel his arm pressed on me.

He had smiled and said that he couldn't make it out, that there were far too many dizzying images in my head while I slept, and he wasn't about to strain himself trying to decipher it all.

On the last day of my grounding, Stacy and Lark both decided that I'd be joining them on a shopping trip in celebration of my freedom. The idea of a day of girly bonding seemed so foreign to me, I was genuinely frightened at the thought; they were shopping mall kind of people—I was most comfortable in a thrift store. But Stacy wouldn't take no for an answer, and Lark could see all of my excuses before they were even out of my mouth, so she always had a reply on the ready if ever Stacy stumbled for one. I knew then that Stacy and Lark had become friends because there wasn't anyone else anywhere who could match wits with the two of them. They were kindred spirits, even if Stacy remained ignorant to what Lark truly was.

It was a point that I brought up on the way to the mall that night. Lark had the highly coveted front passenger seat, while I had the cramped rear. It was, Lark explained, easier for a blind person to enter and exit the car from the front than from the back. I pictured a very large bull and a very large pile of steaming dung that spelled out a very obnoxious phrase after that explanation. She snorted, and I shook my head and laughed.

Will you tell Stacy about what you are?

Lark was quiet for a bit, then she sighed. *I don't know. I've never told anyone what I am. I don't know how to judge a person's character worthy enough to do so.*

In the back of my mind I could hear Ellie's comments about the test that the electus patronus were given in order to prove their loyalty. *What about that? What about seeing if she passes the test?*

Lark seemed to take that suggestion into consideration. *I admit all of this is very new to me. I've never enjoyed your kind; humans are always so depressed and self-destructive. Your wars, your politics, your incessant need to possess gets annoying after a few centuries. And yet, with all your written history, you still repeat it! Einstein was right when he said that insanity was doing the same thing over and over again and expecting different results.*

Stacy, who had been singing along to the radio throughout most of the silent conversation between Lark and I, noticed how quiet we were. "What's up with you two? Are you mad at each other or something?"

Lark and I both laughed; I a bit more nervously, while Lark's was simply one of amusement. "I can't be mad at Grace. If I were, Rob would never let me hear the end of it."

I couldn't help but smile at that, because it was true. She had said it; there was no getting around it. "I'm simply enjoying listening to you sing, Stacy. You know, you've got a pretty good voice." And I meant it. My head perked up at that admission. "I didn't know you could sing."

Stacy shrugged her shoulders. "Fat lot of good singing is going to do me here. My parents have it set in their minds that I'm going to graduate, go to college and become a doctor, or lawyer, and then, when I'm twenty-five, I'll marry a doctor or lawyer—Korean of course—and give up my career and have babies." Lark and I looked at each other. We both knew that she had meant her mini-rant to sound sarcastic, but what it sounded more like was sad and hopeless.

"Well, you could always go away to college and take a few singing courses there," I suggested. "Your parents will be here, so it's not like they'll know, right?"

She shook her head, turning the car to park. "You don't know how lucky you are, not to have been raised by a Korean Mom. She plans on moving with me into the dorms, as my chaperone, because she says American boys cannot be trusted. She forgets that she's the mother of *five* American boys herself."

Lark hissed.

I was about to laugh at her comment when she suddenly slammed on the breaks, sending my head careening into the headrest. "Ow."

"Oh goodness, I'm sorry Grace. I forgot. I shouldn't have said that stuff about not being raised by a Korean Mom. Ugh, how stupid am I?" Stacy moaned, her little face turning red with embarrassment and hurt. "I didn't mean it. Oh dear." She seemed torn between apologizing to me and parking the car. Parking won out when the honking started—her sudden stop had nearly caused an accident behind her.

I patted her shoulder with one hand while rubbing my nose with the other. "It's okay, Stacy. I know you didn't mean anything by it."

Stacy sniffled, disbelief in her eyes.

"Suck it up, Stacy. She said it's okay, so let's go and shop. I've got a great idea for our Halloween costumes, and I want to check out the fabric store," Lark complained, her eyes rolling at Stacy's mini-pity party.

"Yes, let's go and see what Lark's got up her sleeve," I agreed, not knowing what exactly she was talking about, but welcoming the subject change nonetheless.

Stacy laughed, as though I had cracked some incredible joke. "I forgot, you don't know, do you?"

I looked at her, my ignorance obvious. "What?"

"Well…this year's homecoming ball was cancelled and instead, there's going to be a Halloween Carnival with a costume contest, and Lark entered the three of us in it."

"Wh-a-a-at?" My shock was genuine. "When did this happen? And why wouldn't I know about it?"

Lark picked at an invisible piece of lint on her blouse, something that went completely unnoticed by Stacy, and I could almost see the millions of gears in her head working overtime trying to find a way to give an explanation that didn't reveal the truth without it actually being a lie. "Tell me, Lark, or I'll ask Robert."

She threw up her hands. "All right, fine. It happened yesterday, and you wouldn't know about it because I wasn't planning on telling you until Halloween. I guess I just forgot to tell someone *else* that it was supposed to be a secret." She threw daggers at Stacy with her eyes.

Stacy, not realizing the danger she was in, laughed at the comment. "There's a cash prize for best costume, Grace. There won't be a homecoming queen or king this year, so everyone can participate, and Lark's idea sounded awesome, considering the theme."

"What's the theme and how much is the prize for?" I asked, not wanting to know what the actual costume was. I had a strange feeling that the theme would have something to do with agriculture and Stacy and I would end up dressed as the cow to Lark's farmer girl.

Lark snorted as Stacy answered, "It's that song about three being the magic number; isn't that awesome? The prize is for three hundred bucks! Think about what you could do with your share of that money, Grace!"

A hundred dollars? That would go straight into my meager

savings account and accrue pathetic interest, that's where it would go. I shook my head. "What is your idea, Lark? What are you plotting in your head for this costume contest?"

She puffed up and grinned. "We're going as three Goddesses. Greek, to be exact. None of that made-up stuff you see on the internet."

It was my turn to snort. "Like I could ever be a Goddess."

Stacy groaned, "Grace, you don't even realize how much you're envied right now. Not only did you crush Erica at the soliloquy reading last month, but you're dating the hottest guy in school. That does a lot to change the way people look at you."

"Can you not refer to my brother as the hottest guy in school? I have to live with him and I don't want that phrase running through my head when I smell him in his nasty sweats and sneakers," Lark protested, which drew a peal of laughter from me.

I couldn't picture Robert wearing anything that smelled nasty. I couldn't picture Robert wearing sweats for that matter. He was always dressed impeccably, while I was the frump in thrift store shirts and jeans.

Lark, having heard my thoughts, uncharacteristically put her arm around my shoulder. *He doesn't care what you wear, Grace. It wasn't you in a designer gown that he kissed, was it? No. It was you in boxers, with no makeup, no fancy hairdo, no fancy jewelry. Just you.*

I hadn't thought about it that way. I had been so wrapped up in trying to convince him how I felt, what I had been wearing had been of little consequence. I looked into Lark's face, and saw her grin. Stacy came up on the other side of me and wrapped her arm around my waist. The three of us stood there in the parking lot embracing, myself in the middle, and I couldn't help but start giggling. I didn't care if Lark and Stacy both thought I was completely nuts. The giddiness of having girlfriends that I could talk about boys with, and the fact that there actually was one that I could talk about seemed like such an impossibility just a few months ago, and yet here I was, living the impossible.

Looking like an odd set of conjoined triplets, the three of us started walking towards the mall entrance, the topic of costumes on our

343

minds.

Halloween and Homecoming both fell on the same day this year, which explained why the homecoming ball had been cancelled and the carnival set up in its place. The theme for the costume contest was made clear with all of the posters that had plastered the school walls for the past two weeks; Heath's Halloween and Homecoming were clearly visible on every bright yellow and orange piece of paper, each capitalized "H" in big, bold letters.

Lark, who had found some incredibly inexpensive fabric with Stacy the day after our shopping trip—having not liked anything we had seen the night before—had spent most of her free time holed up at home, sewing our costumes. Stacy had offered to help, thinking that Lark's blindness was a handicap to her, but Lark insisted that she could do it herself, that being blind had allowed her other senses to be heightened. It was true, of course, but Stacy couldn't have known that; the rejection had left Stacy miffed and Lark upset that she had hurt her, and confused because she was upset.

Robert and I had spent every day together since the night of the wedding, with him spending most nights lying next to me, innocently holding me while I slept. I had thought that perhaps as time went on, his affections would grow stronger, his kisses more demanding, but everything had seemed to level off for him.

And, though I always felt the incredibly heady rush of blood and fire whenever he would brush his lips gently across mine, there always seemed to be something missing, and I could never place my finger on it; I could tell by the way he was breathing that he was just as affected as I was, but I had come to realize that part of it was due to how I felt. I often took for granted the fact that everything he physically felt, he felt through me. If my reactions to his touch were cataclysmic, his would be as well, although in a much milder sense.

Graham had been distant with me since the night of the wedding, and I understood why. It was difficult for him to watch as

344

Robert and I walked through school, oblivious to most everything else save each other. Although there were no overt displays of affection between the two of us, it was hard to miss how close we were, connected through something other than just something physical, and I knew how that must have felt to Graham, because a couple of months prior, it had been my heart that had been aching.

I wanted to talk to him about our friendship and where it stood in relation to my relationship with Robert, but it seemed that neither of them could deal with my wanting some kind of dialogue with the other. Robert had lamented that until he could control his jealousy, it would be best if I stayed away from Graham, and Graham had insisted that Robert was trying to control me because of the fact that he was jealous. Of course, Robert had been extremely upset that Graham was aware of how he felt, which only further complicated things.

And the one thing that stood at the back of my mind, the thing that worried me the most, was always in my line of sight. Erica hadn't been suspended, but she had been put on probation and received a D on her soliloquy, and that only seemed to fuel whatever form of hatred she felt for me. When Robert and I would arrive to school, especially on that Monday back, she was there. It was as though she had been waiting all weekend at the school to tear my eyes out.

I had been terrified until Lark suddenly appeared, her lips pulled back over her teeth in a nasty snarl, her walking stick folded in her hand. "You will leave Grace alone, or I will make your life a living hell. And believe me when I say this, I can." I knew that the sudden appearance out of nowhere was enough to have startled Erica, but the fierce look in Lark's sightless eyes, and the way her words came out like a growl were what kept Erica from acting on whatever plans she had concocted since that Friday.

However, that did not stop her from making idle threats directed at me to her friends, nor did it keep her from intentionally crashing into me while walking through the hallway. I was constantly on my guard, paranoid that when I least expected it, she'd exact the revenge she seemed to be clinging to with determined desperation.

Being pulled in so many directions, with so many different

emotions running through me was draining. So when Halloween finally arrived, I looked forward to dressing up as something else, pretending to be someone else—escape this life for just one day. Stacy had picked Lark up at the Bellegarde house that morning before arriving at mine, costumes in hand.

My Grecian gown was a knee length mass of soft white fabric that draped in the front and hung low in the back. The straps at my shoulders were twisted knots of the same fabric joined with plum-sized medallions that had been embossed with the head of a lion on its face. A ribbon of gold wound and crisscrossed over my abdomen, finally tying in the back. It was the second most beautiful dress I had ever seen in my life.

Unlike that off the rack design that my brother got you, this was made by me. It's a Lark Bellegarde original, and one day, when you have a bit more fashion sense, you'll appreciate it for what it is.

I rolled my eyes, having heard enough of Lark's sarcasm to know better than to get riled up. As Lark wrapped the golden laces around my waist, Stacy was busy trying to turn my hair into a mass of ringlets. "I don't think your hair wants to cooperate. I'll just pin half of it up and leave the rest down."

I shrugged my shoulders, not really caring either way, knowing that the two of them would look decidedly far more beautiful than I would. I felt something wrap around my feet and glanced down. "You didn't make sandals, too?"

Lark's head bobbed up and down as she wrapped golden straps around my calf, "I've been making these for ages. It would seem that the only way that they'll ever be appropriate is with Grecian fashion, so I finally have a legitimate excuse to wear them."

Knowing that for her, "ages" actually meant "ages", I couldn't argue to the contrary. And I also couldn't fault her on her design either, because when I looked in the mirror to assess her skill at costume design, I was amazed. "Lark, this is beautiful." I turned around to see how the back looked and nearly stumbled over in shock. "There's no back!" I gasped.

Rolling her eyes, Lark handed me something from her bag.

"Here. Put this on your arm."

I looked at it and marveled at what I saw, glad for the distraction. It was a bronze snake that was coiled just so that it would wrap around the bicep. "What is this for?"

Stacy finished pinning up my hair and then clapped her hands. "You're Athena, the Goddess of wisdom. That's your Erichthonius. Lark said it was very important that you had one. Your shield is in the car."

"And who are you supposed to be?" I questioned, looking at her gown, which was the same length as mine only in an ivory shade rather than white.

"I am Artemis. Lark said that with your intelligence you'd suit well for Athena, but my penchant for fighting, and that fact that I have a twin brother made me the perfect Artemis."

Lark nodded, "Yeah, but your brother—from what I've heard, he's no Apollo, so I think that might disqualify you."

"Oh please. And what qualifies you as Aphrodite? Other than your looks?"

Lark smirked, not caring that she really shouldn't know how beautiful she was due to her blindness. "Is there any other reason necessary? Now come on, let's go before we're late for school."

The three of us stumbled outside, having said quick goodbyes to Dad and Janice who both stared in shock as I left the house for the second time in a dress. As we joked about what the reactions would be when we got to school, I caught sight of someone standing by Stacy's car.

"Graham," I breathed.

Lark's head lifted up and Stacy stopped laughing. "Get off my car, Princess."

He backed away, his hands held up as though Stacy were holding up some kind of weapon. He looked all three of us up and down, a lazy smile on his face. "You ladies look nice."

Stacy made a confused sound, Lark's face lit up, and I felt my heart crack a little. "What's up?" I asked casually, fearful that at any moment, a black Charger or motorcycle would appear and then I'd be stuck in the middle of some ridiculous testosterone driven war.

He laughed, and shrugged his shoulders. "I saw that your owner wasn't here, so I thought I'd stop by to see if you needed a ride. When I got outside, I saw that your friends were here, so I figured it was safe to at least say hi. Hi."

Ignoring the swipe at Robert, I smiled at him. And it felt good. It felt very good. "Hi back."

Graham looked over at Lark and Stacy, and then at me again, and grinned. "Are you guys the three Graces?"

Stacy slapped her forehead, the sound visibly pleasing Graham. "*That's* who we should have been! The three Graces!"

Lark shook her head. "Nope. We don't meet the personality requirements. Well…*you* don't, anyway."

Not wanting to have to listen to another argument between the two of them, and not wanting to have it happen right in front of Graham, I quickly changed the subject. "What time is it, Graham," and pointed to his watch.

He glanced at it, "It's a quarter to eight."

"What? We're late! Come on, let's get going guys. Robert expected us fifteen minutes ago," I groaned, my voice tinged with nervousness.

Stacy nodded, and fumbled for her keys inside of her bag. Lark, who always sat in front, waited while I said my goodbyes to Graham.

"I guess I'll see you at school," he said, not trying to hide the sadness in his voice.

"I guess."

I watched as he stalked away towards his car, and then I climbed into the backseat of Stacy's. I leaned my head on the window, and wondered when had everything become so difficult. I waved as we passed him getting into his car, but he didn't see me.

The ride to school was quiet. Stacy kept opening her mouth like she was going to say something, but then closed it. Lark didn't speak at all. I just wondered what else could go wrong today.

As we pulled up to the school, I scanned the parking lot for Robert's car. It wasn't there. Neither was his motorcycle. My gaze

348

travelled to Lark's reflection in the rearview mirror. *Where is he?*

She shrugged her shoulders. *I don't know. I haven't seen him since yesterday when he brought you home.*

I frowned. *He didn't tell you that he was meeting with Sam?*

Lark's eyes widened and then narrowed into suspicious slits. *No. He knew I'd start in on him about it. But damn him for leaving like this, and without saying anything.*

My head jerked at her thoughts. *What do you mean, leaving? He said he was meeting with Sam and that he'd be waiting for me here at seven-thirty.*

Lark frowned. *His meetings always end up with him leaving. Sam has probably taken him on one of his duties. Ugh, that means that we probably won't be seeing him until Monday.* She grunted and slouched in her seat, apparently not pleased with the idea.

It was my turn to frown as I realized that this would be the first weekend that Robert would be away. He had spent a few nights away before, but never more than one at a time, and I had discovered that I didn't sleep as well when he was gone. If he was going to be away for three nights, I'd be a complete zombie by the time he came home! I closed my eyes and tried to reassure myself that I was going to be alright.

After parking, the three of us climbed out of the car, our enthusiasm for the day's events thinned a bit, and walked towards the school's entrance. Everyone was in costume. This year's theme had been widely interpreted, as it had been intended. There were people dressed up as actual number threes, while others came as famous trios. Chips, Dip, and Salsa were dressed up as the three stooges, and three of the girls in our class were dressed up as the three witches from Macbeth.

As the bell rang for class, Lark unfolded her walking stick, sighing as she did so. It was a pain for her, to have to pretend that she needed it when I knew she did not, but her obvious impairment necessitated it, and so she begrudgingly started swinging it back and forth as she started walking, waving a nonchalant hand back at us as she did so.

Stacy quickly opened up her trunk and peered in. "Uh-oh. I

don't know where your shield is. I think we might have left it at Lark's house. That's okay, though. I think all you have to do is say who you are. It's not like people are going to know you're missing your shield, after all."

I couldn't argue the point with her there. We were the only ones dressed as Goddesses, so I simply nodded and waited as she locked up the car. We headed off to homeroom at a leisurely pace, grateful for the return of Mr. Frey's penchant for sleeping during class. It appeared that his being awake the day of my soliloquy had been a fluke, and there would be no more repeat performances.

The day, as it was, passed slowly for me. I hadn't appreciated the fact that with Robert in school, I had something to look forward to. The classes that we shared together dragged without him there, and the classes that we didn't share made me dread leaving because I knew he wouldn't be outside of the door, waiting for me.

Lunch, as well as third period with Stacy offered a respite from the nagging feeling of loneliness that plagued me throughout the day. I hadn't expected that I would feel so…lost. It was overwhelming. By the time the last bell had rung and it was time to head off to the gym for the homecoming assembly, I was feeling quite depressed.

"Snap out of it, Grace. You act as though he's your life force or something," Stacy quipped as we walked to the gymnasium. "He's probably just taking a skip day and hanging out at the mall or something. Besides, he's just a guy—no offense, Lark—and guys really aren't reliable. I should know. There are five of them in my house."

Lark was silent, her thoughts for me alone. *You're not the only one worried. I can't hear him. I can never hear him when he's with Sam. It's one of the reasons why he gets on my nerves.*

I frowned, wondering if she felt the same way when it was my thoughts she couldn't hear.

I know why you protect your thoughts, Grace. I don't understand why Sam and Robert are protecting theirs or how they're doing it. Maybe it's because Sam is winged. I don't know. I just know that it irritates me because I don't know, and I like to know everything.

Well, she was right on that account. She did like to know

350

everything. "So when exactly is the prize for best costume supposed to be awarded?" I asked, looking for anything to change the subject...of either conversation.

"Tonight, after the game at the carnival that the boosters are throwing; the announcement is supposed to be made there." Stacy fiddled with her prop bow as we sat down in the bleachers, intentionally trying to distract herself from something.

"What are you doing?" Lark hissed at her as the tip of the bow hit her arm for the third time. I knew that she was more concerned with the damage that her body would do to the bow than the other way around, and the questions that that might bring up, but Stacy made the proper assumption and put the bow on the floor.

"Sorry. I just don't want Sean to see me."

Sean was Stacy's twin, and older brother by two minutes. Those two minutes meant a lot in Stacy's family, because that left the role of the baby of the family to fall on the shoulders of the only girl, and the five brothers were very protective of their baby sister. "He's already told me that he's telling Mom when we get home, so I don't care what you two say, I'm not going home until after we win the prize money."

Lark's sightless eyes glared across the court at someone sitting high up atop of the bleachers. His face looked similar to Stacy's; his jaw was square, and his forehead was slightly wider, but they shared the same honest eyes, and the same sarcastic twist to their lips. I watched as the perturbed look on his face suddenly changed to one of...apprehension?

What are you doing to him? I could tell by the way Lark was smirking that she was up to something.

I'm showing Sean just what will await him if he tells his mom about Stacy's costume.

I gasped. *Isn't that kind of against the law?*

Lark turned her head towards me, her expression one of annoyance. *Look, I'm an angel in form and function, but I'm not one in behavior, okay? And no, it isn't* against the law. *It's me trying to save our friend here a little trouble from her parents that she doesn't need.*

Suddenly Lark's head turned, her focus right back on Sean. Her

351

brows furrowed in confusion, her eyes widening and narrowing as thoughts that were obviously troubling ran through her mind…and then her mouth opened, shocked. She turned to look at Stacy, who could have been my reflection, our faces both concerned for her strange behavior.

"Why didn't you tell us that you used to have cancer?" Lark blurted.

Stacy's face showed her surprise and also the pain of a silent betrayal. She turned to look at her brother, and whispered, "Who told you? I've never said anything to anyone. I don't even think about it now. Only my family knows…" Her head whipped back to Lark. "How did you find out?"

Lark's lip trembled, and I could see her struggle, the flash of pain in her eyes as she fought the truth from coming out. She stood up, and with methodical steps, slowly left the two of us in the gym, her stick mindlessly waving back and forth with no purpose whatsoever. Stacy grabbed her bow and rushed after her while I followed.

Lark, where are you going? I sent my question out to her, hoping that she'd answer it, but I couldn't hear her response. Stacy and I both stopped in the parking lot, neither of us knowing where Lark could have gone off to.

"Where did she go?" Stacy turned to face me, her eyes full of tears. "I don't understand. Why did she leave? How did she find out, Grace? Did you know?"

I looked in her eyes, and I couldn't say anything. The truth was not mine to tell. Stacy's secret hadn't been Lark's to tell either. I just didn't know what the consequences were for Lark if she couldn't tell Stacy the truth.

I watched as Stacy's head perked up, her brow furrowing with concentration, and then she started walking away from the parking lot. "Stacy?" I called out, but she kept walking. "Stacy where are you go-" She raised her hand up to silence me as she stopped, her head dipping down a bit before straightening, and then she turned, heading towards the baseball diamond towards the back of the school. I followed her, trying to match her pace, but failing pretty miserably. She was in great

352

shape, while I felt like a sack of potatoes.

We kept walking, Stacy much further ahead of me than she had been when she took off, until we reached third base. I was panting, while Stacy seemed irate. "Wh-why are w-w-we h-here?" I wheezed, the air not wanting to cooperate with my lungs to get the words out with the appropriate amount of syllables.

Stacy looked at me as though she hadn't realized that I had been following her. "I heard Lark's voice. She kept saying to come to the baseball field. Then she said third base—go to third base."

"Maybe she's talking about with a guy," I joked, not knowing what else to say because I knew what was coming. I just didn't think it'd be *today*.

Stacy raised her hand again. "Shh. She's saying something." She swung her head around, as though looking for something. Her body turned, following her head like a tail would on a dog, and after three full rotations she stopped, shaking the dizziness away.

And then she screamed.

Because Lark was standing right in front of her.

"Holy Hell and everything covered in chocolate, how did you do that?" Stacy shouted.

Lark looked…fragile. I had never seen her like this before, and it was scary. I could see that she was terrified. Today she would either be gaining a true friend, or losing the first one she had ever cared about. I stepped back, not wanting to intrude on whatever happened.

Stacy's head bobbed up and down as she answered an unspoken question. I saw her eyes widen, her mouth open, and her hand raise up to cover it. She turned to look at me, accusations written plainly in her eyes, and then whipped her head back at Lark, her jaw set stubbornly as this new bit of information set in, obliterating what she had thought was real and what wasn't. Her forehead wrinkled up in concentration, and I smiled at the familiar action, knowing what it was she was trying to do.

Lark's head shook, and a small smile tipped the corners of her mouth. She disappeared, eliciting a shocked "oh" from Stacy, who stared blankly at the empty spot that Lark had occupied just seconds before. When she reappeared a few minutes later, she had something in her hand; it was my shield. Stacy took the shield from her and wiped the tears from her eyes. "Why didn't you ever tell me?"

Lark finally spoke, a strange sense of easiness in her voice. "I didn't know if I could trust you."

Stacy smiled. "With such a huge secret, I guess I can understand that. But why now? What's changed?"

The strain of having to be honest aside, I was curious as well as to what could have compelled Lark to make the decision to finally reveal the secret that she had kept to her for over five hundred years to a human.

"When I heard your brother's thoughts, I realized how long you had kept your secret to yourself. You didn't exaggerate when you said you don't even think about it. I would have seen it. I knew then—knew more than I've ever known anything else that I could tell you. I could tell you everything and it would be okay. I could trust you," Lark's words tumbled out.

Stacy laughed. "How awesome is this secret?" She directed her next question at me, "And I suppose you were never going to tell me?"

I shook my head. "It's not my secret to tell."

Accepting that, she did something that was very Stacy. She reached out and hugged Lark. The small displays of affection that I had been a part of with Lark had told me that it was possible to not be surprised by a similar reaction on her part, but never did I expect to see what happened next. With a loud shout of joy, Lark's arms wrapped around Stacy and they shot straight up into the air, disappearing completely from my sight.

I could hear Stacy's shrieks of excitement, but I couldn't see her. I held my hand above my eyes as I scanned the skyline for any sign of them, but seeing nothing, I sighed and prepared to have a seat on third base. A slight breeze alerted me to their return.

"Don't you dare sit on that filthy base in that dress," Lark ordered.

Stacy's cheeks were ruddy from the wind, and her eyes were glazed over with excitement. "I cannot have imagined a better Halloween. This is better than Christmas."

354

"So did you actually tell her what you are, or have you decided to let her figure it out on her own?" I looked at Lark, and waited for her response.

"She knows everything."

I threw my hands up in the air. "Well that's great. I had to play twenty-one thousand questions with your brother, and she gets a straight answer. What's the difference?"

Lark's lower lip stuck out. "Grace, I really cannot tell you."

"Ugh! She gets all the answers and I get 'sorry, I can't tell you'. Consider yourself high up on the angel social ladder, Stacy. I'm currently cruising here on the second rung."

Stacy smiled. "I'm sitting on that second rung with you, Grace. Besides, you got to find out because Robert loves you. I found out because my brother can't keep a secret. Even in his own head." And that was it. The biggest secret of all was the one even the angel hadn't known about.

"So are you in remission?" I wanted to know.

"Well, technically, yeah. I've been cancer free for over ten years now, but I don't like to think about it. I don't, really." She gazed away towards the woods behind the school. "That was a tough time for my family."

Lark and I stood beside her, the three of us forming an odd, silent trio.

Then the noise of the school crowd took over as we heard the rush towards the football field. The assembly was over. The game would start in an hour, and after that, who knew. It was Halloween. One costumed person had been unmasked already. What else lay in store?

SENSE

We were routed by Newark High. Our poor football team had been completely destroyed before the first quarter countdown had ended. Graham had been sacked so badly, he had to leave the game before the second down. Newark scored three touchdowns and a three point field goal in the first seven minutes of the game. A state record, the crowd murmured, the double meaning not lost on everyone.

By the time the game had ended, Heath hadn't scored a single point, and Newark's three digit score had the newspapers buzzing with talk about world records and professional potential. All I could see was Graham sitting on the bench with his head in his hands, all of his college football dreams seemingly wiped out by one determined defensive lineman.

As the crowd got up to leave and head on over to the carnival, I headed towards the locker room. I couldn't get the image of Graham's dejected face out of my mind. I saw Lark and Stacy watch as I left, disapproval plain on their faces, but I simply couldn't leave him to wallow in his misery alone. I was his friend, and he had chosen to be mine. I couldn't throw that choice back in his face.

Robert isn't going to like this.

I shrugged my shoulders as I kept on walking. *Robert isn't here. He stood me up. I'm not going to worry about him right now. Graham's hurting and I cannot ignore that and let him do it alone.*

I heard the dual resigned sighs and the echoing of footsteps as the two followed me. I smiled and waited. "Thanks, guys."

Stacy grimaced. "I don't know why you feel the need to comfort the Princess. He's probably just going to blame the other team and whine like a baby."

Lark shook her head. "No, he's not." Those three words caused Stacy's mouth to hang open in shock.

356

As we walked towards the locker room that reeked of loss and defeat, I saw a familiar face. Iris Hasselbeck, Graham's mother, stood outside, waiting for her son, a thin line of irritation the only hint that a mouth existed on her face. "Hi, Mrs. Hasselbeck," I called out to her.

She turned to stare at me, her face filled with mild shock. "Oh, hello Grace. I didn't expect to see you here. Did you come to see Graham, too?"

"We all did," Lark responded, holding her hand out to Iris. "I'm Lark Bellegarde, and this is Stacy Kim. We're friends of Graham's."

I turned to gawp at Lark's comment. She had said it, which meant I couldn't refute it, but when did the two of them become friends with Graham?

"Well, that's nice. I'm glad to know that he's been able to keep *some* pretty girls around," Iris said acerbically while looking at me, taking Lark's hand in hers and smiling at the beautiful face that was so different from my own. Of course. She was upset at me because Graham broke up with Erica.

Both Lark and Stacy looked poised to attack, and Lark snatched her hand out from Iris's grip when Graham walked out of the locker room entrance, his pads and helmet in one hand, his jersey in the other. He wasn't wearing a shirt, and I allowed myself the opportunity to look at his bare chest. I felt the short intake of breath as I became aware of just how physically attractive Graham was.

It appeared I wasn't alone. Stacy and Lark were both ogling—Lark through either mine or Stacy's eyes, for sure, but ogling nonetheless—and I could see that Graham was quite pleased by that. He saw me and smiled. "So you brought your guard dog and your fashion coach. Where's the warden?"

I rolled my eyes ignored his question. "We're here to see how you were doing and to see if you wanted to go to the carnival with us. They're going to be announcing the winner of the costume contest soon and I thought you might want to spend time with three Greek Goddesses instead of with thirteen jocks."

Graham's expression was one of skepticism, but also pleasure as he quickly handed his speechless mother his equipment and pulled on his jersey. It hung on his body, which made him appear much like the boy I would rather remember than the young man who had been standing there semi-unclothed. I shook my head to remove the thought from my mind and took his arm when he offered it to me.

He offered his other arm to Lark, probably because he knew Stacy would have refused. "Well, let's go ladies," he said, tossing a quick farewell to his mother as we walked past her, a smug smile on all of our faces. The four of us headed towards the large field that lay between the football and baseball fields. It was lit up with the bright lights from the midway and the various rides that were spinning, rolling, and flipping amid the screams of its riders. The smell of sugar and fried foods assailed the senses, and I became eager to hurry, my stomach rumbling from the lack of breakfast and lunch.

We found out that there was a few minutes left before the announcement of who had won the costume contest, so we rushed quickly to the stage that had been set up facing the school. There was a large crowd of costumed people both sitting and standing around the stage. Lark looked them over and smiled to herself. *We're the best dressed ones here. I'm fairly confident that we'll win.*

I cocked my head to the side and raised a lone eyebrow in mock surprise. *Give it up, Lark. You already know who won, don't you?*

She nodded, her smile growing wider. "Graham, would you mind getting us something to drink?"

Graham, sputtering at the melodic way that Lark spoke, nodded and left. She watched him leave, her smile whimsical and carefree. "He's handsome. I think it might be a good idea to bring him around more often, Grace."

Stacy scoffed at that idea. "He's nice to look at, sure. But he's annoying. I can only handle him in small doses."

"You seemed to have handled that large dose of pecs quite well," Lark quipped.

I started giggling at the way Stacy's face turned beet red. She stumbled for something to say but there really wasn't much she could offer in way of an argument. Her thoughts gave her away. "Oh, I'm going to have to get used to this," she moaned. I wrapped my arm

358

around her shoulder in understanding.

"Shh. They're going to announce the winner," Lark hissed and waved her hand at us, trying to quiet us but succeeding in looking more like a bird high on caffeine.

Stacy and I looked at each other and rolled our eyes as our names were called. Lark couldn't pretend she was surprised because she rarely was, so she didn't. The audience was so mesmerized by her beauty, she *was* Aphrodite to them. Her angelic beauty, her grace, and her lilting voice had everyone so captivated; they didn't seem to notice that she hadn't used her walking stick. She accepted the prize and raced back down, nearly crashing into the two of us as we waited for her at the bottom of the stage.

Graham reappeared with bottles of water for us and then congratulated us on our win. "It was really Lark's win," I corrected, "She's the one who designed and sewed the dresses. If she had made wigs, I think the rest of the competition would have simply dropped out. She made these, too." I pointed to my sandaled feet.

He grunted his amazement, staring at her with puzzled eyes.

We started walking again, the four of us, Graham between Lark and I, while Stacy was on the other side of me. It must have made for an odd picture, the football player between three Greek goddesses. We played a few games and rode on the Ferris Wheel before Stacy started to worry about the time and what her parents would think if she showed up late wearing her Artemis dress. Lark sighed and I looked glumly at the cotton candy and caramel apples that seemed to be calling out my name. Maybe next time.

"I'll take you home, Grace."

Graham, although no mind reader, knew me too well. "I haven't spent any time with you for the past few weeks. Come on; let's have fun while your jailer is missing."

I looked back at Lark, and her face showed no emotion. "You know he's going to be upset about this, Grace…"

I looked away, not wanting to see her face as the thoughts ran through my head. Of course I knew that. But…*I don't really care right now. He knew what was happening today, and he didn't show up. He didn't tell either of us that he wasn't coming. Graham is my friend and I'm not going to just leave him hanging because Robert cannot get a grip on his feelings.*

"I think that's a great idea, Graham," I said grabbing his hand. "I'll talk to you two later." I waved at Stacy and Lark and pulled Graham towards the caramel apples. I didn't look back, and I didn't stop walking until we were standing in line.

"So, I take it that you're not exactly happy with your warden right now."

I didn't want to answer him. I was tired of having to choose sides at the moment and worry about trying not to hurt either of them. I just wanted to have fun. "Let's just get some apples and ride the rollercoaster like we used to, okay?"

He grinned at me and nodded. We ate our sticky treats and walked the fairgrounds, content to talk about what we'd both been up to the past few weeks. He told me about his parents constantly fighting about money, and I told him about Janice putting the house on a health food kick because of an article she had read online. We both laughed at television shows we'd watched, and discussed class assignments we had left to complete.

Deciding that the hour was growing late, and still not having ridden the rollercoaster, he grabbed my hand and started pulling me towards the line, laughing the whole way about the first time we had rode it and I had thrown up. I missed this. I didn't realize how much until now, how much Graham was a part of my new life as he was my old, and this time, I was the one keeping him out.

As we stood in line, my mind started racing through all of the emotions I felt and questions that I hadn't dared to ask myself because I had been afraid of what the answers would be. What was I giving up to love Robert? He had asked me not to share my feelings with him, having wanted to be able to reciprocate, and so I had complied. But, holding them back was not as easy as it sounded when every time he touched my hand, my face, my hair, every time he brushed his lips against mine with his faint, yet intoxicating kisses, I wanted to burst out with the raw emotion that was damming up inside of me.

360

And just for the privilege of doing so, I had to watch as my best friend drifted further and further away. Graham had always been a part of my life; at least, the part that I could remember. His actions had torn us apart completely at the seams, but we had somehow mended it, although it had taken time, but how long until this patch gave out, too? And what would I have to show for it if it did?

Robert's words about not being able to be everything I wanted him to be, about not being here when he finally got his wings, or when he received the call echoed in my mind. I was risking so much just for the opportunity to love him. Not to be loved, but just to love him, and I didn't know if I could accept the answer to the question of whether or not it would be worth it.

"Well, I see you didn't waste any time."

The icy words tore me from my thoughts as I felt the hand on my shoulder tighten and pull be closer. I looked at who had spoken them and saw that Lark, Stacy, and I weren't the only ones who had been dressed in Grecian form. She hadn't been in class today and I hadn't noticed.

"Hello, Erica," I said through gritted teeth. She had on a dress similar to the one Lark had worn, long and flowing with a low neckline and even lower back. It had been cinched in at the waist with gold cord that had been wrapped twice around and tied, ending with golden tassels. But Erica didn't come dressed as Aphrodite. No. She was the gorgon, Medusa, snake-draped head and all, and still unerringly beautiful.

"Robert isn't here for one day and you go running back to your lapdog," she sneered. "Robert's wasted on someone like you. I wonder what he'd say about this...touching reunion. Or are you not going to tell him that you were here with your arms wrapped around each other? Perhaps I should go and find him and tell him the good news myself, eh?" Her smile was arrogant, the maliciousness in her eyes was clear. I wanted to scratch them out.

"Get lost, Erica. You're not going to accomplish anything here except make yourself look like an idiot," Graham ground out.

Her eyes seemed to light up with rage at the Graham's remarks.

361

She opened her mouth to speak, but Graham only continued. "Just so you know, Robert already knows that Grace is here. He told her to have fun tonight because he knew he wasn't going to be able to be here with her. He knows that we're just friends, and that he can trust her. So go ahead and tell him. If you think that doing so will give you a shot at him, I've got an ocean view apartment in Licking I'd like to sell you."

I bit my lip to keep from laughing, not knowing whether it was the pain or the comment that caused the tears to spring in my eyes. I waved as Erica stormed off, knowing that wasn't going to be the last I saw of her, but glad that, at least for tonight, it would be.

"You didn't have to lie like that, Graham," I said after Erica slithered away.

He shook his head. "I wasn't lying—not much anyway. You can be trusted, Grace. I've always known that. And, well, we'll never be anything more than friends. All he'd have to do to know that is to have watched how you were today, walking around school like a complete zombie without him there. I could hate him, you know, for being such an important part of your life that when he's not there, even if it's for one lousy, stupid day, you end up looking so miserable. But then I see your face when he is here, and I can't be anything else but glad that someone has finally made you happy the way that I didn't."

And there it was. Graham had given me my answer. I looked at the rollercoaster that we had been standing in line for so long to ride, and it simply didn't seem that important and necessary anymore. "Graham, could you take me home?"

He smiled and nodded. I wrapped my arm around his waist as we started walking towards the student parking lot. "Hey, remember when we were kids, and you would tease me about my teeth?"

I laughed. "Yeah. I called you Lispy the Rabbit because you thpoke with a lithpp but had teeth like a bunny."

He guffawed. "Man, I used to hate when you did that. I felt so damn self-conscious about my teeth."

"And then you got braces, and now the ladies all love to see you smile," I chided.

"Even your friend?"

I raised my eyebrows, curious at his question. "Which one?"

His smile grew soft, almost wistful. "Lark."

"Lark?" I snorted. "You're interested in Robert's sister?"

He straightened his smile, all humor gone from his face. "No. I was just wondering, that's all."

I smiled a knowing smile, and hugged this new piece of information to myself. If he had feelings for Lark, that would definitely add a twist to the dynamic of my relationship with Robert. It could ease his mind about Graham once and for all or it could only intensify his disapproval.

As we approached the car, I saw something move in the shadows of the school building. I stiffened in fear. Had Erica decided to await us at the car to continue her tirade? Was she plotting something worse? Graham, having felt the sudden change in my mood, dropped his arm from me and pushed me behind him. "Who's there?" he called out.

The moon was high in the sky, and as if on cue, its light cast down as the person emerged from the shadows. "Oh God—Robert."

He looked so striking standing there in the moonlight. His midnight hair looked almost silver and his eyes were—they were full of sadness.

"Robert," I whispered as I heard his thoughts, heard the silent accusations, heard his heart breaking in my mind. "Robert, this isn't what it looks like."

Graham stepped away from me, thankfully knowing that this moment wasn't one that he belonged to. I took a step towards Robert, and then another, my hand reaching out to him, pleading for him to stay.

Robert, please. Listen. Look, look through my mind, please.

I continued until I became lost in the enclosed darkness of the school, my hands reaching out for him. Part of me said to turn around and go back to where the light was still shining, where Graham was still standing, but my heart pulled me forward. I was drawn, like a lodestone, towards the only thing that could make me leave. I plunged onward through the blackness, feeling the slide of walls and doors, walking through them, not knowing where they led, but knowing that they were taking me somewhere I needed to be.

Robert. Robert where are you?

I could feel him, even if I couldn't see him. I could feel him in my mind, searching. He would know, he would see. I kept telling myself that, because it was the only way I knew that I wouldn't lose him. I couldn't lose him. I stumbled over something that was blocking my path and fell to the floor, smacking my elbow on the cold tile.

Picking myself back up, I continued on, rubbing my throbbing arm, sometimes tripping over my own feet as one of the laces on my sandals came undone and flapped beneath me while I walked. I finally saw the shadow of a figure standing in the middle of the hallway, his body outlined by the pale sliver of moonlight that broke through the glass window of a door directly behind him, his glow dark, almost black in appearance. I recognized the door. We were in front of the registrar's office.

"Robert, thank goodness. Why are we here?" I huffed; tired from walking through the maze he had pulled me through, but glad for the privacy that he'd provided for our reunion.

He didn't move. He didn't say anything at all. I continued to walk towards him, reaching my hand out, desperate to touch him, to smell him, feel his breath on my skin—but he held his hand up to stop me. It was a stiff, jerky movement—it was a movement I had seen before. It was a movement that asserted nothing but rejection. It was one that I was all too familiar with, and my blood turned to ice water. I had not been led here for a reunion. There would be no happy kisses, or warm embraces. He had not listened to my pleas, hadn't searched my mind at all. It hadn't been him. He saw only Graham with his arm around me, my arm around him, and our laughter. I could see it in his eyes.

And I laughed. It was a hysterical outburst that quickly turned inside of itself and became something else: A painful, quiet laugh tinged with irony and misery and hurt. How easy it had been for him, to lose all faith in me, while I had been struggling to find fault. Graham had said that I could be trusted. He knew that I could because he knew me, loved me. But Robert couldn't—he couldn't trust me because…

"That's it, isn't it? You can't trust me because you don't love me," I whispered, my voice so soft, no one but God could have heard it; or an angel. "You don't love me-" I felt the twist in my stomach and the burning pain it caused shoot directly to my heart. I shook my head, the words coming out having sealed out any chance for rebuke. I turned around and started walking back the way I came, fighting the pull inside of me that kept wanting me to turn around. It was screaming at me to turn around. It fought with the burn in my heart. My feet moved faster, not trusting the speed of a mere walk to get me out of that building fast enough, not trusting the pain of my perpetually breaking heart.

The darkness seemed blacker, my direction no longer destined, but random. My hands were mindlessly waving in front of me, no longer sliding on walls, but slapping them, bumping into them, crashing into them. I could feel the cuts and gashes caused by the sharp corners from lockers, and the growing throb of bruises yet to form from doorways and doorknobs that had been in my way of escaping the ever growing sound of the fracturing of my world.

I stumbled more often now, the laces of the sandal having grown decidedly longer and more dangerous. I finally surrendered to the exhaustion that my pain had weaned from me, and fell over my own feet, the cold tiled floor biting into my hip. I hissed at the sting, hearing it bounce off of the dark and empty halls, and then moaned in recognition as it was soon joined by the sound of broken sobs. I scooted myself back against a wall and felt my body shake with the crushing pain of loss.

It was far more painful than anything else I had ever experienced. The loss of Graham had been a mild irritation compared to this. It felt like I was drowning in my own emptiness, and the echoes of my pain were forcing me under.

I closed my eyes as I felt my heart slowly being torn apart, each fragment of hope and love being ripped to pieces as the seconds ticked by, each one being claimed by hurt, betrayal, and despair. The only part of me that could ever be truly immortal, truly like Robert's and Lark's was suddenly succumbing to the truth that I hadn't been loved at all. And only now could I admit that, even though he had never said it, I had believed he loved me, and that I was a fool for doing so.

"You're not a fool."

My eyes flew open. His face was just inches away from mine. "Go away," I whispered, my voice cracking with emotion.

He shook his head. "I can't, Grace. Don't you see that I can't?"

I braced myself against the wall and with all of my might, I shoved him.

He didn't move. He was a wall again, his strength too great for me to budge with any part of me…just like his heart. "Just leave me alone!" I cried, no longer able to keep quiet. If he wasn't leaving, I would. I tried to stand, but he placed a firm hand on my knee, preventing me from getting up. I tried to push it off, the anger flowing into me just as quickly as the tears flowed out. "Get your hand off me!"

He yanked his hand away from my leg quickly, his eyes wide with shock.

I tried standing up once more, but again his hand shot out, this time to my shoulder, his fingers touching the bare skin that the straps of my costume didn't cover. I could feel the fabric of my thoughts reach out to him, finding no way in—I was shut out completely, despite his nearness, despite his contact with me, despite how desperately I was still clinging to some kind of hope that I was wrong.

"Will you quit touching me?" I shouted, grabbing his wrist, ignoring the way the tips of my fingers prickled with sensation as I tried to pry it off of me. "Let me go." I cried; the broken sound coming from my lips didn't sound like me at all.

His hand once again swiftly pulled away, and I heard myself sob at the unbearable way I felt more at a loss without it there.

"Grace, I-" he started, his eyes wide, as he looked to me and then to his hand.

I shook my head, not wanting to hear anything else, not wanting to hear his voice which made my dying heart sing, even as it was breaking. "Stop, just stop it and leave. Don't you see how much you're hurting me?"

But he didn't leave. Instead, he placed both hands on either side

366

of my face and forced me to look at him. "Grace, listen! I *feel* this," he said softly—desperately—as he rubbed his thumbs against my tear stained cheeks. "I *feel* it." He lifted one hand away to rub a teardrop between his fingers, and stared in awe at me. He placed his fingertips against my lips, and brushed them, softly, gently. "So…soft?"

My heart was pounding as the realization sunk in that he was talking about actually being able to feel what he was touching. I reached my hand up to his face. "Can you feel this?" I asked as I cupped his cheek. He nodded and turned his face into it, pressing his nose and lips against my palm. He breathed in the scent from my wrist, and kissed the pulse point there. It felt like my skin would burst into flames where his lips had just been.

"Soft. I'll never be able to hear the word soft again without thinking about your skin," he whispered as he grabbed my hand and pressed it harder against his mouth. I closed my eyes, trying very hard to keep from moaning, not wanting to fall into the oubliette of emotion that I could see was beckoning to me. Only one thing would keep me from falling…

"Do you love me, Robert?"

Silence would have been better. Silence would have been wonderful. Silence would have been less painful than the whispered "no" that incinerated any hope that I had somehow been able to scrape up from the bottom of my heart. I swallowed down the sob that choked me and nodded once, feeling my hand drop limply to my side as he let go.

I struggled to stand up, but did so without reaching for his aid. The pain in my side caused me to stumble, but when he reached to help steady me, I hissed and shrank away from him—he might have discovered what it meant to touch something and feel it, but he had also murdered my faith in the process, and I did not want the slaughter to continue.

"I-I'm glad that you now know what it feels like to…to feel, Robert…but that has nothing to do with me anymore. I could have stayed—I *would* have stayed not knowing whether or not you loved me, but I cannot now that I know that you don't. I would have risked everything for the chance, but now that I know there isn't any, I just can't."

I stepped around him, keeping my hands tightly at my sides as I did so, for even now they were traitorous and itched to touch him, his hair, his lips. I started to back away. I paused as I looked into the two pale moons of his eyes, ignoring the pained look in them and, without thinking, I pressed a kiss to my fingertips and then laid my fingers against his lips. "Goodbye, Robert."

I started running. I didn't look behind me; I don't know if I looked ahead of me either. I just kept running, ignoring the aches and pains that were screaming at me to stop. Endless darkness and endless hallways finally relented; I saw the bright light of the moon through the doors that had led me to my dream's end and rushed forward, glad for the exit towards…what? What was I running to? A life without Robert? Was that what I wanted? Was I giving up that easily?

I slowed my pace and my toes stopped at the line that separated darkness from light, Grace before and after Robert. But which was which? Would stepping into the light really mean stepping away from Robert? How could an angel be my darkness? The ache in my heart shouted at me the answer; he had brought the moon down from my sky. Its last gift to me before it was gone was allowing me to find my way out of the suffocating dark that would smother me if I chose to stay. Taking a deep breath, I started to move forward, my feet heavy, as if all of my pain, all of my sorrow and disappointment had settled there, weighing them down like anchors. Slowly, I took a step and watched as the cool light grazed my toes.

From the darkness behind me, a sound tore through my body, through my heart, and into the deepest reaches of my soul. It was a cry of pain, and my mouth opened; the cry felt like it was my own, like it was coming from my lips, my mouth, my throat. It was agonizing and horrific, and I couldn't stop it.

My body whipped around, the sound forcing me to turn towards it. I shook my head, refusing its demand. I tried to turn back towards the fading moonlight, shouting my objections, "This isn't fair! God, this isn't fair, to toy with my heart, to be so cruel! He doesn't love me!

368

Why should I care?" Again, the sound came, frantic and tortured. I shook my head, covering my ears with my hands, refusing to hear it, but it broke through and shattered the last ounce of strength I had left in me to refuse.

Compelled by some unseen will, my feet pushed me forward towards the anguished cry, not caring what I'd find, only that when I got there, I could somehow stop it. I raced through hallways, following the agonizing sounds that echoed and bounced all around me—through me—knowing who was making them, feeling the hurt crash through me as though I was the one suffering them instead—I wanted to be the one who suffered them instead, because my pain seemed so insignificant right now. The sound kept knocking me down, it was filled with so much hurt that it was heavy, weighed down by the intensity of it. I struggled for air as I fought to stand up, as I urged my legs forward.

Rounding the corner that led me back to that fateful hallway, I saw him, bent on his hands and knees, his back arched in pain; I fell down in front of him, slamming my knees against the cold floor. "Robert-Robert what's wrong?" my hands gripped his shoulders, trying to pull him up. Realizing that that was impossible, I allowed my hands to roam his body, trying to find what was hurting him.

He shook his head at my searching and opened his mouth to say something, but another cry erupted from his lips. It sounded like the scraping of metal against each other, and I covered my ears. He was in pain—undeniable and invisible pain—and I couldn't stop it. His body twisted from the force of it, his muscles straining, twitching from unbearable agony. "Robert tell me. Tell me what's wrong!" I pleaded, my voice sounding frantic as I backed away from his flailing limbs.

His reached for me with a shaky hand. I watched as it trembled and fell; he was too weak. Again, he raised it—reaching—and finally fitted itself against my face. I grabbed his wrist with both hands, keeping it there, not wanting to lose this small connection. I tried to pull him up, tried to help him, but even weakened, he was the impenetrable wall. I finally stopped trying and cradled his head in my arms, my mind trying to erase the look in his face, erase the way his eyes had looked so colorless and drained from the excruciating torture. *Please, Robert...*

He fell on his side, his head landing in my lap. I placed my hand on his chest, searching for his heartbeat, finding it weak and desperate. He closed his eyes and moaned.

"I love you, Grace."

And the wall tumbled down.

CHANGE

The sight of Robert collapsed in my arms did things to me that nothing else ever could. The desperation in that moment was suffocating. I couldn't scream for help. Who would hear me? Who could help me?

Lark? Lark! My mind was screaming. It was screaming its denial, its hurt, its misery. I clutched at Robert's still form, not caring that it felt like he was boring me through the floor. I wouldn't leave him. No matter how he had hurt me, no matter how late his final utterance, I would not leave his side. He had said he loved me. He had said it and that meant it was true, and there was nothing that could take that away from me now.

"Don't leave me," I sobbed softly into his hair, my fingers absentmindedly running through it. "Don't tell me you love me and then leave me. Don't break my heart and then put it back together again only to shatter it once more. I'm not strong enough for this."

I tried to find his heartbeat, tried to find his glow, even the one that was pitch and ominous in its darkness, but there was nothing. There was no warmth, no breath, no life. Whatever it was that had cause him to suffer so horribly had taken from him, from me, his immortality—it had killed him.

I kept stroking his hair as a strange sound started echoing in the empty hall. It sounded airy, and harsh. It bit through me, vibrated through me, and I admitted to myself finally that it was the sound of the sobs that were ripping through my chest, splashing the darkness with my colorless grief. I sank into him, pressing my face against his, needing to feel his skin against mine. I brushed my lips across his, once, twice. "Feel this. Feel me. Please, please...feel," I pleaded, not caring about anything anymore.

It was as though I were telling myself to feel; I felt the

numbness of loss settle in me, so familiar, and so hated. First my mother, then Graham, and now Robert. Surely the heart couldn't stand for so much destruction of its reason for beating. It had been robbed of a mother's love, denied the love of a friend, and now, now that I knew what being in love really meant, what it meant to live for love and lose it, to risk for love, and to pay the cost, what was there left to beat for? What else could there be now after this?

"Robert—no!" a voice cried out from the darkness.

I looked up as the gasps of horror reached me and saw the stark white faces of Ameila and Lark—shock and grief battering their beautiful features. They had heard his cries of pain, felt it as deeply as I had. They had come, not caring what they were doing or who saw them. They had dared to hope, praying that they would be in time to help him, save him.

They had lost.

"My son. My son!" Ameila wailed, ripping his body from my arms. She buried her face into his chest, her soprano keening blending with the alto of Lark's sobs, the harmony of their grief filling my ears, but not my arms that now felt empty and cold, useless sticks that hung limp at my sides. I couldn't see anymore, my tears too thick with grief to focus on the orange glow that blazed from their bodies, filling the hallway with the tragic light of their loss. I shut it out. I shut it all out and closed my eyes, pushing myself away into a corner to be alone with my sorrow.

"Oh my God," Lark whispered, her trembling voice mirroring the pain I felt pulling me under.

I wouldn't look. I refused to look.

"Mom, let him go. Let him go, Mom, look!"

I looked.

The body of my beloved angel started to lift, his arms hanging lifelessly at his sides. His legs dangled below him, bending at odd angles, his shoes planted flat on the ground. Ameila reached for his hand, bringing it to her lips and kissing it, while brushing his hair out of his eyes. All things a mother would do to a child who slept soundly. Did she not realize that he wasn't asleep? She began to rise as his body did, never dropping his hand, never breaking contact from him. I felt the heat of jealousy bubble up in me as I stood up, too. He loved me. He loved me and I should be the one holding him now.

But I couldn't say it. The thought alone burned me, and added to the guilt that was slowly starting to build up inside of my chest as I played over and over again in my head the last exchange I had had with Lark about Robert, about not caring about hurting his feelings. I had lied out of anger, and spite, and now I'd never be able to tell him that I was sorry, beg him to forgive me for being so selfish for being so...human.

Another gasp brought my attention to his shirt—one that I didn't recognize—as it started pulling at his front. The buttons were straining against his chest, and one by one, they popped off, sailing into some obscure corner or rolling under a door. Higher he floated, until, as we stood around him, his head was nearly level with ours.

"Robert..." the three of us whispered together.

His shirt hung open behind him, and beneath his back—no, from his back—I could see a grotesque branch-like staining of his flesh bulging and pulsing with darkness. Ameila hissed at it, and lurched forward to—I don't know what she planned on doing, and I probably never would because Lark held her arm out to stop her.

The sound of Ameila crashing into Lark's arm sounded like a giant hammer hitting a steel beam. It echoed around us, but only I seemed to notice it. Lark and Ameila were both staring at the grotesque markings that were spreading across Robert's back. I watched in fascinated horror as the branches started to protrude out towards the floor. The skin was pulled so taut, it was nearly translucent, a dark film of flesh and...bone.

"Oh my God, it's his wings," Ameila breathed, her hand over her mouth in shock, her other hand gripping Lark's shoulder so tightly, I could see a grimace of pain on her lips.

The branches and skin stretched further as Robert's body rotated so that he was upright, his head lolling to the side, like a puppet whose string had been cut. I wanted to help hold his head up, the silly human worry that his neck would get stiff causing me great concern, but Lark shook her head, her hand grabbing a hold of my arm to prevent me from interfering.

As his body rose higher, the branches on his back stretched further. Wings, Ameila had said. Biology class was paying off in a strange way as I could make out the rough skeletal shape of a wing in the base of the branch, but the outer branches, they were not so easy to identify. As the branches grew in number, smaller and smaller still, the dawning of recognition hit me. Each one of the divisions weren't bones. They were feathers.

"Yes," Lark breathed, nodding her head in agreement. Her face was filled with awe.

Fully formed, fully plumed, the span was surely beyond even the width of the hallway. I shook my head in amazement at such an unfathomable sight. Robert's body was still limp, but stretched out behind him—in a magnificent display of unintentional beauty—were his wings. Full, glossy, and...

"Black," Ameila gasped.

Like the wings of a raven.

His body started to lower, his wings folding inward. Lark rushed forward to catch him, her diminutive form belying her strength as she handled him with ease. She gently laid him to the ground, carefully settling his wings around him, shimmering tears falling from her face as she did so. "Brother, you did it. You've got your wings. Open your eyes and see them. Open your eyes and see that those who care the most have shared this moment with you."

Her voice was so soft, I could barely make out what she was saying, and I wanted to ask why she was saying them at all but the answer was already there. She couldn't think them, because he wasn't there. He would not receive her thoughts. He wouldn't receive any of our thoughts anymore.

"But I thought angels didn't die," I murmured, mainly to myself because I knew differently—other angels died, but not mine. "You're not supposed to die."

I felt a pulse of emotion start to softly beat within me as I stared at my beautiful angel lying prone on the ground, his strong and sarcastic sister broken and crying on his chest. Ameila, beautiful even in her sorrow, stood stony, her arms at her sides, as though she accepted this, accepted the fate that had befallen her son. The slow beating within me grew. It grew bold, and loud, and strong, and fierce. It pushed me, jerked me around like a rag doll in the hands of an unruly child. It grew hot inside of me, and it leaked out in scorching tears that ran down my face.

"No!"

The shout echoed around the hallway, the final crack in my heart, the fissure now too large to stem the overflow of emotion. It was angry, fire drenched, and vengeful. "No! No, no, no!" I leaped onto Robert's still form, my intense reaction somehow enough to shock Lark away. I began to beat on his chest, his shoulders. I grabbed his head and looked at his face, perfect and exquisite, even in death, and shook it. "No, you're not supposed to be the one to die, damn you!"

I slapped him. I don't know why, and I'll always question myself later what compelled me to do it, but at that moment, it was the only thing that seemed reasonable. My hand began to throb; I forgot how hard and unforgiving their skin was. Unlike the punch that I had given to Lark, this was *supposed* to cause pain. This was supposed to bring with it hurt and contempt to the abused, and instead I was the one feeling the bite of it. But I didn't care. Pain was better than falling numb again because if I accepted the numbness then that would mean that I accepted Robert's death, and I couldn't accept that. I wouldn't accept that. Instead, I slapped him again.

"You're not dead. You can't tell me you love me and then leave me. You're not dead, do you hear me? You're not, you're not!"

For every crack that lined my heart, for every single tear that I had shed, I hit him. I hit him for things he had had nothing to do with. I hit him for every plan that might have been made but now wouldn't. I hit him for every dashed away hope, for every crushed dream, for every single moment that now stretched out before me, empty and without reason. I hit him for every single time I doubted myself, doubted him. And, mostly, I hit him because if I stopped, if I thought about stopping, I feared I wouldn't know what else there was left for me to do in this world.

A hand grabbed my aching wrist as it rose once more, stopping it before I could cause more damage to my hand. I looked at it, strong, determined, and followed the lines of the wrist, to the arm…to its owner.

Two liquid pools of mercury stared up from beneath me.

Reason would have demanded that I pass out from shock. But there wasn't room for reason in my world anymore. There never had been. There was only room for drowning in those eyes that held mine locked onto them. Oh, I was in shock; the fact that I couldn't move, couldn't breathe was proof enough of that. But I also couldn't blink, afraid that if I did so, those glimmering orbs would disappear when my lids rose. I couldn't let the sight of something so beautiful disappear. I desperately fought the human instinct to close my eyes.

"Grace."

And I blinked. Because apparently shocking one's ears coincides with the need to blink.

"Grace, please stop hitting me."

I shook my head at the absurdity of it. I must be hallucinating, because the dead didn't speak. They didn't gaze up into my eyes and say innocuous things that made me feel like I could leap off the very edge of the sky and never touch ground. I shook my head because forget reason, forget logic, this miracle couldn't possibly be mine.

And yet, the gasps behind me—of a mother's joy, a sister's hope—weren't absurd. They were the confirmation that I wasn't in the midst of a mental breakdown. "You're here," was all I could form by way of recognition. He was alive, he was here, he was holding onto my wrist and that contact was mending my battered hand as surely as it was the other parts of me that I believed had died right along with him.

He sat up, his grip around my wrist loosening, and then made motions to stand while I moved away, making way for his family to embrace him in a way that I couldn't. His mother's arms, strong and firm, gripped him tightly to her chest, his sister wrapped around his neck, the three of them lost in the joy of their reunion. They were silent, their heads pressed together, sharing their thoughts.

It was such a private moment I almost felt like I was intruding. Almost. I had questions of my own that needed to be answered. But, more than anything else, I needed to hear him say those words again. I needed to hear them, to reassure myself that I hadn't imagined them, that it hadn't been a figment of my imagination brought on by shock. I needed them because I had stopped breathing when he had opened his eyes, and without them, I don't think I'd be able to remember how to start again.

Slowly, Lark lowered her arms from around Robert's neck. Ameila gently released him, but held onto his hand. I stood silent as they moved to his side. He was looking directly at me, a concerned expression on his face. He reached a hand out to me but started to pull it back when I looked at it skeptically, hesitantly. Seeing what he was doing, what he had interpreted in my thoughts, I rushed forward to grab it. I knew what chances I had were few, and I wasn't about to miss out on any of them. I held his hand clasped in mine, and looked into his eyes.

"I'm okay," he said softly, and pushed a piece of my hair away from my eyes with the hand that I was holding onto tightly. "I'm better than okay. You're still here. You didn't leave me."

Nervous laughter poured out of me. Hadn't I said the very same thing to him a few weeks ago? What was I supposed to say now? How does one deal with stuff like this? This reality that wasn't…real? Broken hearts were one thing, but I had just watched him die. I watched as his dead body changed, watched as it grew wings—wings for goodness sake! And now, he was talking to me, as though everything was normal. Was there ever going to be a moment when I became comfortable with things like this?

He pulled me closer, and I was hit with a sudden sense of shyness and fear. He sensed my hesitation and eased his hold on me. "I-I don't know how to be with you," I said softly, and I didn't. He had turned my entire sense of self upside down in just a few hours. I didn't understand anything that had happened, and I didn't understand why I couldn't have just walked away.

"You couldn't walk away because your heart knew where it

belonged," Ameila responded to my thoughts, which elicited a gasp from her children. She had not done this for such a long time—why now? She placed a hand at my back and turned my chin to face her. "There is so much you have yet to be told, little one. But let us not do it here. People are coming."

I didn't have a chance to express my objections to leaving when I felt a sharp pull and found myself pressed up against Robert's chest, my face in the small hollow of his neck. His arms were wrapped around me, clamping me to him like a vise. I didn't know what was happening, only that the bite of a cold wind was stinging my back and shoulders. I wound my arms up around his neck, though I'm not exactly sure if it was to keep from falling, or just to be closer to him. I simply didn't care at the moment.

It took only minutes for Robert to finally place my feet back on solid ground. My knees had started to shake from the crush of emotions that were welling up inside of me. For the first time since we had met, Robert didn't let me get used to it on my own. He picked me up again, one arm beneath the bend of my knees, the other around my back, and carried me into his home. This was where I would be told the truth.

He carried me into the living room, but instead of setting me down onto a sofa or chair, he simply remained standing with me in his arms. "There is so much to tell you," he murmured into my hair. "I don't know where to begin."

Ameila appeared then, followed by Lark. I hadn't realized that we had gotten there before the two of them. "Let me explain it, son. She still has feelings of distrust, and I do not blame her." Ameila reached for my hand, and, with all three angels standing in the middle of their living room while I was cradled in Robert's arms, she began to explain to me what it was that I had just endured.

"Sam had misled Robert. He's been mentoring him these past few decades—having him accompany him while he fulfills the duties of his call—and Robert had looked up to his wisdom and experience like any one would of a big brother, for that is what Sam's role was intended to be. But Sam took that trust too far. He told Robert that his wings would come only while suffering a great pain."

378

Ameila's voice grew soft then as she looked at her son. "But what is there in an angel's life that can cause us true pain other than to betray our hearts?"

I looked at her in confusion. "I thought that the only way your kind felt pain was when you lied?"

She nodded her head. "Yes. But you see, it is in our hearts to be honest. We cannot be who we are, fulfill the roles in this world that we're meant to play, if we are not honest with those that we are born to protect, born to care for, and…born to love. You, my dear Grace, are the truth that is my son's heart, and when he denied *you* that, when he denied *himself* that truth by lying to you and saying that he did not love you, it caused him a pain so great, it k-" Ameila's voice caught in her throat as she struggled with the words "-killed him. You see, foolish boy that my son is, he was doing this not only for himself, but for you as well. He thought—he believed that if he could receive his wings, he'd receive the call, and then he'd be able to let you go.

"He thought this would make it easier for you to have the normal life that you craved, and he assumed that you understood he'd have to leave one day when this happened. However, he and Sam forgot that our wings do not come because we will them to, or because we want them to. You cannot tell a lie so blatant and expect the pain of dying to be enough to trigger the change.

"But Sam told Robert that lying to you, the pain that he'd feel through you, coupled with the punishment our bodies dole out when we break one of our own rules would do just that. And Robert paid the price for it. Our wings…they are tied to our emotions as angels. It takes a great catalyst of feeling to bring them forth. Love, hate, anger, jealousy, sadness, compassion…it takes a combination of so many emotions to spark our body's physical change, but one emotion, far more significant than all of the others, always stands out—the trigger to it all."

I felt Robert pull me in closer to him, his cheek resting solidly on the top of my head. I rested my face against the cool material of his shirt, and searched for the soft wooshing of his heartbeat, needing its steady beat to comfort me as my mind fought to sort out all of this new information. His chest was silent.

"Ahh, yes. There is an issue that was confusing me at first, but I understand now why that is. You hear no heart in his chest."

I turned my head to look at her, nodding unnecessarily while swallowing down the fear that was slowly creeping up within me.

"Grace, you know how Robert came into existence—how different he is, even among us. His birth was not like Lark's, in that he was born from a corpse. Do you understand what that means? It means that he has always been on the cusp between life and death, owing his soul to both. Death won out tonight when his body could take no more, but you—you came back for him, and you allowed him his last bit of peace. He knew he was dying, and so to make peace, he could finally tell you the truth. He would see you with a normal life. But, none of us, especially not Robert, knew what would happen as a result.

"You are his salvation, Grace. His love for you brought his wings, and your love for him brought him life. And, to be given life through death, not once, but twice…it must exact a cost, even if only in a minor way. His price was that of the part that makes him the most human—the most human like you."

I turned my head to look up at Robert, whose gaze was pointed down towards me, his eyes focused and intense. I knew it in my own beating heart that it wasn't what made me human. The literal heart could beat forever, but the figurative heart, the romantic heart was what kept love alive. His heart was still there. I could feel it in me, even if I couldn't hear it in him.

"You understand," Ameila smiled. "I am glad for it. But, you must question why his wings are that color…"

I looked at Ameila and she knew that I honestly had not until that moment. "I was always under the impression that angels' wings are supposed to be white."

She nodded her head, and then took a step away from us, her head lowered, and I watched in amazed horror as arm like limbs started to jut out from behind her, tearing through her blouse and lengthened, branching out like Robert's had done, but far more smoothly. The branches splintered and grew outward, each end bisecting multiple

380

times, finally blooming into a pair of immense wings that were a white that reminded me of cotton balls and baby powder—pure and innocent.

"*My* wings are like all of the others. They do not alter in color or shape. Only in size do our wings differ. But no one—absolutely no one else has black wings. Robert is the first of our kind. Our history has never had such an occurrence before, and I do not know what this could mean for him—or for us. I will have to discuss this with the others, but for right now, it is a blessing that he is here."

But what about Sam? What he had done had caused Robert so much unnecessary pain, and I couldn't get around just how much I wanted to cause him that exact same pain. If there was any justice in this world...or his...

"What he did caused both of you great pain, Grace," Ameila said, interrupting my thoughts. "It was misguided and it was a foolish mistake that no one who has lived for as long as Sam has should have made, but it is done, and though the two of you were hurt, the results are much better than I believe any of us could have hoped for."

"Oh please, Mother. Sam did this deliberately to hurt Grace," Lark bristled. She was pacing, her hands curled into tight fists at her side. "He didn't forget what triggers our wings to appear. He just didn't want Robert's to come the same way his did."

Ameila hissed at Lark to which Lark responded with a throaty growl, "I won't keep quiet about this. Sam's stupidity and selfishness nearly cost you your son! Stop defending him!"

The unspoken arguments from Ameila would not be answered silently, as Lark once again shouted, "No, I won't stop talking about it. If Sam has such a problem with me talking about him, let him show up and tell me himself."

Robert's hold on me grew tighter, and I felt the tension in his body as he listened to the exchange between his mother and sister. I locked my fingers together around his neck, not wanting to let go. His face seemed distressed by the direction that the conversation had taken. No longer about explanations, it was all about laying blame, and he wasn't about to allow it to happen.

"This discussion ends now!"

His directive wasn't shouted, but it still rattled the walls and windows with its finality. I had hid my face as the booming sound flowed through my bones and caused my teeth to ache. "The only person to blame here is me, not Sam. I made the decision to hurt Grace, and myself. The blame rests with me. Now, if you two will excuse me, Grace and I have a lot of talking to do. We will be in my room."

Ameila made a motion to stop him. "Do you think that's wise, son?"

Robert's body stiffened and he lowered me so that my feet were once again touching the ground. "Yes, I do think that is wise, but I think it would be in Grace's best interest if she makes the decision herself to come with me."

I looked at the two of them, one with a warning in her eyes, the other with a soft plea in his. I didn't know what the warning was for, but I knew what the pleading was about, and I went with what I know. It's far safer that way.

"Let's talk, Robert."

He held his hand out to me again, and shyly, I took it, following him as he pulled me towards a room at the back of the house. It was past the kitchen, the room I had been in the last time I was here. I didn't want to think about what my foolishness had nearly cost me then, so I simply watched as Robert pulled me through a dark door and into a room that was painted a bright white. The dark hallway that led to the room reminded me of all that had happened at the school, and I could feel it all start to boil up inside of me again. I could feel the sob climbing up my throat, ready to leap out, dragging all of my fear and heartbreak behind it.

"Shh, it's okay," Robert said soothingly, wrapping his arms around me yet holding me back far enough so that he could still look at me while talking. "I'm so-so sorry, Grace. I have so much to apologize to you for. I promised to never hurt you, and I've broken that promise twice now. I'm sorry for being so cold to you…for being so cruel and hurtful. I'm sorry, Grace, for lying to you."

He lifted a hand to my face and smoothed out my eyebrow with his fingertip, the small movement igniting a pilot light within me that I

382

could have sworn had been dampened by the tears I had shed tonight. "I know that this is no excuse, but when I saw you with Graham, it seemed like it was the right time; you were so happy, you were so carefree, and I could see that there would be hope for you after I had left, and that you'd be able to have the normal life that you said you wanted. I used the anger and jealousy I felt, used it to hurt you, and I will never forgive myself for as long as I exist."

His eyes were glossy, and I watched in amazement as two silver tears rolled down his face and landed on the wooden floor beneath our feet with large thuds. I bent down to inspect them and gasped in shock. Not tears. Teardrop shaped crystal. I touched them, feeling their warmth and smiled. "These are just like the ones at the wedding."

He bent down and picked them up, weighing them in his hands. "We've never paid attention to these things. They were always so trivial to us when compared to the causes of them."

"You don't pay attention to a lot of things," I muttered, fidgeting with my hands that were lost for something to do—seeking a distraction.

"I know. It's something that I will spend the rest of my existence making up for." He headed to a small dresser, obviously looking for a replacement for his shirt, and disappeared in a blur of motion.

I stood up, not wanting to continue the conversation as it was, and took a look at his room while he changed. This was the one room that he had not shown me before. It wasn't that large, perhaps just a bit bigger than mine, and its focal point seemed to be a very ornate wooden bed that was stained black with snow white linens; it was always a war between black and white, light and dark with him. I rolled my eyes and continued my observation. There were matching nightstands on both sides of the bed, and a large chest sitting at the foot of it.

The chest reminded me of something you'd imagine in a pirate story—old and wooden with a large keyhole that would suit a skeleton key. "Do you have buried treasure in there?" I asked, wanting to lighten the mood a bit, if only to help ease my frazzled nerves.

He laughed and, taking my hand, led me to the chest. He knelt and pulled me down with him. "This has parts of my past that I chose to keep as mementos; these things that represent people, places, and events that were pivotal moments in my life."

My curiosity piqued, I waited while he lifted the lid. How old were some of these things going to be? Would they be spectacular or ordinary? With the lid open, I peered inside. It wasn't overly full, which was surprising for holding some fifteen hundred years of memories.

"Silly Grace, these are only the moments that were important to me. When you have forever before you, you can afford the luxury to be particular." He reached in and pulled out what looked like a horse carved out of wood. "The farmer who carved this had a little boy who had been very sick; he was the first human I had knowingly healed. In a display of gratitude, he gave me this. He told me that he had carved the toy for his son because he knew the little boy wouldn't live very long, and would probably never grow old enough to ride a real one. I had given his son the one thing he couldn't—time—and now he could grow up and ride all the horses he wanted. The farmer said that the boy wouldn't need the toy horse anymore, so he gave it to me as a thank you; it was the only thing he had to offer me.

"I was humbled by the experience, and through wars and plagues, famine and feasts, I have kept this with me to remind me that what we do is worth it. It can be a hard thing to remember when we hear so much anger and rage and hatred from your kind on a daily basis."

I took the horse and looked at it. Age had softened the stained and chipped wood, but the detail that had been painstakingly carved into it was still there. It had been made to look like it was in thc middlc of a full gallop, its mane and tail blowing out in the imaginary wind. "It's beautiful."

He smiled, pleased that I could appreciate its simple beauty. He started to pull out a quilt—beginning its tale of importance as he did so—when something caught my eye. I reached past his arm to grab it. It was a shirt. I looked at his face as I opened the folded bundle. The absence of a blush didn't diminish his look of embarrassment. "This is my shirt," I said quietly as I gazed down at the object in my hands.

The silly smiley face stared up at me from the front of the shirt, its tongue mockingly sticking out. "I threw this in the trash can," I said, mostly to myself. "I threw it away, and now it's here." I pressed it to my face and inhaled, my nose searching, but smelled only the slight fragrance of fabric softener. "Why?"

Robert grabbed it out of my hands, and tucked it back at the top of the pile of items in his trunk. "It belonged to you."

It was as simple an answer as I could have expected, but he wasn't finished. "I couldn't have taken anything from you. Our nature prevents us from stealing, and I couldn't ask you for something of yours without explaining why. I saw you throw this away, and I knew that I had to retrieve it. I came back after I dropped you off at home that first day and dug through the trash for it. I washed it when I came home and placed it in here.

"You want to know why I kept it, right?" He waited for confirmation before continuing. "It's because I knew that first day that you would change my life, Grace. I knew it the way I felt the burning fire in my heart, the way I could see the light surrounding you shine far brighter than anyone else's, the way I could hear your voice in my head, even though you were nowhere near me.

"I guess I can say that in hindsight, what I felt that day was my entire existence being rewritten—I spent the past fifteen hundred years merely existing, but since you entered my life, I've spent the past few months living. I know that to you, that might sound ridiculous and unrealistic, but it is what I have come to understand and appreciate as the truth. And since I've said it, and I'm still here, it cannot be anything but."

"Robert," I huffed, "what sounds ridiculous and unrealistic is that there are angels in Heath, going to Heath High...dating me." My head cocked to the side as a thought popped into my head then. "If you cannot take something that doesn't belong to you, how were you able to come into my room that night I met your mother? You came in and you took me out of my house."

"You *are* mine," Robert answered simply as he took my hand and laced his fingers with mine. "Mmm." He closed his eyes and squeezed my hand. "I don't think I ever want to get used to this." He looked at my impatient expression after opening his eyes and sighed. "Grace, there's no denying that fact. You *are* mine. I knew it the moment I saw you. I might not have recognized it at the time, but it doesn't make it any less true.

"As to the existence of angels in Heath, the majority of people in this town like to think that my kind exists. They want to have faith in my existence, but whether or not I was real wouldn't matter. The human psyche is set up to only accept what it wants. You have to be willing to believe that you're right or wrong, not just say that you are. What do you think would happen were I to announce to the school body what I was? Would I be feared, or accepted?"

I shrugged my shoulders, not wanting to vocalize my answer, knowing that he'd hear it in my mind anyway.

"See, you know that people wouldn't accept what I am, even though they are taught that my kind are supposedly good." My puzzled expression at his last comment seemed to amuse him. "You don't know much about my kind, do you? Even after all that you have read, after all Lark has told you?"

I shook my head. "You know that I wasn't raised in the church. My mom liked to read the bible, and she loved to sing the psalms, but she was adamant that we never go, and Dad never felt like it was necessary after she had died. Everything that I knew before meeting you came from stories and movies—I admit that I did some research about angels after the accident, but most of it consisted of Botticelli type illustrations with biblical verses and personal accounts that did not sound anything at all like what I have seen so far. Even the wings— there were no descriptions on angels being born without wings with the exception of the Jimmy Stewart movie."

Robert laughed as he recognized what I was talking about. "Ahh yes…that line has plagued us for decades. The children of the electus patronus are always walking around those of us who have yet to receive our wings with bells, hoping that one of them will make them appear."

I giggled. I could see it in my head. I looked at Robert

suspiciously. "Are you doing that?"

He shook his head. "Those images are all yours."

I gazed down at our hands meshed together, and sighed with contentment. "So you can feel this now. Why? What happened that caused this?"

"Grace, I wish I could explain it. Even I don't know. I just know that there has never been a feeling quite like that first time I touched your skin and I could feel it through my own. It might be part of the change. It might have been part of me accepting my love for you. I've been fighting it for so long and when I heard your thoughts, felt your pain, it mirrored my own. I was hurting you, and it hurt me—it killed me—knowing that you were suffering because of me.

"But I thought it was the only way that I could let you have what you wanted. You wanted a normal life, but what kind of normalcy would you have had, always worrying about when I'd get my wings, when I'd get the call, where would I go? I said I was giving you what you wanted. But I was lying to myself, too. No, not exactly lying to myself, but denying an additional truth. I was doing it because I thought I was saving myself the pain of having to leave you later. I thought that if I left sooner, it would be easier for me. It was me being selfish."

I reached my hand up to touch his face, and marveled at the way he pressed his face into my hand, sighing as he did so. For the both of us, it felt as though I was touching his face for the first time. "You know, I wish all of you would stop talking about what I want as if you know how I feel. You don't understand that for me, normal now means that you're in my life. Normal doesn't exist for me anymore without you in it. And yes, you were being selfish. A very un-angelic thing to do."

"Your definition of angelic and mine don't match up. Right now, I want to be very angelic with you," Robert teased.

Feeling nervous, I brought the subject back to a more serious level. "You said that I don't know much about your kind. Do you mind explaining?" I thought I would be prepared for whatever it was that he had to tell me. I was very wrong.

"Grace, the stories of angels are always filled with light and purpose of doing good. Lark and I have told you about some of our rules, we've told you about what we are—to an extent. But, there is a dark side to who we are. There are angels whose sole purpose—their entire reason for existing is to cause pain and suffering to your kind. Their calls may require that of them, but inside, they are wicked—you might even say that they are evil. They enjoy doing what they do, and do not follow the rules that the rest of us have to abide by.

"It would seem that each of us receive the call that is best suited to our inner nature. My mother says that my call will probably involve the healing of the faithful. I have always taken that to mean that I would never have to feel the failure of not being able to heal someone.

"But, I would also be bringing upon me the wrath of the dark ones, because I would be undoing much of their work. It is a symbiotic relationship, but it doesn't mean that either of us have to like it. And unfortunately, I would not be powerful enough to stop the dark ones if they choose to cause harm again. It is up to the faithful to ask for my help."

My mind was reeling at this new revelation. The idea that there were angels who were sadistic in nature and spirit went against everything that I thought I knew. It simply didn't want to register in my mind, as though it was rejecting the information, unwilling to allow it to take root and branch out into its own set of ideas. "But what if you're not supposed to heal anyone? What if your call is something else?"

"It cannot be anything else. Mother's ability to change shapes, to shift her physical appearance is the basis for her call. She becomes what the human needs to see in order to set them on the right path, the right journey. If they need to see the image of a lost loved one, she becomes that person. Whether it's a person, an animal, or a mythical creature, she'll take that form if that is what it takes to accomplish her duty," Robert insisted.

What could I say to that? Robert's gift was to heal. He had demonstrated that to me time and time again—I was alive because of it. If he wasn't destined to be the greatest healer when he received his call, what else was there left for him?

LIFESONG

When Robert finally brought me home, I felt that I understood less now than I had before the day had even begun. We had continued to discuss the dark ones, as he liked to call them, and I questioned him about whether they were different in appearance as some of the fictional books I had read suggested. Although he felt he was reassuring me when he said that there was no real visible difference between them, I wasn't exactly feeling too confident.

"There is only one way a human can tell that an angel is a dark one," he said softly. "They don't have shadows. Our history tells us that it is because their souls are so dark with their task, they cannot bend the light the way everything else can."

"So now I'll spend the rest of my life looking for people with no shadows. I shouldn't have asked," I grumbled.

He squeezed my hand gently as he drove me home. "You should have asked, and I'm glad that you did. I would have read your mind anyway, but it is much better knowing that you are asking, rather than just wondering."

As we pulled up to the driveway, I looked at the clock on the dashboard. "Oh no, I'm past curfew," I moaned, looking at the door and knowing that behind it was an angry father ready to ground me until I was thirty.

I turned to look at Robert, the silent question passing between us. "You'll be fine. I will be back in a little while," he said reassuringly.

I grimaced, not knowing what to do. It wasn't that I didn't trust Robert—because after witnessing what it cost him to tell a lie, I would never doubt him again—but rather, I didn't trust Dad's reactions versus his thoughts.

I stepped out of the car and waved as Robert drove off, a knowing smile on his face the last image of him left in my mind. I took a deep breath and walked towards the front door, opening it as quietly as I could. I turned the outside light off as I closed the door, and tip-toed into the living room, my only goal: heading up the stairs to my room.

"How was the carnival, Grace?"

Damn.

"It was fine, Dad. We won the contest."

Dad, in his tattered robe I had gotten him for Christmas about three years back, stood up from his favorite chair and gave me a hug. "I'm glad, kiddo. Stacy called me and told me that you were going to be a bit late, that you were hanging out with Graham since Robert was out of town or something."

Stacy had called? She was covering for me? The thought warmed me up on the inside. Just when I thought I had experienced all there was to having a girlfriend, something new popped up. "Yeah. Robert's back, though. He was with a family friend earlier today, but he came back a short while after the announcement for the winner was made," I rushed. I frowned at the words that poured out of my mouth. It was as if I had a compulsion to tell the truth, now more than ever. I started silently praying that he wouldn't ask me about what happened after Robert came back.

"Well, it's late, and I have to work tomorrow. I just wanted to make sure you got home alright. I'll see you in the morning, Grace."

My head perked up, and I said quickly, "Okay Dad. Good-night!"

I watched as he walked up the stairs, his steps heavy with purpose. Relief and confusion were battling it out to see which one I would feel first, but before a winner could be decided, I started to feel very giddy. I turned off the lights in the living room and climbed the stairs to my room.

I closed the door and prepared to change out of my now tattered costume. I hadn't realized until I saw my reflection in the mirror as I was retrieving a change of clothes that the dress that Lark had made was no longer white, and it definitely looked like it had seen the corners of

390

one too many objects. I was so grateful, I sent a silent prayer of thanks that Dad had been too tired to focus on the damage to the dress.

After changing, I sat on the bed and waited, staring at the window for Robert to appear. It felt different this time, almost new.

I felt my eyes start to close, the pull of exhaustion fighting with my desire to remain awake. I forced my eyelids to fly open in a last ditch attempt to stay up, and spied the slow creep of mist crawling through my window. It wasn't the gray that I was used to, but a sinister black, and I pulled my feet up on the bed before I could stop myself.

The black haze swirled around my bedroom floor, crawled under my bed, and finally, around me. I felt the soft wisps turn solid as the embrace became strong and possessive.

Are you grounded until you're thirty?

I giggled. It sounded so girly and feminine, I suddenly stopped. "No." I cocked my head to the side, not understanding what exactly was wrong with me.

I think the answer to that question is that you're finally sure of how I feel, and it's nothing that you feared at all.

Well, he was right about that. I knew now, knew that he loved me, and that feeling sent my pulses racing. It was knowing he loved me that made me feel giddy, and girly. How odd love was. I had always known that it was supposed to change you in some ways, but I never expected this. My love for him had put me in a dress. His love for me made me giggle like I was a little girl. I wasn't sure if I was thrilled with that part.

Grace, you're being ridiculous. Come, I wanted to talk with you a bit more about what happened this evening. There was something I wanted to say to you that I should have said before any of this had ever started.

I nodded my head, allowing him to pull me back against his chest, and listened as his thoughts flowed through my mind.

I wanted to let you know that I was very wrong to have been jealous of Graham. I admit that when I saw the two of you this evening, seeing how you were holding each other, and enjoying each other's company, I felt very angry, very jealous. But I also heard the words that he said to you, and I realized that I was foolish. Far, far more foolish than any human person could ever imagine, for allowing my inability to contain my emotions to dictate how you live your life.

It is especially wrong of me to have done so when I know what will happen when I do receive my call. You will have to endure me constantly leaving you for reasons I won't be able to explain-

"You won't have to explain them to me, Robert. My God, I watched you die in my arms. There is nothing else in my world—or yours—that could ever make me feel as alone and helpless as I did then. I think I can deal with you leaving to do what you were meant to do if I know you'll be coming back to me." I turned in his arms to look at him.

There was a stubborn set in his jaw, but he also had a smile that quite possibly melted every single bone in my body, including the ones that he had healed. *Grace, what kind of a normal life is this? What seventeen-year-old has a boyfriend who keeps leaving for reasons he cannot explain?*

I twisted my body around so that I was fully facing him, and took his face into my hands. "*This* seventeen-year-old has a boyfriend who will be leaving to do what he was born to do, and I will be waiting for him when he gets back. Robert, I know I kept saying that I want a normal life, but what I think what I failed to communicate to you is that I have it. Normal is having friends, and falling in love with someone who loves you back. I have that. I have *more* than that. I have *you*. If you don't want me, if you don't want me in your life, then you are going to have to say it, otherwise I'm stuck with you for the rest of my life."

Robert leaned in and placed his hands on my face, mirroring my hands on his. *Not want you in my life? You are the reason I exist!*

With our faces just inches apart, there was no hiding our emotions. We could see it in each other's eyes, see it in the tug of our smiles. He pulled my face closer, while raising his. I let go of him and closed my eyes as he gently kissed my eyelids, one after the other. I felt his cheek press against my forehead, and heard him sigh, felt his breath blow across my skin.

You do not know how unbelievably decadent this is. I can feel the blood beneath your lids, feel your eyes move beneath them.

392

He brought his face down level with mine again and brushed my nose with his. With a soft exhalation, he kissed the tip of my nose, and then brushed his nose against my cheek. Everywhere he nudged with his nose, he kissed. Once, twice, even three times, each time sighing, as though it was his first kiss. Of course, I sighed, too. It wasn't like the first time. There was so much…more. There was just more.

When he reached my lips, he just tickled the corner of my mouth, and then very lightly brushed it with his lips. It wasn't dissimilar to all of the kisses we has previously shared in its manner, but there was something lurking behind it, something that I could sense that caused a shiver to run up my spine. I inhaled his heavenly scent as he exhaled slowly before leaning in and carefully molding his lips to mine.

I had known exquisite joy before in Robert's kisses. I had felt the electricity and the fire that ran through my body, under my skin, out through my limbs with each one of his kisses, each one of his embraces. But this time…this time it felt as though my bones had melted away, and the white heat of my core had replaced them with pure, molten fire. As always, I had a difficult time breathing, but this time I knew that if he stopped, I wouldn't even be able to restart until he kissed me again.

I tried to raise my hands to tangle in his hair, wanting to bring him closer, be closer—the need to have him be engulfed in the need within me so strong I knew I was going to suffocate in it if I didn't let it have its way—but they were being held firmly in place. I moaned my distress as Robert pulled away from me, a strange look covering his face.

This is dangerous.

I knew it was. We were both breathless, and I was willing to allow him to rip my arms out if it meant he'd kiss me again.

Grace, I'm being serious here. I-I don't know how to handle myself—these feelings are too new. They're my own and I don't know what to do; I never thought I'd be able to feel so much, feel so intensely. Your feelings are mixed with them too, and its combination is—it's just so strong.

"You're strong. I think I'm fairly adequate for a human. Let's be strong together," I panted, and leaned up to kiss his chin.

He laughed quietly, but pulled away. *Grace, please. Allow me some time to get used to this. I promise it won't be like the last time I needed to get used to my emotions.*

Knowing that there really wasn't anything that I could do to change his mind, I sighed and relaxed; my heart was still racing and my breathing still ragged, heady with the knowledge that I was affecting him the same way that he was affecting me, the same way that he had always affected me.

I'm far more affected than you could possibly know.

He leaned back and pulled me with him, resting my head on his chest. I placed my hand over the spot where his heart was; I was overcome with a deep sadness as I realized the sacrifice that he had made just to live. He placed one hand on my head, the other captured the one on his chest, and he took a deep breath, his exhale perfumed and warm against my ear. *I won't miss it. Your voice is the only sound I need to hear to know that I'm alive.*

ଓ

We went back to school the following Monday two different people. While before, we'd walk side by side but not touching, or we'd sit in classes together, our bodies facing forward but our faces turned towards each other; now Robert enjoyed holding my hand as we walked together, his body would be turned towards mine, and mine to his in class. His chaste kisses on my forehead remained, but they no longer felt that way. It didn't matter that he had yet to kiss me on the lips again after that Halloween night. I had faced losing him forever. A few days or weeks wasn't going to make that much of a difference anymore.

And that Monday held for me something that I had been desperately wanting. Robert and Graham somehow came to an understanding about their differences.

"Thank you, for saying what you did to Grace," Robert had told him during lunch. He had walked over to the football table with me in tow, and held his hand out to Graham. "You're her best friend, and you know her best. You were right when you said that she can be trusted, and now I know that when she says you can be as well, she's right."

Graham stood up and looked at me standing shyly behind Robert, my face peeking out from underneath his arm. He winked at me and took Robert's hand in his. "No problem. I meant what I said, too. I'm glad that you're able to make her happy in the way that I can't. I don't think you deserve her, of course. I don't think anyone really does. But you come close, and I can't hate you for that."

With the two of them smiling at each other, it was easy to imagine that they could be friends; the two most handsome guys in school, one blonde and effervescent, the other dark and broody.

I again felt that bubble of giddiness within me as I finally saw the pieces of my life fall into place. Normal was feeling very good indeed.

The rest of the week went by in a blur. We had amassed our own little group during lunch as Graham had taken to sitting with us now that the feud between him and Robert had come to an end. Lark had all but abandoned the gaggle of girls who had followed her around like little ducklings to sit with us, and Stacy had swallowed her distaste for Graham just enough to be able to laugh once in a while when he cracked a joke.

This group would eventually move to my house after school, with Graham and Stacy trickling in after their respective practices. Stacy had insisted that I finally start taking classes at her dad's Tae Kwon Do school. Of course, when she told me about the payment, I nearly balked.

"I have to scrub the floors?"

Stacy smirked. "What? I do it every day! At least this way, you can help me and we'll get out faster. Come on! You said you wanted to learn, and now you can for free! I told you I'd give you the family discount—I just didn't tell you that it'll just cost you a little elbow grease."

"That's not free," I muttered, but agreed to starting the following week.

I wasn't prepared for the drastic change in Stacy when I showed up for my first class. Standing among five and six-year-olds, I had already felt foolish, but these kids had been with Stacy for at least a month, and they were already far more knowledgeable than I was and she never seemed to fail to point that out.

It took me that entire first week to learn the terms and commands, not to mention the motions and positions. I estimated it'd take me until my twenty-first birthday to be able to catch up to the level that they were at now. And boy, did those kids like to remind me of that fact.

And, as if it weren't bad enough that I had to learn with basically infants who were far more skilled at this than I was, I had to practice what I was learning with Stacy, whom I knew could take out a quarterback without touching him. It was like living in a sitcom, and I was the running gag.

By the time Thanksgiving had arrived, I looked like a walking eggplant. I had never felt so bruised and useless in my life. Robert had wanted to heal me after each and every grueling practice, but I insisted that he leave me to heal on my own. It wasn't that bad, really. For whatever reason, the pain was far easier to deal with than I had thought. After one particularly rough session, I thought back to the punch I had thrown at Lark, and recalled how shocked Robert had been that I hadn't felt any tenderness.

Though I was sore and stiff, I knew that I should have felt worse. I should have been incapacitated in some way, because Stacy hadn't held back during sparring. I could see it in the intensity in her face, and the way her body moved way too fluidly. She wasn't applying any tension, just letting the movement flow from her into me. I should definitely have felt worse.

On Thanksgiving Day, Robert, Ameila, and Lark arrived at my house for dinner, each of them wielding a casserole of some kind; Janice had invited them, insisting that they were now part of our family. Robert liked that idea a great deal, and I admitted to myself that I enjoyed the sound of that as well.

With the six of us scattered around the living room and kitchen, eating, cooking, and talking, the house was filled with a warmth that it hadn't seen in a very long time. I could sense it, feel it absorbing the

396

conversation and the emotion that it had been missing for so long. Our cozy little house needed this, I realized.

As we all sat around the folding table that Dad had set up in the living room to eat, I realized how thankful I was. So much so that when we started going around the table to announce what we were thankful for, all I could say was "I just am".

"Well, that's...erm, nice, Grace," Dad mumbled.

Robert winked at me and squeezed my hand underneath the table. "I'm thankful to you, Mr. Shelley, and to Grace's mother, for bringing her in into the world. She has changed my life, and I cannot begin to express my gratitude to you for making that possible."

Dad seemed to puff up with pride at Robert's statements, and Janice smiled at his reaction.

"I'm also thankful for your father, Grace," Ameila spoke up then, and raised her glass of water to Dad. "You have blessed us with your gracious hospitality, and I ask that your home always be blessed with an abundance of love and warmth such as we feel here today."

Dad stared mesmerized at Ameila, as most men were, and raised his glass, stuttering out a broken "thank you" before nervously taking a sip of water. Janice seemed amused by the display and turned to Lark, waiting to hear what she was thankful for.

"I'm thankful for meeting genuine people who don't want anything from me that I can't give." It was matter of fact. It was succinct. It was Lark.

"Well, I guess that leaves me then, huh?" Janice laughed. "I'm thankful for this opportunity at having a family, with James and Grace, and with the new baby on the way, too. I am also thankful that you are here, Mrs. Bellegarde, as well as your children, who have become such an important part of Grace's life.

"You have done so much for us just by being there for her, and I don't think either James or I could ever repay you for any of it. I also think it would be safe for me to say that Grace's mother would thank you as well. And, I am thankful for you, Grace. If not for you, I wouldn't be here today. I know what it took for you to welcome me into your life, and for that, I will always, *always* be thankful."

I could feel the blush rise up in my cheeks as the words reminded me how foolish and selfish I had been. I turned to look at Robert, remembering that the day that had been the turning point in my relationship with Janice had also been the day that I had first met him. He had changed my life in so many ways, in such a short amount of time, it seemed like there wasn't enough time to appreciate or experience it all. I wasn't about to waste a single moment.

The rest of the meal was filled with light conversation between Ameila and Janice. Dad and Robert discussed the virtues of standard transmissions versus automatic ones, and Lark and I were left to our own silent conversation.

So how's the butt kicking going? Lark looked at me, a smirk tilting up one side of her face.

It's going. I responded, lifting up my arm to show the nice smattering of bruises that spread across it. *I know it's not as pretty as the one that you gave me, but it's still quite fun to poke and watch it change color.* I demonstrated by pressing my finger into the center of one, causing the purple color to push away, leaving behind a small yellow dot that quickly faded through reds, greens, and finally back to its original purple when I removed my fingertip.

Hold on now, let's get one thing clear. You punched me, which means you gave yourself that nice little bruise.

I grinned. *It doesn't explain why my hand bruised the way that it did, though. Maybe I'm just allergic to you.*

She snorted. It was a typical Lark response. I was waiting for her to reply with some snappy remark but instead her eyes darted to Robert, who had suddenly gone quiet. Ameila, too, had suddenly stopped talking. Dad and Janice both became aware of the eerie quiet that had quickly taken over the house.

"I'm very sorry, Janice—James, but we have to leave. There's something urgent that we have to take care of," Ameila said apologetically as she stood up, Robert and Lark mimicking her motions with perfect synchronicity. "Thank you very much for such a wonderful meal. I hope that we can do this again sometime soon."

The rest of us stood up as well, although not as gracefully or with as much purpose—well, Dad and Janice didn't anyway. I could see the urgency in Robert's eyes. *What's wrong?*

He turned to thank Dad and Janice for dinner and then grabbed my hand, pulling me towards the door. *It's time.*

I looked at him, confusion and fear flooding back to me in one familiar tidal wave of panic. *Time for what?*

He touched my face with the back of his hand, calming my jittery nerves. *Grace, it's the call. I can hear the singing. I'm being called up.*

Suddenly, all my postulating about being okay with him receiving the call went out the proverbial window as I clung to his arm, my hands suddenly slick with nervousness and fear. *Will you come back? Will you come back to me?*

He lowered his face to mine, still brushing cheek with his knuckles, and gently pressed his lips to mine. It had been our first kiss in four weeks—and it was in farewell.

In that moment, I didn't care that Dad was probably right behind me, or that it might seem desperate. I threw my arms around his neck and pressed myself into him. I felt his body tense, and prepared myself for his rejection, prepared myself to fight for just a few seconds more of being close to him. Instead, his arms wrapped around my waist and pulled me in closer than I was able to against his solid steel frame.

His lips, once light and nearly imperceptible, became hard and insistent. I could feel the pulse in my lips flow through his, taking with it all of my love, and returning with all of his. When he finally pulled away, I realized that I hadn't been breathing, and I gasped, the air rushing through my lungs like a bittersweet elixir.

It had only been a few seconds of time, and there had been no thoughts shared, but I knew—I knew that this wasn't a "see you later" kiss. It was a goodbye. I stood at the doorway as he rushed out, Lark and Ameila already in his car, their faces somber, both knowing what I already knew. I felt the tears flow down my face, mixed tears of joy that he had finally received the only thing he had ever truly desired, and tears of sadness because I did not know if I'd ever see him again because of it.

I wiped them away quickly and waved as they pulled off. I knew this was coming, I told myself. If I was having buyer's remorse now, it was my own fault. I stayed at the door until long after they had driven out of sight. Convinced that there had been no mistake, and that they wouldn't be returning, laughing at the bad little joke they had played on us, I quietly closed the door and helped Janice clear away the food, methodically putting the food into baggies for leftovers and freezing for later.

"Grace, I'll wash the dishes. Why don't you go upstairs and finish that paper you've got to do," Janice suggested, her face a mixture of concern and sympathy. She might not have known what was going on, but she surely knew that whatever it was that had happened had changed things for me.

Slowly, I climbed up the stairs, each step getting harder and harder, my feet feeling heavier as I went. I opened the door to my room half hoping that he'd be there, sitting on my bed like he normally was, a "just kidding" poised on his lips. Seeing that it was empty, I felt my heart sink even further. I should be feeling happy for him. I knew that this was coming. I just wasn't expecting it to happen so soon.

I walked over to the window and stuck my head outside of. I knew it wouldn't be there—no motorcycle, no Charger, and no dark mist slowly creeping to come and find me and make things better—but I still had to look.

I pulled myself back in and sat on the edge of the bed. Something crumpled underneath me, and I shifted over, grabbing a piece of paper from beneath me. I recognized Robert's handwriting immediately. The flowing, flourished script was unmistakable.

Wait for me.

On the bed where the paper had been was something long and dark. I picked it up and gasped. It was a black feather. I clutched the letter and the feather to my chest and laid down on the bed. He loved me enough to come back from the dead, but did he love me enough to come back to me from Heaven?

POE-TRY

As if nothing had happened, the day after Thanksgiving started with breakfast, followed by a long shower. I grabbed my book bag and went downstairs and into the garage. I rolled the used bike that Dad had bought to replace my old one outside, got on it, and started pedaling towards the library.

It was the first time in months that I had ridden one, and I don't care how the saying goes. You do forget how to ride a bicycle. I fell off before I had even made it past the driveway.

"Stupid bike," I grumbled, standing up and brushing off the dirt and grass from my jeans. I righted the bike back up and got back on. A few not so pretty starts, followed by a few more quite horrendous falls, and I was about ready to give up. I looked around me and I could see some curious faces peeking through their windows. Well, if I was going to give up, it surely wasn't going to be in front of an audience.

Picking the bike up one last time, I climbed on it, and prayed: Balance—that is all I want. I placed my foot on the pedal and pushed off, and smiled as the bike rolled smoothly down the street.

I rode the bike the few miles up the old wooded road towards the library. If I was going to finish my paper about Poe, I would need to borrow a few books, and the quiet would be nice. Graham's dad and a few of Dad's work buddies were coming over to watch the multitude of football games that would be playing today. A house full of loud, drunk men was not my idea of a good place to write an essay.

I nearly felt sorry for Janice until she told me that she was going to visit her sister up in Newark for the day, and wouldn't return until later on in the evening. Instead, I found myself feeling quite jealous of her freedom.

As I pumped my legs, I came upon the area where I had been hit. I slowed the bike down and stopped on the side, looking at the two lane road with the small dirt road shoulder. There were no street lights here, but I hadn't been hit during the evening—just found then. I hopped off of the bike and knelt down to pick up something that sparkled in the morning sunlight. It was a piece of a blinker light. The orange, reflective piece of plastic wasn't exactly hard to place. I put it in my pocket to inspect later, and got back on my bike and continued towards the library.

It felt good to walk through the door when I finally made it there ten minutes later. I felt at home here, felt comfortable among all of the books that had been my constant companions for so long throughout my lonely childhood, even with Graham in it.

I headed towards the back of the library, the poetry section being one of the least frequented sections there, and began looking for the books I had searched for online earlier that morning. Finding just one of them, I pulled it out and settled into a chair to start reading.

The first poem was too long to read, but a few of the others that weren't caught my attention. I pulled out a notebook from my book bag and started taking notes, copying the poems themselves first, and then segmenting out specific lines that stuck out.

Miss Maggie toddled over to me, her spindly little legs peeking out from beneath her dress, and said happily, "I'm so glad to see you back here, Grace! You're looking quite healthy and chipper."

I couldn't help but smile back at her. She was always so sweet and sincere. There really wasn't anything one could do to avoid feeling "chipper" whenever she spoke to you. "Thank you, Miss Maggie. How have you been?"

She waved her hand at me, as if to brush off my question. "You know how I always am, and yet you always ask. What are you reading there? Ooh, Poe. Good stuff that one. Have you read the first poem? It is the best one. Might interest you a bit." She winked at me and toddled off, disappearing amongst the shelves.

I put my notebook down and flipped the book back to the first poem, the one that I had avoided because it seemed to go on forever. Miss Maggie had never steered me wrong before when it came to things to read, so I took her word for it and settled in.

As I read, I realized that this poem was about angels, and that I had read it before. I read further and stopped at a verse that sounded so familiar, much more familiar than having simply read it once in passing. It was an intimate familiarity. I continued reading, figuring that the memory would come back to me as I kept going.

The further I read, the more personal the dialogue became, and I found myself imagining that I was the angel named Ianthe, who shone brightly and was madly in love with her angel lover Angelo. My mind took me into their world, and I felt the incredible emotion that surrounded the two lovers, their love being so strong, so demanding of their energy and attention, they failed their duty as angels, and were locked out of Heaven.

I realized that deep inside of me, I secretly wished that Robert would do the same for me, for love. I was instantly filled with shame at my selfishness, and closed the book, not wanting to read anymore of angels or the price one paid for loving someone too much. Robert had already paid a price for loving me. I couldn't demand he sacrifice again because I wanted him near me. I couldn't even think it. But I did. I thought it, and then I hit myself for thinking it. I must have looked like a complete idiot, smacking myself in the forehead and talking to myself while doing it.

Taking my little moment of insanity as a sign that it was time to leave, I went to place the book back on the shelf, but found that Miss Maggie was standing there, her hands full of some ancient looking books.

"Ah, Grace, there you are. Did you read the poem? Wasn't it lovely?"

I shook my head. "Not really. I think that there are some things that you simply don't sacrifice for love."

She looked at me in shock. "Really? Like what, dear?"

The inability to lie paid off for me then because it was a question that I had wanted answered myself. "Your dreams. You don't sacrifice your dreams for love. Especially if you've had them for your entire life."

She smiled a knowing smile and patted me on my shoulder.

"You know, dear, sometimes the things we dream about are merely the heart's way of protecting us from what we really want, and what we're really afraid to lose."

I watched as she placed her books on the shelf and took the book from my hand and placed it back in its original slot without even having to look. I suppose that is what comes from being a librarian for so long.

"I'm gonna get going so I can start on this paper of mine, Miss Maggie. It was really nice seeing you, and thank you for the little talk."

She waved her hand, "Bye Grace. I hope you found what you were looking for."

☙

When I arrived home, I rushed to the stairs, raising my hand in a mute greeting to the loud male chorus of "hey Grace" that arose from the living room, and headed up to my room. I threw my book bag onto the bed and took out my notebook, needing to read the notes that I had jotted down.

The poems that I had copied for my dissection essay were no longer holding my attention. My mind kept drifting back to that first poem, and how selfishly I had reacted to it. It was like it was pulling all of the worst possible feelings I had inside of me and laying them on top of everything that made me who I was. It smothered everything, and all I could think about was Robert and me, tumbling through the sky.

I tossed my notebook onto the ground and placed my face into the mattress. The whole day had started out as a mission to complete an assignment, and it had turned into a life-altering experience where I was suddenly the bad guy, and I didn't like it.

☙

It took me another week before I was able to finish the final draft of the essay. I took the easy way out, and wrote about the Raven and Lenore. I knew that it would just disappear amongst all of the other essays about the Raven and Lenore, but I didn't really care at that point.

404

I just wanted to get the assignment done and out of the way so that I wouldn't have to think about any Poe poems anymore.

When I turned it in, I felt relief when I saw it disappear under another essay, exactly as I expected it. I didn't think about it again until that Friday, when Mrs. Muniz called me to her desk before class began to discuss it.

"Grace, I would like to ask you to consider doing this paper over again," she said matter-of-factly, holding out my neatly typed, double spaced essay in her hand while tapping it with the other.

My head jerked back in response to her suggestion. Do it over again? "Any reason why, Mrs. Muniz?"

She pulled open a manila folder on her desk and pointed at the contents inside. More essays. "You have an incredible gift for writing—a passion for it—and yet there isn't even an ounce of emotion in this. You might as well have been writing about earthworm mating habits."

I took the insult in stride because I knew that she was right. I hadn't put as much effort into the writing as I did with avoiding the thoughts that were running rampant in my mind. I took the essay from her hand. "I guess I could do better."

She seemed annoyed by my response. "You can do more than better, Grace. If you want to turn that in, and accept the grade it would receive, then that's fine. But, if you want to turn in something that will get you the grade you deserve, then please do. You have until the end of next week to decide."

I nodded and returned to my desk with my essay, unsure of what I was going to do.

The answer came by way of Lark, who had been avoiding me since we returned to school the Monday after Thanksgiving. Stacy, who had learned about what had happened and had repeated the same story that Lark had told to explain Robert's absence from school, had been acting as a slight go-between, understanding that I was full of questions that Lark just couldn't answer, and Lark was full of answers that I just didn't want to hear.

Stacy had continued with my Tae Kwon Do classes in the same

upbeat and yet violent manner since Robert's call, but today, she was giving, or should I say, she was more open to my getting in a few good hits without feeling the need to retaliate in some painful manner.

"What's up, Stacy?" I asked once class was over and we were on our hands and knees wiping the floor and mats. "You're not usually this…nice."

She threw her rag on the ground and placed her hands on her thighs as she sat on her heels. "Lark has been bugging me to get you to talk to her. She doesn't want to just pop up in your head, or at your house, and so she's been doing it in mine. She has a lot of stuff she has to say to you—stuff about Robert."

My heart started racing when she said that Lark had something to tell me about Robert. Was he coming home?

Stacy held her hands up, her face screwed with what looked like too much information. "Ugh—Lark wants to know if she can come and talk to you now, because I'm kind of done with this mind-telephone operator thing."

I nodded my head, and then there she was, as if she had been there the whole time. "You were hiding out nearby, weren't you?"

"Well, I'm not as quick as my brother, plus I get a kick out of seeing the two of you beat each other up," she replied. Looking at her was painful. She was so beautiful in her own way, but she was also so similar in appearance to Robert, I had to look away. I didn't want to see anything that looked like him until it was him. I didn't want to ruin his face in my mind.

"Well, thanks," Lark huffed, "I'm glad I'm able to ruin Robert's perfection in some way." She took a step towards us and Stacy shrieked.

"Take your shoes off! No shoes on the floor!"

Lark rolled her eyes and removed her sneakers. She padded over to us in her socked feet and then gracefully knelt down and assumed a very ladylike seated position that I knew I would have never been able to pull off.

"I wanted to tell you, Grace, that Robert is coming back-"

"When?" I grabbed her arms, interrupting her, too anxious to hear anything else but a time, a date, anything.

Her eyes narrowed as she pulled her arms out of my grasp with a slinky, effortless movement that made my grip—the strongest I could have ever formed—appear weak hearted.

"He doesn't know for sure. His call wasn't what he expected. It wasn't what I expected, that's for sure." I detected a little bit of dismay in her eyes, but then her eyes widened and she smiled widely. "He says that he loves you, and that you'll see him soon. And, he says to read it again."

Her smile was infectious, made more potent by the news that Robert loved me—even after achieving his greatest dream—and that he was coming back to me soon. But that last part, about reading it again. What exactly did he mean by *it*?

Lark shrugged her shoulders. "He just said to read *it* again."

I looked at her with doubt written plainly on my face. How could she not know what he meant?

She shook her head, annoyed by my thoughts. "He's going through a lot right now; a lot of information is flowing through his mind, the entire history of our kind, things that we only find out after we receive the call. There is too much information in there to sift through, Grace, and I'm sorry if I didn't stop and take the time to run through everything to find out what he meant."

Immediately contrite, I reached my hand out to hold hers. "I'm sorry, Lark. I'm being an ingrate. I was trying so hard to not think about Robert and here you are, with so much of him in your head. I'll figure out what he meant on my own. It shouldn't be so hard, right?"

And, it turned out that it wasn't. The next day, Stacy, Lark, and I went back to the old library. I was convinced that whatever *it* was, it was something that I had read here. I scoured the fiction section, looking for anything of importance that I might have read. Stacy sat on the floor with a book in her hand and proceeded to read. I asked what she was reading, and she held the book up. I rolled my eyes. "Don't you think you're a little old for that?"

She grinned. "No one is too old for a little Seuss."

Shaking my head in disbelief, I headed towards Lark, who had posited herself in the poetry section. "I found a few books that might interest you." She held up a couple of books with worn covers. One of them I recognized as the Poe book that I had read a week ago.

"I read this one already," I mumbled.

Read it again.

Confused, I took the book, ignoring the other one in Lark's hand, and went to find my own corner to sit down. I flipped the first few pages until I came upon the first poem. It was the one that I had avoided that first time, the one that I had gone back to read after Miss Maggie had insisted, the one that had made me start to imagine being enough to leave Heaven behind.

I found myself once again becoming immersed in the rhythmic verse as I was swept away by the tale of an angel doing as she had been commanded, and two who had not. I read it twice, and had started to read it again for the third time when something struck a chord within me.

That feeling of familiarity that I had felt the first time I read the poem had returned, this time with far more clarity. I could hear the voice in my head, see his face.

Somehow, Robert knew that I had read the poem, and he knew that I'd figure it out. "He loves me," I mouthed to myself as I rubbed my fingers against the words that he had spoken to me that night after the wedding, after I told him that I loved him. That first night I had slept in his arms. He had recited a verse from this poem because he couldn't tell me directly that he loved me. But now I knew.

I hugged the book to my chest, my newfound knowledge wedged deep between the two, and I looked over to Lark. She was smiling at me, relieved that I had figured it out.

When they dropped me off at home later that afternoon to rewrite my essay, my mind was ready to flow onto the paper, and I spent the next few hours typing away on the computer in the living room. I waved away any mention of food, and refused calls from Stacy and Graham. I was going to complete the twenty pages that evening, while the words were still fresh in my mind and the emotions still new in my heart.

It was one thing to know that Robert loved me. It was something completely different to know that his love hadn't been something that he discovered when near death, as romantic as that notion might be, but rather something that had been in him for as long as it had been inside of me. I was giddy—there's that word again—with my newly discovered piece of information.

As my essay printed, I ran upstairs to grab the note that he had left me. I had taped it to my mirror—at the time, it was a masochistic thing to do. I flipped on my bedroom light and rushed over to grab the note, but it wasn't there. Instead, an envelope had been taped to the mirror in its place.

My name had been written on it in the same fluid script, and so I tore it open and pulled out the small sheet of folded paper inside.

I will be home on the following Friday. Please meet me at the retreat at four. With love, Robert.

He would be home in a week! That was just before Christmas break; the thought of spending two weeks with Robert, unfettered by homework and school nights sounded like my own piece of heaven. I put the little piece of paper back in the envelope and left it on the dresser. I silently made a promise to myself that I wouldn't touch it again until Friday.

And I kept it.

CB

My alarm went off screaming like it always did: loud, loud, and way too early. But, today was different. I jumped out of bed, quickly gathered up my things, and headed to the shower. I stood there for what felt like ages. In reality, it was only about a half an hour, which is usually how long it takes before the water runs cold.

I performed all of the normal girlish rituals that involved a razorblade and foam in a can. I needed to feel feminine, even if only underneath my clothes.

I dressed in a pair of jeans and my Skellington shirt, and put my hair up into a neat ponytail. With the exception of the shirt, I was

409

dressed in the exact same manner that I had been when we had first met, although with the weather being as cold as it had been, I would need to wear a thick jacket over everything. Fortunately, it hadn't snowed yet, which meant no need for boots and gloves.

I rushed downstairs to grab a quick bowl of cereal and ate it standing up, leaning against the counter as Janice walked in to make Dad his breakfast.

"You're up early," she said while yawning."

I nodded, my mouth full of milk and cereal flakes. I finished and washed my dishes, leaving her to fry the eggs and bacon before my stomach started complaining about my choice of breakfast fare. I was halfway up the stairs when Dad started coming down. "You're up early, kiddo. Must be an important day."

I bit back the grin that wanted to spread across my face with enthusiastic glee. It would look more psychotic than ecstatic. I simply nodded quickly, and continued to my room.

I took the envelope with Robert's note in it off of the mirror, and put it in my book bag. I stuck Robert's feather, which I had been keeping under my pillow, in my binder, and placed that in my book bag as well. I sat down on the edge of my bed and looked out of my window. The sky was changing from the bruised purples and blues to the blush of morning's pinks and oranges.

The clock on the dresser said half past six. That gave me almost an hour before Graham would arrive to pick me up—I still hadn't found out who it was that had told him about Robert leaving, but he had shown up that first day back to school after Thanksgiving and had so ever since—and drive the two of us to school. After he had eaten a second breakfast, of course.

I double checked to make sure that my essay was in my binder and, satisfied that I had everything I thought I would need, I went back downstairs to wait for Graham, opening the kitchen window…to let out the smoke, I told Janice, smiling as I saw a light come on over at the Hasselbeck house.

಄

School the day before a long vacation always felt more like one large party. The teachers were lenient in ways they never were on a normal day. Rules weren't just bent or broken; they were tossed out of the window, or decimated and written out of the books completely. The bells ringing at the beginning and end of classes were now just a mere annoyance as we all shuffled lazily from one class to the other.

During lunch, Lark seemed annoyed that Robert hadn't told her about coming home this afternoon, and she took out her annoyance on nearly everything she could. She snapped at Graham for complimenting her British accent, and she criticized Stacy for being obnoxious to Graham. Both things had always pleased her before so it was especially shocking to actually hear her demand that it stop.

As the end of the day drew near, the excitement in the school was at its peak. The only time it was ever rivaled was the last day of school, and that was still over six months away. I turned in my essay to Mrs. Muniz in fourth period, who seemed pleased after skimming the contents, and I even smiled at Mr. Branke, who was not his usual touchy-feely self today. That was cause enough to be charitable. Sixth period Theater class with Mr. Danielson had gone over well as we acted out Christmas carols in different moods and accents—another exercise in humility, Mr. Danielson told us. It definitely was an exercise, trying to sing Jingle Bells as though it were a funeral march rather than a jovial tune.

When that final bell rang, the school emptied out rapidly, everyone excited for Christmas shopping, parties, and parades. I rushed out of the school and headed towards Stacy's car. She had agreed to drop me off to meet Robert, even though it was in the opposite direction from the Tae Kwon Do school.

"Thank you, Stacy. I really appreciate this," I told her as she pulled into the gravel parking lot.

She pulled her lips into a half-hearted smile and shrugged her shoulders. "Hey, at least one of us gets to be happy today."

I saw her grip the steering wheel tightly, her knuckles turning white as she fought against something inside of her. "What's wrong,

Stacy?"

"I'm just annoyed by the way Lark's been acting ever since you told her about Robert coming back. She's not just verbally angry, but she's also mentally angry. She doesn't seem to realize that her thoughts cut worse than anything else."

I understood what she meant. Lark could control what came out of her mouth, just like most people, but her thoughts ran free, and if we were granted the access to hear them, sometimes it was just too harsh and cold to deal with for a normal person. A lifetime of being teased and ridiculed had given me a slight advantage over Stacy, but I knew that it hurt. I placed my hand on her shoulder and squeezed it reassuringly. "I know she doesn't mean to hurt your feelings, Stacy."

Stacy turned to look at me, her eyes red with tears. "It's not my feelings that are hurt, Grace. She's physically hurting my mind when she thinks about Robert coming home and not telling her."

My own eyes widened in shock. "She must not be aware that she's doing it, Stacy."

She nodded, more a patronizing motion than anything else. I couldn't do anything else but hug her. "You're a good friend, Stacy. Thank you for being mine.

She hugged me back, her smile tinged with a bit of sadness. "Anytime, Grace."

I climbed out of the car, glancing at the little clock on the radio as I did so, and closed the door. I watched as she drove off and then walked over to the bench where Robert and I had had our first conversation. Where I had first learned he could read my thoughts. Where I knew that I had first fallen in love with him. That little revelation brought a smile to my lips, because it wasn't silly teenage romanticism as some might call it. It was real. What else could have brought my heart back from the cold and ashy death that it had suffered?

I looked up at the sun in the sky. It was slowly retreating into some light clouds, the afternoon light dimming as the weather gave a hint that things weren't going to be so clear for long. The clock in Stacy's car had said it was a quarter past three. I had forty-five minutes left before Robert would show up. I closed my eyes against the warmth of the sun's rays and thought of Ianthe and Angelo as the clouds moved across the sky, taking with them each minute until I would be reunited with my own falling star.

REVELATION

I waited for Robert until the sun had nearly set. I waited for his mind to fill my own with his love. I waited for him to wrap his arms around me and kiss away all of the trepidation that had settled around me since he had left. I hadn't realized just how unbelievably bereft I felt without him near, how it had changed me. It was as if there were two Graces, and the one that stood here was merely the photocopy: flat, 2D, and monochromatic, while the real Grace was off floating somewhere with an angel up among the stars and the clouds. And I envied that Grace. I hated her, too.

When the last of the sun's rays had succumbed to the ever constant pull of the night, finally losing its grip on the horizon, and the colors of the sky changed from the beautiful pinks and oranges of dusk to the mauves and purples of twilight, when the lights of the parking lot automatically popped on, illuminating me with the false brightness that made everything seem sickly and dead, I stood up. He wasn't coming.

The disappointment washed over me, drenching my skin with embarrassment, pinking my cheeks with anger, and overflowed onto my face in the form of tears that I had promised myself an hour ago I wouldn't shed. I couldn't afford to be upset by this. It wasn't like he was getting off of a shift at the Dairy Queen, I had to remind myself.

This was something that he had been born to do, born to fulfill. It was his destiny, long before he had ever met me, and would be long after I had died. I couldn't make demands of him, or have expectations that he'd be able to do everything that he said he would when there was something far more important than me he had to concern himself with now.

Sighing, I bent down and reached for my book bag. When I couldn't feel it, I looked under the bench—behind it—but it wasn't there.

414

The clichés in novels and movies about the hair on the back of your neck standing up when something isn't right really should be taken more seriously because I suddenly realized that I wasn't alone when that same, creepy feeling appeared on mine.

I heard the rush of air behind me and my heart started racing. "Rob-" I turned, searching for his familiar eyes, and stopped.

They weren't silver.

It wasn't Robert.

"Sam." I said, stunned. "What are you doing here?"

He smiled at me...sly, sinister. I shivered, but not because of the sudden chill in the air. "I came here to tell you that Rob isn't coming."

"I figured that much out already, Sam," I said, annoyed by the way he was looking at me. "I was just about to start heading home. When you talk to him, tell him—no, don't worry about it." I changed my mind about giving him a message to give to Robert. I knew it would probably never reach him anyway.

I looked down at Sam's hands. He had my book bag in one, the feather that Robert had left me in the other. Its glossy black color contrasted dramatically against the pristine white of Sam's clothing. Night and day. Good vs. Evil. But Robert wasn't evil—what was missing?

I glance at Sam's face and it was as though he had made the same comparison because he smiled in such a manner that I felt the hair on the back of my neck rise up again. My hand automatically went up to pat them down, as if they were sticking straight up, a warning flag to anyone who passed by. But no human would have noticed the reaction. It was too minute to be anything but a feeling one brushed off as silliness.

"I've got to get going now, Sam. Could I have my things back?" I told him, not wanting to stay around any longer than necessary. I held my hand out expectantly, an impatient sigh coming out as I did so. Impatient was better than annoyed.

His gold eyes had started to grow warmer, the hard, cold metal in them turning into liquid. "Why in such a rush, Grace?" he asked, his voice dripping with artificial sweetness, saccharine in its falseness.

Not wanting to show the sudden fear that had taken a hold of me, I pointed to my book bag, as if the answer to his question were quite obvious. "I have to walk home, Sam, and it's not like I live right down the street."

I could feel my heartbeat picking up, the nervousness and fear that were starting to overwhelm my thoughts was affecting its rhythm. I walked towards Sam, my hand outstretched, shaking. "Could you give me back my book bag, Sam?" Instead of the book bag, he handed me the feather.

It was then that I noticed that the light from the parking lot was casting my shadow across the grass. It stretched before me, reaching out its dark fingers towards the bench and the trees.

It was alone.

"You—you have no shadow," I breathed. The words, unbelievable, yet the absence of his confirmed it.

He nodded, surprised at my reaction, but knowing what path my mind was leading me on.

"You're…one of the dark ones," I whispered again, more a revelation than an accusation. My mind raced back to when Robert told me that the dark angels bore no shadow because they were all darkness and couldn't shape the light the way the others could. I searched the grass once more for any tell-tale sign of a shadow, anything that would calm the screaming accusations in my head—I found none.

He bowed then, his left knee bending, right leg pulled behind him. He had one arm draped across his abdomen, while the other was raised up at his side. It was a very elegant, gentlemanly bow, but I forgot all of that when he started talking. "One of the many angels of death, at your service," he said, his smile dark, his voice mocking.

I took a step back, shock sending shivers throughout my body. My blood felt a degree colder. It felt like it was thickening beneath my skin. How could Robert have been friends with him? He had called them wicked and evil. How could he call someone who was evil a brother?

I looked at him, at his beautiful face, and I wondered how many

416

people had been fooled by such treacherous beauty? Robert had been just one of many, no doubt. Sam's mistakes had cost Robert his heart, and if he were willing to do that to someone who called him a brother, I was suddenly very suspicious of what he was planning for me. "You can't touch me." I told him, my voice cracking in its fear. "Lark and Robert told me that there are laws that you have to follow, rules you cannot break."

"I don't have to touch you, Grace…to kill you. Didn't Robert tell you that we're not subject to the same rules as the rest of them are?" He smiled, the diabolical gleam in his eye causing me to catch my breath as I nearly choked on his words.

I took another step back, even as he took one towards me. "Why—what are you doing here, Sam?"

He shrugged his shoulders. "I was bored."

The way he said it—his unaffected tone—was too perfect. He was lying. "I thought angels couldn't lie," I said, the accusation clear in my voice, as I continued to back away from him.

He laughed, but the annoyance was plain to see in his face, hear in his tone. He didn't like the fact that I already knew so much about his kind, his world.

"Silly girl. One of the things I can do, and do with ease, is lie. It's quite a gift of mine, actually," he said, an evil smile causing his lips to curl up, revealing the slickness of his teeth, as though his mouth was watering for something.

"And don't worry your silly little head about that whole wing-bringer nonsense. No one is going to punish me for removing you from this life, Grace. Your little soul isn't as valuable as you think." I watched as the tip of his tongue peeked out from behind his teeth to touch the sharp point of an incisor, the corner of his mouth curling up as he did so.

"Your silly little romance has been amusing to watch, though, if that's any consolation to you. So unlike all the other girls of this earth, you are, and yet so similar. So quick to fall into what you think is love. So quick to fall out of it. You don't know what love is, how it can burn inside of you for an eternity, how it changes you physically, into something you can never reverse." His words hinted of loss and pain, but I wasn't brave enough to ask what he was talking about.

Instead, I took a different route, placing my hands on my hips in defiance. "I don't know what loving someone for an eternity feels like, Sam, but I know that if it were possible for me to do so, I would love Robert for at least that long. And contrary to your statement, I am completely aware of how love can change someone physically, because his love for me *has* changed me physically. It's just not obvious to someone who's lived for centuries in his own perfect little world. It's ironic that with your incredible gifts, you're unable to see that." My voice was sad. I hadn't meant it to be, but the sadness was there just the same.

He leered at my little speech, completely unaffected. "You say that as if he's actually changed you in some way. You think that the way you feel something somehow eclipses the way that we feel? That it can alter your very makeup the way it can for us?" he sneered, his lips pulling up over an angry snarl.

"You are pathetic. You haven't changed physically, you stupid girl. Your hormones are just working overtime. He hasn't even lain with you yet; I can see *that* quite clearly!" His eyes roamed up and down my body, his laughter echoing around us, it was so loud. I almost felt violated by the way his eyes lingered on certain parts of me, and angered at how he could just continue talking the way he did. Each word felt like a nail being pounded into my heart and my dignity.

He saw the pain in my face, and took advantage of it. "Has he even tried? Has he made any attempts to seduce you, Grace? Does he not find you suitable to bed?"

I didn't want to answer, but I couldn't deny to myself that he had not, had never tried.

"Ahhh…and you probably think it's because you're human, right, you silly girl?" He smirked again.

This time I did answer. "I know that he's been with others. He has told me everything. And I don't think that's any of your business!" I tried to keep from sounding hurt by his statements, but I couldn't help but sense the slight truth in the insinuation that Robert didn't find me

418

desirable in that way.

I closed my eyes to calm myself. I didn't need to be feeling all of these other emotions when I needed to focus on Sam and what exactly he wanted with me.

And then he was in my face, so close, I could feel the warmth from his chest, smell the odd sweet smokiness of his breath. "How you must disappoint him. All of the secrets he told you, and you didn't even listen to any of it. He told you that he couldn't take things from you, didn't he, And yet how quick you were to believe that he took his little note from you. How little faith you had in him."

My mouth opened in a small gasp, the obvious lapse in my judgment clear to him, but I had been oblivious to it, and it shamed me. I had accused Robert of not paying attention and yet I had failed in the same regard. My failure only angered me further as Sam continued, enjoying the shift in my emotions immensely.

"Of course, he also said that he'd keep you safe, too. He made himself a liar when he told you about me," he whispered before leaping back to his original position.

"He didn't keep you safe from me, Grace, even though he knew what I was. He shouldn't have brought you to the wedding—shouldn't have allowed you to see so much, especially knowing that the possibility was so great that he would need to keep you safe from himself."

I was confused. Despite the abhorrence I felt listening to him, I had to ask, "What do you mean, keep me safe from himself?"

The anticipation of telling me some long unknown truth changed his presence wholly. He became relaxed, where before he was poised, on the verge, ready to spring at a moment's notice.

Whatever he was about to tell me was something he had wanted me to know for some time.

"I'm not just a minion of death, Grace. I am Samael. I am a *dark* angel of death. But your N'Uriel, ahh…he is something special— unique even. His position is much more desirable than mine among my fellow dark ones. Why do you think I was sent to mentor him, Grace? Why do you think I was chosen to teach him, to lead him to this path? He has the power to decide; he is a judge, a throne, a punisher, a savior.

I may be an angel of death, but your N'Uriel…he *is* Death." The smile was wide on his face as he took in my shock.

"I don't believe it," I said, shaking my head in denial. "I won't believe it. Death isn't a person—it's not Robert."

Sam laughed, "You stupid girl. His name isn't *Robert*. His name is N'Uriel. You've asked so many useless questions about us, and yet you failed to ask the one question that would have answered everything for you."

Again, he was in front of me, the span of fifty feet crossed in less than a second, with one firm, cruel, iron hand holding my chin so I couldn't look away from him, his other placing something in mine. "Ameila gave N'uriel his name because of who he would become when he got his call. Oh yes, she's known since the moment of his conception—how could she not when she chose to create his life in that of a walking corpse?"

He sneered at the shock in my eyes and continued with his lurid tale, "Did he tell you what his name meant, Grace? No? N'Uriel is the fire of God. His soul crossed through the fires of hell in order to be born. He was born amid flames, emerging from that woman's corpse as though he were Lucifer himself. What else could he be *but* Death? Did you never stop to ask yourself what the consequences were of such a birth? Of course not, you stupid girl. Even *he* assumed that the most he'd have to suffer would be to not be able to heal someone.

"Such naiveté. I blame his mother for not educating him sooner. It would have made my job much easier. Instead, I've had to try and wean him away from you because of *her* ridiculous guilt and belief that you humans are worth loving and caring about. And look where that has gotten me? He no longer trusts me. Because of you."

My nostrils flared in anger as I remembered the consequences that came as a result of trusting and loving Sam. "You didn't deserve his trust, and you definitely didn't deserve his love and friendship. I watched him *die* because of his trust in you; you *killed* him with your lies. You knew-"

Suddenly, I was unable to speak, the darkness in Sam's eyes and the words that were stuck in my throat causing my breath to catch. In a flash of comprehension, I knew that Sam had never intended for Robert to get his wings at all. He hadn't intended for Robert to have lived. "You *wanted* him dead," I whispered, my breath rough with the depth of the accusation.

He snarled at me, his teeth snapping in anger. "Yes. I almost had Death's soul! Do you know what that would have meant for me?"

I shook my head, still clamped in his grip, knowing that he simply couldn't see how wrong about everything he was. "No. You never came close to having Robert's soul, Sam, because his soul, his heart, his life belongs to me. It was why he came back to me."

He smirked again. "I'm sure that matters little to him now that he's achieved the one thing that matters more to him than you do. Let me remind you, Grace, that there has never been an angel who chose his *girlfriend* over fulfilling the call. The taking of souls is far more pleasurable than dealing with a whiny, grasping female in need of attention," he let go of my chin, and again, returned back to his original spot, instantly, as though he had never moved at all; the only evidence that he had been near me at all were the bruises that were slowly appearing on my skin.

He smiled from his perch, and called out, "But, in all your uselessness, you still manage to test his loyalties, Grace. You tempt him. He is distracted by you and it angers those of us who had to make the sacrifice that he has not yet done."

I didn't understand what he meant by sacrifices. What did one sacrifice when you were one of the divine? "What did *you* sacrifice, Sam, that makes you so jealous of what Robert and I share?"

His anger had melted the cold gold in his eyes, and it bubbled now, dangerously on the edge of spilling over. "How do you think I found *my* wings, Grace?" he seethed. "Do you think that the love you and Robert share is unique? That it is the only one of its kind to have ever existed? You are nothing special, Grace. You're not even beautiful. It would have been slightly tolerable if you had at least been that."

In a movement so quick I didn't see it, he had flown to one of the lights in the parking lot and shattered its bulbs. I shook at the sound of the glass falling to the gravel below, and the growing darkness that I knew he planned to have slowly consume me.

"The woman who brought along my wings was Miki. She was beautiful, with a laugh that freed my mind from the thousands of others that crowded in there. I vowed to never leave her side so that we'd always be together.

"But there aren't many options for immortals when it comes to turning a human into one. Did N'Uriel tell you how it's done? No? Ahh…he's wiser than I thought. We have to ask the seraphim for permission to do it safely, or we use what gifts we possess in freakish experiments behind their backs. But, if we create something that the human world cannot tolerate, we're bound by a universal law to destroy what we create, even if it means destroying our own children.

"Miki was denied immortality by the seraphim—those self-righteous, sanctimonious… I'm losing track here—your kind are always so good at bringing out the worst in us. Where was I? Ah, yes—I did not want Miki to die. So I began searching." He flew to another light. More shattering and the sound of glass raining down on gravel prickled my skin, as though it were the beginning of a countdown to something dark and tragic.

"I had heard that some immortals had succeeded in changing humans into other things, to keep them around, whether for amusement or for other purposes, but I didn't have the power in me to be successful; I turned Miki into a mindless monster that didn't recognize me, or our love. I had to destroy her and whatever humanity I had been given from this human form was destroyed right along with her. It was from that loss, that act of destroying what I loved the most that brought my wings," he sneered at me, his glow dark now.

He flew to the second to the last lamp, destroying those bulbs with a loud cry, and moved to the remaining set of glowing lights, looking down on me with glee as he floated overhead.

"I know you think that N'Uriel will choose you, that he'll realize that being one of us isn't what he thought he wanted—what he waited all these centuries for—but you are wrong. No one can resist the call, not even those in love. Why else do you think you're here alone…with me?"

And the last set of lights went out.

RETRIBUTION

I stared out into the darkness—the immeasurable fear pounding a fierce staccato rhythm in my heart—wondering where he had disappeared to. With all of the lights smashed out, I was swallowed by blackness; there were no stars, no moon to help my eyes see in the dark, wintry sky above me.

I could hear his laughter, though; the mocking tone in it, the savage disgust he held for me. He was near, and I was ready, my sneakers dug into the gravel beneath them, bracing myself, planting roots to prevent me from running should the feeling overtake me.

"Did you really believe that N'Uriel would give up his dreams for you? That he thought your life was worth more than the rest of us? Did you really hope that he was planning on deserting his obligation to all of humanity for you, a mere girl who is nothing but disgusting and weak? What is it they call you at school? Grace the Freak?" Sam taunted from the darkness.

"Did he truly tell you about all of the others, Grace? Of the countless other girls there have been? There were centuries of them—a millennia of girls who kept him occupied, busy while waiting for the call. Girls who gave him *everything*. Did you think that after all of them, that him not wanting to be with you in that way meant you're special? Was that what you told yourself in order to make yourself feel better when he wanted to *cuddle*?" he laughed cruelly.

"Did you think that you'd mean something because you were the one who brought around his change? You mean no more to him than all of those who came before you, those who have died for him, died because of him. You're *nothing* to him, Grace."

I shook my head, knowing he could see me, wanting him to see that I was defiant, while the tears in my eyes fogged up my eyesight. I brushed them away with one hand; I needed my vision to be clear, needed to be able to see his face, even if the evil and hate there would also reveal that there was some truth in his words. I needed to see my fate—whether I lived or died—because my time for running and hiding on my bed were long gone. I would face all of it head on.

I was stronger than he thought. I was stronger than I had ever imagined myself to be. Love and hope had helped me to realize that.

And then he was there. He stepped from behind a tree, his snow white wings folded behind him, his face pale, his glow a deep, satisfied blue. His hands were open at his sides and his eyes were a hard, icy gold. He bared his sharp, angry teeth at me, and then stepped forward. His wings spread wide, as he prepared himself. I saw the fingers in his hands twitch.

Behind my back, my fingers twitched, too. In my grip I held onto the only reminder I had of Robert, of what it meant to be loved: the lone, black feather that Sam had returned to me filled my hands. It comforted me, knowing that at least a part of him were with me. And yet, at the same time, my hurt curled inward, knowing that should I die, he might be the very one who came to collect my soul.

But I wasn't ready to die today—not without a fight at least; and strangely, I did not fear it, either. Both roads would lead me to Robert.

I held the feather in my hand, tilting the plume up towards my elbow, the quill end in my palm, hidden behind my arm. I silently thanked Robert for figuring out and showing me how to close off my mind so that my thoughts could remain my own as I felt the sharp tip press into my calloused skin. I readied myself, taking deep, calming breaths. I silently thanked Stacy for drilling enough calming exercises into me during classes, otherwise I was quite certain that I'd be hyperventilating right now. I nodded my head towards the angel of death, ready.

He came at me slowly, his cat to my mouse, his wings spreading wider with each step like an eagle ready to swoop down on its prey. He wouldn't do this as quickly as possible, though. He wanted to see me suffer for what I had done—to pay for the great crime of daring to love an angel, and for the audacity of having that angel love me back.

I knew he wasn't going to fight fair—if ever a fight between a human girl and a vengeful angel could be so—when I noticed that I was suddenly cold; he had begun to slowly draw the warmth from me, from my blood. My veins felt like my blood had turned into slush.

"W-why d-do you need to u-u-use y-your ab-bi-lities, S-S-Sam?" I stammered, feeling the chill rattle me from teeth to toes. "A-are y-you afr-raid that w-w-without them, y-you'll lose to a-a h-human girl?" Angel or not, human or not, he was still a male, with male pride and male ego.

Immediately, I felt the chill recede. He smiled cruelly, nodding, his head at an angle keeping his gaze on me, conceding to my questions. "You're right. I don't need anything to kill you, Grace, other than my bare hands." As if to emphasize the point, he flexed his hands, squeezing them into a fist and then releasing them. "I haven't had the pleasure of doing so in centuries…since that glorious period of the Crusades when soul after soul came to lie at my feet. But then again, those deaths were all young boys or old men, too ready and willing to die, the fools. I don't think I enjoyed their deaths half as much as I will yours."

His wings were fully extended now, and I watched, confused, as he pulled them forward around himself, as though he were shielding himself from me with them. For whatever reason, my body curled inward, my arms around my head, as though it knew separately before I did what was coming.

With a rush of sound and air, he flung his massive wings open; the force of the motion sent me flying backwards.

I hit the hard gravel of the parking lot on my back, the impact causing all of the air to shoot out of me, the gravel slicing through my shirt, burrowing into my skin. I could hear him laughing again as I stared up at the cloudy night sky, trying to catch my breath and gather my wits which seemed to have scattered to the trees. If only there had been one star in the sky to focus on…

"I'm going to do this so slowly, Grace," he spoke softly, almost lovingly. I could hear the crunching of gravel as he slowly walked towards me. "I will have you begging for me to be quick. You'll even be willing to trade your very soul for the pain to be over. I will enjoy

426

the taste of your tears as you beg for me to finish, but I won't. I'm going to take my time and make you suffer."

He appeared over me and knelt down; his large wings surrounded us like arms, keeping us in...keeping me in. He had his head cocked to one side, his long, dark-golden hair hanging over his shoulder, touching my face. It smelled of smoke and ashes...and blood.

He brought his hand to touch my cheek, almost as gently and lovingly as Robert would. He caressed it, his thumb softly stroking the crest, as though appreciating the texture, the warmth—and then with surprising cruelty and speed, he slapped me, the brutality of it splitting my lip, and causing me to bite into the inside of my cheek, the taste of blood burning a strong memory into my mind.

I let it collect in my mouth, that vile, metallic flavor filling my senses. It pooled against my tongue, while the blood from my lip dribbled down the side of my now throbbing face. My nostrils flared as I tried to breathe without choking.

He continued talking, satisfied that I hadn't yet cried out. "You are more tolerant than I thought. How tolerant will you be when you learn what I will do to you, I wonder." He looked at me as though I were some odd curiosity.

He brushed my cheek again, this time with his knuckles, clicking his tongue, as if the bruise that was most likely forming before his eyes had somehow been my fault. He turned my face, looking at one side then the other, comparing them it seemed, and then smiled a beautifully vicious smile. I could feel my eye starting to swell, and I knew that soon it would shut, cutting off that side of my vision, handicapping me even more than I already was.

"I think I will break your bones, one by one," he said calmly, his voice soothing, as though he were describing how to paint trees. "I will slice you here-" he brushed a finger against the bottom of my ear and traced a path across my cheek towards the corner of my mouth "-to here, so that your screams will remind forever anyone who dares to take from me what is mine what will be coming for them." He watched me— looked into my eyes, trying to read the thoughts that I had kept hidden away, see if I felt the pain, enjoying it as much as he enjoyed the inflicting of it.

His finger was still against the corner of my mouth when he started to press into my skin, his claw-like nail cutting through. I flinched at the sting as I anticipated the action he had just promised, prepared to keep my screams from rushing out, but he pulled back. I glared at him defiantly. I let my mental guard down just long enough to let one word through before he could flood my mind with his own. *Coward!*

He stared at me in shock, and then his face grew amused. For an immeasurable moment, he looked so beautiful, it was easy to forget that he was going to kill me and would do so with great satisfaction. He was once again the beautiful angel from the wedding, a golden god, the epitome of angelic beauty. The cruel irony wasn't lost on me, and I started to laugh.

When he started laughing in response, I seized the opportunity. With as much force as I could, I spit the blood and saliva I had collected into his face, turning the golden god into the monster, finally revealing him for what he truly was.

Momentarily caught off guard by this benign attack, he eased his wings back, licking his lips and savoring the taste of my defiance. That little movement gave me just enough room to raise my hand, my only weapon, my only hope against an immortal angel of death—the hard end of lone feather—was gripped and ready. With all the strength I had, with all the will I had in me to live and the desperation to see Robert again alive, I rammed the quill into Sam's left eye. Surprise and shock filled me as it sunk in.

The screech that erupted from him tore through me, his pain became mine, worse than mine, unbearable as all of the nerve endings in me reacted to his cry. Reflexively, I pulled the quill out, my hand falling to the ground to brace myself for the pain that racked my body.

Sam gripped his eye with both hands while a golden liquid poured from between his fingers and dripped hotly onto my face. His pain and his anger were vibrating throughout his body, and his wings were spread wide, as though reaching for help from some unknown source. I bit through my pain, forcing it it down with a deep gasp, and

428

quickly brought my arm up again, ramming the end of the quill into his other eye, blinding him completely.

His scream, the scream of an angel in pain, caused blood to rush out of my ears and my nose. The scream seemed to grow louder, more frantic. It echoed all around me, bouncing off of me before returning, and I grabbed my head, trying to keep it all out but only succeeding in trapping it inside of me—like a bumblebee in a jar—bumping around harder and harder in its quest to break free, but there was no freedom from this sound.

I rolled on the ground in agony. I tried kicking my feet against the gravel in a feeble attempt to crawl away while he wailed with his hands over his now blinded eyes; the two of us, pitiful creatures wallowing in our own pain. I shook and convulsed with the unbearable way it felt as though my entire body was imploding, tiny explosions beneath my skin like a million stab wounds biting into my flesh. I could see the blood pooling beneath my fingernails through the red mist that covered my eyes. I began vomiting the blood that had collected in my stomach, and struggled to breathe when my blood began to slowly drown me as it filled up my lungs.

I could feel the gravel cutting through my hands and my knees as I fought to get as far away from the sound as possible. I knew that the loss of sight wouldn't be enough to stop him, but I hoped it was enough to slow him down long enough for me to get away and die peacefully. I moved an inch—a small victory—and moved another.

Suddenly, I could feel a sharp pulling at the back of my head. My time was up. I was drawn to a standing position and then my feet were no longer touching the ground, while a tremendous pain radiated from my head.

He had lifted me off the ground by my hair, his fist knotted into my ponytail.

He placed his other hand around my throat, and brought my head to his. I could feel his hot and ragged breath in my ear, and shivered as he began talking in a hoarse voice. "You are going to pay for that, you walking corpse. I'm going to tear you into bite sized pieces and then feed you to your boyfriend. And when he's done eating your flesh—thanking me for an exceptional meal—I'm going to serve him your tongue for dessert." He laughed maniacally at that last line, knowing the unspoken irony was far more hurtful than anything else he could have said.

I felt the hand on my throat start to squeeze, the fingers biting cruelly into my skin, and I wrestled weakly knowing I had no ounce of fight left in me.

I had only my love for Robert left, and he could not take that away from me, no matter what he said or did. I had fought the angel of death, and I had lost. With what strength I had left, I began to recite the only bit of scripture I knew; my mother's favorite, Psalm 91. I sent a silent prayer that she'd help me find my way to Robert again as I teetered on the edge of consciousness.

I felt my limbs start to go numb, saw the flashes and spangles in front of my eyes, recognizing the signs that I was losing consciousness. I could feel the light as it surrounded me. I saw it, and marveled at it. It truly was as glorious as it is described.

My star had appeared after all.

The light, small and far away, seemed to grow brighter as it came closer. It was radiant, beautiful. I was in complete and utter awe, and I welcomed it as much as I feared it. Weakly, I raised my hand to block some of the brightness from my eyes and gasped in shock when I realized that beams of divine light were shooting out of my fingertips. I brought my other hand to my face and saw that it, too, looked as though the stars themselves had been contained in my hands, their brilliant light exploding out of the tips of my fingers like spotlights.

I became aware then that the hand around my throat had suddenly let go; my hair was no longer held up above my head in a callous grip, but was flowing all around my head in the warm, swirling air that vibrated around me. My skin was glowing, the light growing brighter and brighter with each heartbeat. I wasn't touching the ground—the light was keeping me afloat, and it was spreading out, an extension of my limbs, my hair, my breath, even my scent. It smelled like sunshine, and it was wrapped around me, warm and comforting, like a mother's embrace.

I looked at Sam—saw the black orbs that were once the golden pools of light that were his eyes, saw the agony on his face—and became instantly aware that the light was causing him an unbearable pain just as his cries had done to me. It was burning him…and he couldn't do anything to get away from it. He had become trapped in it and it was now clinging to him like honey.

He was screaming again, but the light changed the way the scream sounded; instead of causing me to beg for death, it sounded like the bells one hears ringing in a church on Sunday.

His face was twisting, his body curling and contorting as the light changed him, but the movements were slow and graceful; it would be quite easy to mistake his suffering for a strange sort of dance. I watched in fascinated horror as his wings began to disintegrate, turning into ashes that floated away like a light mist of dust into the distant light. His once beautiful dark-blonde hair changed, becoming white, thinner. His skin began to pull up against itself, wrinkling in such a drastic way; it reminded me of the crumpling of aluminum foil. All of the things that had made him beautiful were now gone, but the punishing light wasn't done with him yet.

He began to shake and writhe from the invisible torture, the sound of bells belying the suffering in his voice, but I could make out the word that seemed frozen on his lips; he was screaming "No".

I felt the sharp intake of air as the light that stretched from between us caused his chest to crack like glass, the sound unmistakably hollow like the shattering of a million crystals with no void for it to travel off to. It crept into him through the multiple fissures and drew out tiny blue orbs from deep within. I watched as he writhed in agony while the opaque light smothered the orbs until their inner glow died out, and Sam was left on the ground—devoid of power, devoid of beauty, devoid of immortality.

The mysterious light began to fade, pulling back into me by the same unseen force that had pushed it out in the first place. There was no danger anymore. I knew I was safe.

"Thank you, Mom," I breathed as I saw him—my own guardian angel—shielded from the intense light by his black wings; the dark plumes had been given to him for a reason after all. And then I collapsed to the ground, my battered and dying body simply incapable of supporting me. "Thank you for saving me," I wheezed, the crushing weight of my chest starting to squeeze the air out of my lungs.

As soon as the light had completely receded into my body, he was at my side, his face looking astonished, unbelieving, his arms lifting me and holding onto me so tight, I half feared he'd break whatever bones had yet to be shattered. He wrapped his wings around the two of us, cocooning us in our own private reunion. He buried his face into my hair and inhaled deeply as his body was racked with violent sobs.

I was so tired, I didn't care that the motions were causing me excruciating pain. I just wanted to close my eyes and let everything go. I was with Robert. I knew everything was over.

Through my exhausted haze, I could feel his tears tumbling through my hair, falling in my lap and scattering on the ground around me, the soft tinkling of crystal hitting stone sounding like tiny bells. I felt a need to protest, but was cut off for he had his hands on my face then, and was kissing my hair, my forehead, my nose, each touch causing my skin to alight, the flames joining each other until they formed a fire of feeling within me.

He fed that fire by brushing my cheek and my chin with feather soft kisses, torturous and wondrous, until finally, he reached my lips, and the world became one large, blazing sun. With a strength I did not know I possessed, I wrapped my arms around his neck, winding my fingers in his hair, locking them there, trying to keep his mouth pressed against mine.

His intent, I knew, was to heal my wounds but I didn't care. I didn't care about anything except the way he felt holding me, the way my heart now beat loud enough and strong enough to drown out the silence that was left behind by his lack of one, the way I knew that he felt everything I was feeling. I knew that I'd do anything, even break every single bone in my body over and over again just to keep his lips on mine, just to have him stay with me.

He pulled back from me, frowning at that thought. "Grace, don't. I cannot stay. I will already have to answer for what happened

432

here with Sam. I have to bring him back with me. I just wanted—I need to make sure that you are safe, that you are well."

When he began to expand his wings and loosen his hold on me, the day's revelations, the truths I had learned today all crashed in on me, and I remembered what Sam had said he was

"Robert, I have too many questions for you to leave me now. You have to-"

He pulled my arms from his neck as easily as if he were pulling a stray thread off of his shirt, separating us. "I cannot answer your questions right now, as much as I want to—and yes, Grace, I do want to. What Sam did will anger many of the others who would seek to blame someone other than him for what happened, and I have to try and fix this. I have to fix this for us."

He walked swiftly to where the small, white form lay and lifted him with ease. The contrast between the white, withered shell and the dark, strong angel was startling. With his wings pulled back like a cape, the black clothing blending in with his dark hair and white gold eyes, I knew then that there was no mistaking it—Sam's words had been true.

"You really are Death," I breathed before letting the darkness swallow me whole.

IMMORTAL FAILING

I awoke in my bedroom, the covers pulled over me. My window was sealed shut. I looked at the clock on the dresser; it was nearly two in the morning. I sat up on the bed and pulled the covers down. I saw that I was still wearing the same tattered and blood stained clothes.

"Robert?" I whispered, but I knew that he wasn't there. Would I have wanted him to be? Knowing now what he was, what his calling was? He wasn't just someone's guardian angel, a healer or…or a dark one—an angel of death. He was Death itself, darkness incarnate. And death had touched my life too deeply once before to take my mother from me. How could I let that into my life now? How could I love *that*?

I stood up and walked over to the window. I lifted it, letting the chilled air come through. The sky that had refused to give up a single star earlier was now filled with what looked like every single star that ever existed. Their bright light was brilliant and beautiful, filling up the sky in a stunning white glow that rivaled the full moon and penetrated the dingy yellow that floated from the street lamps.

Yes. Stars were beautiful, and brilliant, and glorious. But they were also hot, and deadly, and all consuming. Everything that was beautiful had a cost. Even the poor stars couldn't just simply be beautiful in our sky.

I shivered as I felt the chill creep in a bit more, but I was hesitant to close the window. The sky could have been falling and I knew that I would still feel compelled to keep the window open. I folded my hands together and searched the sky for something, anything that would signal to me that someone was up there, listening. The brightest star that I could see became my focal point and I tried to remember the silly little rhyme that my mother would say.

434

I believe it went 'star light, star bright'.

I whipped around, the source of the voice in my head was sitting on my bed like he normally did, as though nothing had happened and he had been there the whole time.

"How did you get in here?" I mouthed, my voice lost in my surprise. He reached for me, but I pulled away. "Don't touch me," I rasped, and turned away quickly, not wanting to have to look at his face and see his reaction to my rejection.

Grace, you don't have to be afraid of me. I won't hurt you.

I knew that was true. He wouldn't hurt me. But that didn't change the fact that what he was already had. "You're..." The words were lost. I couldn't say it.

I knew he was standing behind me only by the tickle of his breath against my hair. He placed his hands on my shoulders and I jumped at the electricity that flowed between us at the contact, my body betraying what my mind was screaming out loud. *I'm Robert, the person who loves you and has endured far too much time away from you to keep me sane. I have not changed who I am, Grace.*

"I know," I whispered, because he was right. He had not changed who he was because he had always been *what* he was. He just hadn't known it. And that was who I fell in love with. I buried my face in my hands, the betrayal of my own heart racking my body with sobs.

Why are you crying, Grace? What has changed between us?

I looked up into his face and saw the hurt there, saw that I was the cause of his pain. I couldn't accept that I, of all people was causing Death pain—I turned away. He reached out his hand and caught my chin, bringing my face back towards his. *Grace, please. I love you, and I need you to talk to me. Don't pull away again. Not from me.*

"Don't you see? You're...*Death*. You're the reason why people die. You're the reason my mom is dead. And I'm in love with you, and I hate it. I hate it, and I can't do anything about it because I know that I can't live without you in my life. Don't you see how that's a betrayal to my mom?" I bawled softly, my tears unstoppable rivers, my face hot with revulsion and anger. "Don't you see how much I hate myself?"

435

Robert pulled me against his chest and took a deep breath, letting it out in a long, desolate sigh. *I feel your shame and your hurt. I feel how even now you're fighting with the mixed emotions within you. But mostly, I feel that my life has no meaning without you in it, Grace.*

I laughed in spite of myself. "How can you speak of the meaning of life when you take it?"

I don't take life, Grace. At least, I wouldn't. It isn't up to me who lives or dies. It is only up to me who gets a second chance or not.

I pulled my head away from his chest, and looked up at him. "What do you mean? Sam told me-"

I know what Sam told you, but he also told you that he's a very good liar, and that's the only thing that Sam said that was one hundred percent true. Sam was an angel of death. A dark one--one of many. But there are also good ones, Grace. Both groups carry off the souls who were destined for their eternal afterlives, whether that would be in Heaven or elsewhere.

I'm the middle ground. I'm the one who decides who gets a second chance at Heaven, or who has earned himself a one way ticket to Hell. Sometimes I'm given the ability to grant them a second chance at life itself, as was given to me. The situations are all different, and all warrant their own decisions. The divine nature of my call allows me to do so within the reaches of their minds for a great deal of them. But, there are moments when I have to be there physically. With a great majority of them, though, it is not my decision as to when they die. That is up to God.

And the one thing that you should remember most of all, Grace, is that the whole time, I am fighting the gift within me that demands I heal them. I told you that I thought of my ability as a penance for my birth, and I was right, only now instead of not being able to heal some people, I'm not allowed to heal any of them.

"But you healed me," I murmured.

He nodded and smiled sadly. *Yes, but you're a part of me now.*

I shook my head and tried to pull myself away from him, planting my hands on his chest and pushing against him. I might as well have been pushing against a mountain. "You're still the reason why my

436

mom died. I don't think I can get over something like that."

Robert gripped my shoulders again and forced me to stop squirming. *Grace, I did not kill your mother. I was born to be Death, but that isn't who I am. I am fulfilling a duty to your kind as well as mine, but I did not take your mother from you. You have to see with reason here. I have yet to take a single soul. I have been reluctant to do so; it goes against everything that I am. Do you not see how difficult this is for me?*

I shook my head because I couldn't—not yet anyway. He let go of me then, his arms dropping to his sides in defeat. *I cannot change who I am, Grace. I can only tell you that I do not look forward to the taking of human life, and most importantly, I am not responsible for your mother's death.*

"I don't even remember what happened, if she even said goodbye," I whimpered. "I don't remember anything about that night, Robert. Don't you see? Lark said that you learned everything, shared everything, and now you know what happened to my mother because what you are—what *Death* is—took her from me. And *I* still don't know."

Robert raised his hands to my face, holding me softly and looking at me with his eyes, two pools of unmoving silver. *Grace, I would tell you if I could.*

"I know. You would if you could, but you can't, so you won't. I've heard it time and time again, Robert. I've heard it enough times to know that we'll never be on equal footing. You'll always have your secrets, and I'll always be an open book. You might be the middle ground between light and dark, good and evil, but there isn't any middle ground for us." I pulled my face out of his hands; he didn't protest.

I walked away from him to stand near the dresser, seeing his reflection in the mirror and trying not to focus on how beautiful he was, but rather on the slow coldness that was spreading through me like an infection. "And you lied, Robert. The fact that you've seen my mother's final moments, and you won't tell me about them *is* the very definition of you taking my mother away from me. You're taking her away from me now just as much as she was taken from me all those years ago."

I saw the way his face changed, how hard it became, the way his jaw set stubbornly. His eyes turned cold and stony, his eyebrows drew closer together, the space between them pinched with frustration and anger. I watched as his reflection disappeared from behind me, reappearing in front of me and blocking my view of the mirror in a split second.

He grabbed my arms and placed them around his neck. He slowly picked me up, walked over to the window, and leaned out of it, lifting one leg to stand on the sill. We started floating upwards, and I saw the branch-like limbs start to sprout from his back. They brushed against my fingers and I flinched at the strange smoothness of the bare skin. In one breath, his wings were fully formed, and we were gliding through the night sky.

"Where are you taking me?" I asked, feeling the cold bite against my body and reluctantly pulled myself closer to him.

He was silent and I didn't ask any more questions; the dark look on his face terrifying me into a mutual silence. We traveled through the frigid night with an eerie stillness between us, the icy air nipping at me through the tears in my clothing. When he started to drift downwards, I realized that he had brought me to the spot where the accident that had taken my mother's life had occurred. I had been here many times since in my own journey to discover for myself what had happened. It hadn't changed much in eleven years.

Robert's feet landed on the ground softly, his wings ruffling behind us, but he did not put me down. Instead, he walked over to a small section of brush and turned so we faced the road.

He was looking away from town so I stared in the same direction. I saw the bright beam of headlights approaching and I lifted a hand to shield my eyes from the glare. Suddenly, I heard the tires screech and watched in horror as the car swerved to the right before it went careening out of control towards a utility pole. Just before it hit, an intense light filled the inside of the car that looked like an explosion. Robert was moving quickly. He brought me to the side of the vehicle and I peered in. In the driver's seat with her seatbelt still on was my

438

mother.

Comprehension dawned on me then—Robert was showing me what had happened the night my mother had died. This was a vision that he was sharing with me...but it felt all too real.

I turned to look at his face but he motioned for me to watch. I turned my face back to see what I had been trying for so long, so hard to remember. And like pressing the play button after a long pause, it all came back to me.

"Grace, Grace baby, are you okay?" the woman called out to the little girl in the back seat.

"Yes, Mommy," a small voice answered.

The woman unbuckled her seat belt and turned around, reaching a bloody hand out to the little girl who took it and held onto it fiercely with dogged determination. "Grace, I want you to listen to Mommy, okay?" the woman asked in between the rough, fluid filled coughs that shook her body. "Listen, honey, I want you to say Mommy's prayer with me, okay? Can you say Mommy's prayer?"

The little girl nodded her head. "Yes, I can say it."

"Good girl."

They began reciting the Psalm, and I recited with them. "...He'll cover you with his feathers, and under his wings you will find refuge..."

The vehicle once again began to fill with an intense light. I heard the woman's voice as it spoke again, "Grace, my precious baby girl. Mommy's got to say goodbye now, okay? It is time for Mommy to go to Heaven, but I promise...I promise that you will be safe. You will be safe and you will be happy. Everything will be alright."

The little girl in the car began to cry, her hands tugging on the woman's with frantic urgency. "No, Mommy. You only go to Heaven when you die. You're not going to die, Mommy. Don't leave me, Mommy!"

"Sweet Grace," the woman cooed, her voice growing faint with each breath. "Don't fear death. Death is a blessing, remember? One day, death will be your savior, and you will understand everything. Now, close your eyes to the light, sweetheart; let the darkness protect you. I love you. I never wanted anything more than you. I love you, Grace."

And then the bright light became so intense, I could no longer see. An explosion scorched the brush around us, and I watched in horror as a monstrous ball of fire engulfed the car, consuming it. I cried out for my mother, but she couldn't hear me. The force of the explosion had knocked over a utility pole, which set off a domino effect of poles tumbling down sideways along the shoulder. The sound rattled my teeth, but I did not feel the shaking of the ground as they landed.

I couldn't feel the heat of the flames, and I didn't know if it was because this was only a vision, or if it was because my entire body had grown cold with the knowledge that for the second time in my life, I had witnessed my mother's death.

Out of the corner of my narrowed eyes I saw a movement on the ground several dozen feet in front of the flames. I scrutinized the motion and saw that it was body of the little girl. She was laying peacefully in the road as if someone had laid her there, her hand held out for comfort even in unconsciousness. I didn't know how she got there, but I felt an urge to hold that hand; I gasped in surprise when Robert put me down, understanding my need. I ran towards her, slowing down to kneel on the crumbling asphalt beside her and held her outstretched hand. She continued to sleep, a sweet smile now on her face.

Far off behind the burning car, I could see advancing lights; the first person on the scene was arriving. I had never known who it was that had arrived and called the police—Dad had never told me—but now was my chance to see for myself who was responsible for saving my life that night.

The lights belonged to a large maroon van; the driver got out and started speaking in a foreign language to the passenger. I watched as the he walked hesitantly around the blazing car, taking note of the burning debris scattered all around him, and then gasp and run over to where I was kneeling. He ran completely through me, as if I wasn't there—in truth, I wasn't—and grabbed the little girl's hand. He felt how warm she was, saw the rise and fall of her small chest, that she was still

440

alive, and picked her up, running with her in his arms towards the van. I couldn't help but follow him, the little girl now my only lifeline to this entire scene.

He shouted more words that I didn't understand as he was running and the sliding door of the van opened up to reveal an extremely large amount of children inside, all of them dark headed boys with mischievous grins. The person sitting in the front-passenger seat, a woman, was speaking into a large cellular phone, repeating in broken English that a little girl had been found on the road next to a horrible car fire. The boys were all staring in awe at the little girl; one of them looked strangely familiar.

"Sean, get your water from the back. We have to give her some water," the driver told the familiar looking boy and I recognized then that this was Stacy's family. She wasn't in the van with them, I acknowledged, because she had been sick in the hospital at the time.

Sean did as he was instructed and the father gave the little girl a small swipe of liquid against her mouth. He felt her skin and shook his head in surprise. "She isn't burning up. I don't understand. She was so close to the fire, she should be hot to the touch, but she isn't."

And so the first of the superfreak stories would begin, I thought to myself.

I felt Robert's hand on my shoulder and I turned to face him. "Stacy's family was the one who called for help. I didn't know that." I turned around to watch what would happen next, but it was all gone. "Where did it go? Bring it back, Robert! I need to see the rest!"

"That is all that I can show you, Grace. I shouldn't have even shown you that. It isn't good to bring you back to your past, especially when you're so undecided about your present." His voice was brusque, distant.

I nodded reluctantly, understanding what it was that he had meant, and turned my face back to his. "Thank you."

He gave me a curt nod and repeated the same motions he had in my room, placing my arms around his neck and then picking me up, placing an arm beneath my knees, the other at my back. He leapt into the air and then we were flying again, his wings spread out behind us like a cloak of midnight against the starry sky. I placed my head into the hollow of his neck, feeling strangely at ease and content as I listened to the air rustle against his feathers. "Thank you, Robert. Thank you for giving my mother back to me."

He didn't say anything on the way back to my room. As we floated in through the window, I noticed that his wings had disappeared. I felt disappointed; I was getting used to seeing them.

When his feet softly landed on the floor and he began to lower me, I held on, not wanting to let him go without first telling him...

"Robert, I don't know how, but my mother knew—she knew that one day you'd come into my life. That's what she was telling me. I remember now. At the cemetery before she died, she told me that death brought love. She told me that I had to appreciate it, and accept it. I was too young to understand what she meant, but now I do. She was telling me to welcome you, to not blame you for what you had to do."

I lifted a hand to his face to make him look at me. His beautiful eyes seemed so lost, and I knew that I was the reason. I squirmed enough so that he set me down and I pulled him to the bed to sit. I grabbed his hand and placed it over my heart while placing mine over the spot where his would have been. "But my mother was wrong— death doesn't bring love. You *are* love. You...your love, it's a part of me."

I watched as the cold steel of his eyes, like quicksilver, melted into two pools of mercury. He covered my hand on his chest with his, and brought it to his lips. *You are the only thing that tempts me into acts that would lead me to fall from grace. I cannot even begin to explain to you just how great a weakness you are for me. When I learned what Sam had done-*

"How did you know?" I asked, interrupting his thoughts.

Lark. She was in pain, I could feel it, but I didn't know why. She didn't know why until she tried to reach out to you and saw Sam's face in your thoughts. She knew then why she had been in pain; she had been lying when she kept saying that I was going to be meeting you without telling her. The lie hadn't been hers, which is why the pain was more an annoyance than anything else, but she didn't recognize it for

442

what it was, didn't think that you'd be lying to her about me.

But, when I learned what Sam had done—when I learned that he had deceived you—I knew that you were in danger and the call stopped. The singing stopped, Grace, and I left it all behind to get to you. You are my first priority. I couldn't hear anything, focus on anything while knowing that you were in danger.

He pulled me into his lap, his hand still pressed against my heart, and kissed my forehead. *I tried to get to you as fast as I could. I knew I was close when I could hear your thoughts. I could feel your fear, and I heard your prayer. I heard it and it was like driving a burning stake through my heart because I couldn't do anything to help you.*

He pressed his forehead to mine and I saw the visions in his head as he relived the moment again. He was traveling so fast, everything was a blur of lines and colors. He slowed down as he approached the field, and was taken aback by the scene that lay before him. The field was awash with the combined light of two figures who struggled with each other. The larger of the two had his hand around the other's throat, and was lifting her off of the ground.

The smaller figure's pale glow began to spread out quickly, and her attacker let go with stunning speed. As his arm retreated, it pulled with it the light that was now all over his victim, a sticky string of radiance that grew as it fed on his own. The light crept up his arm, increasing in size until it engulfed him completely, drowning out his own yellow glow.

As Robert moved closer to the two figures, the heat from the light began to scorch his skin. He looked down and felt the stinging of a pain he'd never felt before on the tips of his fingers. He looked up and immediately shut his eyes to the intense light that threatened to burn him blind. His wings quickly, instinctively pulled around him, blocking out the light, but not the screams.

Through Robert's ears, what had sounded like bells to me was the same shrieking cries that had incapacitated me when I had stabbed Sam; I could feel the blood in me start to churn again, though the pain was much duller with Robert there holding me, shielding me from the full force of the destruction that I was far too familiar with.

I could hear the thoughts in Sam's mind as his body twisted in wretched agony, the expletives that streamed out were harsh and grating, and the images in his mind were not of remorse for his acts, but at taking too long to kill me—he was mad at himself for being selfish and greedy in wanting to draw out my suffering.

In the darkness of Robert's winged shelter, the smell of something burning was palpable. Only when the microscopic slivers of light were gone did his wings unfold, allowing him to take in the scene that lay before him in. In a fraction of a second, he was able to see the damage done to the field.

Grass that was in desperate need of being cut had been pushed down in a wide arc, but otherwise completely unaffected by the heat that the light had used to singe his fingers. There was a book bag in the middle of the field, and a large, black feather lay on the gravel that looked as though it had been dipped in gold. A pool of gold had solidified next to it. A few feet away, the gravel was stained and speckled with the reddish-brown that he knew was blood.

He rushed over to the smaller of the two figures lying on the ground, and gasped as he saw the blood soaked jeans and the dried blood on her face. Her eye was nearly swollen shut; her bottom lip was split open near its apex.

A gurgled sound was trapped in his chest as he saw the dark bruising around her neck; the grip had been so strong he could see each finger, each crease in the palm that had tried to crush the tiny throat. He took in her blackened fingers where the blood had pooled and congealed, the bruising across her chest from the impact of being hit by the force from the opening of the other's wings, and the odd angles that her limbs lay out around her.

He could see within her, and the scene was familiar: The injured organs, the broken bones, the bleeding were all sights that he had seen before. And there in her chest, her weak heart, struggling to beat. There had been too much lost blood, and its faint pulsing was slowly waning. Everything was familiar but this; if this heart stopped beating, he knew it as sure as he knew his name that his life would end

444

as well. She was his heart, she was his soul—if she ceased to exist, then he would, too.

Gingerly he picked her up and cradled her, the frail and broken body hanging limply in his arms. He brought his wings forward, wrapping them around him, as though to protect her from any more dangers from his own kind, and in the darkness gently hugged her to his chest.

When she gave no reaction to his holding her, he couldn't hold his emotions back any longer and buried his face into her hair, the sorrow of a friend's betrayal and the threat of a lost love tearing down the dam inside him. His whole body shook with each sob, and each one tore from him a silent prayer that he could save her, that he'd not lose her, that she'd live to see another day, even if it meant rejecting him for what he was.

And taking his love and faith in his hands, he began to kiss her, the ebbing heat from her dying body still warm enough to give him hope. He felt the sparks of feverish need grow in him as he pressed his lips across her face, not daring to go near her mouth, but feeling the pull much stronger than anything else he'd ever experienced before.

Finally, unable to fight it, his will lost among the countless other emotions he had tossed out to make room for the overwhelming feeling of love he felt for her, he brushed his lips against hers, intending only to give them a fleeting moment of contact. Instead he leaned in, pressing harder, and by some miracle, she found the strength to raise her hands, to hold him, to weave a fabric of ownership with her fingers and his hair.

He rejoiced when he could hear her heart beating strong and fast, hear her thoughts, feel her response to him. He pulled away as he heard one of her thoughts, the reality of the situation suddenly screaming for center stage in this second act. The heroine was now safe, but the villain needed to be dealt with, and swiftly. He placed her feet on the ground.

Time was not on his side. She was upset, he felt it. "Grace, don't. I cannot stay. I will already have to answer for what happened here with Sam. I have to bring him back with me. I just wanted—I need to make sure that you are safe, that you are well," he told her, and slowly opened the shelter of his wings, easing her arms off of him with no effort at all.

She was hurt and confused. "Robert, I have far too many questions for you to leave me now. You have to-"

He had to cut her off. "I cannot answer your questions right now, as much as I want to—and yes, Grace, I do want to. What Sam did will anger many of the others who would seek to blame someone other than him for what happened, and I have to try and fix this. I have to fix this for us," he told her, unable to bear hearing her voice so pained.

He bent down to pick up the wasted remains of the fallen angel that cowered on the ground. Even in defeat, his thoughts were defiant. With his burden in his arms, he turned to face her, a good-bye poised on his lips.

The shock and recognition that filled her eyes silenced him, as she uttered the phrase that caused more fear in him than seeing her broken and bleeding had done. "You really are Death."

He watched in horror as she crumpled to the ground. He rushed to her, dropping the body in his arms to the ground with a thud, and quickly picked her up—the exchange swift and heart wrenching. He was torn between fulfilling his duty to return his former friend, and seeing her safe. Knowing that she wasn't in any danger, he sent out his thoughts to the one person who he knew could hear him and who he trusted. He waited for her to appear and spoke wordlessly to her as he again picked up his withered burden.

He looked on as the beautiful angel who had arrived gently lifted the fainted girl from his arms and, nodding, flew off in the direction of the girl's home. Satisfied, he then took off himself, glad for her safety, and saddened by the betrayal that had nearly cost her life.

Robert lifted his forehead from mine, the vision gone. He lifted his hand to my face, cradling it and gently caressing my cheek with his thumb. I turned my face into his palm, kissing the deep line that marked it. He sighed, and pulled me towards him again, pressing my head against his chest.

"So it wasn't you-"

446

No. I don't know who it was that came to help you. Your prayer for help...there are those whose calling is to answer prayers such as yours. I just don't know who it could have been. Their thoughts have remained hidden from me.

I nodded, and half-smiled at the mystery that just added to the endless list of questions that I wasn't sure would ever be answered. There never seemed to be a moment without complication for us; whatever fate had decided for the two of us, it certainly wasn't supposed to be a walk in the park.

Robert's hand brushed against my cheek, and wrapped against the column of my neck, holding the pulse point against the deepest and longest line in his palm, its steady rhythm soothing him somehow. *I have so much to apologize to you for, so much to make up for, Grace. I do not know where to begin, but I will do whatever it takes to make this up to you. You're the only thing in my life worth protecting. I would give up an eternity in Heaven for just one moment with you.*

I pressed my hand against his lips, knowing that he'd understand my intent. "You have me. Don't you dare give up what you have been waiting so long for just for me."

My sweet Ianthe, don't you see? I've already fallen, and it's for you. Heaven is only where you are.

I smiled and laid my head on his chest. "And mine is with you, Angelo."

EPILOGUE: FESTIVE

Christmas time in my house was never so lively—or so decorated. Janice had gone to great lengths to set up as many baubles, knick knacks, and wreaths as one could possibly fit into our little house, with wrapping papered doors, and garland draped over windows. Every table had a green and red something or other. This was also the first year since mom had died that we had a tree in the house. It was fake, cost three times as much as the real one Graham wanted to chop down, and came with built-in lights that did not blink, and were all white. Oh. And it spun around, slow and lazily, like a drunken, demented top. This, of course, made Janice very happy, and so Dad made sure I said nothing.

The most noticeable difference this Christmas, however, wasn't the abundance of faux greenery bedecked with ribbons and glass around the house, or the white fiberfill blankets beneath miniature towns that graced the only bookshelf in the living room. It was the fact that Janice was with us, as was her very prominent belly. It seemed impossible that it had grown so large in just a few days, but there was no denying that she now fit the description of rotund quite nicely.

Robert, Lark, and Ameila were once again invited to the house for the holiday meal, and they brought with them this time a bright red jell-o mold in the shape of a wreath. Ameila held the jiggling form up proudly and announced that it was the first time she had ever made one; her impossibly white teeth poised in the perfect smile while I shuddered as I recalled the images of what she could do with that smile. Janice thanked her as she took the mold, and placed it in the refrigerator.

They had brought with them more gifts than we'd had under the fake, spinning tree to begin with, which made me feel wholly inadequate, but Dad and Janice were very gracious as we sat around and

448

opened gifts, Robert and I seated on the floor near the tree, passing them to each recipient. Janice marveled at the teardrop shaped crystals that adorned the earrings that she received from them, while Dad seemed to be quite pleased with his authentic writing quill.

"I can't believe how perfect this feather is. Look at its color. What a gorgeous shade of ebony. That gloss is a sign of a very healthy bird. I'm thinking Ostrich," he said to me, while I nodded knowingly, trying very hard not to laugh.

I received a skirt from Janice in the same style as the one she had lent me. "It's perfect for your figure, and I thought that if you were willing to borrow one, maybe you'd be willing to own one as well," she said when I thanked her for it, a genuine smile on both of our faces. Of all the changes that have occurred in my life these past few months, this was the one that I still felt the least comfortable with, but that was my problem and not Janice's; she was a good person with a good heart, and she loved my dad. That was more than enough.

Dad had done his usual thing and simply gotten me a gift certificate to my favorite thrift store. I thanked him profusely. I was in need of some new—okay, so not exactly new—shirts after the past few months.

I glanced over to Robert to see his face, and knew that he was trying not to think about that almost as much as I was. I just wasn't sure if it was for the same reasons.

I handed Dad and Janice their gifts; Dad's was a stopwatch—for counting the contractions, I told him—while Janice's gift was a scrapbook for the baby. "I figured you'd want to start doing that whole collecting of memories thing that so many parents do now," I told her, shrugging my shoulders when she held it up with a puzzled look on her face. "You know, this was your first Easter, first Halloween, or first hangover. The stuff that parents like to remember."

She smiled and hugged me, "Thank you, Grace. I wouldn't have thought about that. I'm going to put some of the wrapping paper that this came in here for the baby's first Christmas."

I had given Lark a CD from some foppish boy band that she had taken to, and she gave me an old copy of *Al Aaraaf, Tamerlane, and*

449

Minor Poems, which made me speechless because I knew that old meant first edition. They didn't even print this book anymore, so I knew that when I told her that I would treasure it, it wasn't because I had no choice—rather, it was because I meant it.

Ameila handed us all gift cards to some outrageously expensive department store and Janice gave her an antique brooch that she had found while out shopping for the baby.

Robert, knowing that I had nearly destroyed my favorite shirt during the fight with Sam, had bought a few to replace it. "I think these will fit you better, too," he added when I tried to find reasons why my old shirt was still in wearable condition, not wanting to part with what had always felt like an old friend. He kissed my hair and silently thanked me for the pillow I had made from the front of my favorite shirt—the only part to have remained unscathed, which made him smile at my feigned difficulty earlier. *You'd make a bad angel; you lie too well.*

"I think I'm going to go and check on the bird and see if we can get started on eating because this little guy is getting hungry." Janice said, patting her belly.

My jaw dropped. "Little guy?" I crawled on the floor over to her, quickly putting my hand on her stomach. It was the first time I had touched her pregnant belly, having never accepted any of the prior invitations given so many times to feel the baby squirm and kick; I pulled my hand back immediately. I looked up at her, apologetic at my rude behavior. She grabbed my hand and placed it back on the rounded mound, patting it as she did so.

"Yes, it's a little guy. We found out last week but didn't want to tell you until tomorrow, it being your birthday and everything."

I had completely forgotten that it was my birthday. So many things had happened these past few months, let alone these past few days that it had completely slipped my mind. Turning my attention back to the amazing belly that contained my baby brother, I stared at it in awe; this large, round mound draped in red jersey fabric held within it a tiny person who would be half Dad, half Janice, and 100% Shelley.

"What's his name?" I asked, feeling the slight movements beneath my hands.

"Your dad and I have settled on Matthew James," she answered, proudly smiling down at my hand. "He likes your voice. I can tell already that you're going to be an amazing big sister, Grace." She pulled something out from underneath the couch cushions and gave it to me. "Happy Birthday from your Dad and me."

It was a little red box. I looked at Janice, unsure, but she nodded her head reassuringly. "Go on. Open it."

I removed the lid from the box; nestled within the red satin lining lay a small silver object. I lifted it out with nervous fingers, a long, silver chain attached to it. It was a pendant in the shape of a wing. An angel's wing.

"We have one for Matthew when he gets older. Your dad and I both thought that if you two had the wings, maybe the guardian angel who belongs to them will always be there to keep you two together long after we're gone," Janice said, her eyes glassy with the tears she couldn't stop from overflowing. "Oh these darn hormones. Now I'm really going to go and check on that bird." She got up, dabbing her eyes with the back of one hand, the other resting on her belly, patting it reassuringly, and headed into the kitchen.

I sat on the floor staring at the silver wing in my hand. I held it up to examine it. It was almost a miniature replica of the wings that were owned by my very own guardian angel, the lines just as delicate, although they'd never come close to matching his graceful beauty.

I was just about to say the same thing about you. He came to sit beside me on the floor to admire the gift, his hand at the small of my back. Now that Robert and I had resolved the issue between us regarding what exactly his calling had been, what *he* was, whenever he was around me he always had to touch me in some way: a physical connection that complimented the mental one. It was, he had said, the only way he could feel life flowing through him, especially after the first time he had had to take the life of someone just two days after the fight in the park.

I never asked who it had been—I didn't want to know—but I knew that he had returned to me in need. In a reversal of roles, it had been I who had comforted him as he lay in my arms. I couldn't help but imagine a lifetime ahead of me comforting Robert as I got older. After all, my life with him was already set in stone. I might as well begin writing my name with his adjoined to it… Did I really just think that?

I looked at Dad—sitting in his favorite chair that had been strategically positioned near the kitchen for today's meal—as he was engaged in a deep discussion with Lark and Ameila about the importance of eggnog at a Christmas meal, and wondered when it was that he had done the same thing, if ever, with mom. When was he able to look at her and see into the future without having it appear frightening or claustrophobic?

I watched him, his smile so bright and wide, his eyes twinkling with happiness that I hadn't seen in him since I was a child, since before mom died; I saw that he could see his future stretched out before him now, and that he'd be stepping into that future with Janice and Matthew at his side. I looked once again at the silver wing in my hand and knew that guardian angel or not, they would live a healthy and happy life together.

I was going to have to thank Dad for the gift later, when he wasn't busy. Right now I didn't want to do anything that would disturb him; he was enjoying himself so much.

It doesn't look like my wing at all. Robert smiled, his hand reaching out to remove the pendant from my hand. I already knew that he'd seen enough of it in the few seconds that I had exposed it to have scrutinized its every minute detail. He wanted to help fasten the necklace around my neck; the tiny clasp was too difficult for me to do it on my own. When he had secured it, he turned me around and lifted the wing with his fingers. *It isn't even shaped correctly.*

I snorted at his mock offense. *Your wings aren't made out of sterling silver either, so quit with the comparisons, okay? It's symbolic. That's what matters.*

He snaked his arm around my waist, pulling me into the nest his arms and legs made on the floor, and nuzzled my ear. *I know, I was kidding. All kidding aside, I would like to tell you that I would be honored to be your little brother's guardian angel. We never get a chance to choose this for ourselves, and what better choice than him? I'm in love with his big sister, so I have incentive to keep him safe.*

I turned my head to look into his eyes. I could see the reflection of my face in those large, molten pools; it had taken me some time to realize that who I was in his eyes was different from who I had always thought I was. What better choice indeed to be the guardian angel for little Matthew? *Thank you.*

He kissed the tip of my nose, and looked over at Dad, an impish grin on his face. "Do you think your dad would mind if I stole you away for a few minutes?"

I followed his gaze and shook my head. "He's never had someone he could talk to about anything and everything before, not even Mom, so he's way too involved to notice anything else. Ugh, your poor mom—poor Lark! I don't think she'll forgive me if she's forced to strangle Dad for talking about the importance of Meowing Christmas Carols."

I heard that. Her voice appeared in the back of my mind like a…well, a bird, coming to sit on a branch for a short visit with a tree. A rude, loud, obnoxious bird. *Go on, I'll keep your Dad occupied here and Mom can keep Janice busy in the kitchen.*

I nodded at her, thankful that she hadn't heard that last part about being obnoxious—I valued having all of my fingers in proper working order—and slowly crawled to the staircase and slinked up the stairs. I didn't care what it looked like, even though I know it was probably an amusing sight to Robert.

I walked into my room, Robert on my heels, and carefully closed the door. It was messy, as usual. There were clothes strewn all over the floor, blanketing the wooden surface, and the bed was unmade; mismatched sheets and blankets making for one confused looking place of unrest. Janice's efforts at trying to make my room look presentable, while initially successful, had ultimately failed miserably due to my complete lack of effort—I simply wasn't as concerned with the state of my room as I was with the state of my life.

There were stacks of books on the dresser, and the closet doors were open to reveal an even scarier mess of clothes and junk haphazardly piled in there because if not, I'd most likely have killed myself many times over from tripping on them when they'd been on the floor.

I suddenly felt very embarrassed at the mess, knowing that even though Robert had seen it all before, today felt like a day important enough for me to have at least made an effort at cleaning it up.

"I could clean this room up in about ten seconds if you'd let me," he suggested smugly, and leaned against the door to watch me turn around in circles, assessing what could be done in the quickest amount of time.

"Nobody likes a showoff, Robert," I reminded him, deciding to try a miracle sweep and clean of my own in exactly fifteen seconds…and succeeding in only managing to knock a pillow off of the bed and onto the ground, and pushing some clothes into a corner by the dresser, hiding it from plain sight.

Pleased with my lack of change, Robert sat on the edge of my bed and patted the spot next to him. I stared at him, confused, but willing to oblige him. He reached for me as soon as I was near him and pulled me into his lap. He pulled my face towards his and began planting fluttering kisses on my forehead, the space between my brows, my nose—he was trailing a path of searing fire towards my lips, and damn if I couldn't be anything but patient when he was holding my head so still.

Finally, when I knew that I'd probably scream if he didn't press his lips on mine, he did, and I knew that there was nothing anyone could do that would tear me away from him in that moment. I felt the surge of electricity shoot through me the instant our lips touched—the blood in my veins felt like it was boiling from the heat radiating within me, my heart pounding an ever increasing tempo as I pushed myself deeper into his embrace, even as he pulled me closer.

I could feel his hands in my hair, holding my head captive as I did the same to him. I relished the way his hair felt between my fingers, thick and silky, and the knowledge that it and all of him was mine only

454

further set my heart racing. I was breathless, gasping for air when he pulled away, ignoring my whimper of protest as he pressed his forehead to mine.

My only consolation was that he appeared just as flustered as I was, his breathing ragged, his chest rising and falling at its own rapid pace. "Grace, we have plenty of time for kisses," he said, his voice rough and strained with something that sounded a lot like need. "Right now I have a birthday present of my own to give you; I didn't want to give it to you downstairs. I think your father might become apoplectic if he saw it."

When his breathing had slowed down enough for him to move without causing too much disturbance, he reached into his pocket and pulled out a small box. My breathing didn't help when I started to hyperventilate at its size. There was only one reason why boxes were that small, and only one reason why guys kept boxes that small in their pockets. I looked at him with my eyes wide open, a stuttering sound coming out of my mouth.

He put his fingers over my lips, pressing them together to shut them. "It's not what you think, so don't get all panicky on me. Open it." He nudged the box into my hands and then settled his arms around me, a sly half-smile crooking the corner of his mouth upward. I looked at him with skeptical eyes, not exactly sure whether or not I could trust him.

He rolled his eyes at my thoughts, and motioned with his head to stop stalling and open the box.

I lifted the hinged lid with my eyes closed, the fear of what lay within its confines feeling far more real than what I had felt facing off with Sam. Finally, hesitantly, after taking a deep breath I opened them. "Oh," I said—the contents taking me by surprise. It *was* a ring, but not like anything I had ever seen before. The stone was a deep, almost midnight blue, rounded like an egg, but with a brilliant white, six pointed star at its center. It was set very plainly in a silver band without any additional ornaments or stones. It was, quite simply, the most beautiful ring I had ever seen in my life. I touched the stone gently with my finger, tracing each arm of the star as it trailed across the face of the stone and down its sides.

"What is it?" I asked when I finally remembered that he was still in the room with me.

He took the box out of my hand and removed the ring from its wedged perch. He placed the box on the side of him and then grabbed my right hand, spreading my fingers out and slid it onto my ring finger, the cool metal contrasting with the heat from his hands…and the heat that I always felt whenever he touched me.

"This is a star sapphire. It's not a common stone, and the star disappears if you look at it in any way other than directly. I chose this stone because I wanted you to have something that would remind you of me when I'm not here with you. Sapphire is my birthstone, and, like me, you have to look closely with your eyes open to see the true nature hidden within." He had tried to sound smug, but instead I could hear the hesitant tone in his voice, as though he feared that I wouldn't be able to see what exactly he had meant for the ring to represent.

I felt tears well up in my eyes and rubbed them away with clumsy hands, unable to speak. I was stunned. Aside from the pendant I had just received downstairs, no one had ever given me something that involved such thought and emotional investment. I felt ready to refuse the ring, feeling the need to remove it from my finger. What had I ever done to deserve so much from him?

His love, his friendship…he had even gifted me with my own miracle by giving me back the last memories of my mother. Now he'd given me a symbol of who he was that I could keep with me always, my own star in a midnight sky. What was there in this world that I possessed that I could give to him besides my heart?

"That is all I will ever need, Grace. Your heart and the love that you hold in it," he whispered into my ear.

I nestled my head on his shoulder, and stared at the ring, knowing now what I wanted to say. "I know, but what is there that you can keep with you when *I'm* gone? What will *you* have to remember me by?"

I felt him stiffen beneath me at my words. The topic of my

456

death had never really come up and stayed around long enough to fully discuss it, mostly due to his insistence that we could always talk about it later. Well, it was later.

"Robert?"

He started to rub my back, his voice soft as he spoke, "I don't want to think about you dying, Grace. I've told you before, you are my life. You are the reason I exist; if you're no longer here, I don't want to be either. You give me peace when everything in my head is just chaos. You've helped the days stop blending into each other so that I can appreciate each one. Each moment of my future is one that I look forward to spending with you. I am who I am because of you. Without you, I will cease to be."

His hand stopped rubbing. He shifted my body and I felt his hands on my face as he turned my head to look at him, giving me the full impact of his quicksilver gaze. "I wanted to wait to ask this until you were used to what I am, but I think that the longer I do so, the more stubborn you'll become. I want to know, Grace, if you would consider becoming an immortal." He held himself still as his words sunk in. He didn't even breathe.

I didn't either. I could hear the slowing down of my heart as it struggled in my chest beneath the weight of his words; my lungs were burning for oxygen, and still I couldn't do anything but stare into Robert's eyes. If I were to die right now, I'd probably have been able to say that I was far more loved than anyone had a right to be. That Robert was willing to risk so much so that we couldn't be separated by time felt like he was offering me the world.

"I can't."

He nodded, knowing before I had even spoken the words what my answer would be. "Can I ask you why?"

I looked down at my hand, lifting up the right one and stared at the ring on my finger. The star in the dark stone had disappeared, just like Robert had said it would. "I know that I've told you many times that all I want in this life is to be normal. I've pretty much realized that loving you and being with you sort of cancels out the possibility of that happening, so I gladly accept not being normal in that instance. But, to

457

everyone else, I'm still Grace. I still fit here somehow, even if it is somewhat awkwardly.

"Right now, I'm happy being me. I've struggled for a long time to accept who I am, what I am. Eighteen years of never knowing where exactly I belonged, where I fit in—I was always the outsider who wasn't even comfortable in my own skin. And then you came into my life, and you helped me to see beyond what people had labeled me, beyond what I had labeled myself; you helped me to see that inside, I'm just as beautiful as Erica, just as funny as Stacy, just as likeable as Graham. You made me realize that although I was content to settle for mediocre, I'm much more than that.

"But, if I were to become immortal, all of that would be gone because all of that belongs to the human Grace. If you were given permission to change me, what would I be in your world? What would I be in mine? You're an angel; people paint you on ceilings and send out postcards with your picture on them. They create statues and-" I held up the pendant that dangled from my neck, "-and jewelry in your likeness because you are important. What would I be but a nobody who can live forever? I wouldn't fit in anywhere. Not in your world, and definitely not in mine. I'd be able to live forever, but where would I *live*?"

I fiddled with the hem of my blouse as I let my words sink into him, knowing that he'd have some kind of rebuttal ready to unleash on me. I wasn't sure how long I'd be able to hold up when that happened. Instead, he sighed, the sound sad—melancholy.

"I love you," he whispered as he kissed the top of my head, his arms wrapping around me tightly. "I love you, forever."

I tucked my head even tighter into his chest. I felt myself smile, in spite of the tear that slid down the side of my nose, betraying the words that I had just spoken. "I love you, too."

He could sense the trembling in my words and placed his fingers beneath my chin, lifting my face away from his chest and up towards his. When he spoke his voice was tinged with regret. "Please don't cry, Grace. It was the wrong time to talk about it—I'm sorry." He said this with his eyes full of mercury tears, threatening to spill over at any moment into my lap in a shower of crystals. I could see the sadness that

458

my words had caused him etched into his face, and I wanted to snatch them back, to erase them from his memory just to see him smile again.

"I'm the one who should be sorry, Robert," I murmured, my hand gently cradling his face, my thumb grazing just beneath his lower lashes. "I'm being selfish for thinking of only what I want. I'd have you for the rest of my life, but you wouldn't—I'm just a flash in yours. If the tables were turned, I'm not sure just how I'd react, but I know it wouldn't be with your patience. You've waited fifteen hundred years for what you wanted, while I complain about waiting a measly eighteen."

I leaned my head back down and nestled it in the hollow of his neck. I pressed my lips against the spot where his pulse should be, another tear slipping out as I thought back to what he had sacrificed to try and give me what I had wanted; a normal life, I had told him. And yet, I couldn't help but recall what Sam had told me, about what it had cost him to try and make the woman he had loved into an immortal. She had become a monster and consequently, he had to destroy her. That fear was too much…the cost for both of us was not something I could risk, not when I finally had everything I could ever want.

"Can we not talk about this again? At least for a while?" I said to him in a small, diffident voice.

His arms tightened around me again, his sigh of concession feeling more like a groan of defeat. "Whatever it takes, Grace." He hadn't heard my thoughts, and I was relieved. It would only make him more adamant about changing me…but I was already different.

I pulled my head up to his and tilted my face to kiss him, but he held me back. "I think we should go back downstairs, now," he said, his eyes brimming with sadness and…plotting?

Feeling my lips pull forward in a pout, I nodded, understanding that we had risked being away long enough. "Poor Lark. I'm afraid you'll probably never see me again after tonight—what with all of the favors I'm going to have to owe her for putting her through this," I said with a half-hearted laugh.

Robert stood up, easing me into a standing position with him, his arms still wrapped around my waist. "I'm afraid that you're probably right, but don't be too upset if I play the hero once in a while and rescue you from whatever horrible human task she has set out for you to do." He smiled, the humor and enjoyment in his eyes returning quite swiftly. He leaned forward and softly kissed my pouting lower lip. "And when I do rescue you, I will demand a reward."

"Oh dear bananas," I panted, my heart thundering inside of my chest like no storm ever had.

Laughing at my reaction, Robert loosened his hold and, grabbing my hand, pulled me towards the door. I dug my feet into the ground when something caught my eye. Sitting on the corner of my dresser was a little object. I walked closer to examine it and bit my trembling lip. A small, lopsided whale with an odd protrusion from its head was seated on my dresser, the pink of the whale contrasting with the green of anomaly.

"I broke this…the day we met—I don't even know what happened to it afterwards," I breathed as I picked up the figurine with shaking fingers. "How?"

Robert reached for it and looked at it closely, his eyes seeing far more than I ever could. "Janice had put it away in a small box in your closet. I knew it had meant a great deal to you, and it still does to Graham. He just doesn't want to ask for it back. So, I fixed it."

I took it back with careful fingers and looked at it, though with far more scrutiny. I had made this, after all. "You can't tell where it broke, or that it had broken at all."

Robert smiled and touched the corner of my eye with his thumb, taking away a drop of moisture with it. "It's much stronger than it was before. Just like its maker."

"Thank you," I mouthed, unable to form words or sounds. I leaned into his chest as I replaced the small whale on the dresser. He didn't need to hear me or see my lips moving to know that I was grateful. I was more than that. I was unbelievably blessed. "Okay, let's go back downstairs now," I whispered when I could finally manage the emotions that overflowed within me.

With the blinding speed that I was slowly getting used to, he picked me up and flashed down the stairs until we were back in the living room, sitting on the floor beside the couch as though we had never left.

I heard a melodious noise fill the house that sounded a bit…off. I looked at Robert—his shoulders were shaking with laughter as he pointed in the direction of the wall across from the couch that held the television and Dad's stereo. There, standing with her arm around my dad, was Lark—she was meowing the harmony to the second chorus of Jingle Bells, Dad meowing the melody.

Ameila and Janice were both still in the kitchen, laughing at the antics of the two meowers in the living room, and I shook my head at the impossibility of it all.

There was no helping it now. How normal could I possibly be with an angel meowing Jingle Bells in my living room? I glanced over at Robert and saw that his eyes were sparkling with genuine joy. He grabbed my hand and pressed his lips against my fingers, smiling at me when he saw the flush suffuse my face—roses and freckles.

This *was* my normal. Being in love with an angel, listening to cat Christmas Carols, and…possibly contemplating living forever was as normal as it was going to get for me, I realized. I smiled at my acceptance of this, and stood up. "I think I'll go and sing along with Lark and Dad," I said cheerfully, and did just that. *Meow*.

ACKNOWLEDGEMENTS

Special thanks go out to Tia, Kerri, and Alan, without whom I would not have had the feedback and criticism to know what needed fixing and what needed to be left alone and never touched ever again. You guys rock.

ABOUT THE AUTHOR

S.L. Naeole spends most of her time writing, reading, and living life to the fullest with her husband, four children, and fuzzgut the cat in her home in the Aloha State.

She is the author of Falling From Grace and Bird Song,, books one and two in the Grace Series.